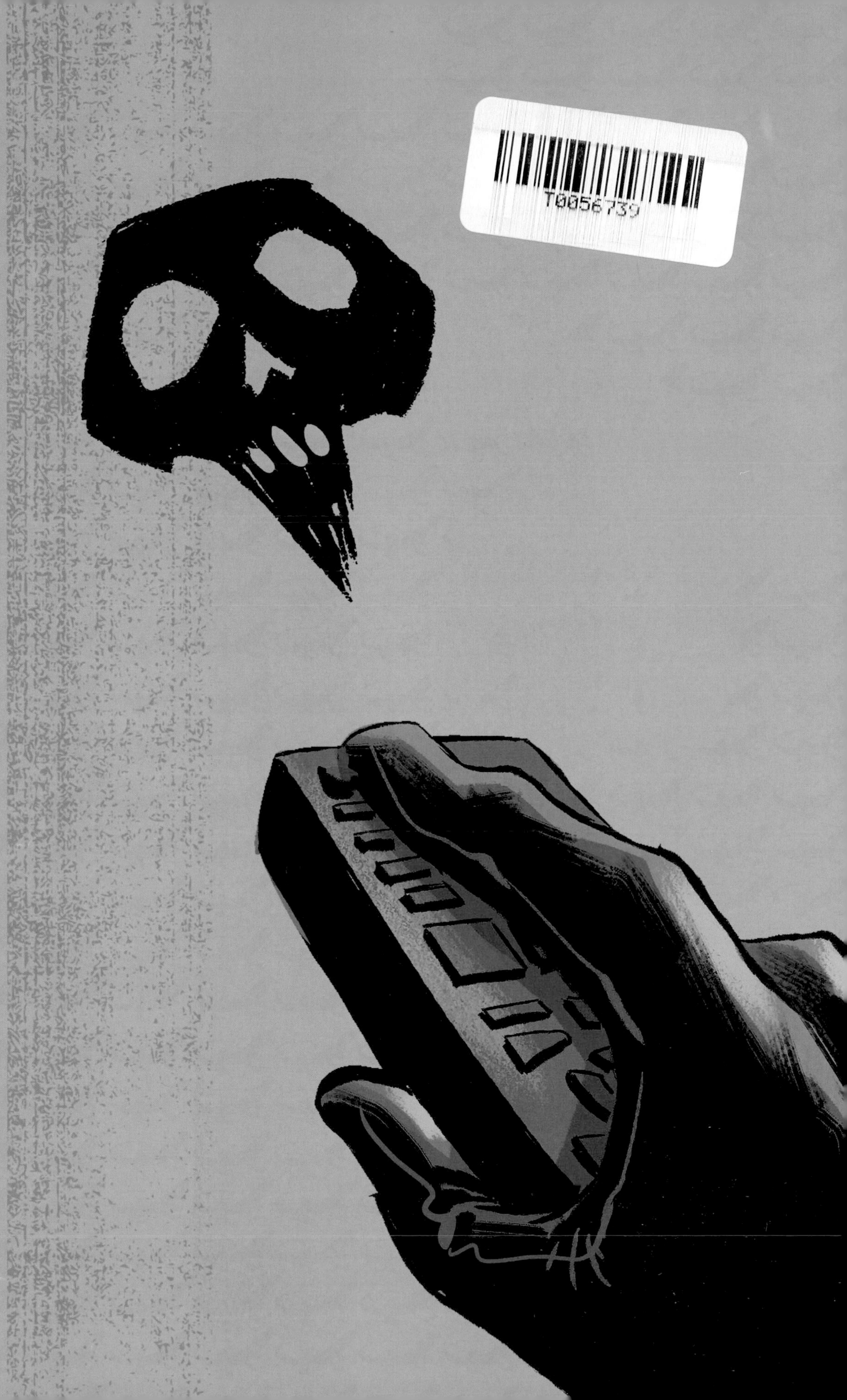

VILLAINOUS™

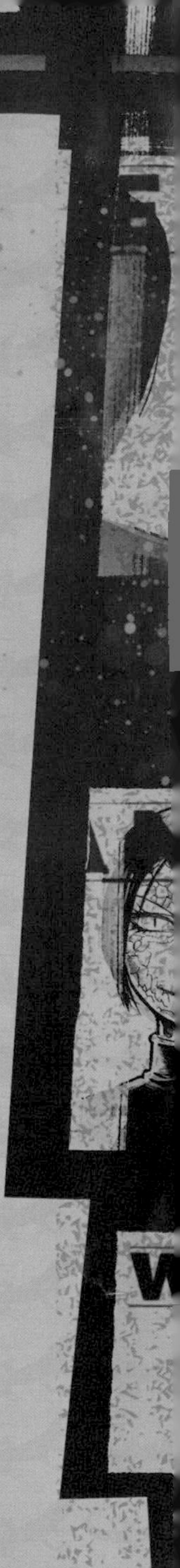

WRITER:
STONIE WILLIAMS
ART:
JEF SADZINSKI
COLORS:
JOANA LAFUENTE
LETTERS:
JUSTIN BIRCH
COVERS:
JOANA LAFUENTE & MIGUEL ANGEL ZAPATA
BOOK DESIGN:
MIGUEL ANGEL ZAPATA
LOGO DESIGN:
DIANA BERMÚDEZ
EDITORS:
GIOVANNA T. OROZCO & CHRIS FERNANDEZ

MAD CAVE

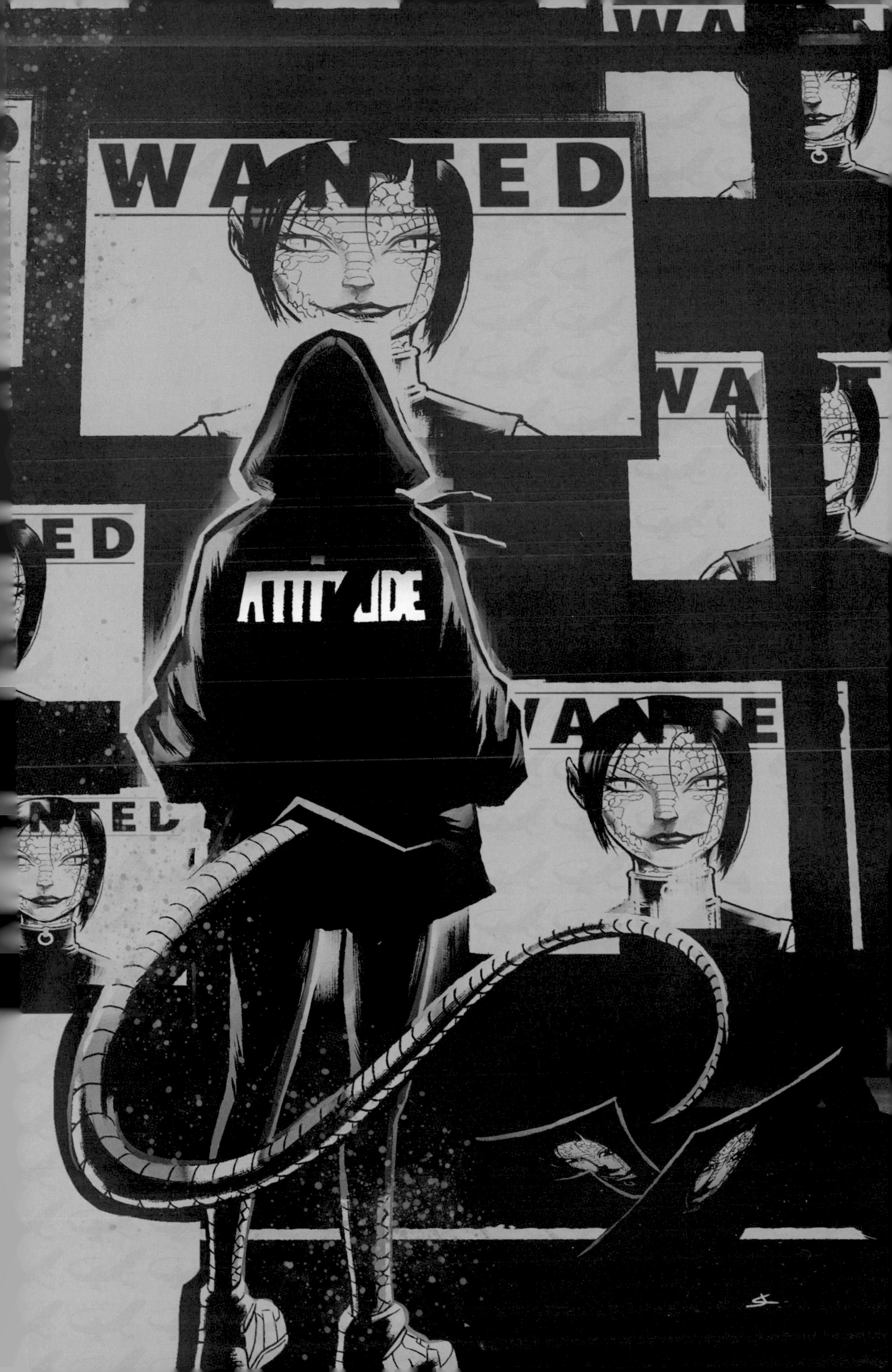
WANTED

"To my wife, April, and our children, Kate, Zane, Xander, Zakk & Chloe.
For being my constant source of support and inspiration.
To my Mom, Janece;
For always encouraging my creativity and comic book reading.
I love you all."
- Stonie Williams.

"To all those who supported me and wouldn't let me give up.
To all those who taught me precious lessons, especially to my teacher and friend Ibraim Roberson. Thank you."
- Jef Sadzinski

Laura Chacón - Founder
Mark London - CEO and Chief Creative Officer
Giovanna T. Orozco - VP of Operations
Chris Sanchez - Editor-in-Chief
Chris Fernandez - Publisher
Cecilia Medina - Chief Financial Officer
Manuel Castellanos - Director of Sales and Retailer Relations Manager
Allison Pond - Marketing Director
Asia Hirschenson - P.R. and Communications
Miguel Angel Zapata - Design Director
Diana Bermúdez - Graphic Designer
David Reyes - Graphic Designer
Adriana T. Orozco - Interactive Media Designer
Nicolás Zea Arias - Audiovisual Production
Frank Silva - Executive Assistant
Stephanie Hidalgo - Executive Assistant

FOR MAD CAVE COMICS, INC. Villainous™ Published by Mad Cave Studios, Inc. 8838 SW 129 St. Miami, FL 33176. © 2021 Mad Cave Studios, Inc. All rights reserved. Contains materials originally published in single magazine form as Villainous™ (2020) #1-5.

Printed in Canada. First Printing. ISBN: 978-1-952303-06-7 **COMICS WITH A MAD TWIST.**

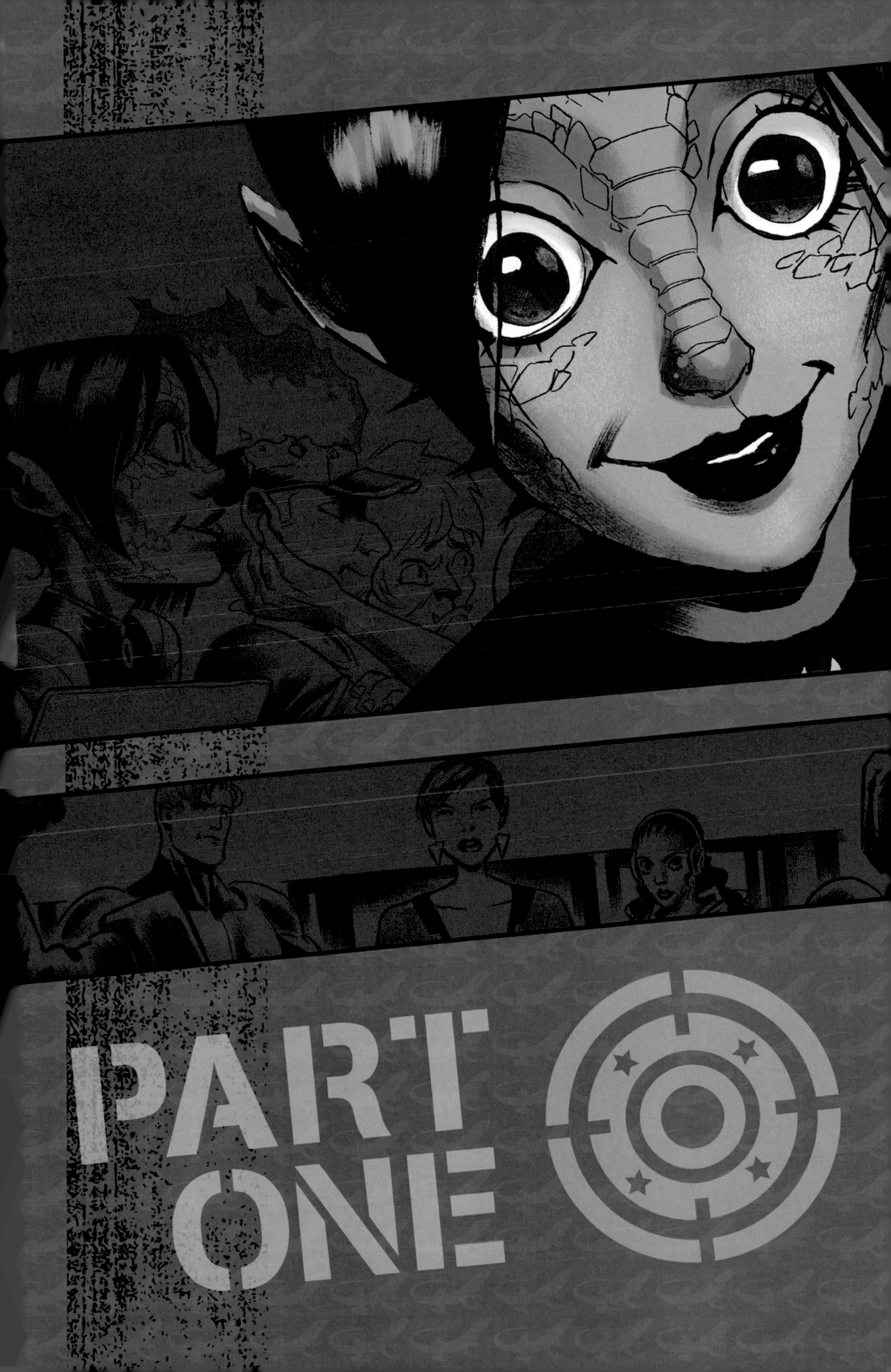
PART
ONE

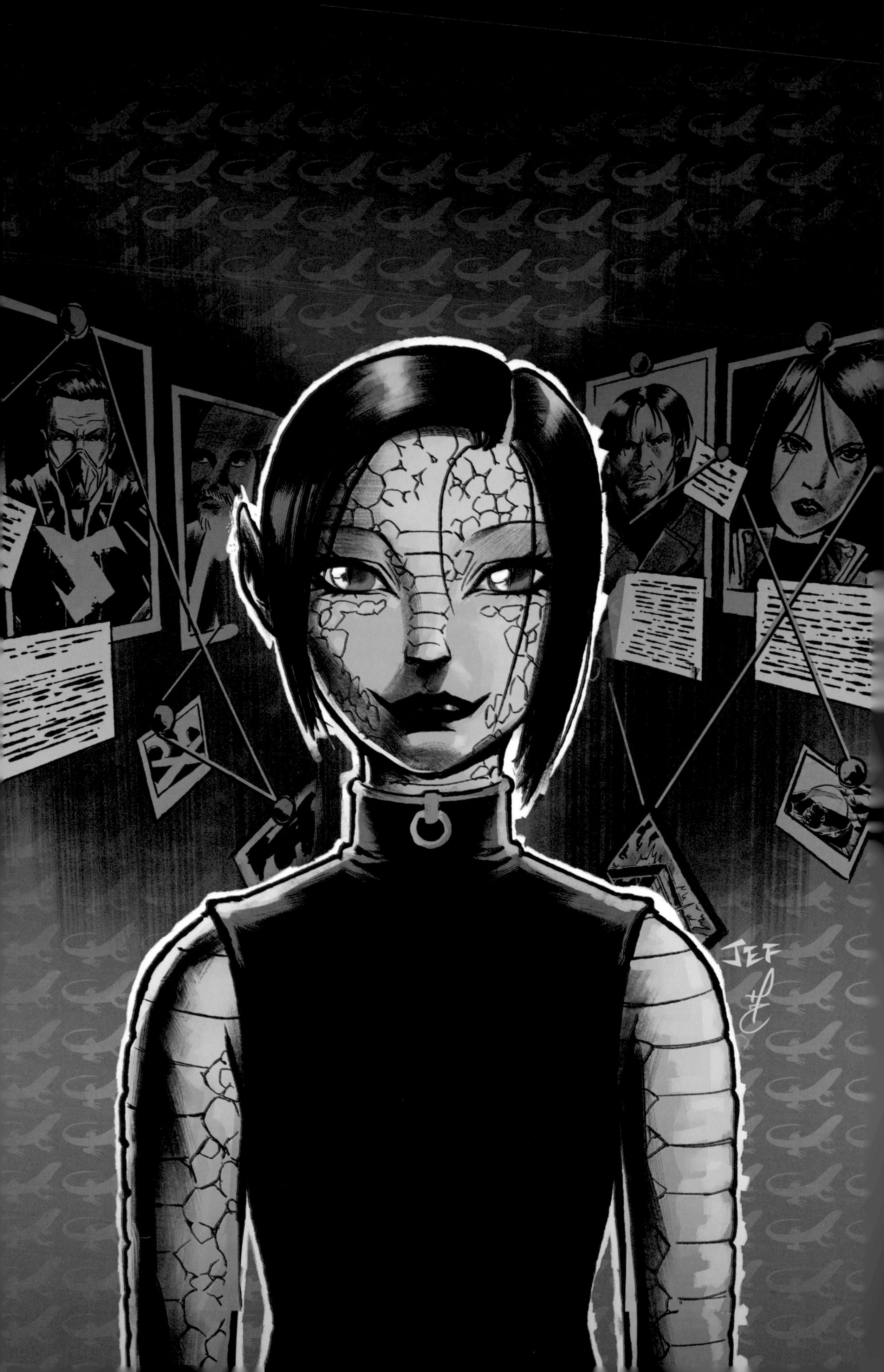

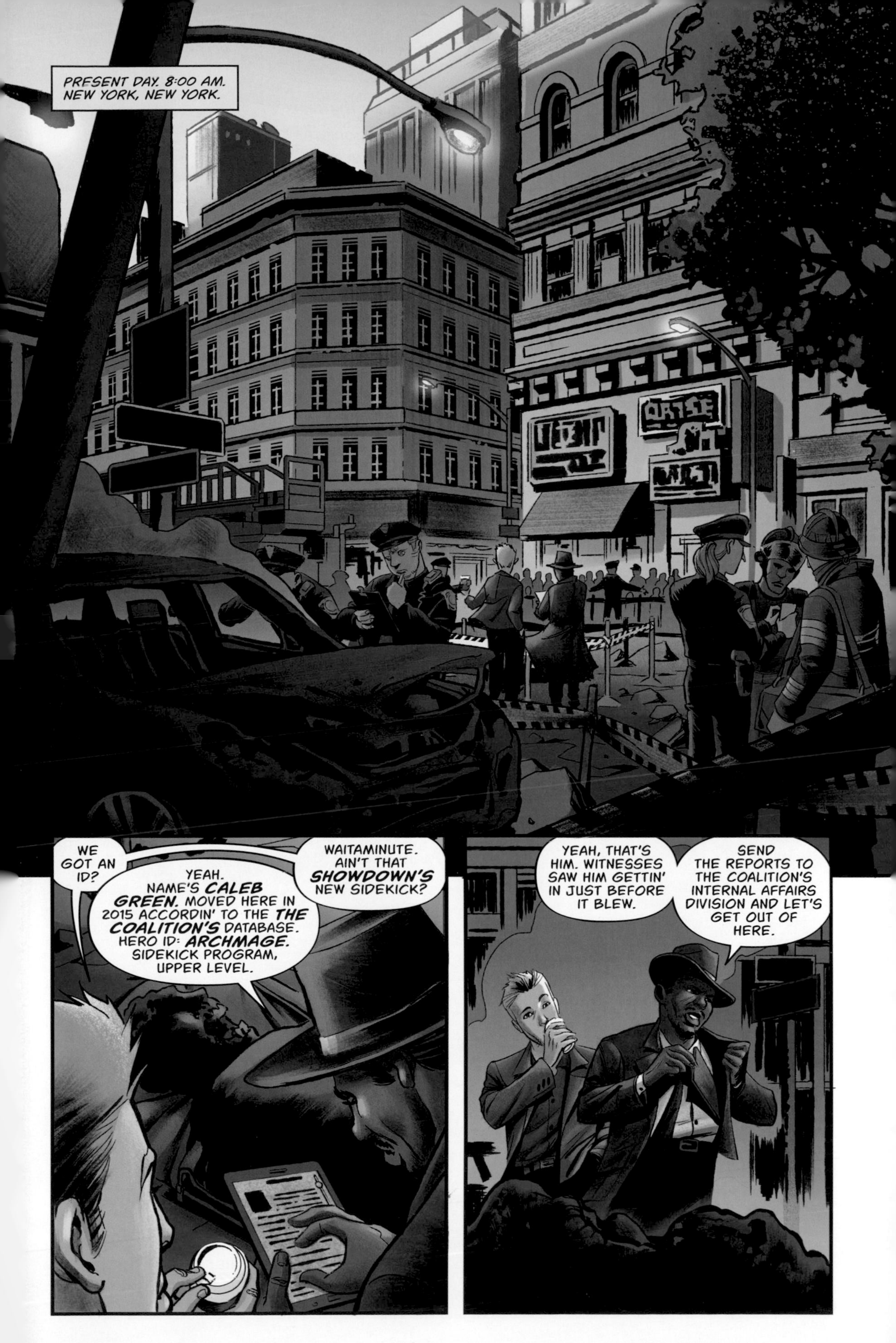
PRESENT DAY. 8:00 AM. NEW YORK, NEW YORK.
WE GOT AN ID?
YEAH. NAME'S CALEB GREEN. MOVED HERE IN 2015 ACCORDIN' TO THE THE COALITION'S DATABASE. HERO ID: ARCHMAGE. SIDEKICK PROGRAM, UPPER LEVEL.
WAITAMINUTE. AIN'T THAT SHOWDOWN'S NEW SIDEKICK?
YEAH, THAT'S HIM. WITNESSES SAW HIM GETTIN' IN JUST BEFORE IT BLEW.
SEND THE REPORTS TO THE COALITION'S INTERNAL AFFAIRS DIVISION AND LET'S GET OUT OF HERE.

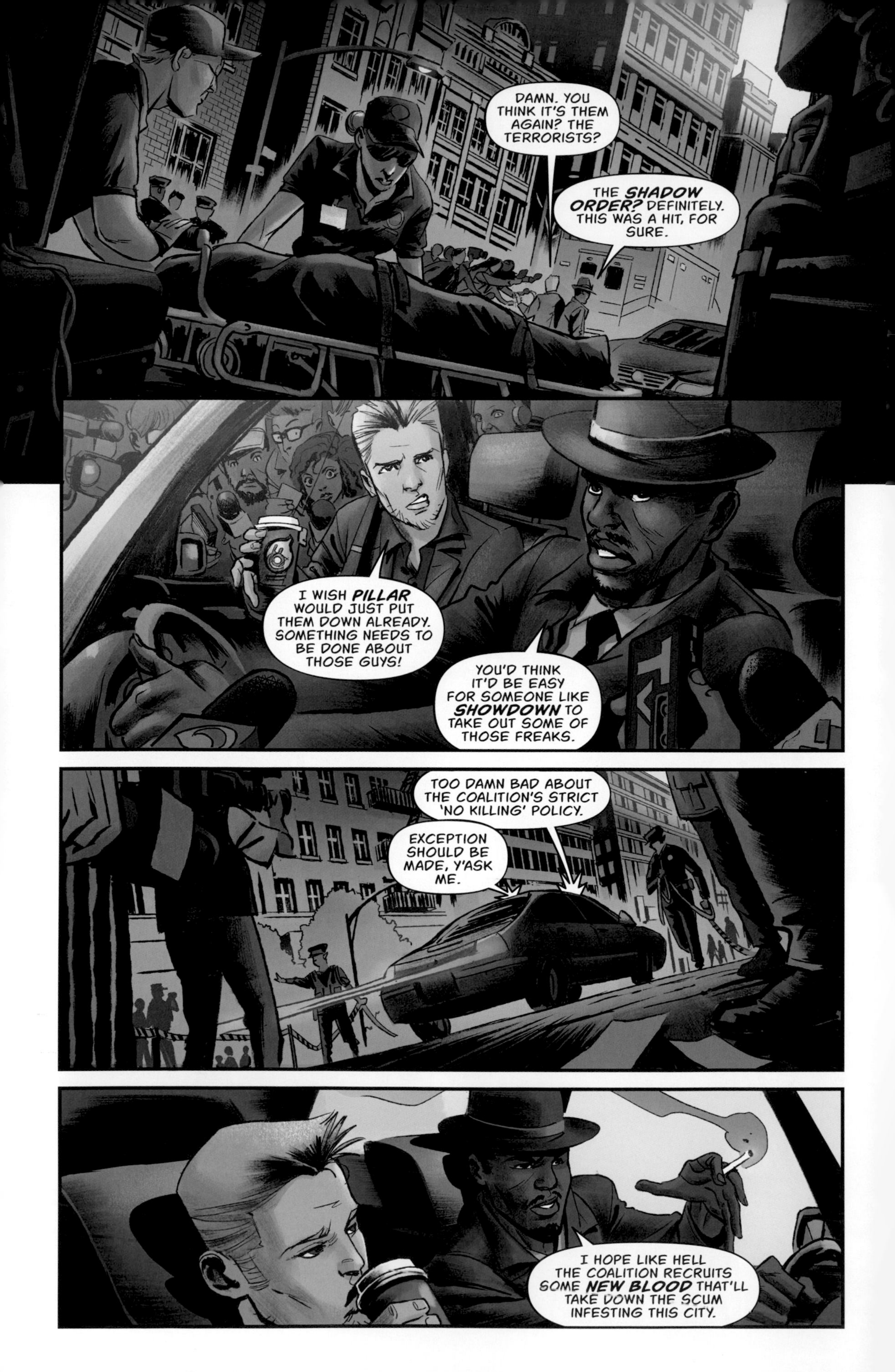

DAMN. YOU THINK IT'S THEM AGAIN? THE TERRORISTS?
THE SHADOW ORDER? DEFINITELY. THIS WAS A HIT, FOR SURE.
I WISH PILLAR WOULD JUST PUT THEM DOWN ALREADY. SOMETHING NEEDS TO BE DONE ABOUT THOSE GUYS!
YOU'D THINK IT'D BE EASY FOR SOMEONE LIKE SHOWDOWN TO TAKE OUT SOME OF THOSE FREAKS.
TOO DAMN BAD ABOUT THE COALITION'S STRICT 'NO KILLING' POLICY.
EXCEPTION SHOULD BE MADE, Y'ASK ME.
I HOPE LIKE HELL THE COALITION RECRUITS SOME NEW BLOOD THAT'LL TAKE DOWN THE SCUM INFESTING THIS CITY.

ONE WEEK LATER. **THE COALITION OF HEROES** HEADQUARTERS.

HELLO, AND WELCOME TO THE COALITION OF HEROES' APPRENTICE PROGRAM TRAINING SEMINAR. I'M PILLAR, FOUNDING MEMBER AND ADMINISTRATIVE DIRECTOR FOR THE COALITION.

BASED ON YOUR ASSESSMENTS, I HAVE ASSIGNED EACH OF YOU A HERO THAT YOU WILL BE SHADOWING AS COH SIDEKICKS.

DO YOUR BEST AND YOU'LL BE **FULL-FLEDGED HEROES** IN NO TIME!

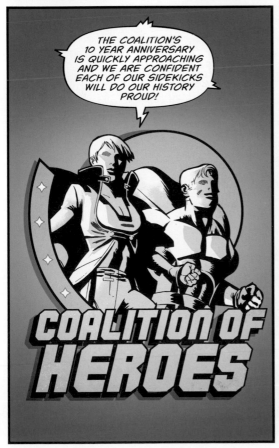

THE COALITION'S 10 YEAR ANNIVERSARY IS QUICKLY APPROACHING AND WE ARE CONFIDENT EACH OF OUR SIDEKICKS WILL DO OUR HISTORY PROUD!

COALITION OF HEROES

THE COALITION OF HEROES--PROTECTING YOU, YOUR WORLD, AND YOUR FUTURE!

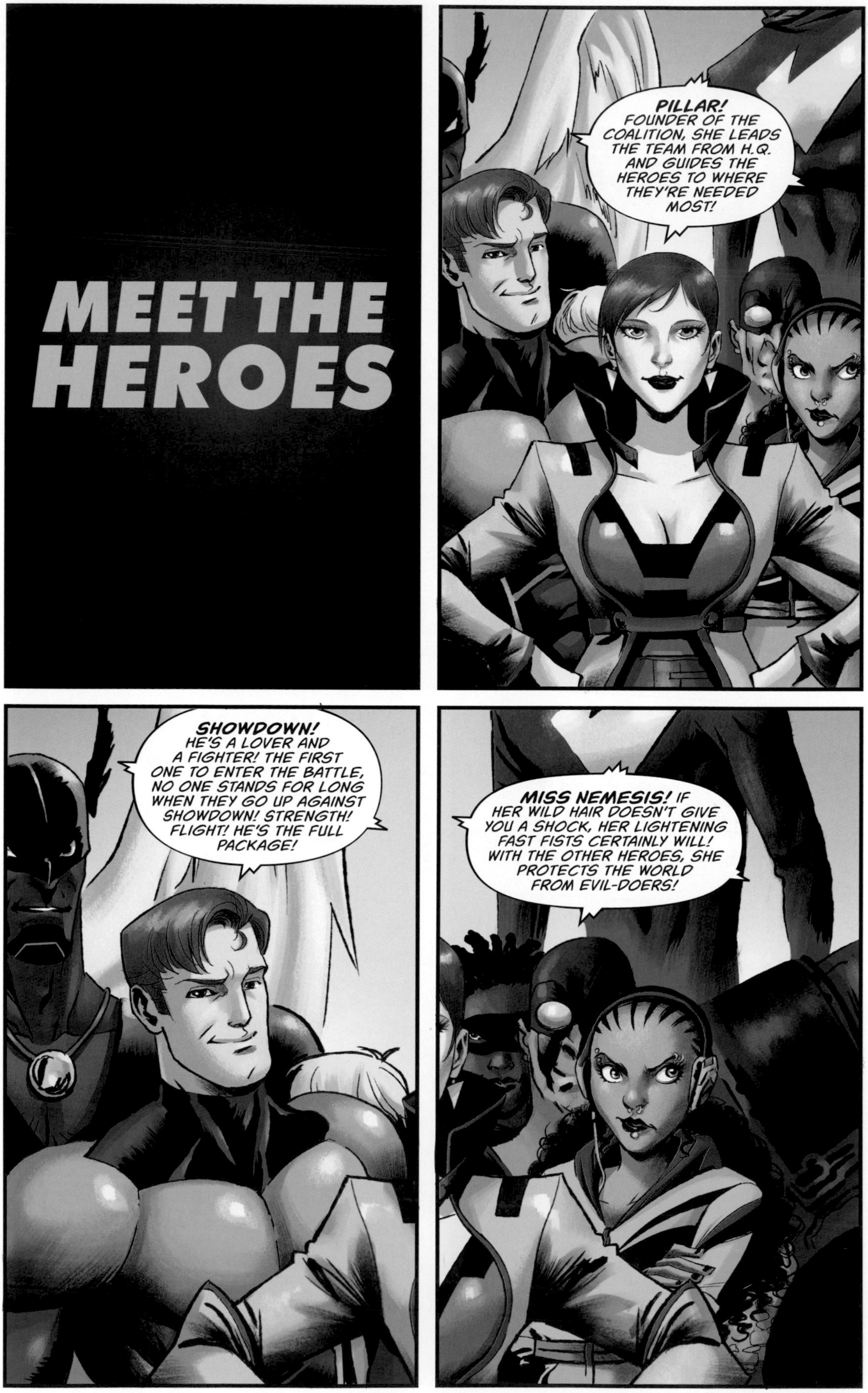
MEET THE HEROES
PILLAR! FOUNDER OF THE COALITION, SHE LEADS THE TEAM FROM H.Q. AND GUIDES THE HEROES TO WHERE THEY'RE NEEDED MOST!
SHOWDOWN! HE'S A LOVER AND A FIGHTER! THE FIRST ONE TO ENTER THE BATTLE, NO ONE STANDS FOR LONG WHEN THEY GO UP AGAINST SHOWDOWN! STRENGTH! FLIGHT! HE'S THE FULL PACKAGE!
MISS NEMESIS! IF HER WILD HAIR DOESN'T GIVE YOU A SHOCK, HER LIGHTENING FAST FISTS CERTAINLY WILL! WITH THE OTHER HEROES, SHE PROTECTS THE WORLD FROM EVIL-DOERS!

THE SHADOW ORDER

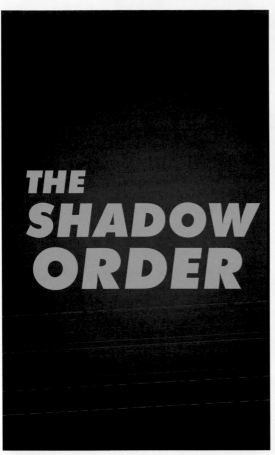

THE EVIL **SEDITION** KNOWS NO SHAME. SOME SAY HE TRIED TO CORRUPT THE COALITION IN THE EARLY DAYS. ONE THING IS FOR CERTAIN-- SEDITION WORKS TIRELESSLY FOR THE COALITION'S DOWNFALL!

DECEMBER, THE WINTER WITCH, CASTS HER FROZEN SPELLS IN HOPES OF CHILLING THE HEARTS AND MINDS OF EVERY WARM-BLOODED CITIZEN AS THE LEADER OF THE SHADOW ORDER!

THE HEADHUNTER USES HIS POWERS TO TWIST AND DECAY EVERYTHING THAT COMES NEAR HIM. HE HELPS THE VILLAINS AND THE CORRUPT TYRANTS THEY WORK FOR TO FIGHT AGAINST TRUTH AND FREED--!

CLICK

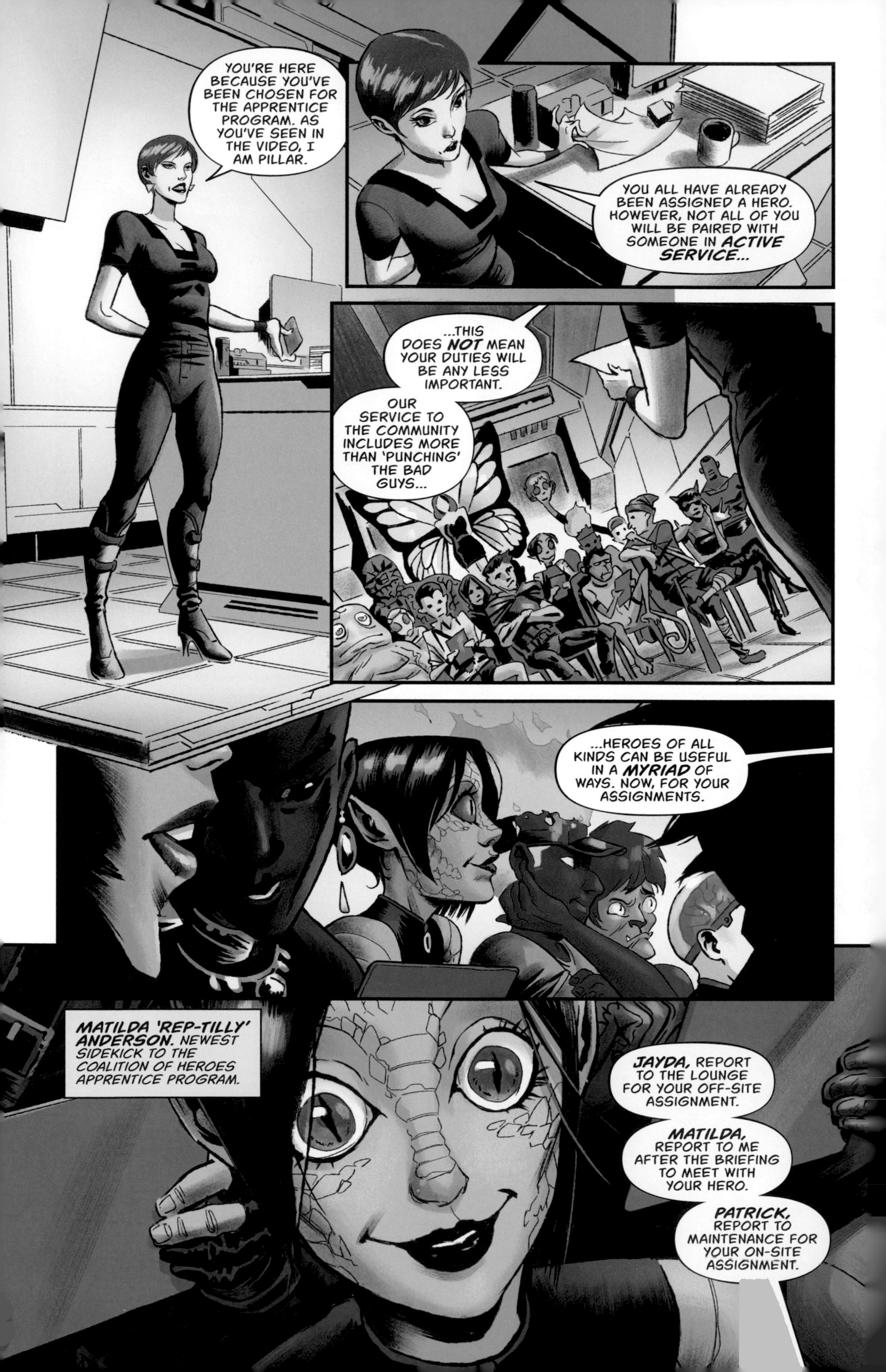
YOU'RE HERE BECAUSE YOU'VE BEEN CHOSEN FOR THE APPRENTICE PROGRAM. AS YOU'VE SEEN IN THE VIDEO, I AM PILLAR.
YOU ALL HAVE ALREADY BEEN ASSIGNED A HERO. HOWEVER, NOT ALL OF YOU WILL BE PAIRED WITH SOMEONE IN ACTIVE SERVICE...
...THIS DOES NOT MEAN YOUR DUTIES WILL BE ANY LESS IMPORTANT.
OUR SERVICE TO THE COMMUNITY INCLUDES MORE THAN 'PUNCHING' THE BAD GUYS...
...HEROES OF ALL KINDS CAN BE USEFUL IN A MYRIAD OF WAYS. NOW, FOR YOUR ASSIGNMENTS.
MATILDA 'REP-TILLY' ANDERSON. NEWEST SIDEKICK TO THE COALITION OF HEROES APPRENTICE PROGRAM.
JAYDA, REPORT TO THE LOUNGE FOR YOUR OFF-SITE ASSIGNMENT.
MATILDA, REPORT TO ME AFTER THE BRIEFING TO MEET WITH YOUR HERO.
PATRICK, REPORT TO MAINTENANCE FOR YOUR ON-SITE ASSIGNMENT.

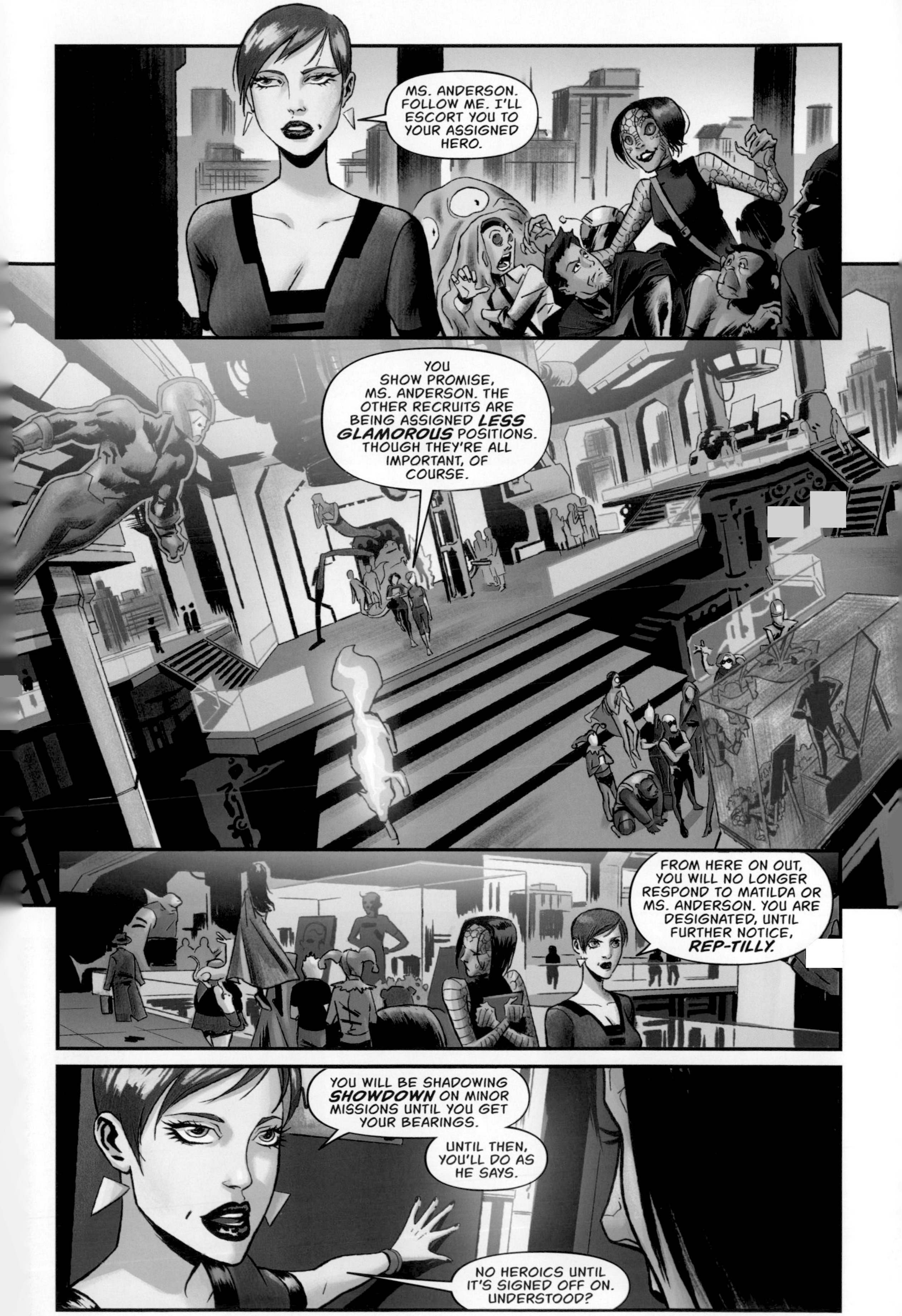
MS. ANDERSON. FOLLOW ME. I'LL ESCORT YOU TO YOUR ASSIGNED HERO.
YOU SHOW PROMISE, MS. ANDERSON. THE OTHER RECRUITS ARE BEING ASSIGNED LESS GLAMOROUS POSITIONS. THOUGH THEY'RE ALL IMPORTANT, OF COURSE.
FROM HERE ON OUT, YOU WILL NO LONGER RESPOND TO MATILDA OR MS. ANDERSON. YOU ARE DESIGNATED, UNTIL FURTHER NOTICE, REP-TILLY.
YOU WILL BE SHADOWING SHOWDOWN ON MINOR MISSIONS UNTIL YOU GET YOUR BEARINGS.
UNTIL THEN, YOU'LL DO AS HE SAYS.
NO HEROICS UNTIL IT'S SIGNED OFF ON. UNDERSTOOD?

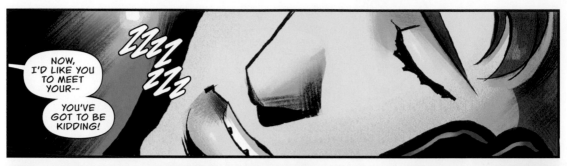

NOW, I'D LIKE YOU TO MEET YOUR--

YOU'VE GOT TO BE KIDDING!

SHOWDOWN!

HUH? WHAT? I MEAN, YES, MA'AM!

THIS IS YOUR NEW SIDEKICK, REP-TILLY. I WANT HER TRAINED AND READY FOR FIELDWORK AS SOON AS POSSIBLE.

ABSOLUTELY! YOU CAN COUNT ON ME!

COME ON IN, RECRUIT.

NOW THEN, REP-TILLY. FIRST, LET ME WELCOME YOU TO THE COALITION. SECOND, LET'S START WITH GROUND RULES. ARE YOU READY?

YESSIR! I'VE NEVER BEEN MORE READY FOR ANYTHING IN MY LIFE! THIS IS MY DREAM! THIS IS--

THAAAAT'S GREAT. SO, MY YOUNG SQUIRE, MY TRAINING MAY SEEM STRANGE, BUT I PROMISE THERE'S A METHOD TO MY MADNESS.

HERE'S A LIST OF THE TASKS I NEED DONE BY THE END OF THE DAY.

IF YOU CAN'T MANAGE THIS LIST, YOU'RE OUT. NO SECOND CHANCES.

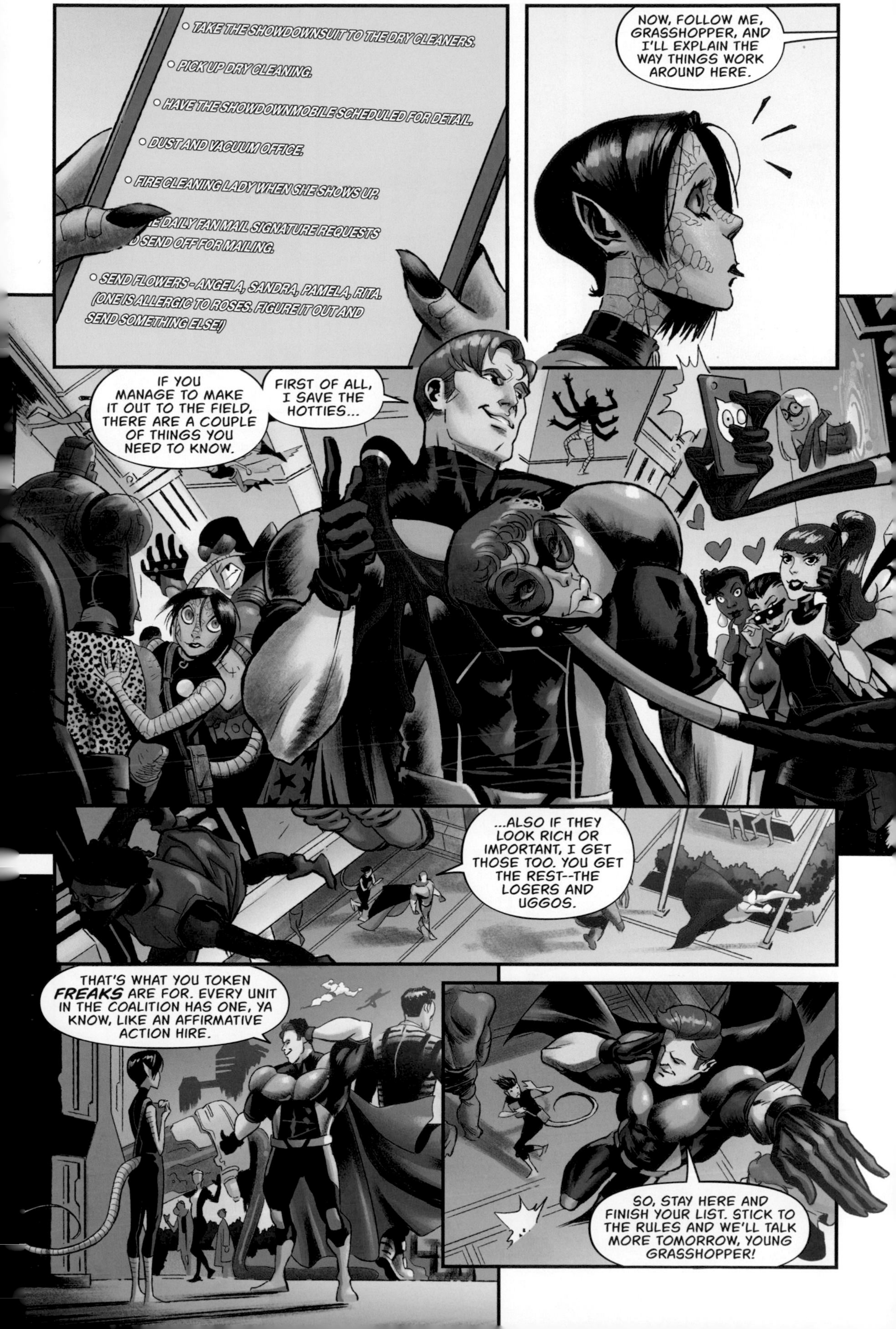
• TAKE THE SHOWDOWNSUIT TO THE DRY CLEANERS.
• PICK UP DRY CLEANING.
• HAVE THE SHOWDOWNMOBILE SCHEDULED FOR DETAIL.
• DUST AND VACUUM OFFICE.
• FIRE CLEANING LADY WHEN SHE SHOWS UP.
E DAILY FAN MAIL SIGNATURE REQUESTS
D SEND OFF FOR MAILING.
• SEND FLOWERS - ANGELA, SANDRA, PAMELA, RITA. (ONE IS ALLERGIC TO ROSES. FIGURE IT OUT AND SEND SOMETHING ELSE!)
NOW, FOLLOW ME, GRASSHOPPER, AND I'LL EXPLAIN THE WAY THINGS WORK AROUND HERE.
IF YOU MANAGE TO MAKE IT OUT TO THE FIELD, THERE ARE A COUPLE OF THINGS YOU NEED TO KNOW.
FIRST OF ALL, I SAVE THE HOTTIES...
...ALSO IF THEY LOOK RICH OR IMPORTANT, I GET THOSE TOO. YOU GET THE REST--THE LOSERS AND UGGOS.
THAT'S WHAT YOU TOKEN FREAKS ARE FOR. EVERY UNIT IN THE COALITION HAS ONE, YA KNOW, LIKE AN AFFIRMATIVE ACTION HIRE.
SO, STAY HERE AND FINISH YOUR LIST. STICK TO THE RULES AND WE'LL TALK MORE TOMORROW, YOUNG GRASSHOPPER!

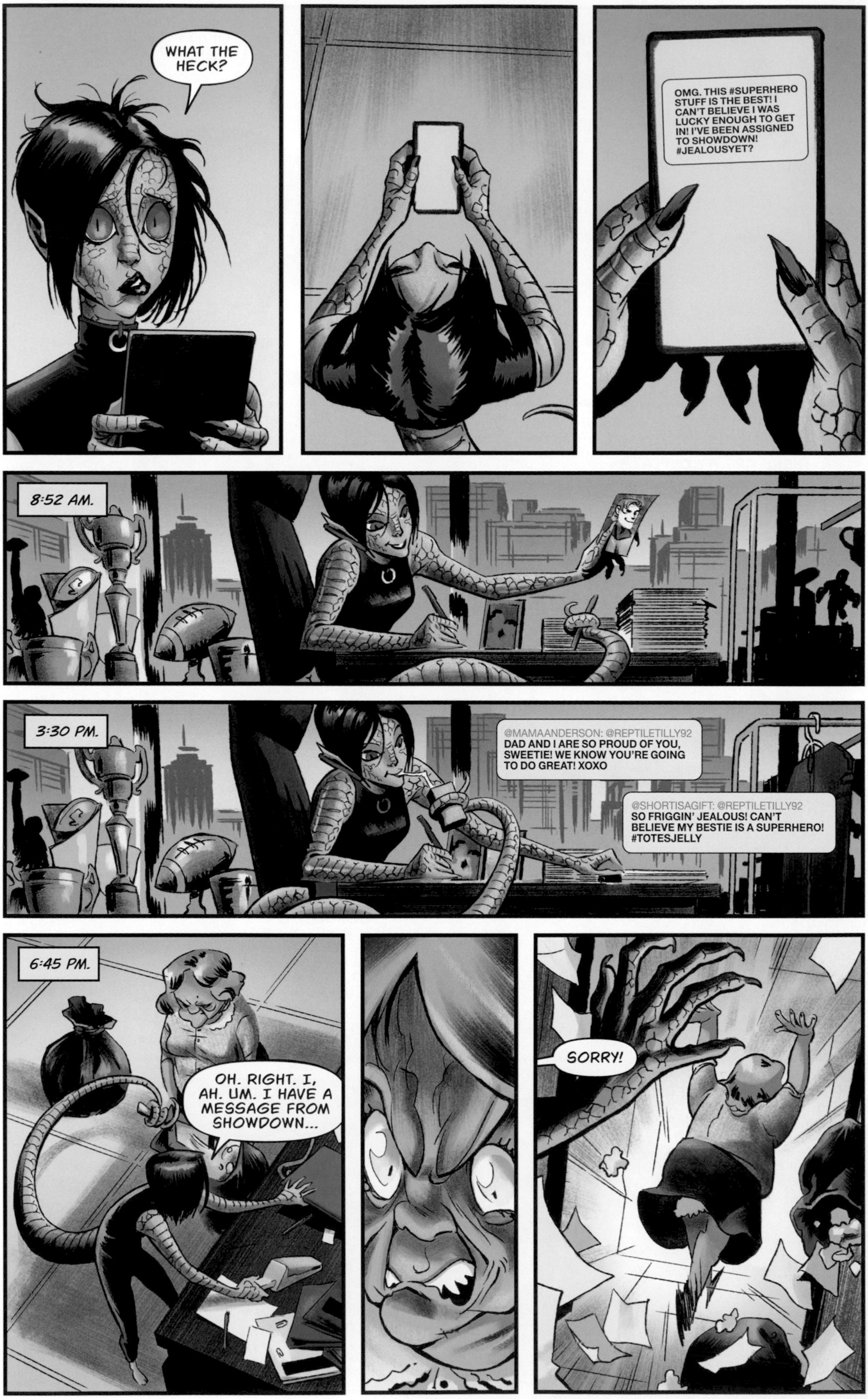
WHAT THE HECK?
OMG. THIS #SUPERHERO STUFF IS THE BEST! I CAN'T BELIEVE I WAS LUCKY ENOUGH TO GET IN! I'VE BEEN ASSIGNED TO SHOWDOWN! #JEALOUSYET?
8:52 AM.
3:30 PM.
@MAMAANDERSON: @REPTILETILLY92 DAD AND I ARE SO PROUD OF YOU, SWEETIE! WE KNOW YOU'RE GOING TO DO GREAT! XOXO
@SHORTISAGIFT: @REPTILETILLY92 SO FRIGGIN' JEALOUS! CAN'T BELIEVE MY BESTIE IS A SUPERHERO! #TOTESJELLY
6:45 PM.
OH. RIGHT. I, AH. UM. I HAVE A MESSAGE FROM SHOWDOWN...
SORRY!

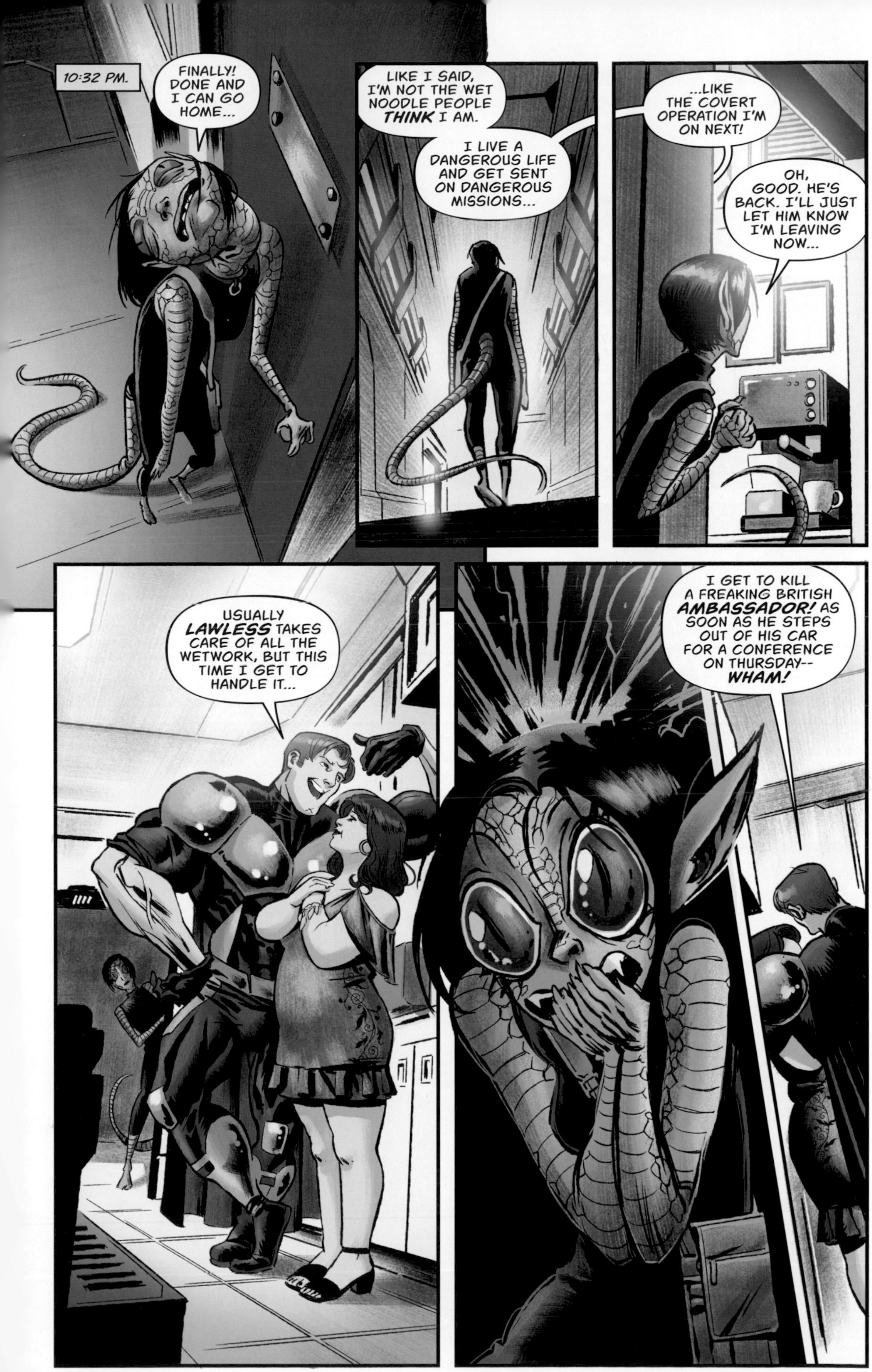
10:32 PM.
FINALLY! DONE AND I CAN GO HOME...
LIKE I SAID, I'M NOT THE WET NOODLE PEOPLE THINK I AM.
I LIVE A DANGEROUS LIFE AND GET SENT ON DANGEROUS MISSIONS...
...LIKE THE COVERT OPERATION I'M ON NEXT!
OH, GOOD. HE'S BACK. I'LL JUST LET HIM KNOW I'M LEAVING NOW...
USUALLY LAWLESS TAKES CARE OF ALL THE WETWORK, BUT THIS TIME I GET TO HANDLE IT...
I GET TO KILL A FREAKING BRITISH AMBASSADOR! AS SOON AS HE STEPS OUT OF HIS CAR FOR A CONFERENCE ON THURSDAY--WHAM!

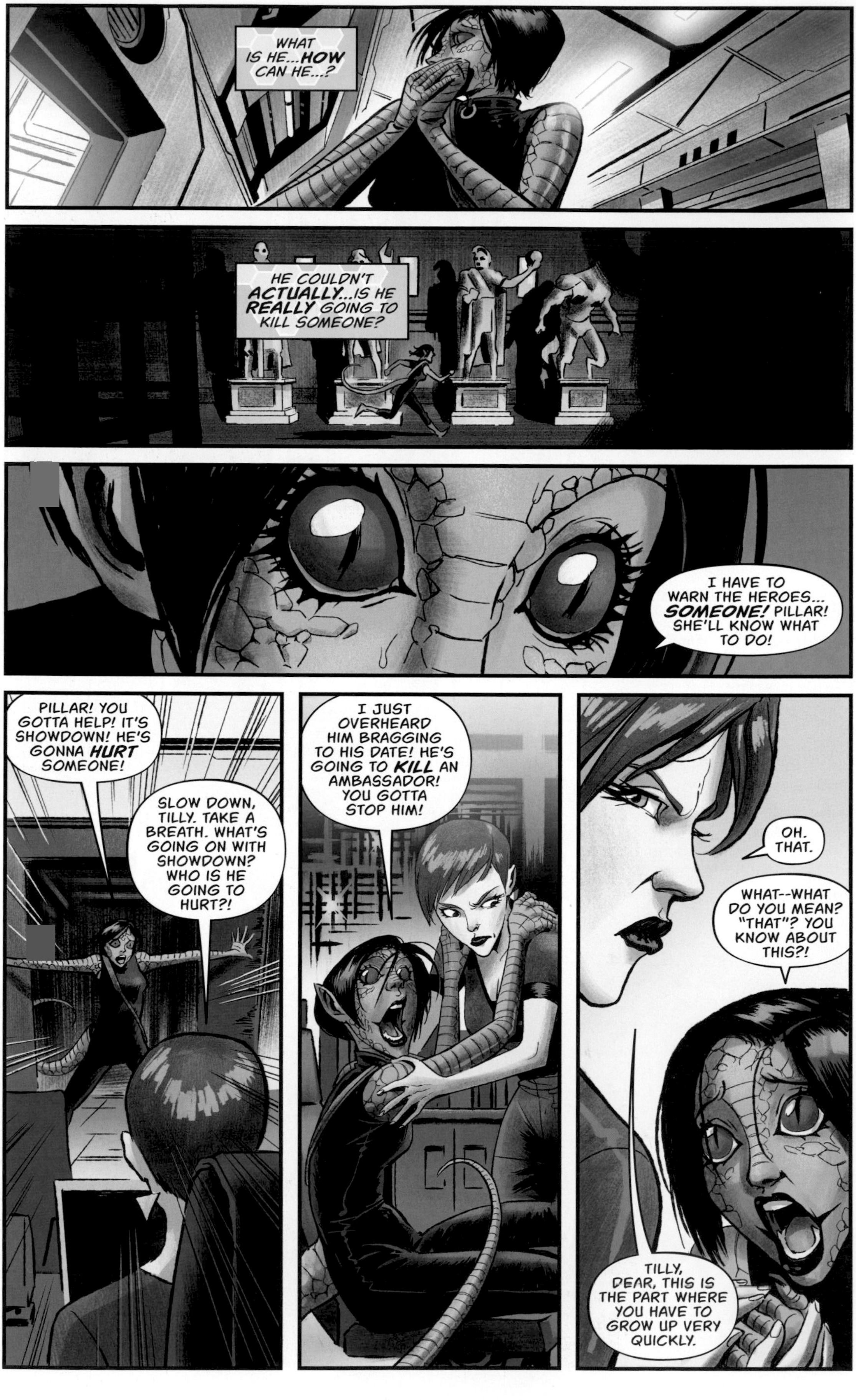
WHAT IS HE...HOW CAN HE...?
HE COULDN'T ACTUALLY...IS HE REALLY GOING TO KILL SOMEONE?
I HAVE TO WARN THE HEROES... SOMEONE! PILLAR! SHE'LL KNOW WHAT TO DO!
PILLAR! YOU GOTTA HELP! IT'S SHOWDOWN! HE'S GONNA HURT SOMEONE!
SLOW DOWN, TILLY. TAKE A BREATH. WHAT'S GOING ON WITH SHOWDOWN? WHO IS HE GOING TO HURT?!
I JUST OVERHEARD HIM BRAGGING TO HIS DATE! HE'S GOING TO KILL AN AMBASSADOR! YOU GOTTA STOP HIM!
OH. THAT.
WHAT--WHAT DO YOU MEAN? "THAT"? YOU KNOW ABOUT THIS?!
TILLY, DEAR, THIS IS THE PART WHERE YOU HAVE TO GROW UP VERY QUICKLY.

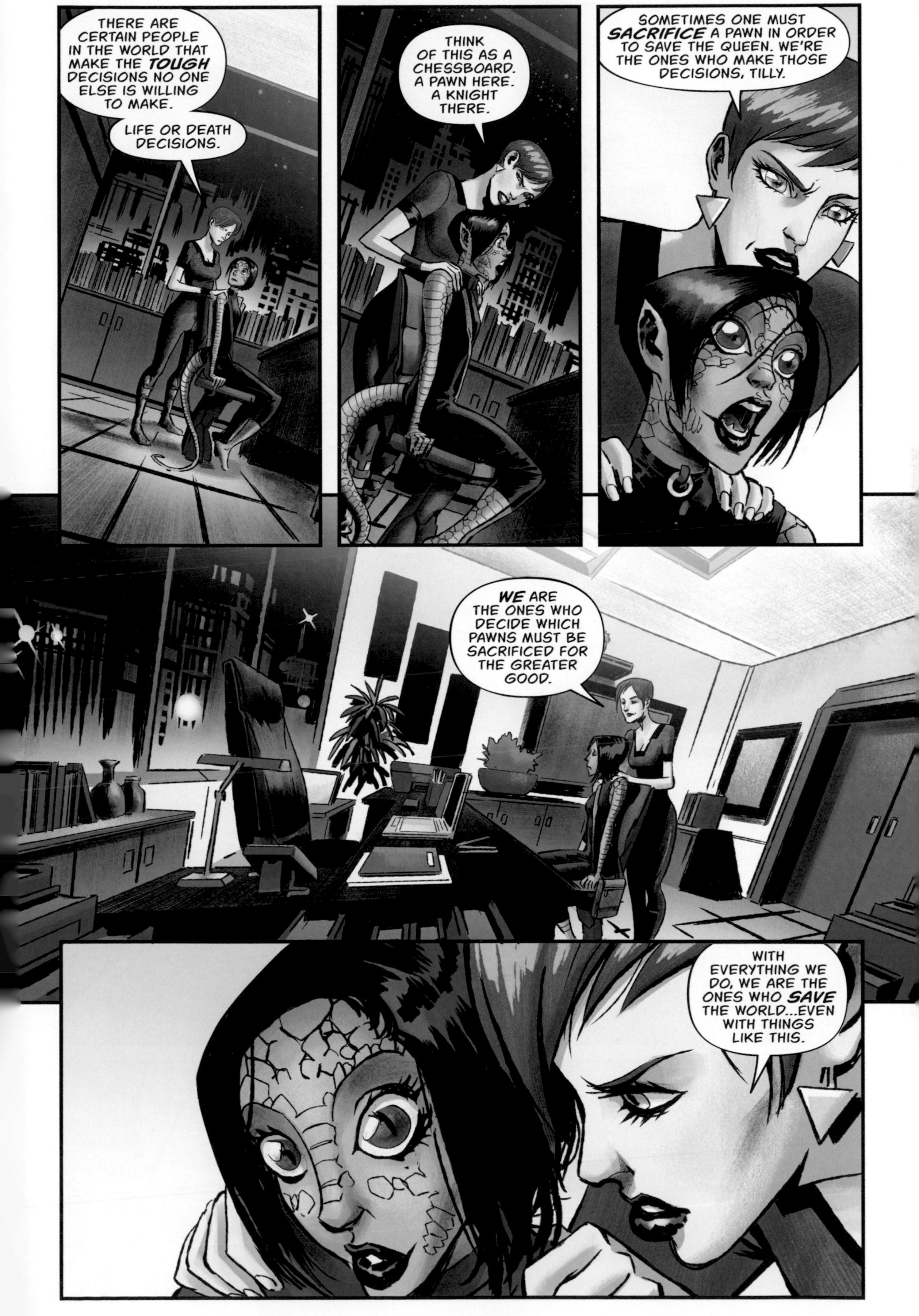
THERE ARE CERTAIN PEOPLE IN THE WORLD THAT MAKE THE TOUGH DECISIONS NO ONE ELSE IS WILLING TO MAKE.
LIFE OR DEATH DECISIONS.
THINK OF THIS AS A CHESSBOARD. A PAWN HERE. A KNIGHT THERE.
SOMETIMES ONE MUST SACRIFICE A PAWN IN ORDER TO SAVE THE QUEEN. WE'RE THE ONES WHO MAKE THOSE DECISIONS, TILLY.
WE ARE THE ONES WHO DECIDE WHICH PAWNS MUST BE SACRIFICED FOR THE GREATER GOOD.
WITH EVERYTHING WE DO, WE ARE THE ONES WHO SAVE THE WORLD...EVEN WITH THINGS LIKE THIS.

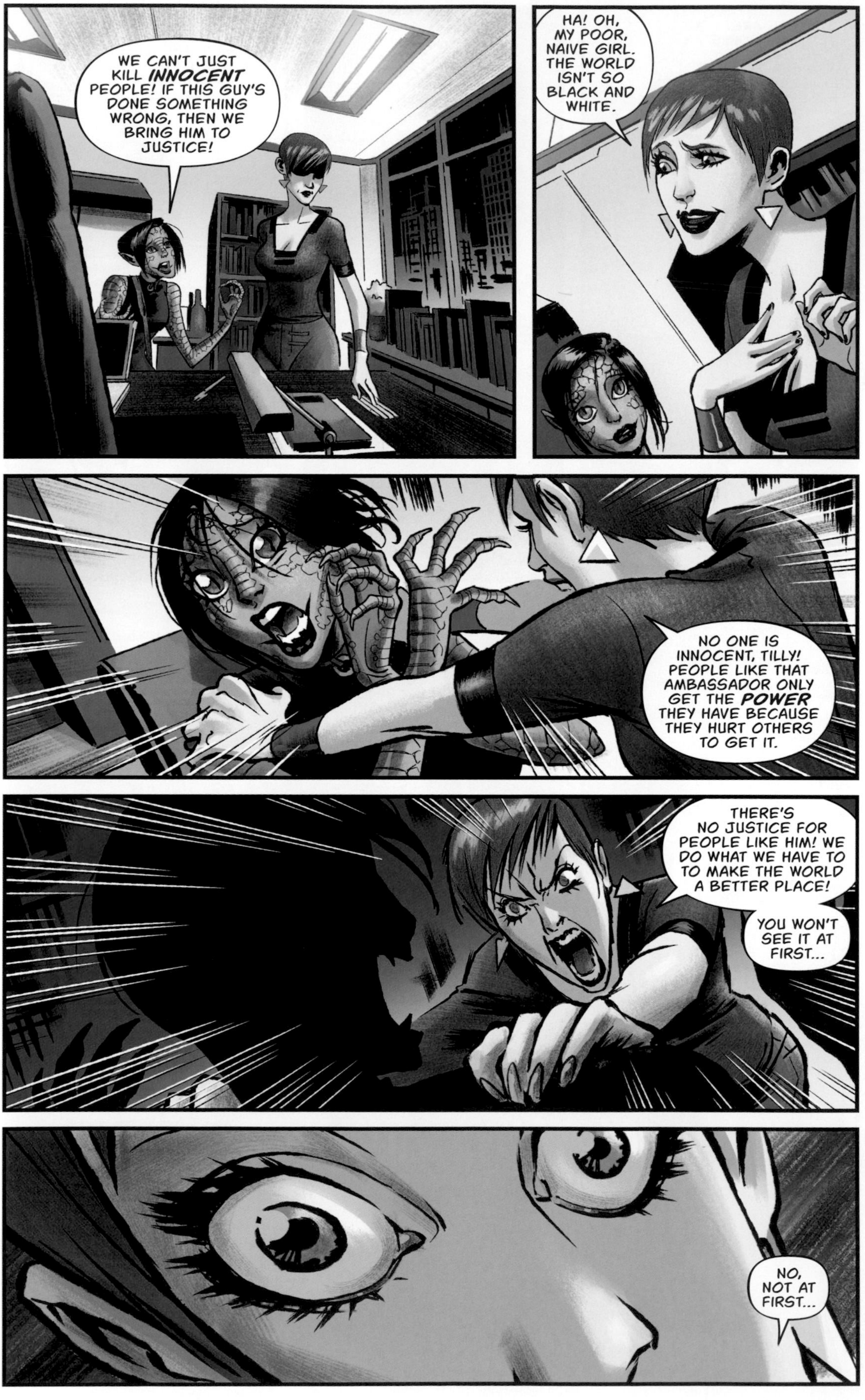
WE CAN'T JUST KILL INNOCENT PEOPLE! IF THIS GUY'S DONE SOMETHING WRONG, THEN WE BRING HIM TO JUSTICE!
HA! OH, MY POOR, NAIVE GIRL. THE WORLD ISN'T SO BLACK AND WHITE.
NO ONE IS INNOCENT, TILLY! PEOPLE LIKE THAT AMBASSADOR ONLY GET THE POWER THEY HAVE BECAUSE THEY HURT OTHERS TO GET IT.
THERE'S NO JUSTICE FOR PEOPLE LIKE HIM! WE DO WHAT WE HAVE TO TO MAKE THE WORLD A BETTER PLACE!
YOU WON'T SEE IT AT FIRST...
NO, NOT AT FIRST...

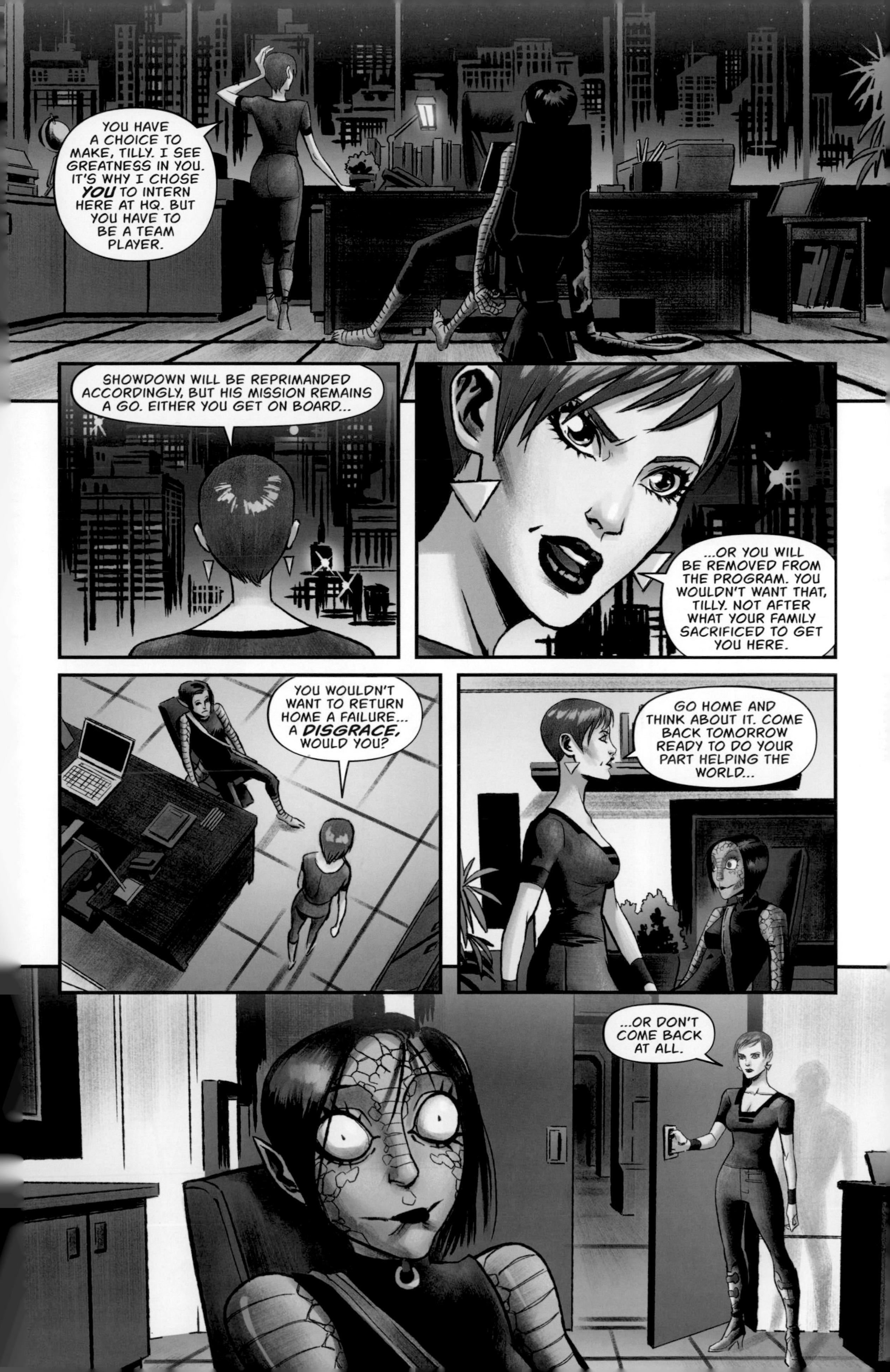

YOU HAVE A CHOICE TO MAKE, TILLY. I SEE GREATNESS IN YOU. IT'S WHY I CHOSE ***YOU*** TO INTERN HERE AT HQ. BUT YOU HAVE TO BE A TEAM PLAYER.
SHOWDOWN WILL BE REPRIMANDED ACCORDINGLY, BUT HIS MISSION REMAINS A GO. EITHER YOU GET ON BOARD...
...OR YOU WILL BE REMOVED FROM THE PROGRAM. YOU WOULDN'T WANT THAT, TILLY. NOT AFTER WHAT YOUR FAMILY SACRIFICED TO GET YOU HERE.
YOU WOULDN'T WANT TO RETURN HOME A FAILURE... A ***DISGRACE,*** WOULD YOU?
GO HOME AND THINK ABOUT IT. COME BACK TOMORROW READY TO DO YOUR PART HELPING THE WORLD...
...OR DON'T COME BACK AT ALL.

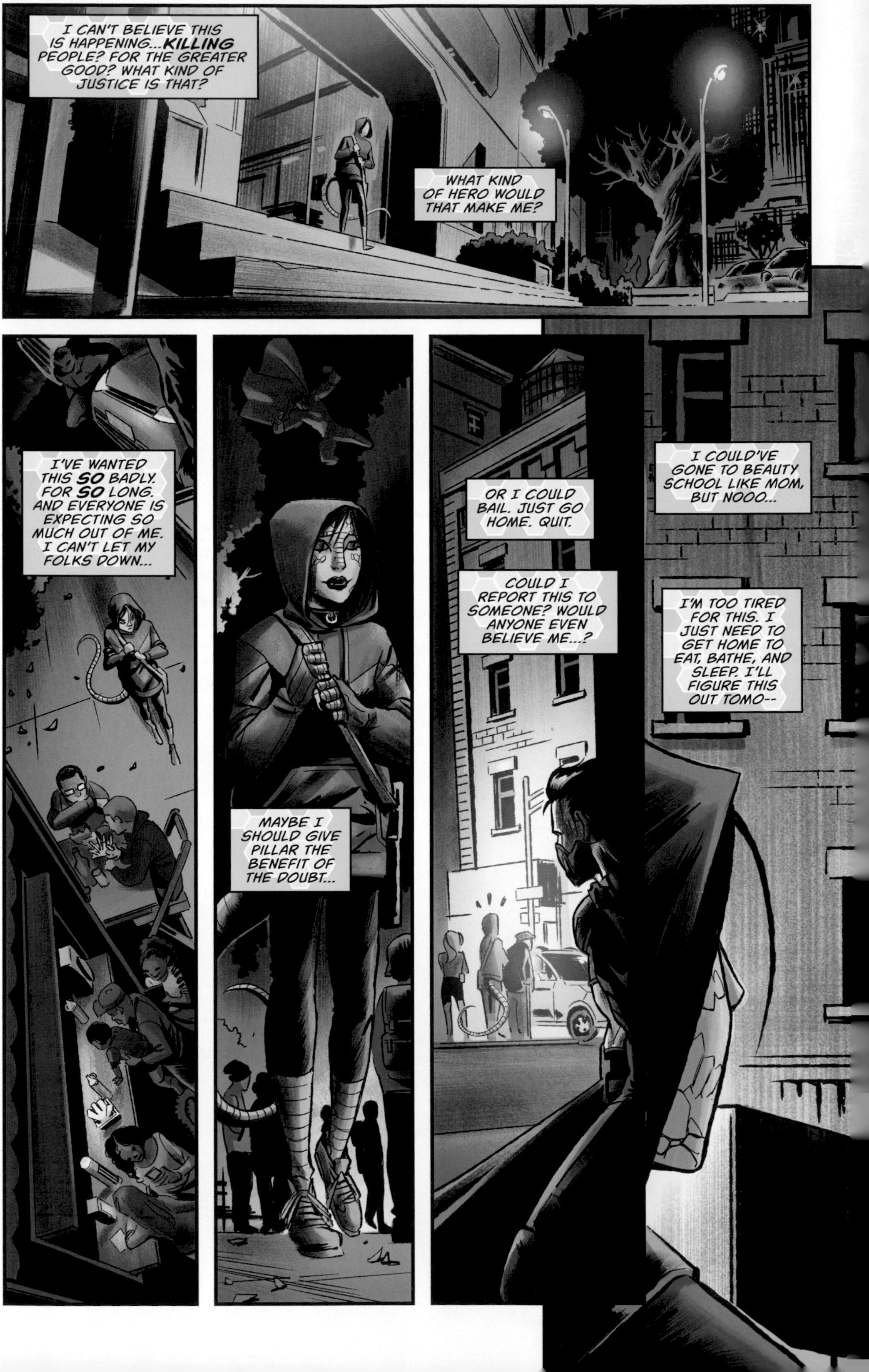
I CAN'T BELIEVE THIS IS HAPPENING...KILLING PEOPLE? FOR THE GREATER GOOD? WHAT KIND OF JUSTICE IS THAT?
WHAT KIND OF HERO WOULD THAT MAKE ME?
I'VE WANTED THIS SO BADLY. FOR SO LONG. AND EVERYONE IS EXPECTING SO MUCH OUT OF ME. I CAN'T LET MY FOLKS DOWN...
MAYBE I SHOULD GIVE PILLAR THE BENEFIT OF THE DOUBT...
OR I COULD BAIL. JUST GO HOME. QUIT.
COULD I REPORT THIS TO SOMEONE? WOULD ANYONE EVEN BELIEVE ME...?
I COULD'VE GONE TO BEAUTY SCHOOL LIKE MOM, BUT NOOO...
I'M TOO TIRED FOR THIS. I JUST NEED TO GET HOME TO EAT, BATHE, AND SLEEP. I'LL FIGURE THIS OUT TOMO--

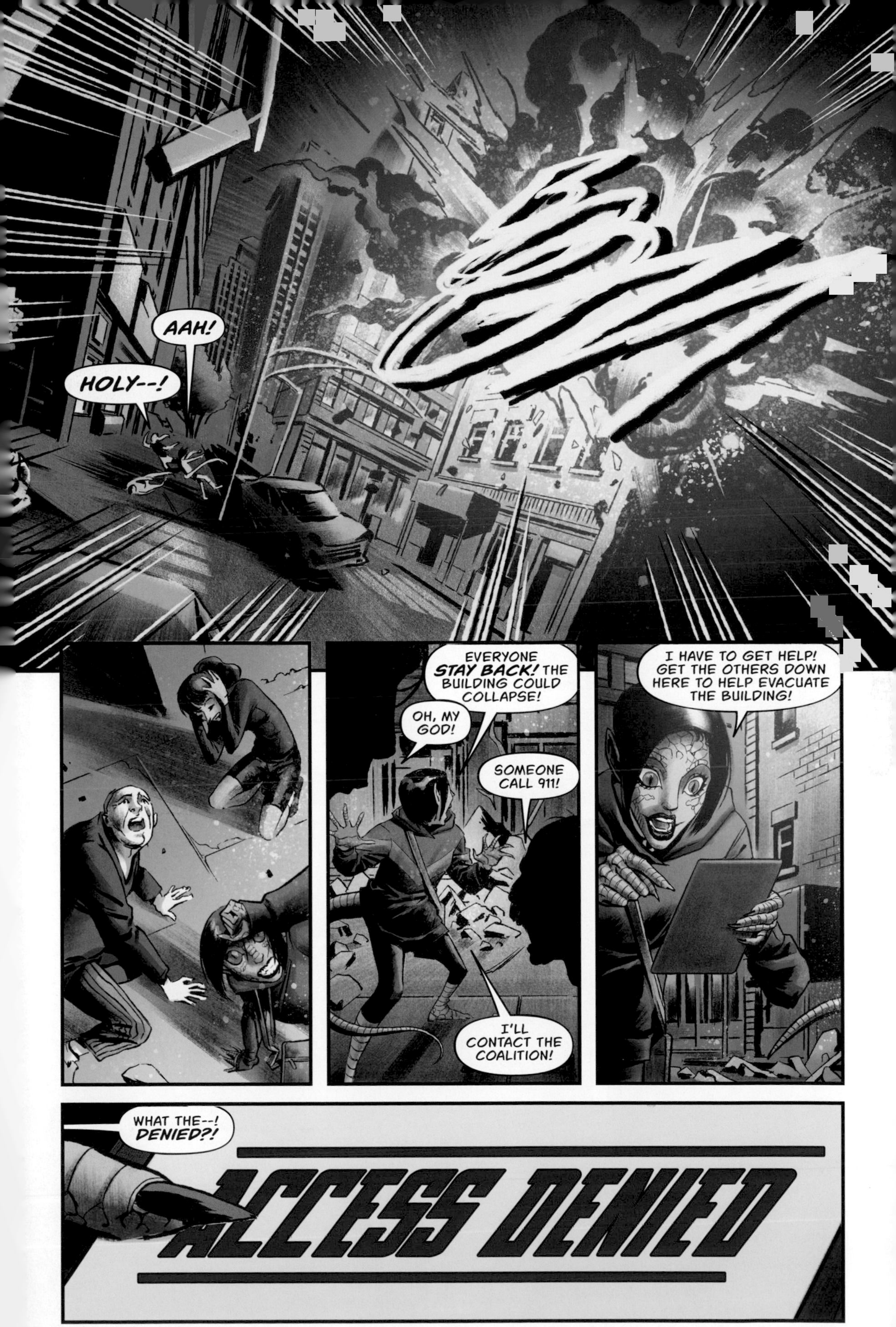
AAH!
HOLY--!
EVERYONE STAY BACK! THE BUILDING COULD COLLAPSE!
OH, MY GOD!
SOMEONE CALL 911!
I'LL CONTACT THE COALITION!
I HAVE TO GET HELP! GET THE OTHERS DOWN HERE TO HELP EVACUATE THE BUILDING!
WHAT THE--! DENIED?!
ACCESS DENIED

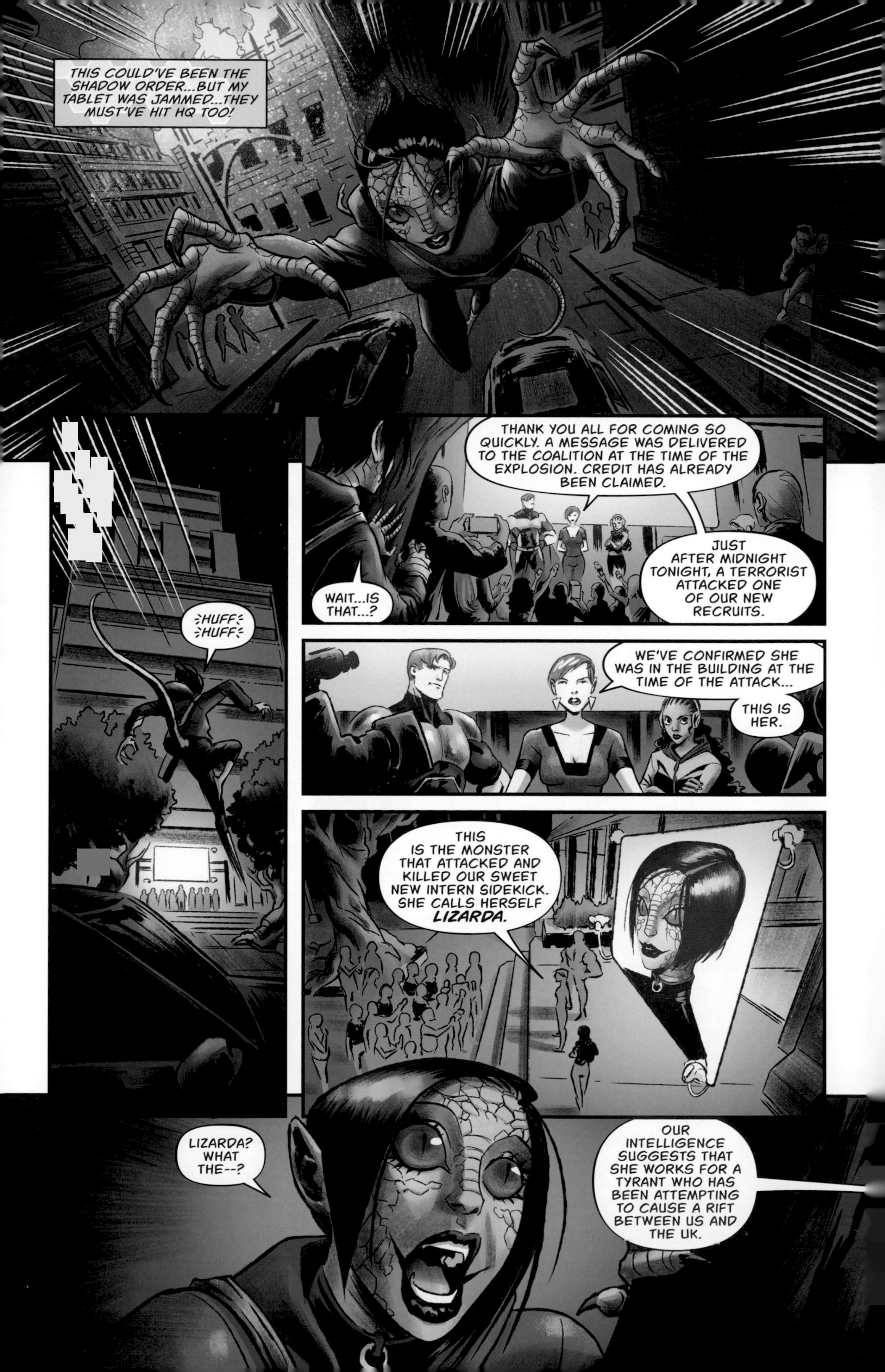
THIS COULD'VE BEEN THE SHADOW ORDER...BUT MY TABLET WAS JAMMED...THEY MUST'VE HIT HQ TOO!
HUFF HUFF
THANK YOU ALL FOR COMING SO QUICKLY. A MESSAGE WAS DELIVERED TO THE COALITION AT THE TIME OF THE EXPLOSION. CREDIT HAS ALREADY BEEN CLAIMED.
WAIT...IS THAT...?
JUST AFTER MIDNIGHT TONIGHT, A TERRORIST ATTACKED ONE OF OUR NEW RECRUITS.
WE'VE CONFIRMED SHE WAS IN THE BUILDING AT THE TIME OF THE ATTACK...
THIS IS HER.
THIS IS THE MONSTER THAT ATTACKED AND KILLED OUR SWEET NEW INTERN SIDEKICK. SHE CALLS HERSELF LIZARDA.
LIZARDA? WHAT THE--?
OUR INTELLIGENCE SUGGESTS THAT SHE WORKS FOR A TYRANT WHO HAS BEEN ATTEMPTING TO CAUSE A RIFT BETWEEN US AND THE UK.

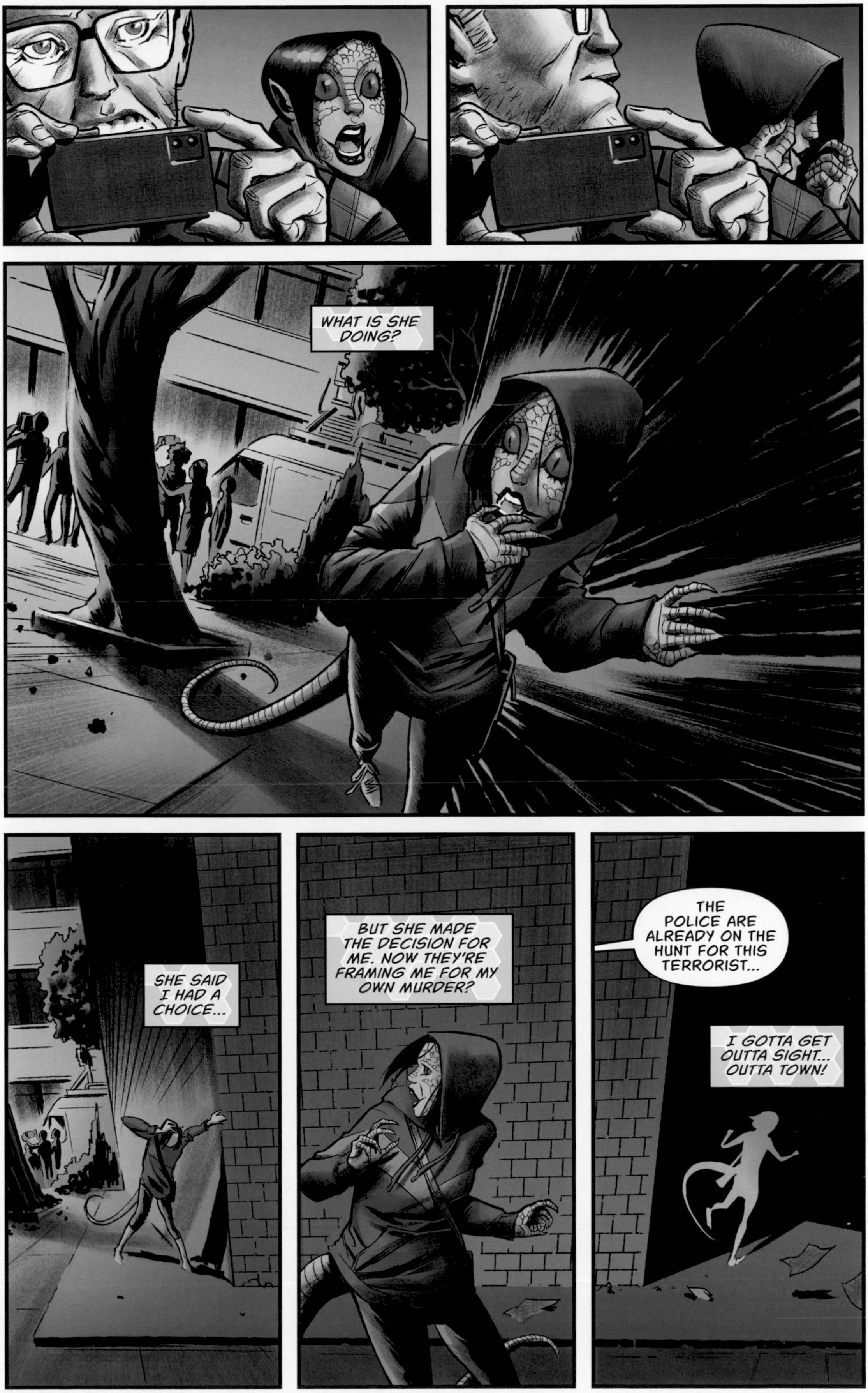

WHAT IS SHE DOING?
SHE SAID I HAD A CHOICE...
BUT SHE MADE THE DECISION FOR ME. NOW THEY'RE FRAMING ME FOR MY OWN MURDER?
THE POLICE ARE ALREADY ON THE HUNT FOR THIS TERRORIST...
I GOTTA GET OUTTA SIGHT... OUTTA TOWN!

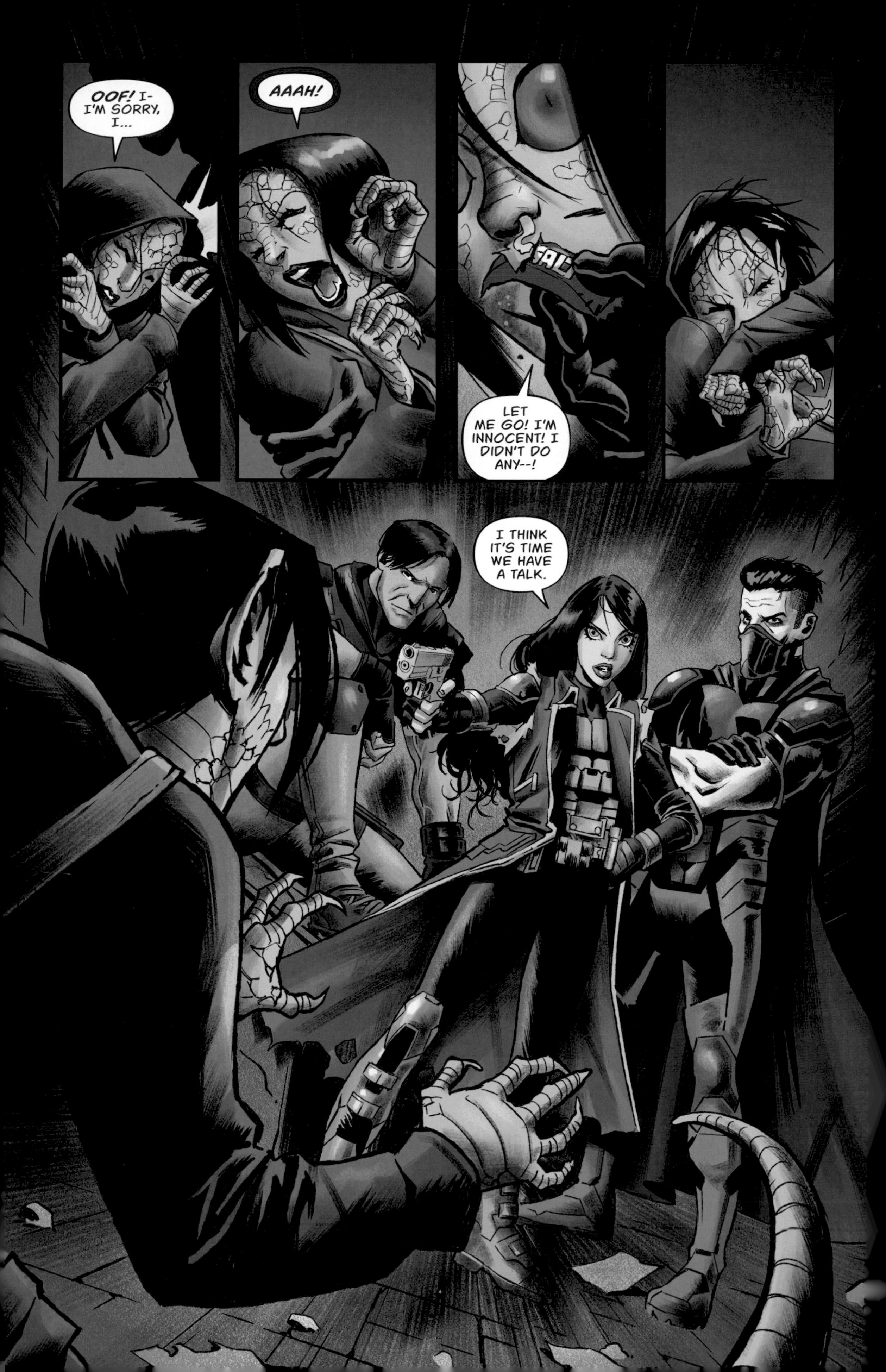
OOF! I-
I'M SORRY,
I...
AAAH!
LET ME GO! I'M INNOCENT! I DIDN'T DO ANY--!
I THINK IT'S TIME WE HAVE A TALK.

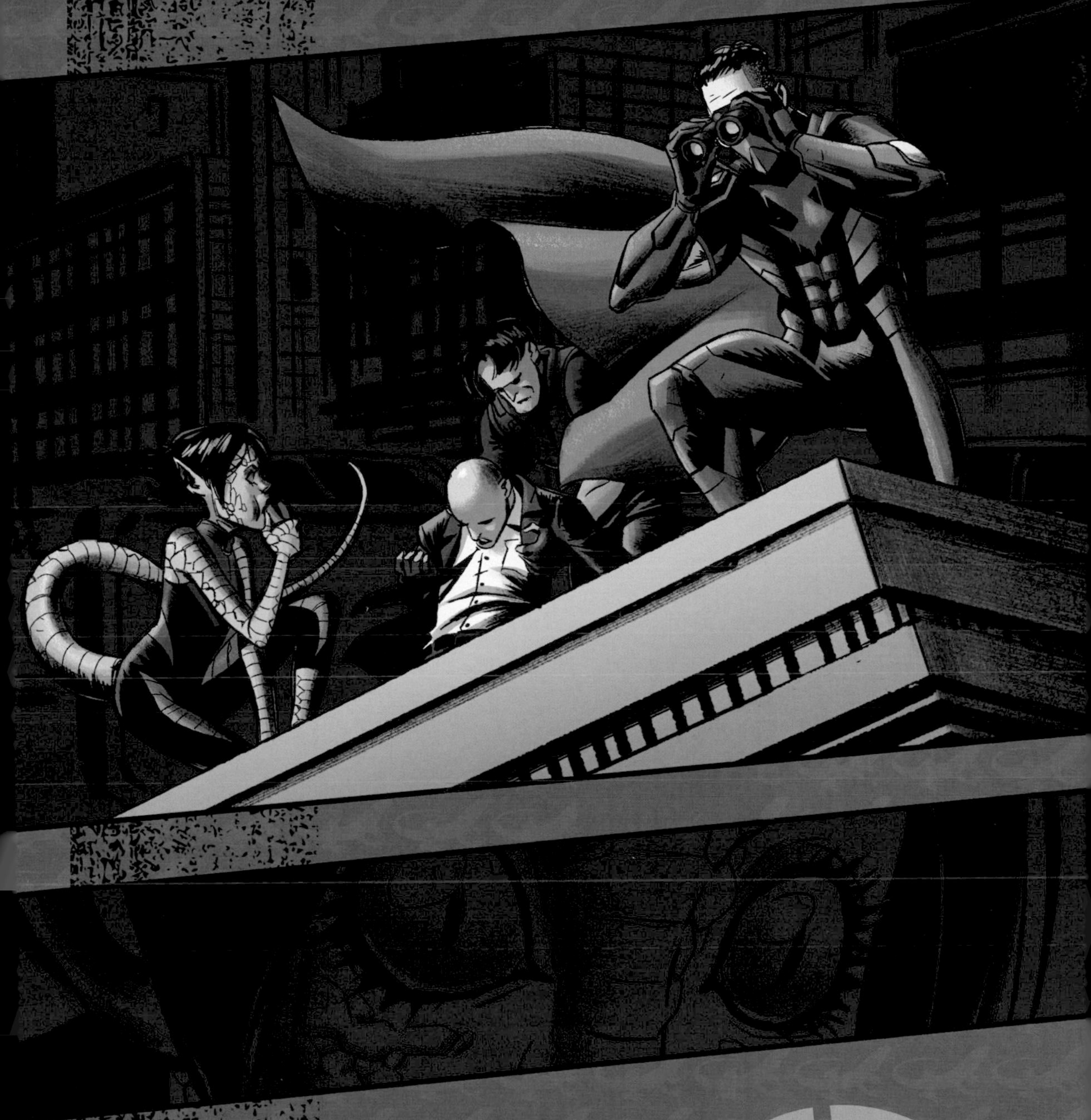

PART TWO

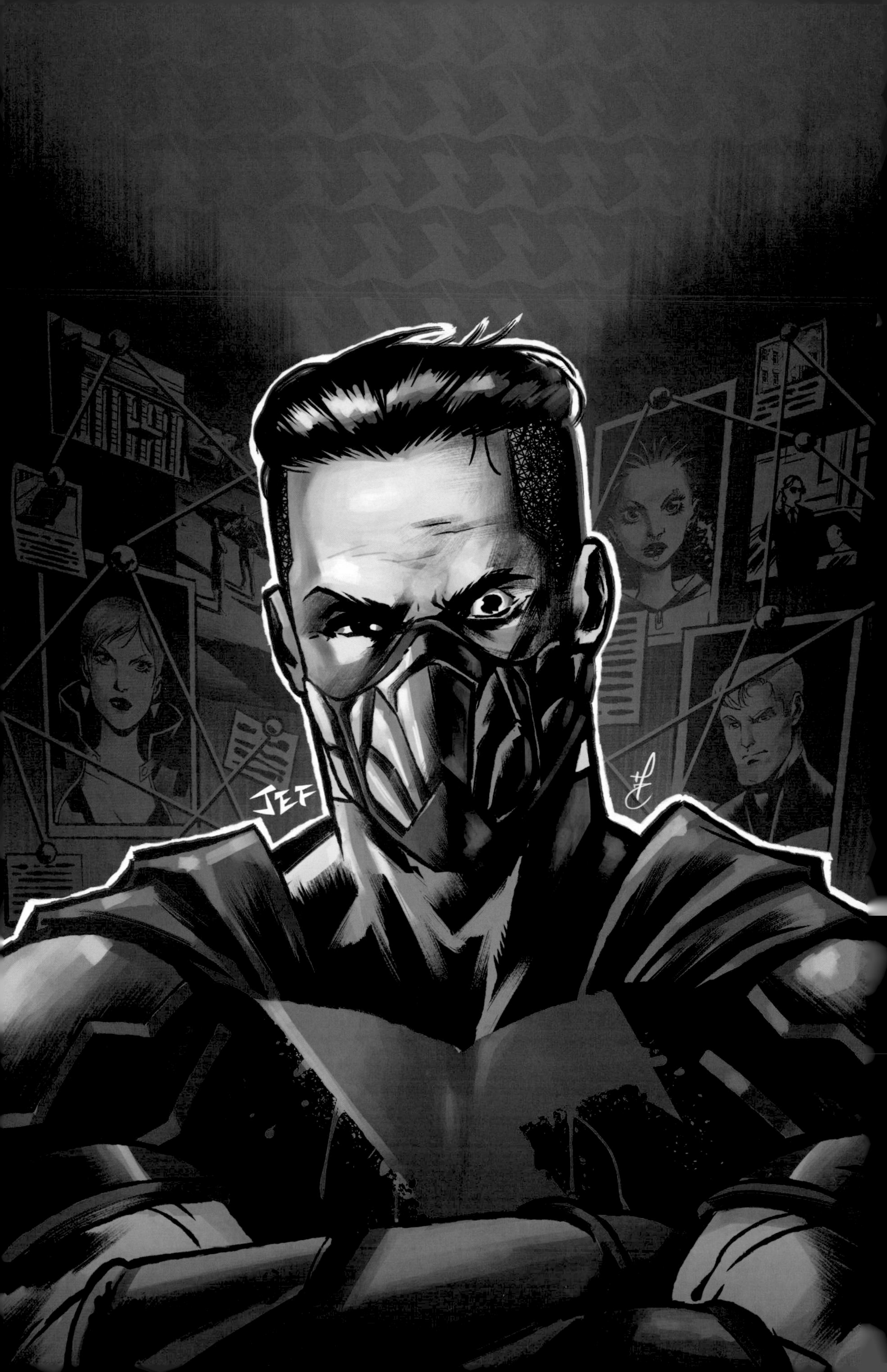
JEF

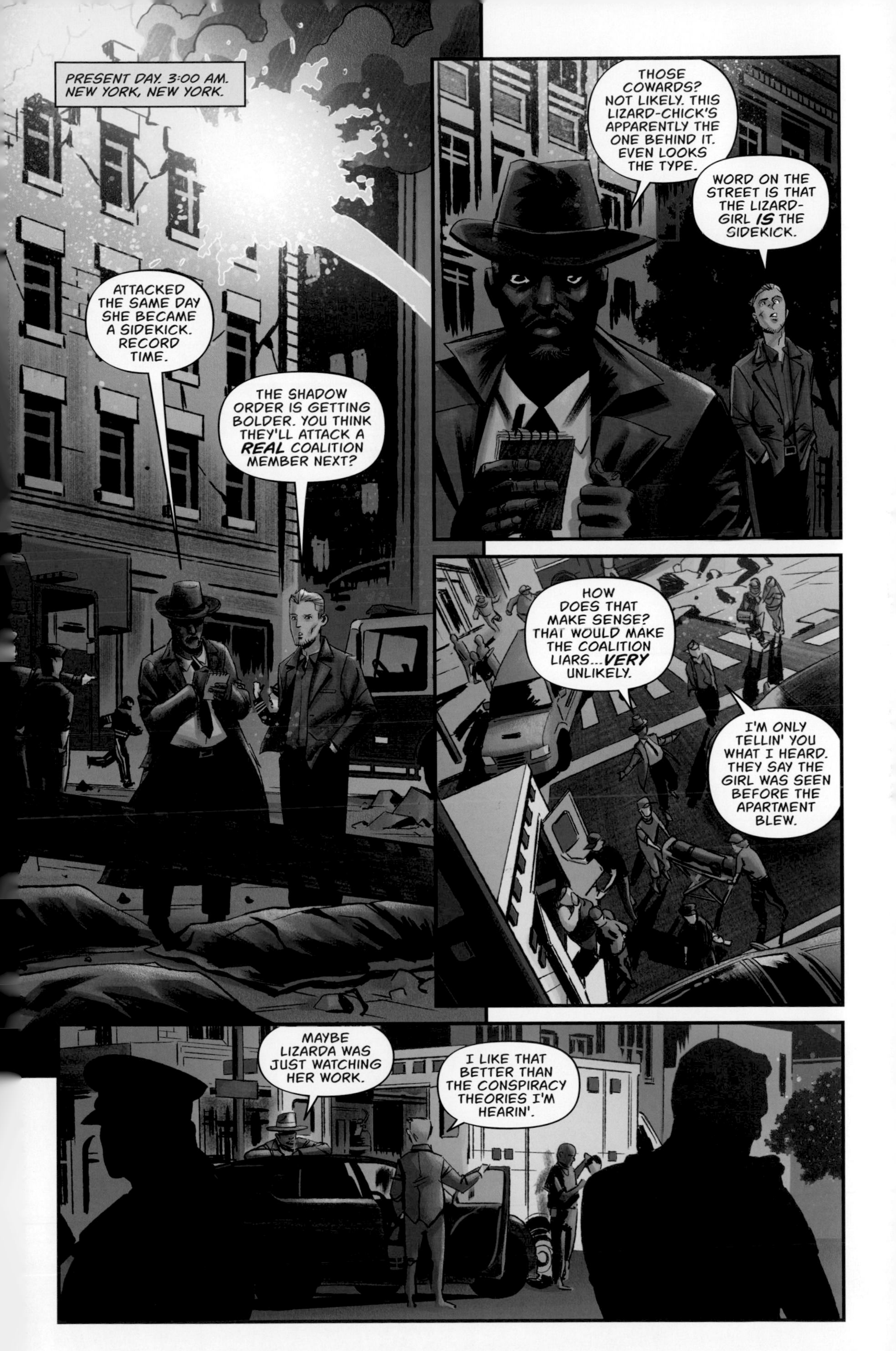
PRESENT DAY. 3:00 AM. NEW YORK, NEW YORK.
ATTACKED THE SAME DAY SHE BECAME A SIDEKICK. RECORD TIME.
THE SHADOW ORDER IS GETTING BOLDER. YOU THINK THEY'LL ATTACK A REAL COALITION MEMBER NEXT?
THOSE COWARDS? NOT LIKELY. THIS LIZARD-CHICK'S APPARENTLY THE ONE BEHIND IT. EVEN LOOKS THE TYPE.
WORD ON THE STREET IS THAT THE LIZARD-GIRL IS THE SIDEKICK.
HOW DOES THAT MAKE SENSE? THAT WOULD MAKE THE COALITION LIARS...VERY UNLIKELY.
I'M ONLY TELLIN' YOU WHAT I HEARD. THEY SAY THE GIRL WAS SEEN BEFORE THE APARTMENT BLEW.
MAYBE LIZARDA WAS JUST WATCHING HER WORK.
I LIKE THAT BETTER THAN THE CONSPIRACY THEORIES I'M HEARIN'.

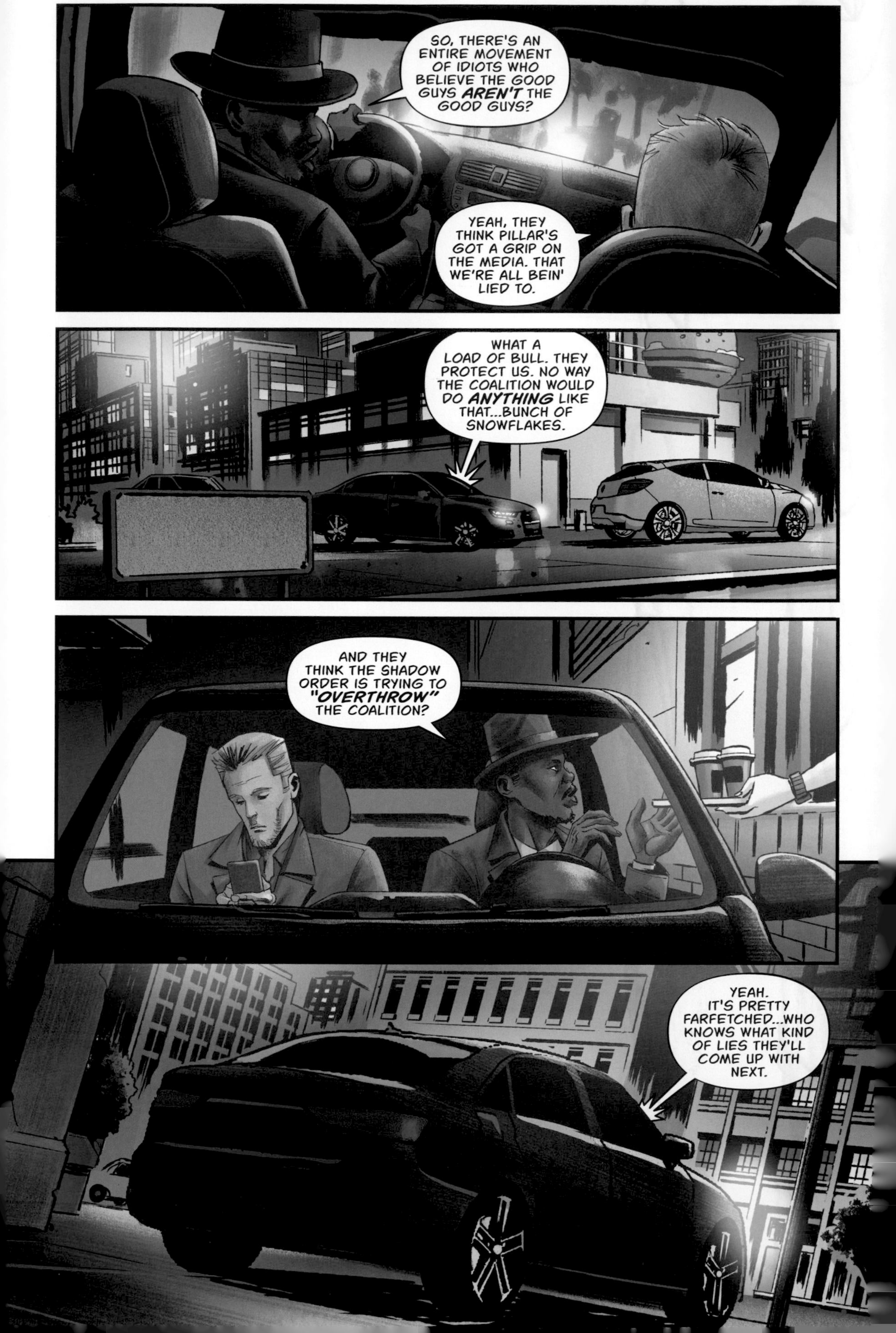
SO, THERE'S AN ENTIRE MOVEMENT OF IDIOTS WHO BELIEVE THE GOOD GUYS AREN'T THE GOOD GUYS?
YEAH, THEY THINK PILLAR'S GOT A GRIP ON THE MEDIA. THAT WE'RE ALL BEIN' LIED TO.
WHAT A LOAD OF BULL. THEY PROTECT US. NO WAY THE COALITION WOULD DO ANYTHING LIKE THAT...BUNCH OF SNOWFLAKES.
AND THEY THINK THE SHADOW ORDER IS TRYING TO "OVERTHROW" THE COALITION?
YEAH. IT'S PRETTY FARFETCHED...WHO KNOWS WHAT KIND OF LIES THEY'LL COME UP WITH NEXT.

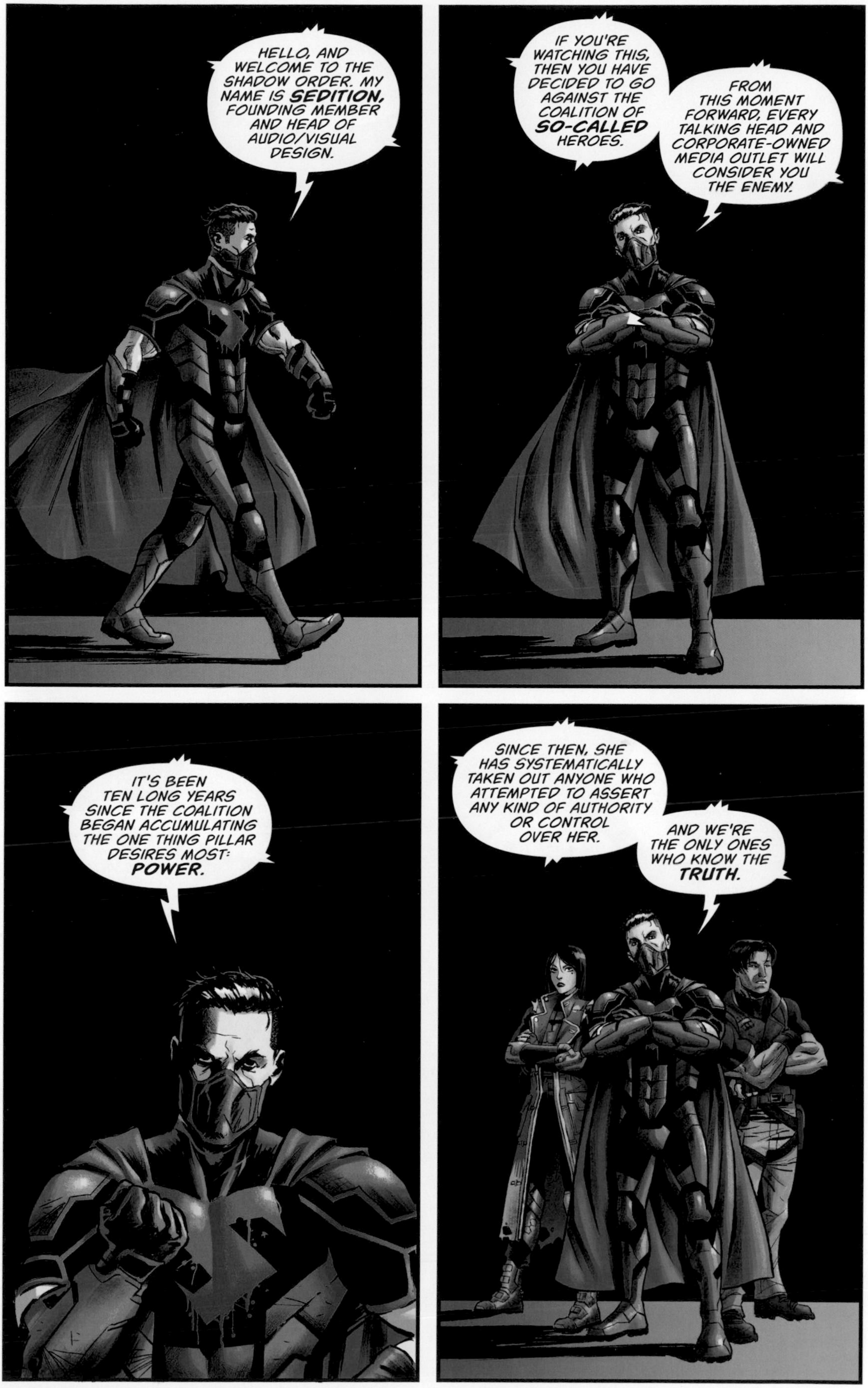
HELLO, AND WELCOME TO THE SHADOW ORDER. MY NAME IS SEDITION, FOUNDING MEMBER AND HEAD OF AUDIO/VISUAL DESIGN.
IF YOU'RE WATCHING THIS, THEN YOU HAVE DECIDED TO GO AGAINST THE COALITION OF SO-CALLED HEROES.
FROM THIS MOMENT FORWARD, EVERY TALKING HEAD AND CORPORATE-OWNED MEDIA OUTLET WILL CONSIDER YOU THE ENEMY.
IT'S BEEN TEN LONG YEARS SINCE THE COALITION BEGAN ACCUMULATING THE ONE THING PILLAR DESIRES MOST: POWER.
SINCE THEN, SHE HAS SYSTEMATICALLY TAKEN OUT ANYONE WHO ATTEMPTED TO ASSERT ANY KIND OF AUTHORITY OR CONTROL OVER HER.
AND WE'RE THE ONLY ONES WHO KNOW THE TRUTH.

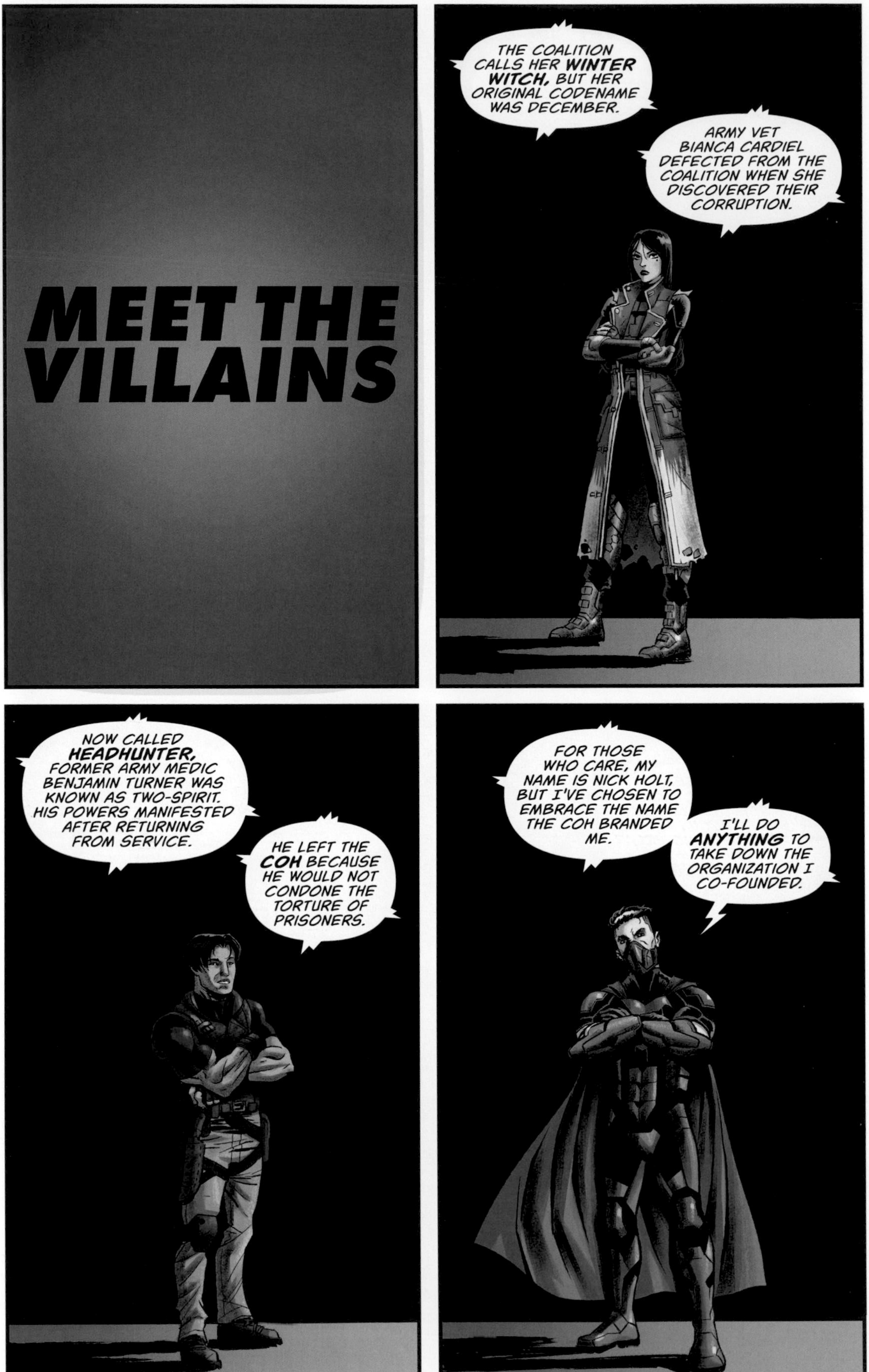
MEET THE VILLAINS
THE COALITION CALLS HER WINTER WITCH, BUT HER ORIGINAL CODENAME WAS DECEMBER.
ARMY VET BIANCA CARDIEL DEFECTED FROM THE COALITION WHEN SHE DISCOVERED THEIR CORRUPTION.
NOW CALLED HEADHUNTER, FORMER ARMY MEDIC BENJAMIN TURNER WAS KNOWN AS TWO-SPIRIT. HIS POWERS MANIFESTED AFTER RETURNING FROM SERVICE.
HE LEFT THE COH BECAUSE HE WOULD NOT CONDONE THE TORTURE OF PRISONERS.
FOR THOSE WHO CARE, MY NAME IS NICK HOLT, BUT I'VE CHOSEN TO EMBRACE THE NAME THE COH BRANDED ME.
I'LL DO ANYTHING TO TAKE DOWN THE ORGANIZATION I CO-FOUNDED.

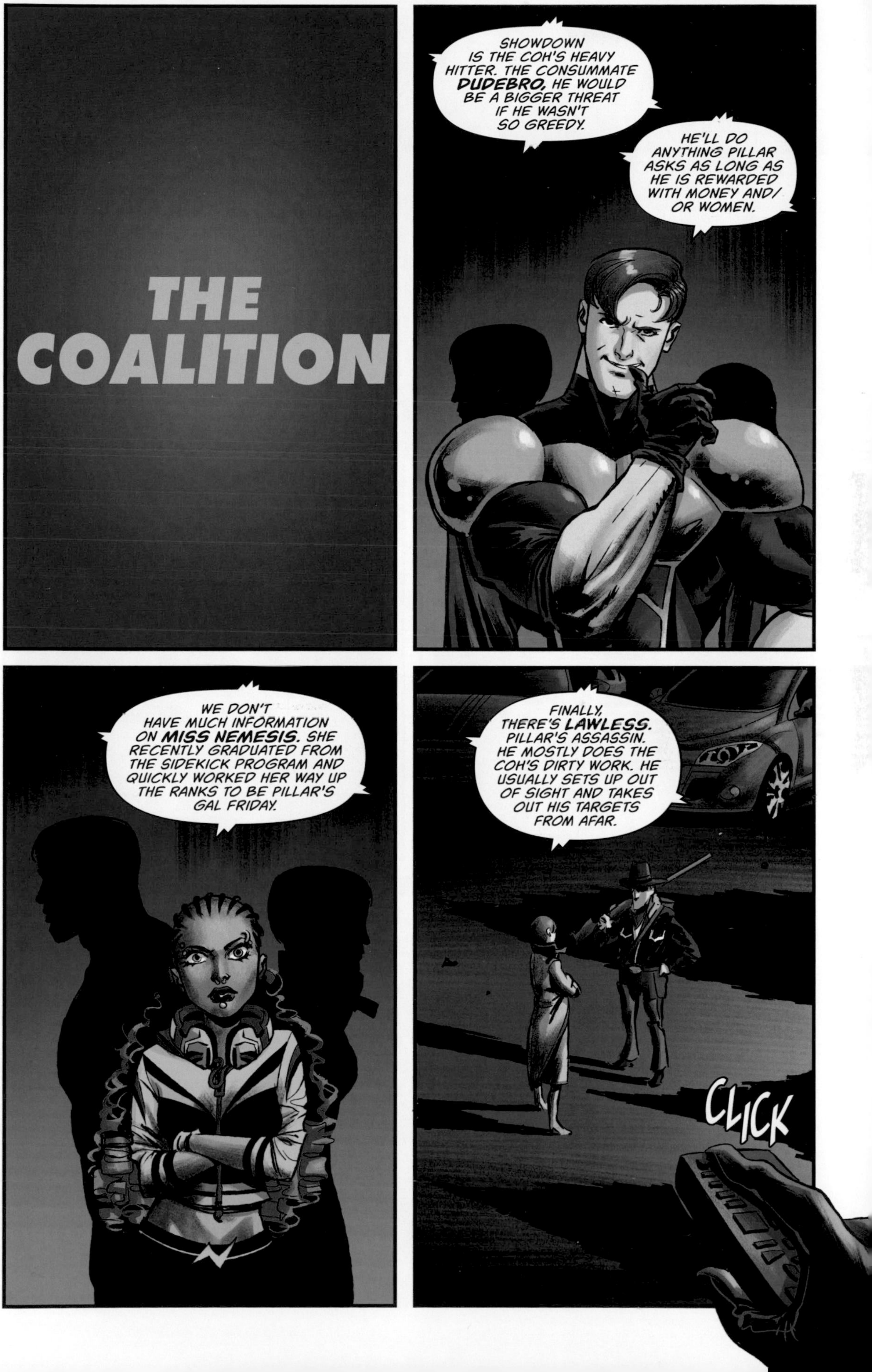
THE COALITION
SHOWDOWN IS THE COH'S HEAVY HITTER. THE CONSUMMATE DUDEBRO, HE WOULD BE A BIGGER THREAT IF HE WASN'T SO GREEDY.
HE'LL DO ANYTHING PILLAR ASKS AS LONG AS HE IS REWARDED WITH MONEY AND/ OR WOMEN.
WE DON'T HAVE MUCH INFORMATION ON MISS NEMESIS. SHE RECENTLY GRADUATED FROM THE SIDEKICK PROGRAM AND QUICKLY WORKED HER WAY UP THE RANKS TO BE PILLAR'S GAL FRIDAY.
FINALLY, THERE'S LAWLESS. PILLAR'S ASSASSIN. HE MOSTLY DOES THE COH'S DIRTY WORK. HE USUALLY SETS UP OUT OF SIGHT AND TAKES OUT HIS TARGETS FROM AFAR.
CLICK

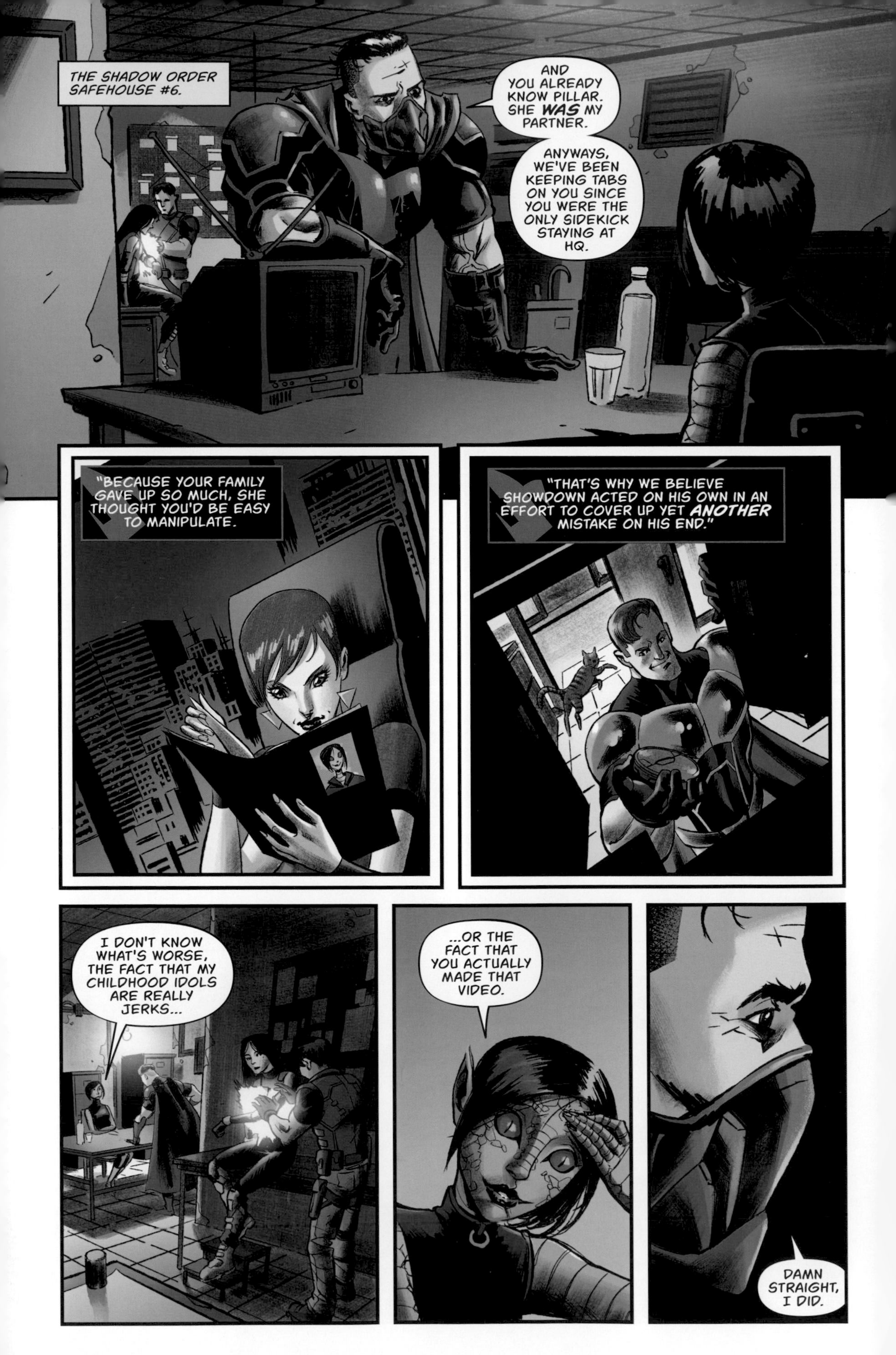
THE SHADOW ORDER SAFEHOUSE #6.
AND YOU ALREADY KNOW PILLAR. SHE WAS MY PARTNER.
ANYWAYS, WE'VE BEEN KEEPING TABS ON YOU SINCE YOU WERE THE ONLY SIDEKICK STAYING AT HQ.
"BECAUSE YOUR FAMILY GAVE UP SO MUCH, SHE THOUGHT YOU'D BE EASY TO MANIPULATE.
"THAT'S WHY WE BELIEVE SHOWDOWN ACTED ON HIS OWN IN AN EFFORT TO COVER UP YET ANOTHER MISTAKE ON HIS END."
I DON'T KNOW WHAT'S WORSE, THE FACT THAT MY CHILDHOOD IDOLS ARE REALLY JERKS...
...OR THE FACT THAT YOU ACTUALLY MADE THAT VIDEO.
DAMN STRAIGHT, I DID.

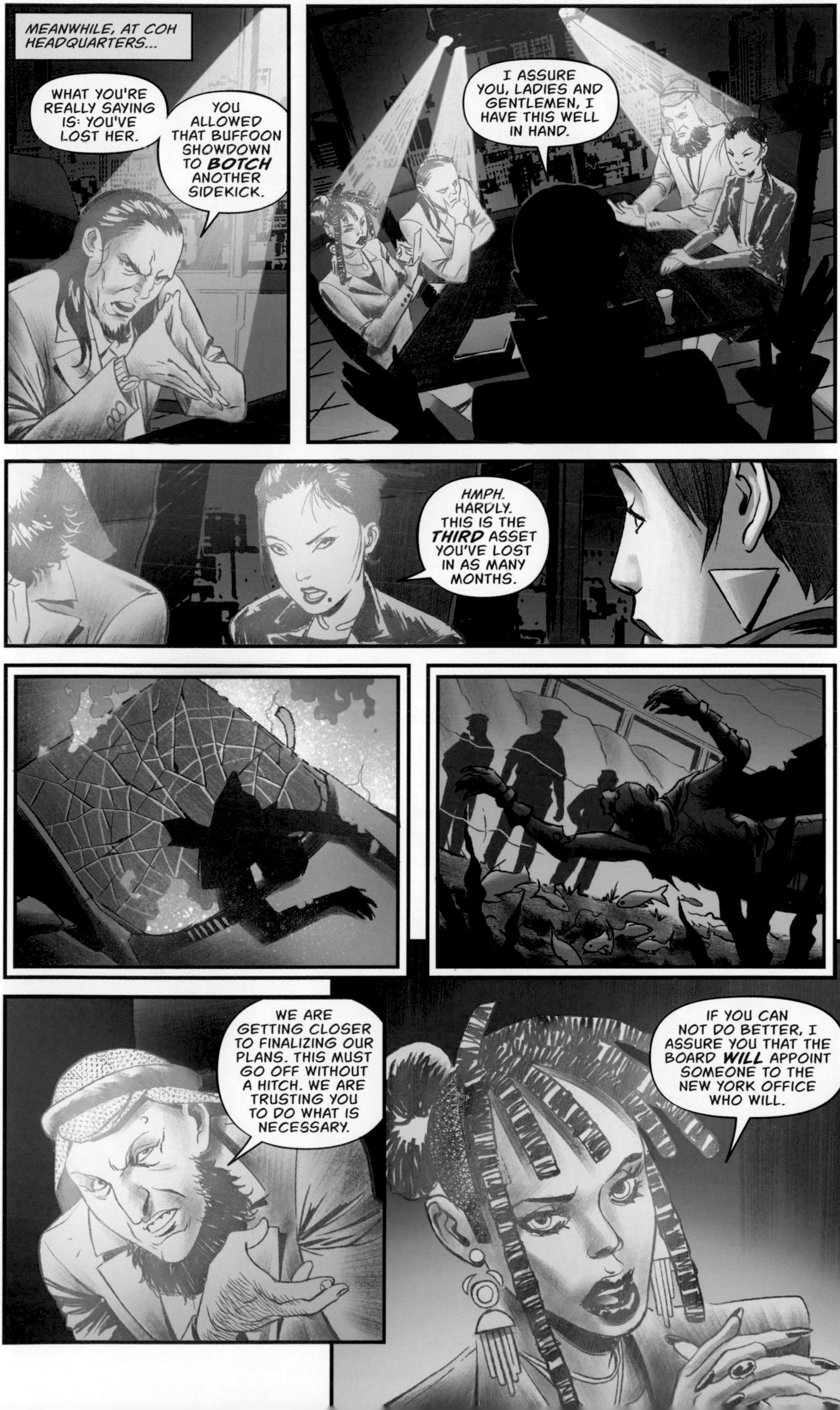
MEANWHILE, AT COH HEADQUARTERS...
WHAT YOU'RE REALLY SAYING IS: YOU'VE LOST HER.
YOU ALLOWED THAT BUFFOON SHOWDOWN TO BOTCH ANOTHER SIDEKICK.
I ASSURE YOU, LADIES AND GENTLEMEN, I HAVE THIS WELL IN HAND.
HMPH. HARDLY. THIS IS THE THIRD ASSET YOU'VE LOST IN AS MANY MONTHS.
WE ARE GETTING CLOSER TO FINALIZING OUR PLANS. THIS MUST GO OFF WITHOUT A HITCH. WE ARE TRUSTING YOU TO DO WHAT IS NECESSARY.
IF YOU CAN NOT DO BETTER, I ASSURE YOU THAT THE BOARD WILL APPOINT SOMEONE TO THE NEW YORK OFFICE WHO WILL.

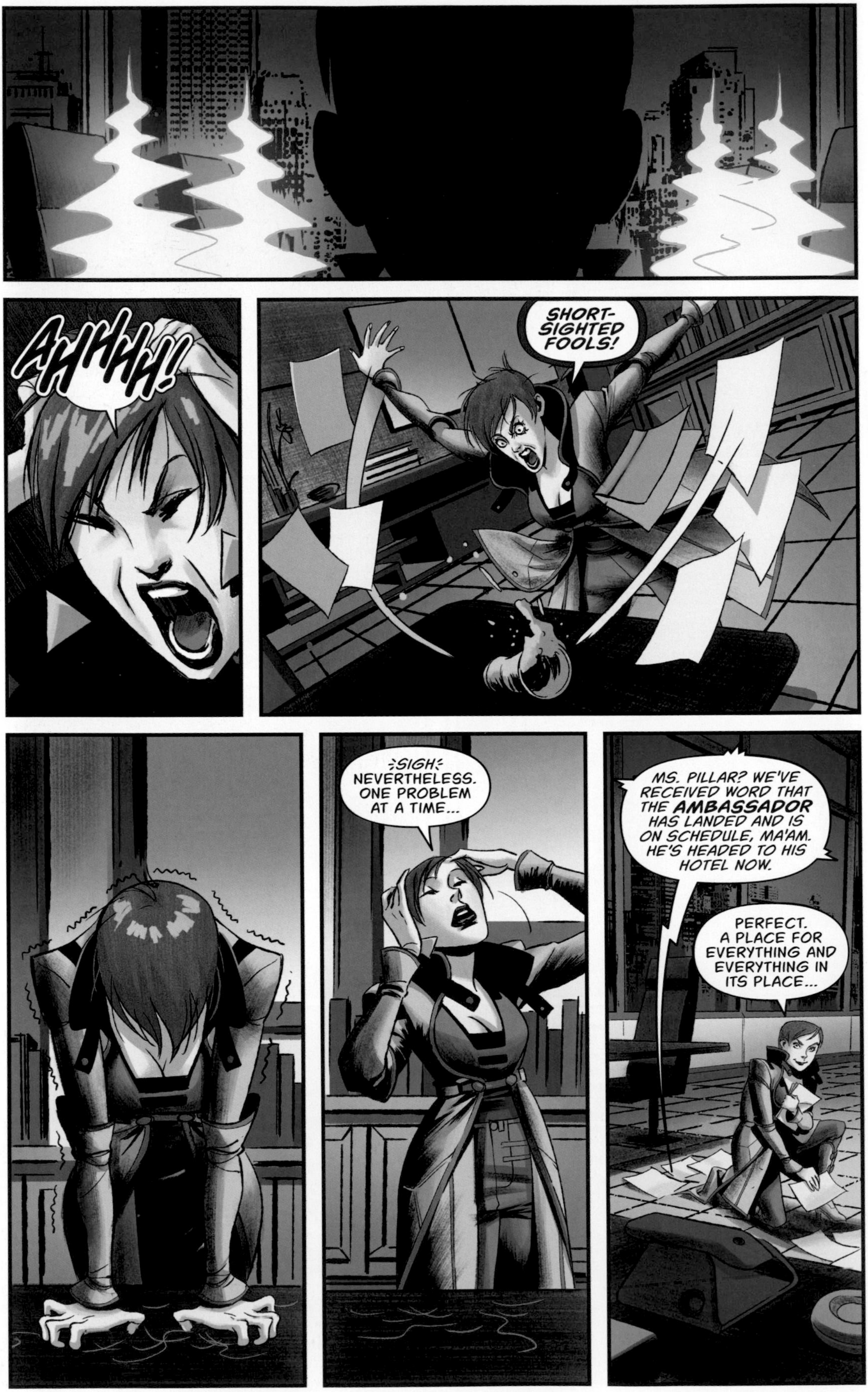
AHHHHH!
SHORT-SIGHTED FOOLS!
SIGH
NEVERTHELESS. ONE PROBLEM AT A TIME...
MS. PILLAR? WE'VE RECEIVED WORD THAT THE AMBASSADOR HAS LANDED AND IS ON SCHEDULE, MA'AM. HE'S HEADED TO HIS HOTEL NOW.
PERFECT. A PLACE FOR EVERYTHING AND EVERYTHING IN ITS PLACE...

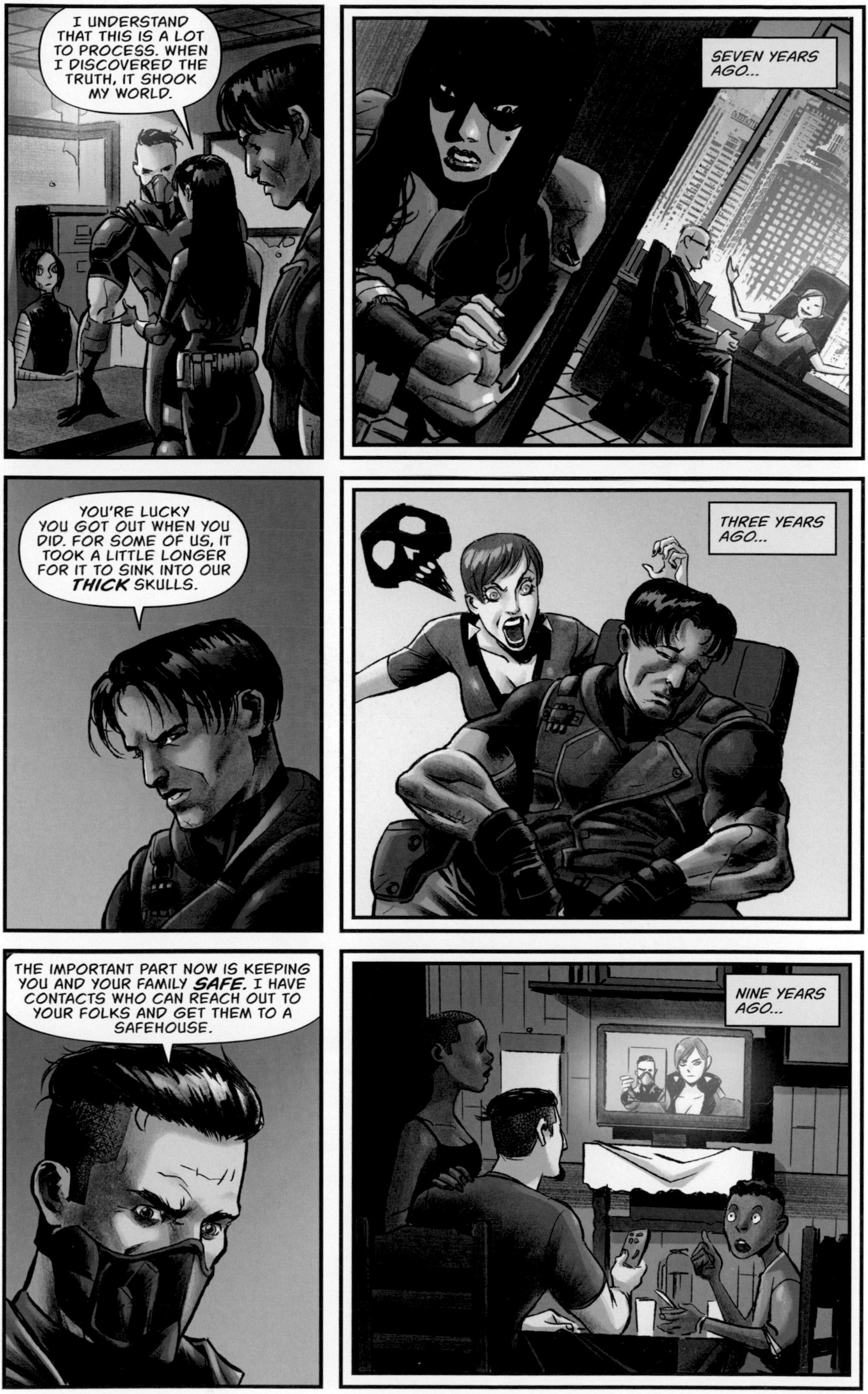
I UNDERSTAND THAT THIS IS A LOT TO PROCESS. WHEN I DISCOVERED THE TRUTH, IT SHOOK MY WORLD.
SEVEN YEARS AGO...
YOU'RE LUCKY YOU GOT OUT WHEN YOU DID. FOR SOME OF US, IT TOOK A LITTLE LONGER FOR IT TO SINK INTO OUR *THICK* SKULLS.
THREE YEARS AGO...
THE IMPORTANT PART NOW IS KEEPING YOU AND YOUR FAMILY *SAFE.* I HAVE CONTACTS WHO CAN REACH OUT TO YOUR FOLKS AND GET THEM TO A SAFEHOUSE.
NINE YEARS AGO...

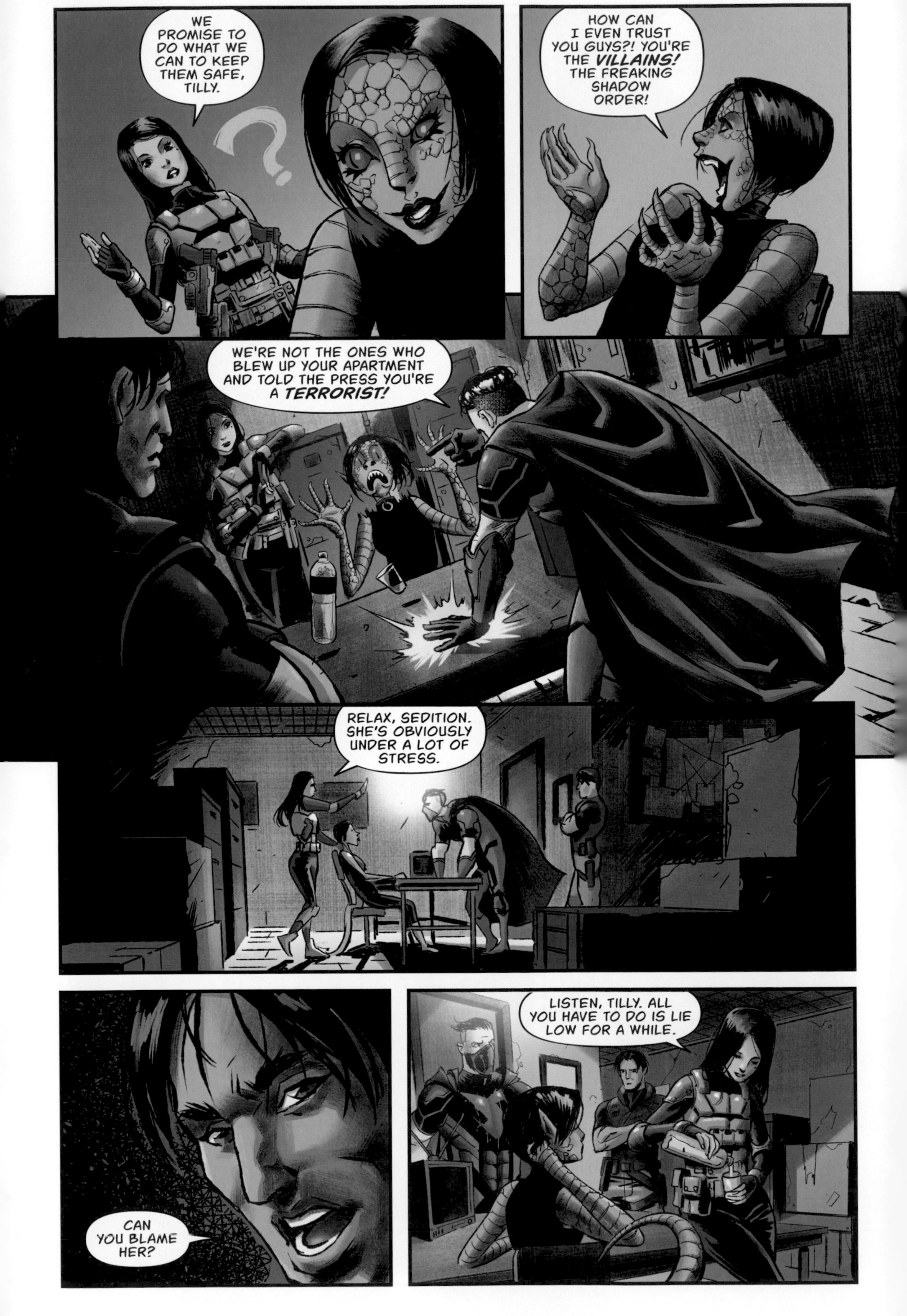
WE PROMISE TO DO WHAT WE CAN TO KEEP THEM SAFE, TILLY.
HOW CAN I EVEN TRUST YOU GUYS?! YOU'RE THE VILLAINS! THE FREAKING SHADOW ORDER!
WE'RE NOT THE ONES WHO BLEW UP YOUR APARTMENT AND TOLD THE PRESS YOU'RE A TERRORIST!
RELAX, SEDITION. SHE'S OBVIOUSLY UNDER A LOT OF STRESS.
CAN YOU BLAME HER?
LISTEN, TILLY. ALL YOU HAVE TO DO IS LIE LOW FOR A WHILE.

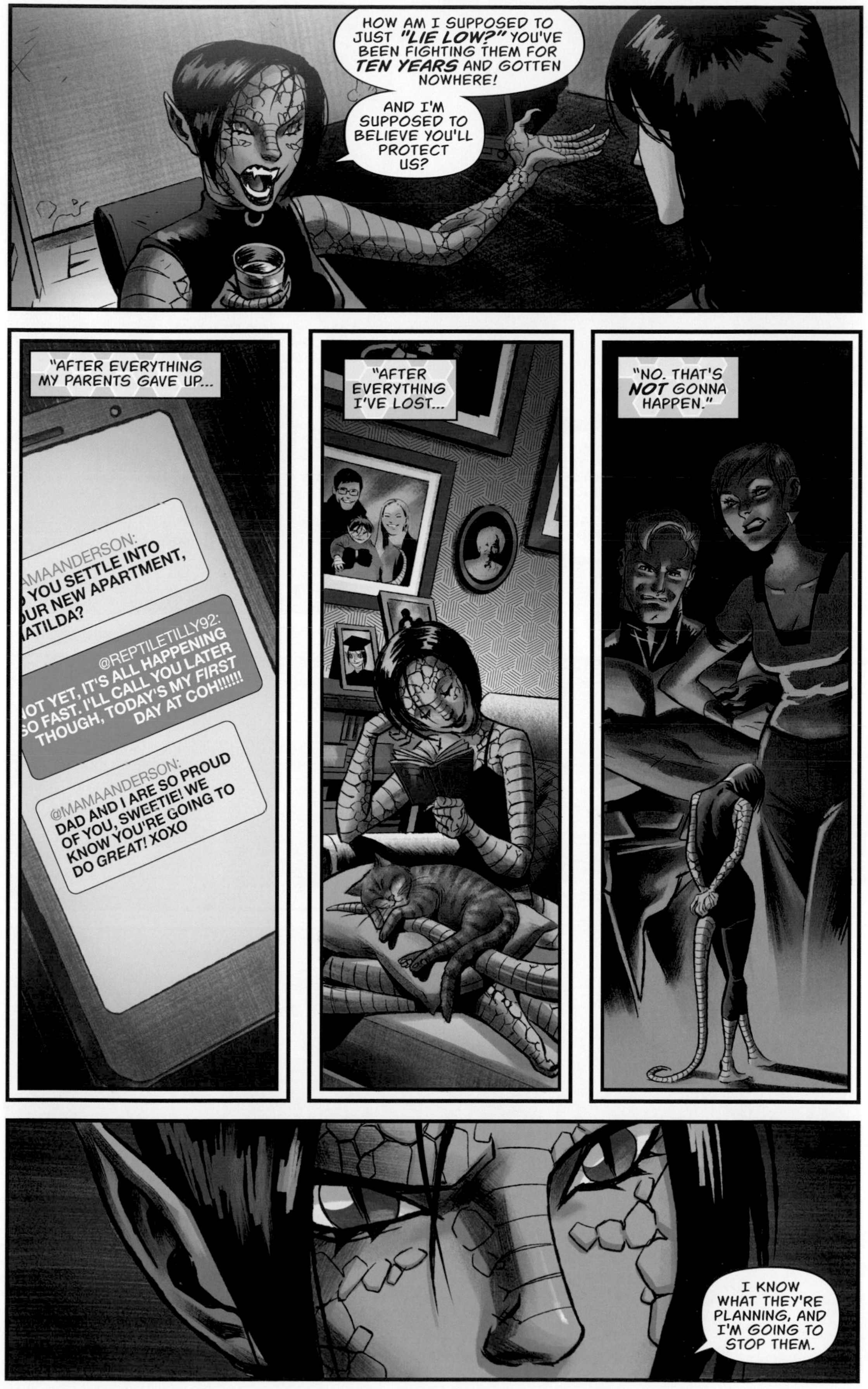

HOW AM I SUPPOSED TO JUST "LIE LOW?" YOU'VE BEEN FIGHTING THEM FOR TEN YEARS AND GOTTEN NOWHERE!
AND I'M SUPPOSED TO BELIEVE YOU'LL PROTECT US?
"AFTER EVERYTHING MY PARENTS GAVE UP...
MAMAANDERSON:
D YOU SETTLE INTO
OUR NEW APARTMENT,
ATILDA?
@REPTILETILLY92:
NOT YET, IT'S ALL HAPPENING SO FAST. I'LL CALL YOU LATER THOUGH, TODAY'S MY FIRST DAY AT COH!!!!!!
@MAMAANDERSON:
DAD AND I ARE SO PROUD OF YOU, SWEETIE! WE KNOW YOU'RE GOING TO DO GREAT! XOXO
"AFTER EVERYTHING I'VE LOST...
"NO. THAT'S NOT GONNA HAPPEN."
I KNOW WHAT THEY'RE PLANNING, AND I'M GOING TO STOP THEM.

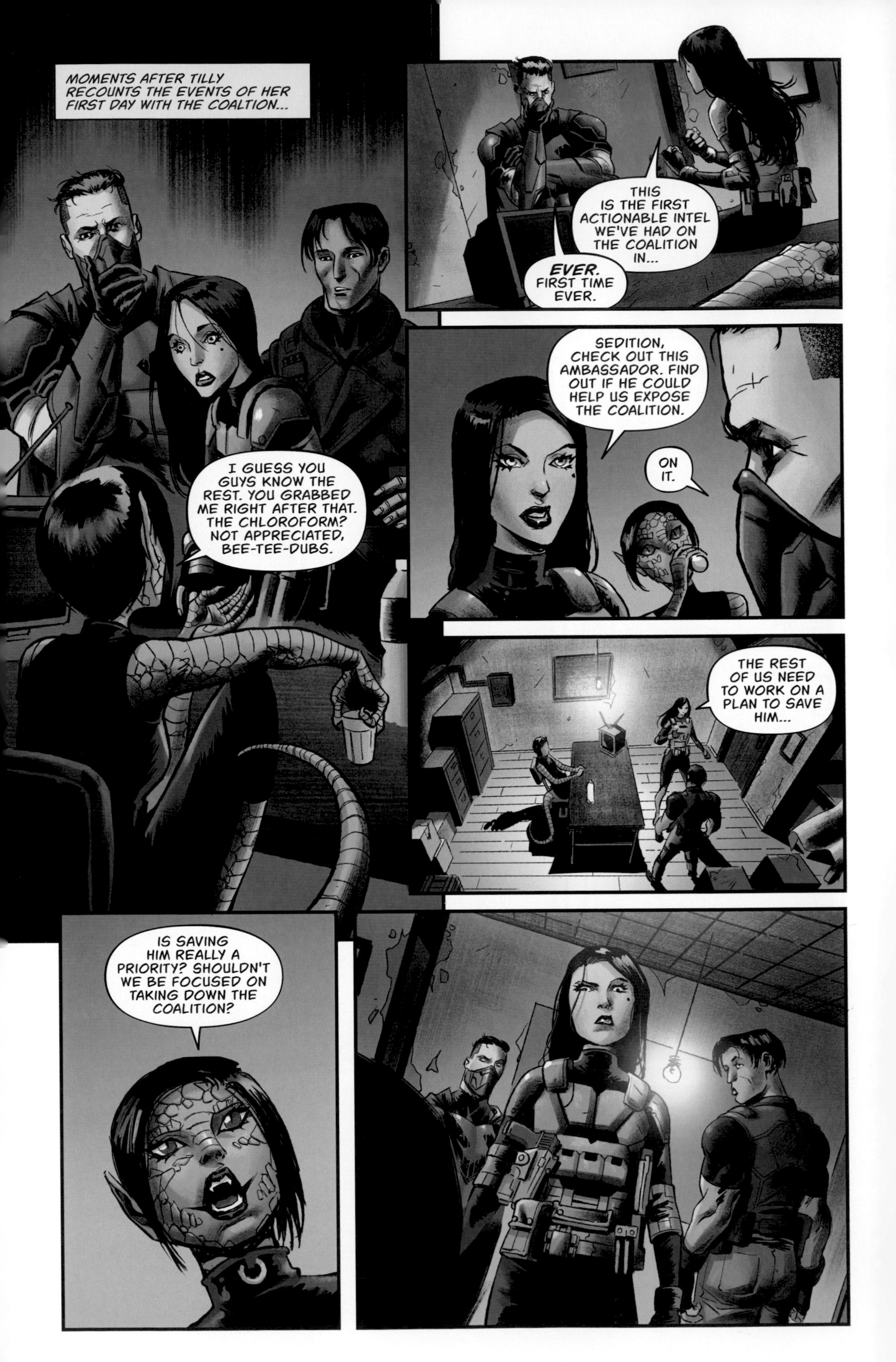
MOMENTS AFTER TILLY RECOUNTS THE EVENTS OF HER FIRST DAY WITH THE COALTION...
I GUESS YOU GUYS KNOW THE REST. YOU GRABBED ME RIGHT AFTER THAT. THE CHLOROFORM? NOT APPRECIATED, BEE-TEE-DUBS.
THIS IS THE FIRST ACTIONABLE INTEL WE'VE HAD ON THE COALITION IN...
EVER. FIRST TIME EVER.
SEDITION, CHECK OUT THIS AMBASSADOR. FIND OUT IF HE COULD HELP US EXPOSE THE COALITION.
ON IT.
THE REST OF US NEED TO WORK ON A PLAN TO SAVE HIM...
IS SAVING HIM REALLY A PRIORITY? SHOULDN'T WE BE FOCUSED ON TAKING DOWN THE COALITION?

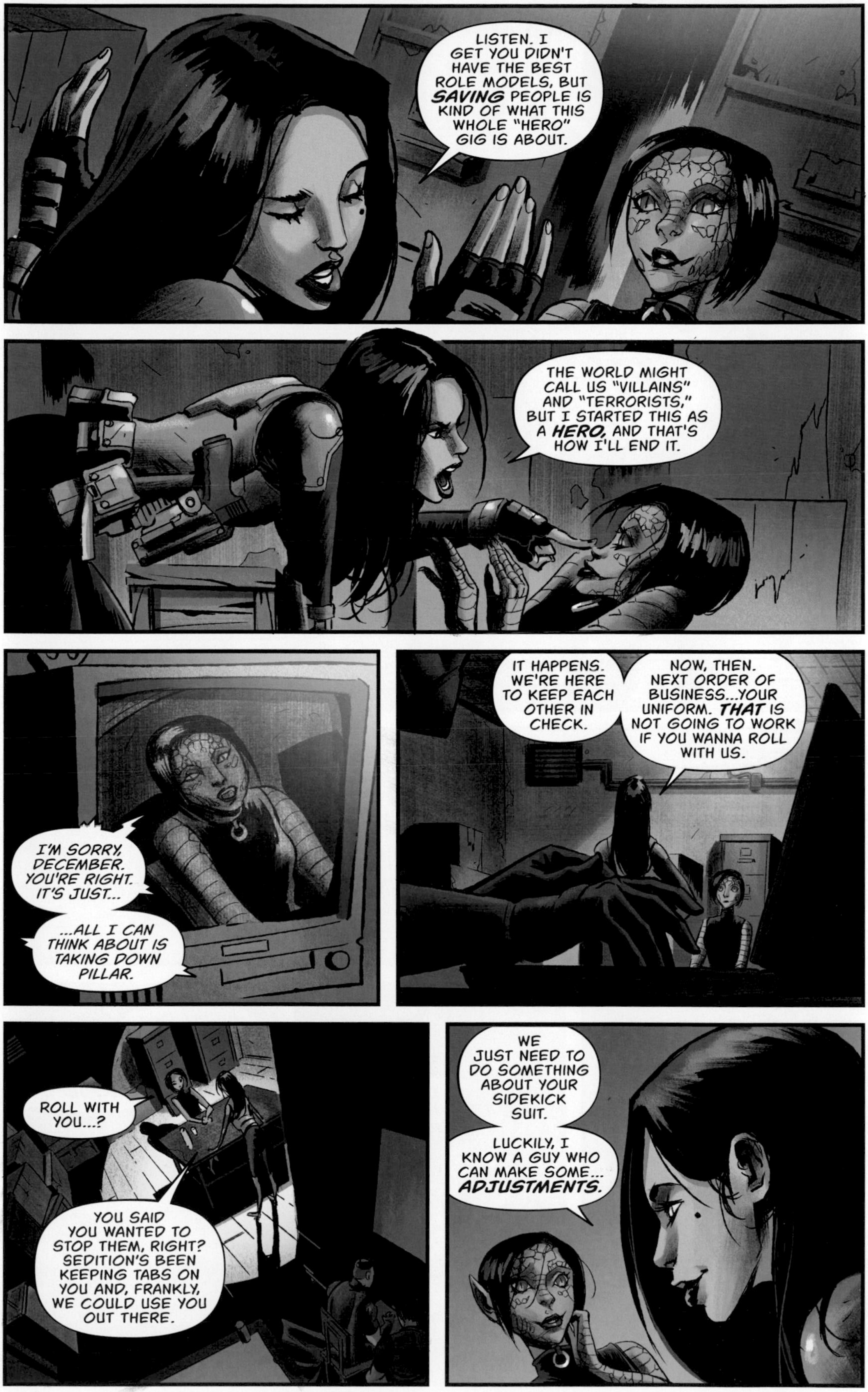
LISTEN. I GET YOU DIDN'T HAVE THE BEST ROLE MODELS, BUT **SAVING** PEOPLE IS KIND OF WHAT THIS WHOLE "HERO" GIG IS ABOUT.
THE WORLD MIGHT CALL US "VILLAINS" AND "TERRORISTS," BUT I STARTED THIS AS A **HERO,** AND THAT'S HOW I'LL END IT.
I'M SORRY, DECEMBER. YOU'RE RIGHT. IT'S JUST...
...ALL I CAN THINK ABOUT IS TAKING DOWN PILLAR.
IT HAPPENS. WE'RE HERE TO KEEP EACH OTHER IN CHECK.
NOW, THEN. NEXT ORDER OF BUSINESS...YOUR UNIFORM. **THAT** IS NOT GOING TO WORK IF YOU WANNA ROLL WITH US.
ROLL WITH YOU...?
YOU SAID YOU WANTED TO STOP THEM, RIGHT? SEDITION'S BEEN KEEPING TABS ON YOU AND, FRANKLY, WE COULD USE YOU OUT THERE.
WE JUST NEED TO DO SOMETHING ABOUT YOUR SIDEKICK SUIT.
LUCKILY, I KNOW A GUY WHO CAN MAKE SOME... **ADJUSTMENTS.**

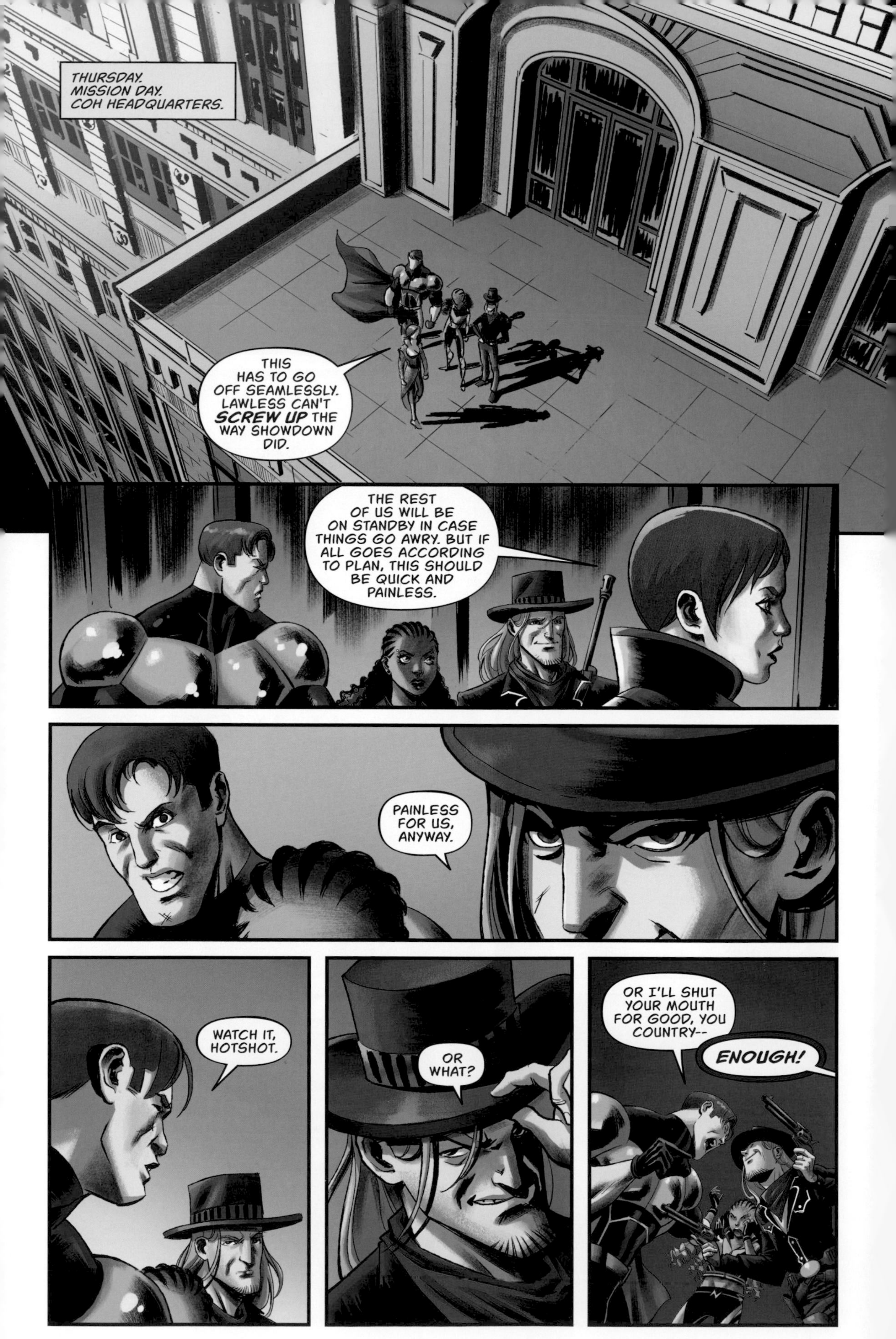
THURSDAY. MISSION DAY. COH HEADQUARTERS.
THIS HAS TO GO OFF SEAMLESSLY. LAWLESS CAN'T SCREW UP THE WAY SHOWDOWN DID.
THE REST OF US WILL BE ON STANDBY IN CASE THINGS GO AWRY. BUT IF ALL GOES ACCORDING TO PLAN, THIS SHOULD BE QUICK AND PAINLESS.
PAINLESS FOR US, ANYWAY.
WATCH IT, HOTSHOT.
OR WHAT?
OR I'LL SHUT YOUR MOUTH FOR GOOD, YOU COUNTRY--
ENOUGH!

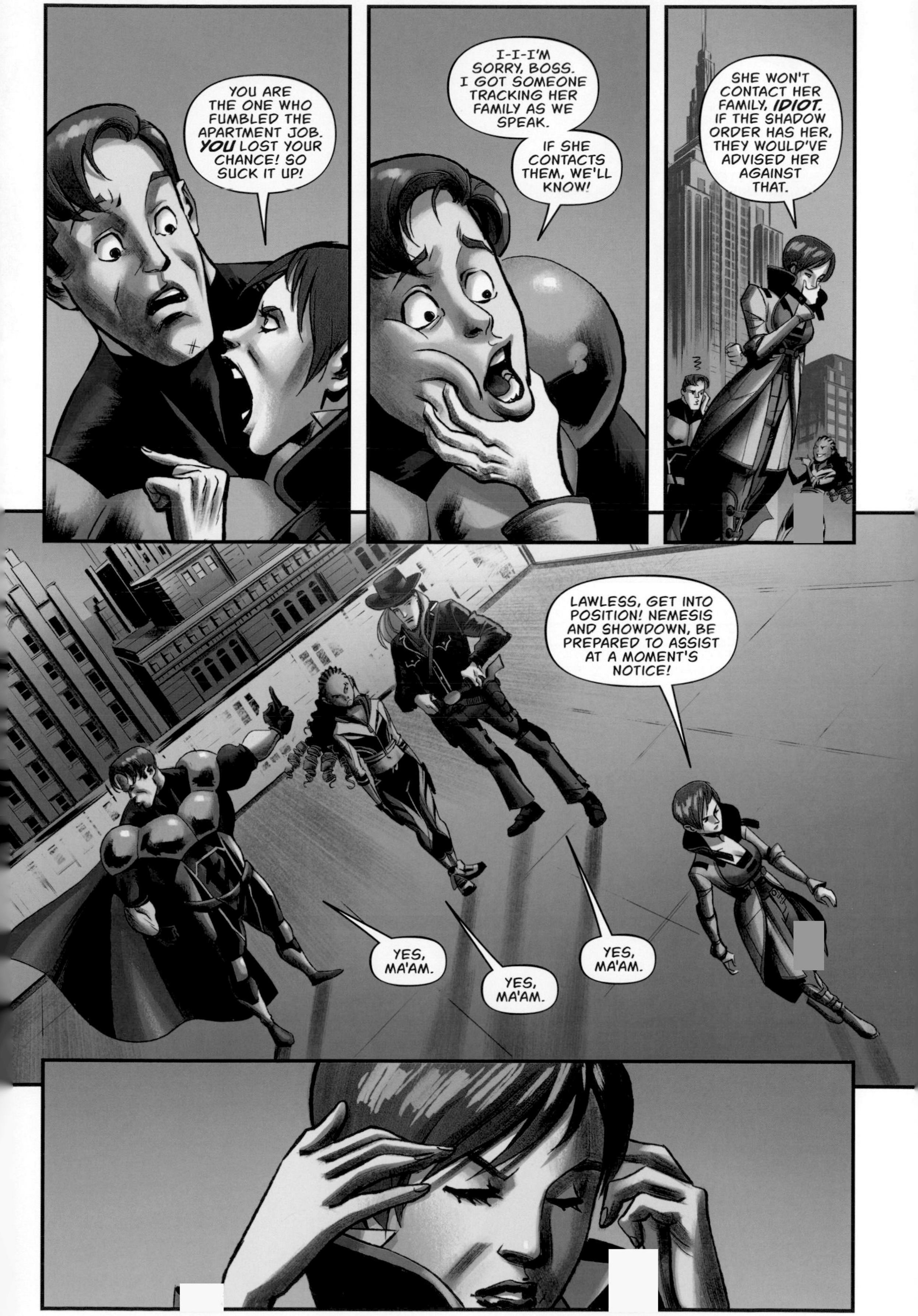
YOU ARE THE ONE WHO FUMBLED THE APARTMENT JOB. YOU LOST YOUR CHANCE! SO SUCK IT UP!
I-I-I'M SORRY, BOSS. I GOT SOMEONE TRACKING HER FAMILY AS WE SPEAK.
IF SHE CONTACTS THEM, WE'LL KNOW!
SHE WON'T CONTACT HER FAMILY, IDIOT. IF THE SHADOW ORDER HAS HER, THEY WOULD'VE ADVISED HER AGAINST THAT.
LAWLESS, GET INTO POSITION! NEMESIS AND SHOWDOWN, BE PREPARED TO ASSIST AT A MOMENT'S NOTICE!
YES, MA'AM.
YES, MA'AM.
YES, MA'AM.

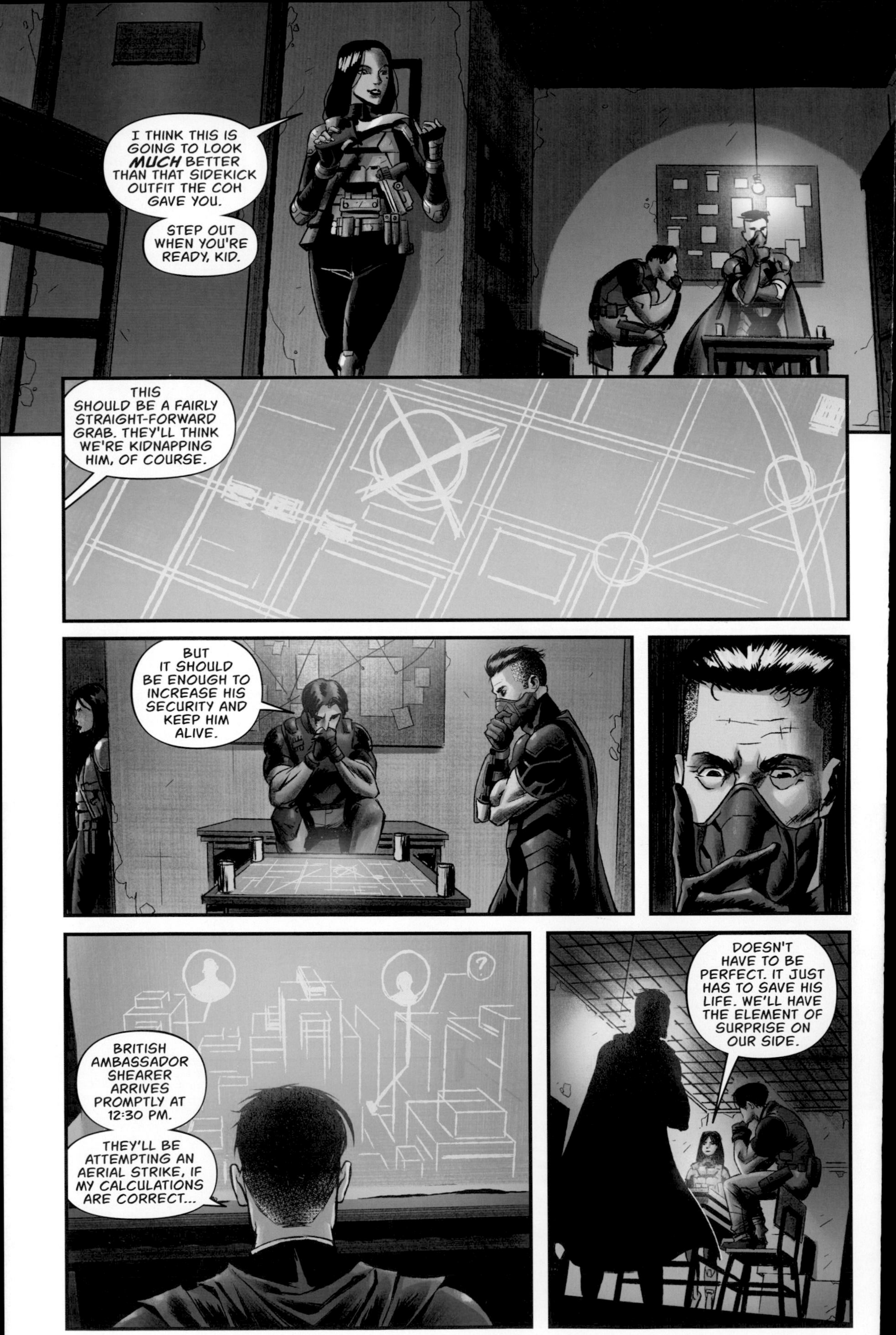
I THINK THIS IS GOING TO LOOK MUCH BETTER THAN THAT SIDEKICK OUTFIT THE COH GAVE YOU.
STEP OUT WHEN YOU'RE READY, KID.
THIS SHOULD BE A FAIRLY STRAIGHT-FORWARD GRAB. THEY'LL THINK WE'RE KIDNAPPING HIM, OF COURSE.
BUT IT SHOULD BE ENOUGH TO INCREASE HIS SECURITY AND KEEP HIM ALIVE.
BRITISH AMBASSADOR SHEARER ARRIVES PROMPTLY AT 12:30 PM.
THEY'LL BE ATTEMPTING AN AERIAL STRIKE, IF MY CALCULATIONS ARE CORRECT...
DOESN'T HAVE TO BE PERFECT. IT JUST HAS TO SAVE HIS LIFE. WE'LL HAVE THE ELEMENT OF SURPRISE ON OUR SIDE.

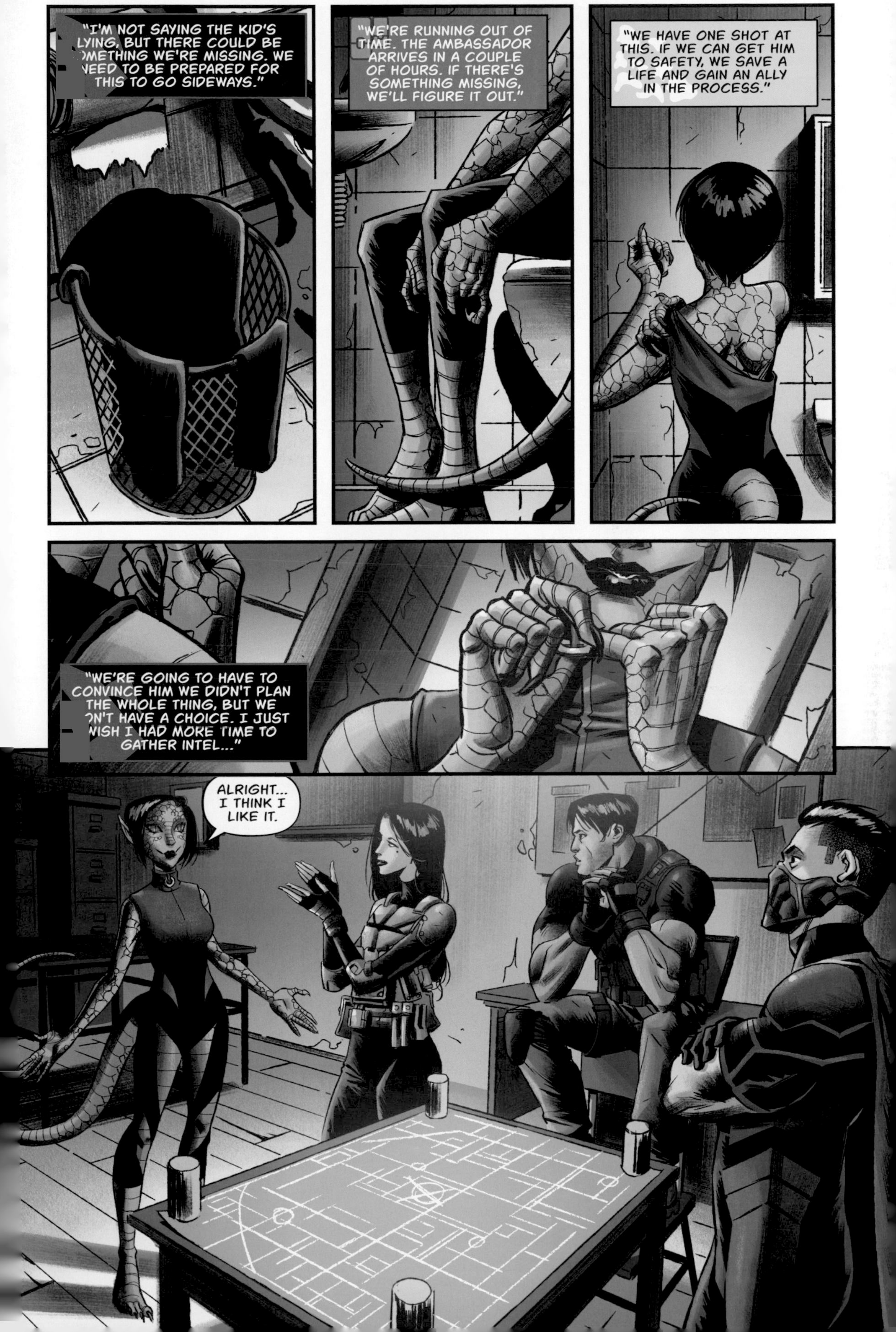
"I'M NOT SAYING THE KID'S LYING, BUT THERE COULD BE OMETHING WE'RE MISSING. WE EED TO BE PREPARED FOR THIS TO GO SIDEWAYS."
"WE'RE RUNNING OUT OF TIME. THE AMBASSADOR ARRIVES IN A COUPLE OF HOURS. IF THERE'S SOMETHING MISSING, WE'LL FIGURE IT OUT."
"WE HAVE ONE SHOT AT THIS. IF WE CAN GET HIM TO SAFETY, WE SAVE A LIFE AND GAIN AN ALLY IN THE PROCESS."
"WE'RE GOING TO HAVE TO CONVINCE HIM WE DIDN'T PLAN THE WHOLE THING, BUT WE ON'T HAVE A CHOICE. I JUST WISH I HAD MORE TIME TO GATHER INTEL..."
ALRIGHT... I THINK I LIKE IT.

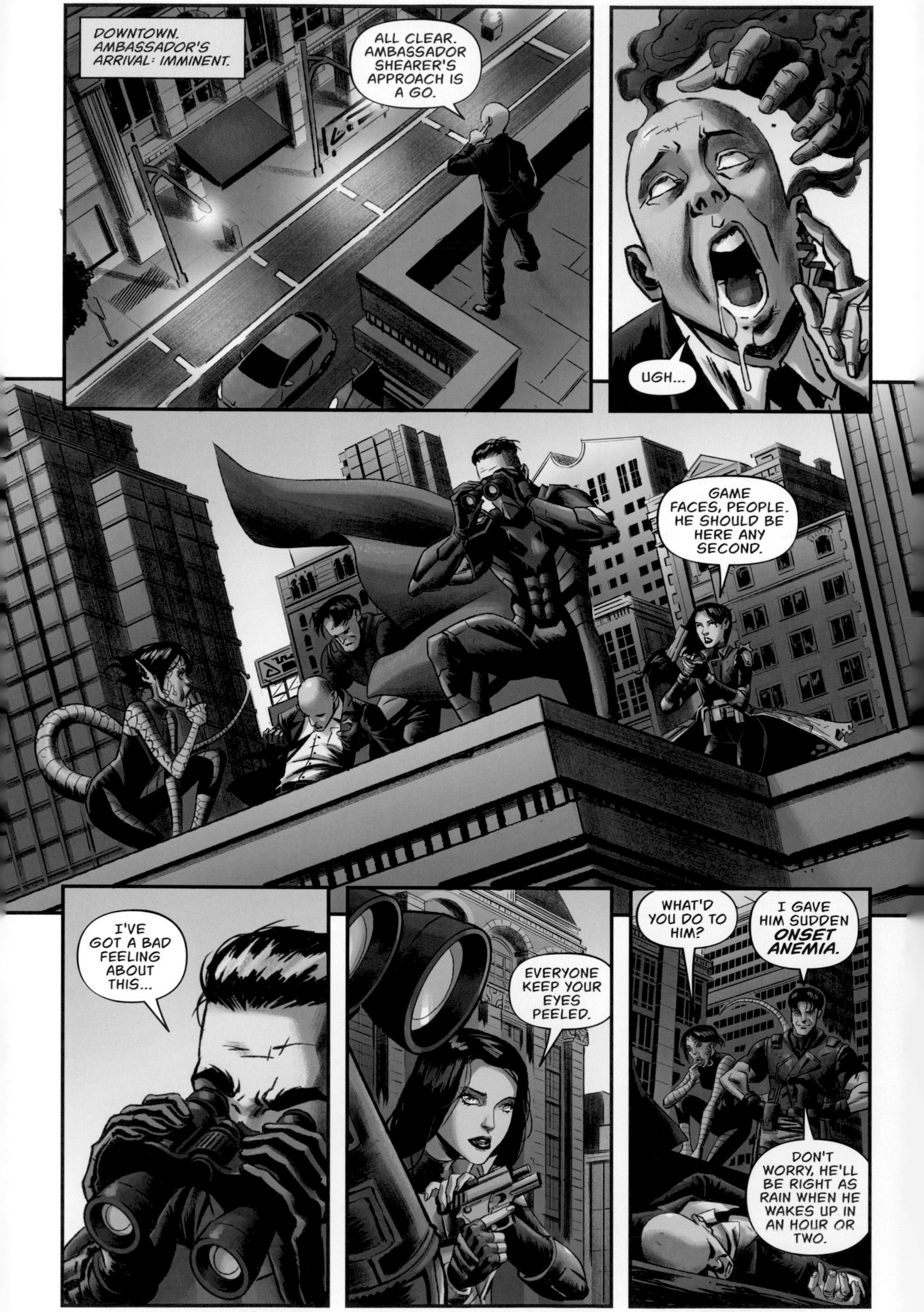
DOWNTOWN. AMBASSADOR'S ARRIVAL: IMMINENT.
ALL CLEAR. AMBASSADOR SHEARER'S APPROACH IS A GO.
UGH...
GAME FACES, PEOPLE. HE SHOULD BE HERE ANY SECOND.
I'VE GOT A BAD FEELING ABOUT THIS...
EVERYONE KEEP YOUR EYES PEELED.
WHAT'D YOU DO TO HIM?
I GAVE HIM SUDDEN ***ONSET ANEMIA.***
DON'T WORRY, HE'LL BE RIGHT AS RAIN WHEN HE WAKES UP IN AN HOUR OR TWO.

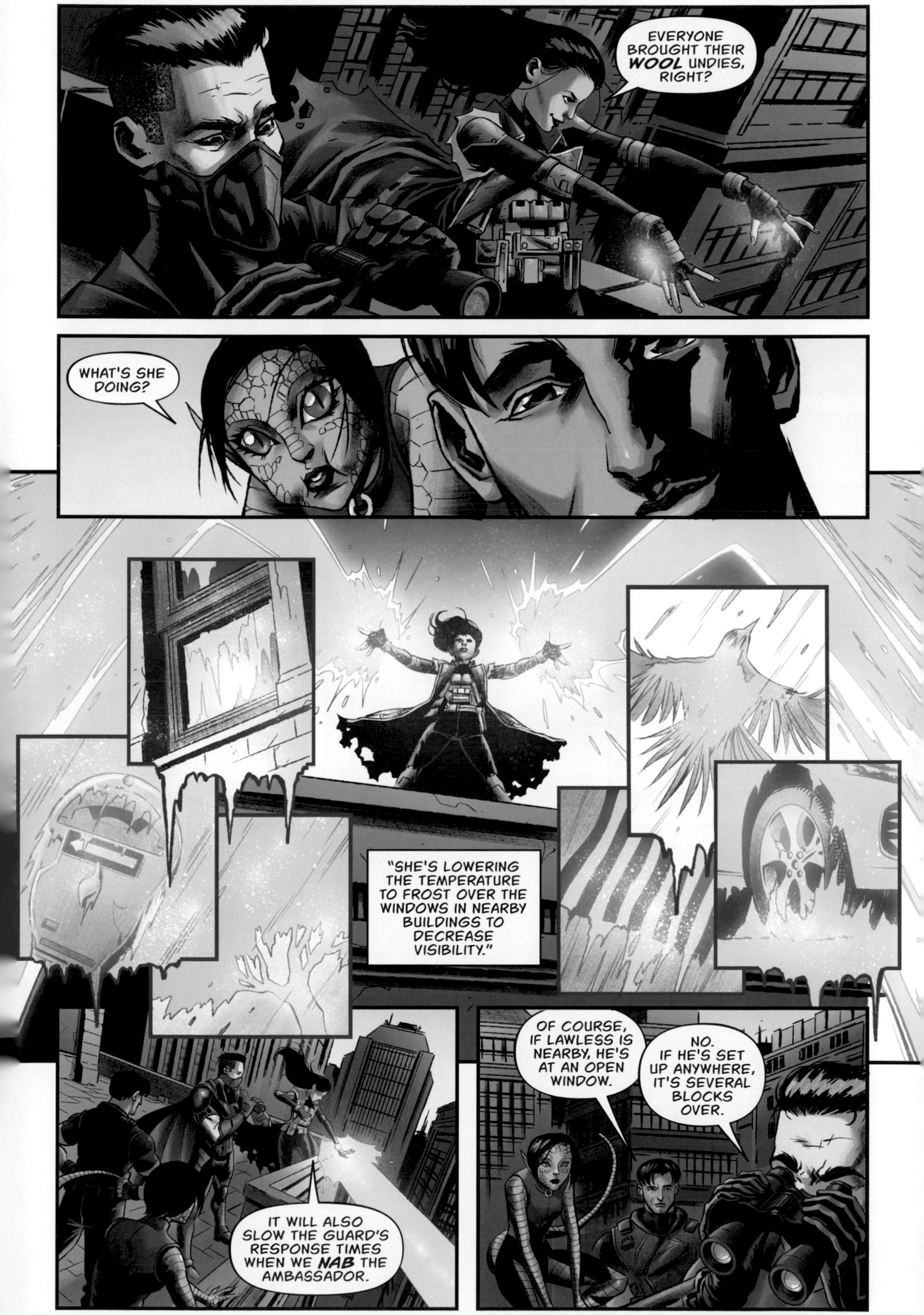
EVERYONE BROUGHT THEIR WOOL UNDIES, RIGHT?
WHAT'S SHE DOING?
"SHE'S LOWERING THE TEMPERATURE TO FROST OVER THE WINDOWS IN NEARBY BUILDINGS TO DECREASE VISIBILITY."
IT WILL ALSO SLOW THE GUARD'S RESPONSE TIMES WHEN WE NAB THE AMBASSADOR.
OF COURSE, IF LAWLESS IS NEARBY, HE'S AT AN OPEN WINDOW.
NO. IF HE'S SET UP ANYWHERE, IT'S SEVERAL BLOCKS OVER.

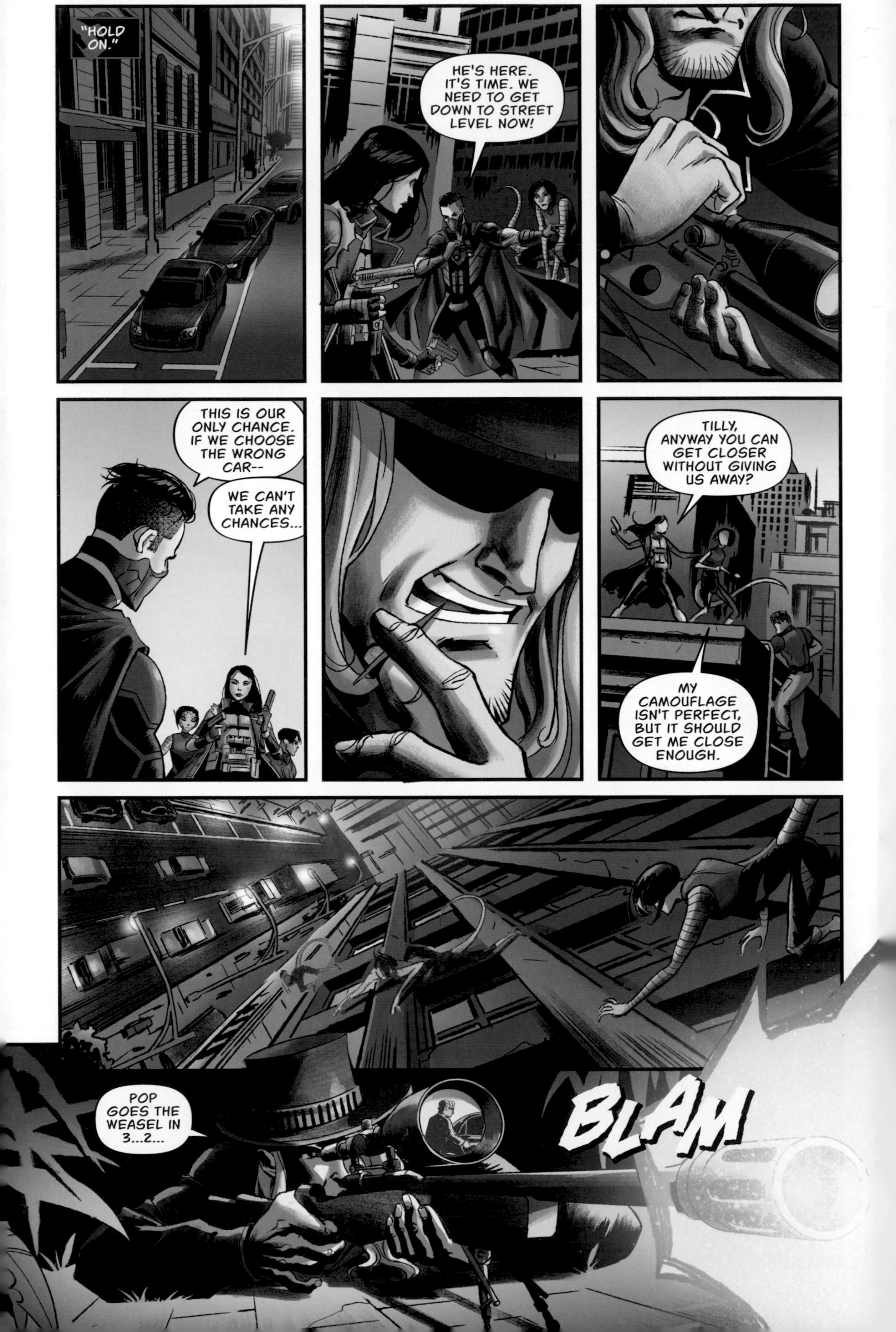
"HOLD ON."
HE'S HERE. IT'S TIME. WE NEED TO GET DOWN TO STREET LEVEL NOW!
THIS IS OUR ONLY CHANCE. IF WE CHOOSE THE WRONG CAR--
WE CAN'T TAKE ANY CHANCES...
TILLY, ANYWAY YOU CAN GET CLOSER WITHOUT GIVING US AWAY?
MY CAMOUFLAGE ISN'T PERFECT, BUT IT SHOULD GET ME CLOSE ENOUGH.
POP GOES THE WEASEL IN 3...2...
BLAM

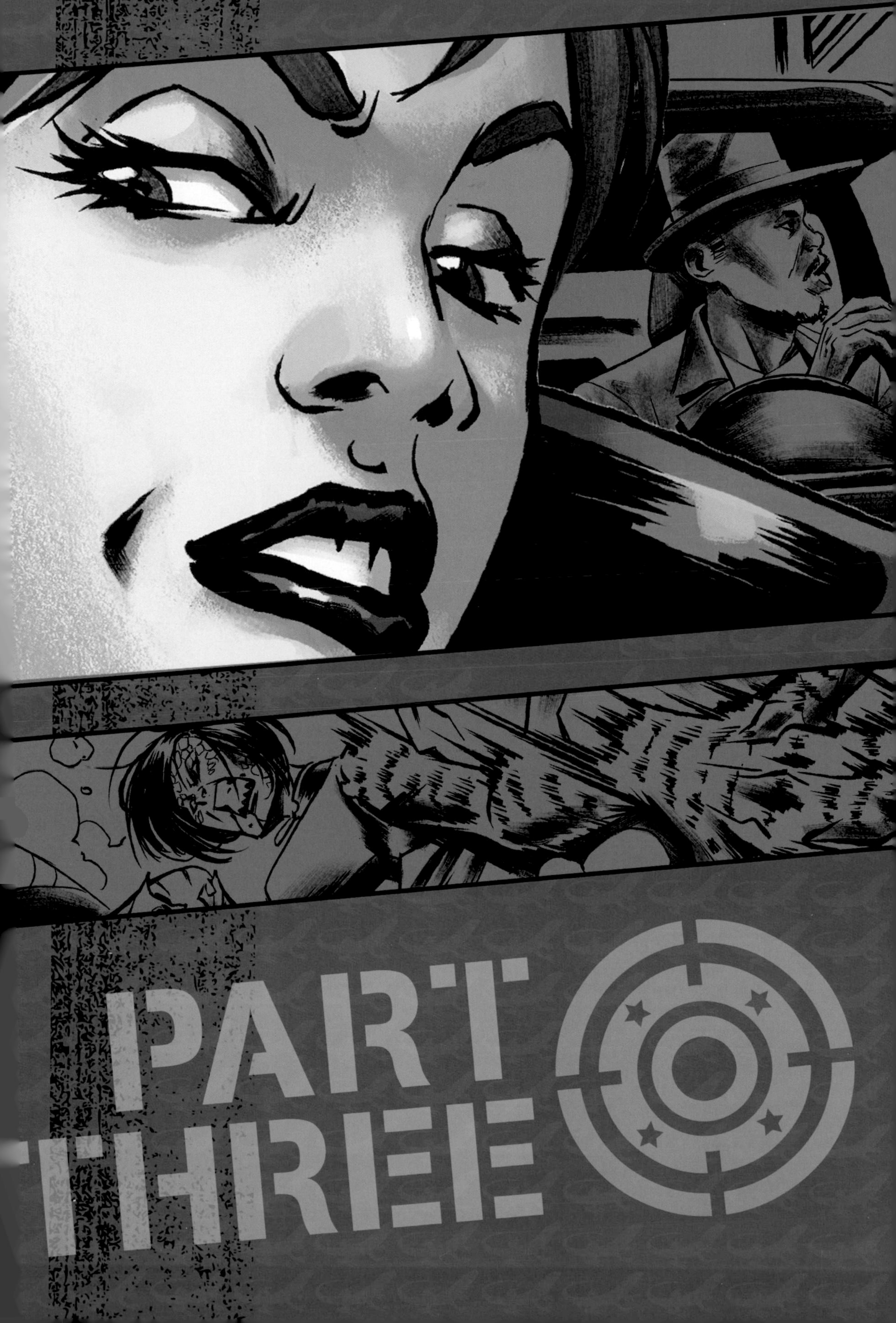

PART THREE

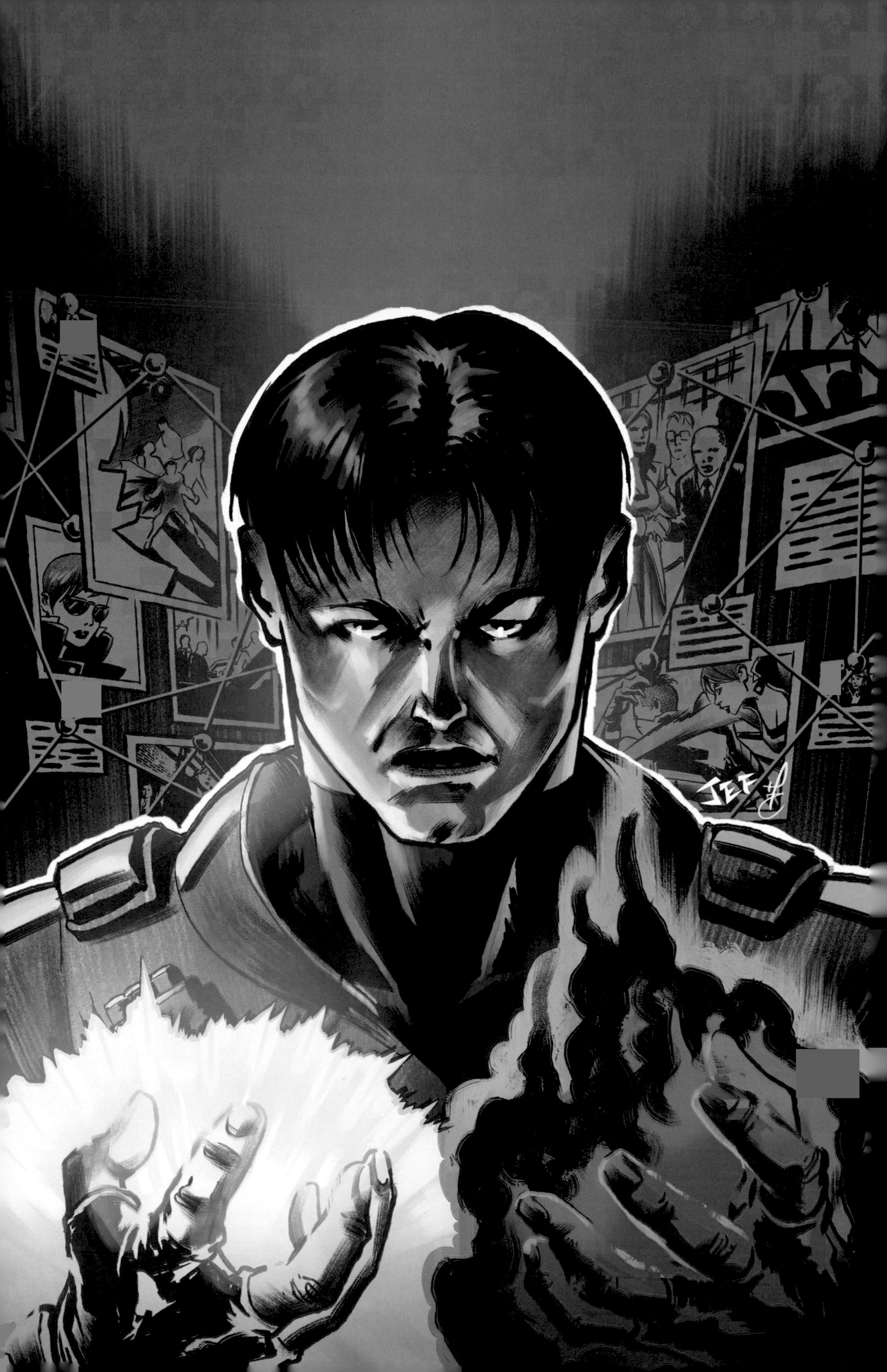
JEF

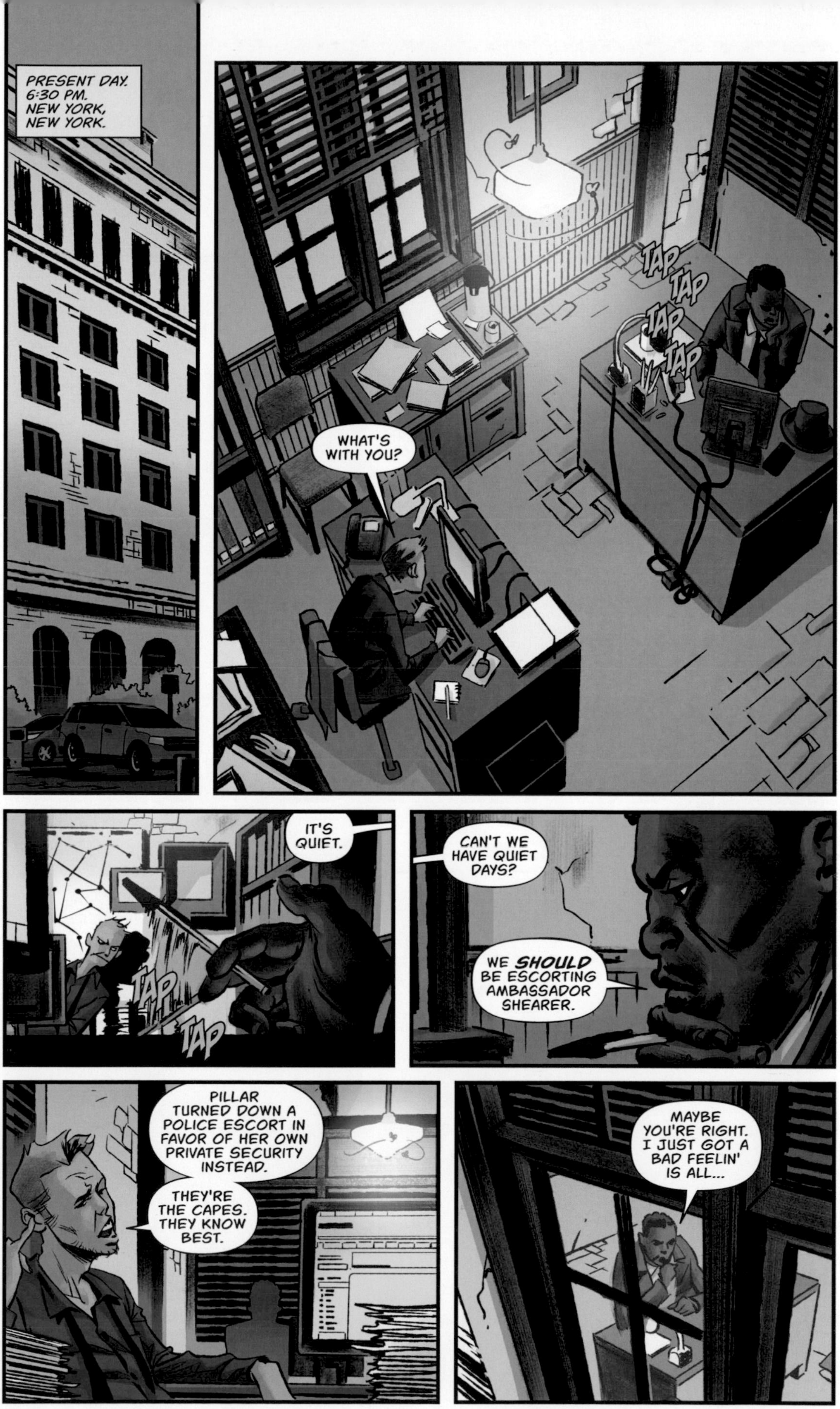

PRESENT DAY. 6:30 PM. NEW YORK, NEW YORK.
TAP TAP TAP TAP
WHAT'S WITH YOU?
IT'S QUIET.
TAP TAP
CAN'T WE HAVE QUIET DAYS?
WE SHOULD BE ESCORTING AMBASSADOR SHEARER.
PILLAR TURNED DOWN A POLICE ESCORT IN FAVOR OF HER OWN PRIVATE SECURITY INSTEAD.
THEY'RE THE CAPES. THEY KNOW BEST.
MAYBE YOU'RE RIGHT. I JUST GOT A BAD FEELIN' IS ALL...

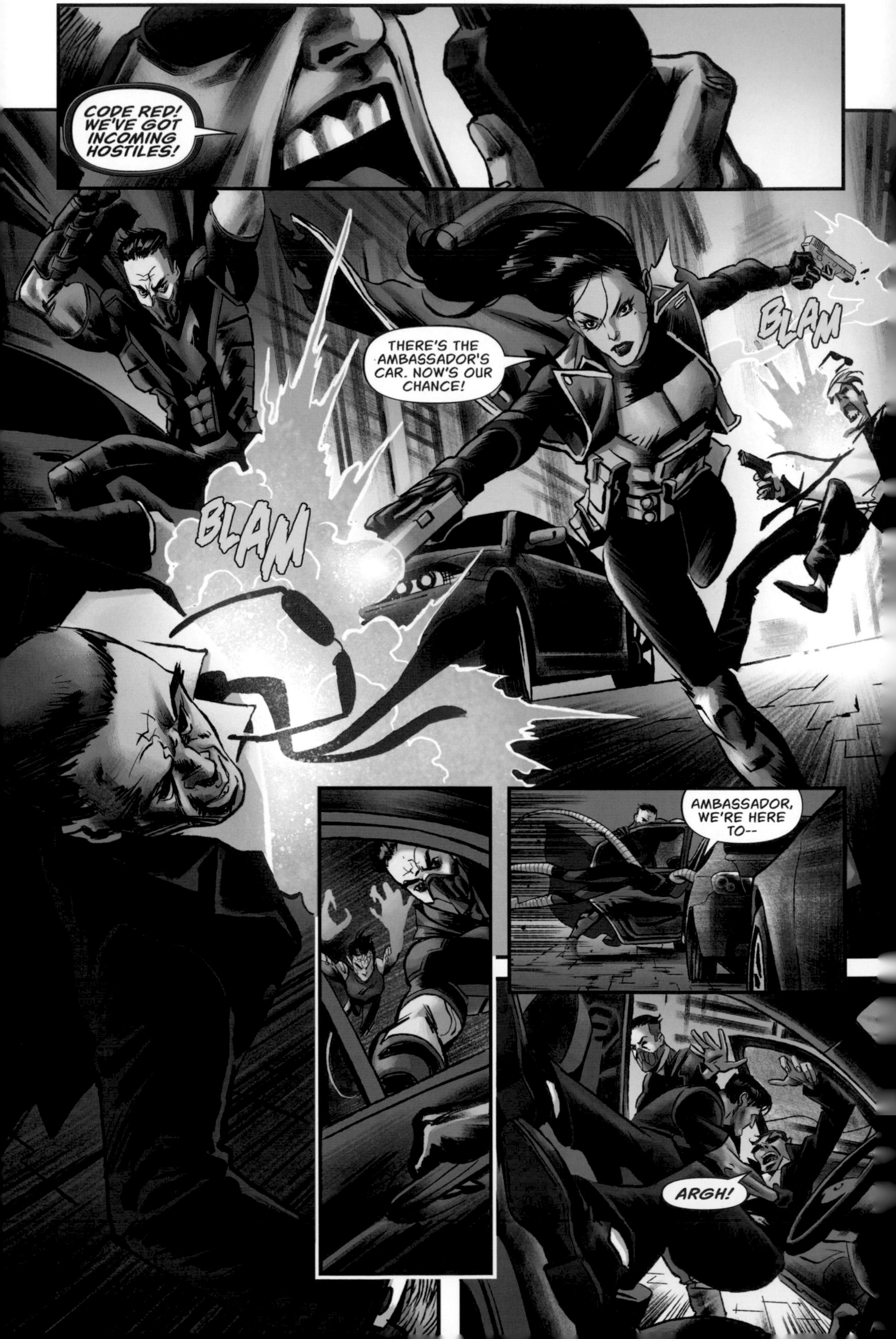
CODE RED! WE'VE GOT INCOMING HOSTILES!
THERE'S THE AMBASSADOR'S CAR. NOW'S OUR CHANCE!
BLAM
BLAM
AMBASSADOR, WE'RE HERE TO--
ARGH!

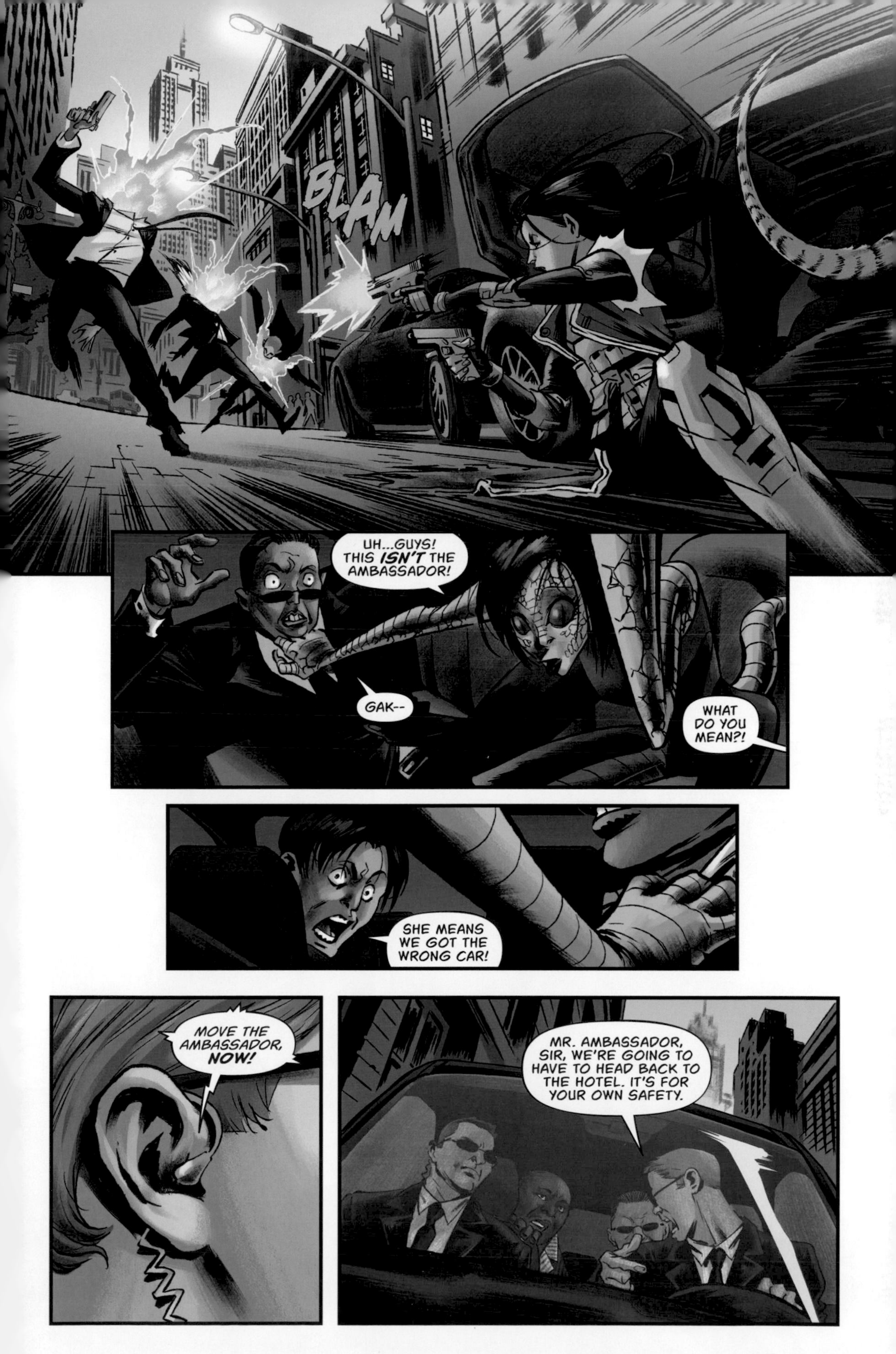
BLAM
UH...GUYS! THIS ISN'T THE AMBASSADOR!
GAK--
WHAT DO YOU MEAN?!
SHE MEANS WE GOT THE WRONG CAR!
MOVE THE AMBASSADOR, NOW!
MR. AMBASSADOR, SIR, WE'RE GOING TO HAVE TO HEAD BACK TO THE HOTEL. IT'S FOR YOUR OWN SAFETY.

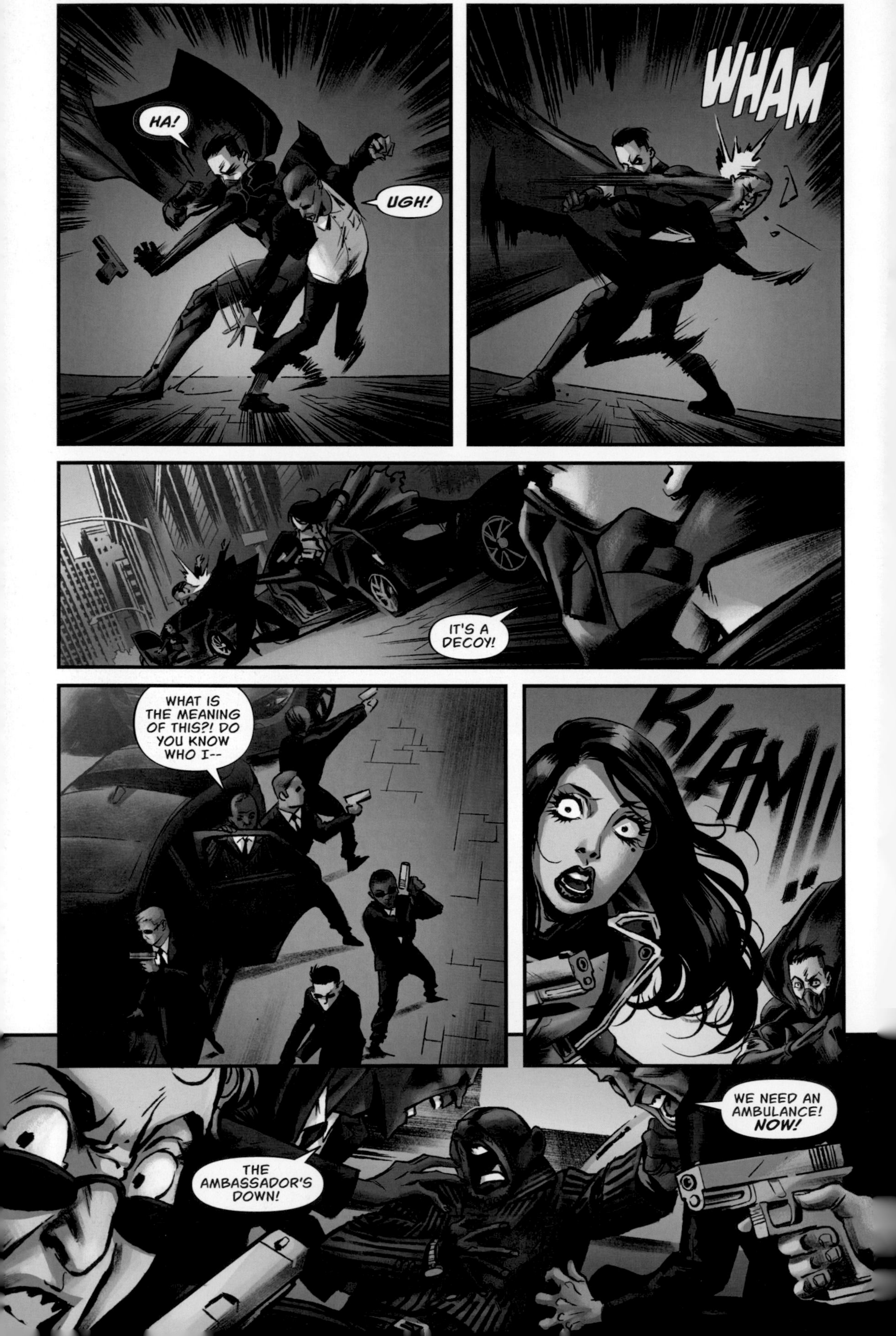
HA!
UGH!
WHAM
IT'S A DECOY!
WHAT IS THE MEANING OF THIS?! DO YOU KNOW WHO I--
BLAM!!
THE AMBASSADOR'S DOWN!
WE NEED AN AMBULANCE! NOW!

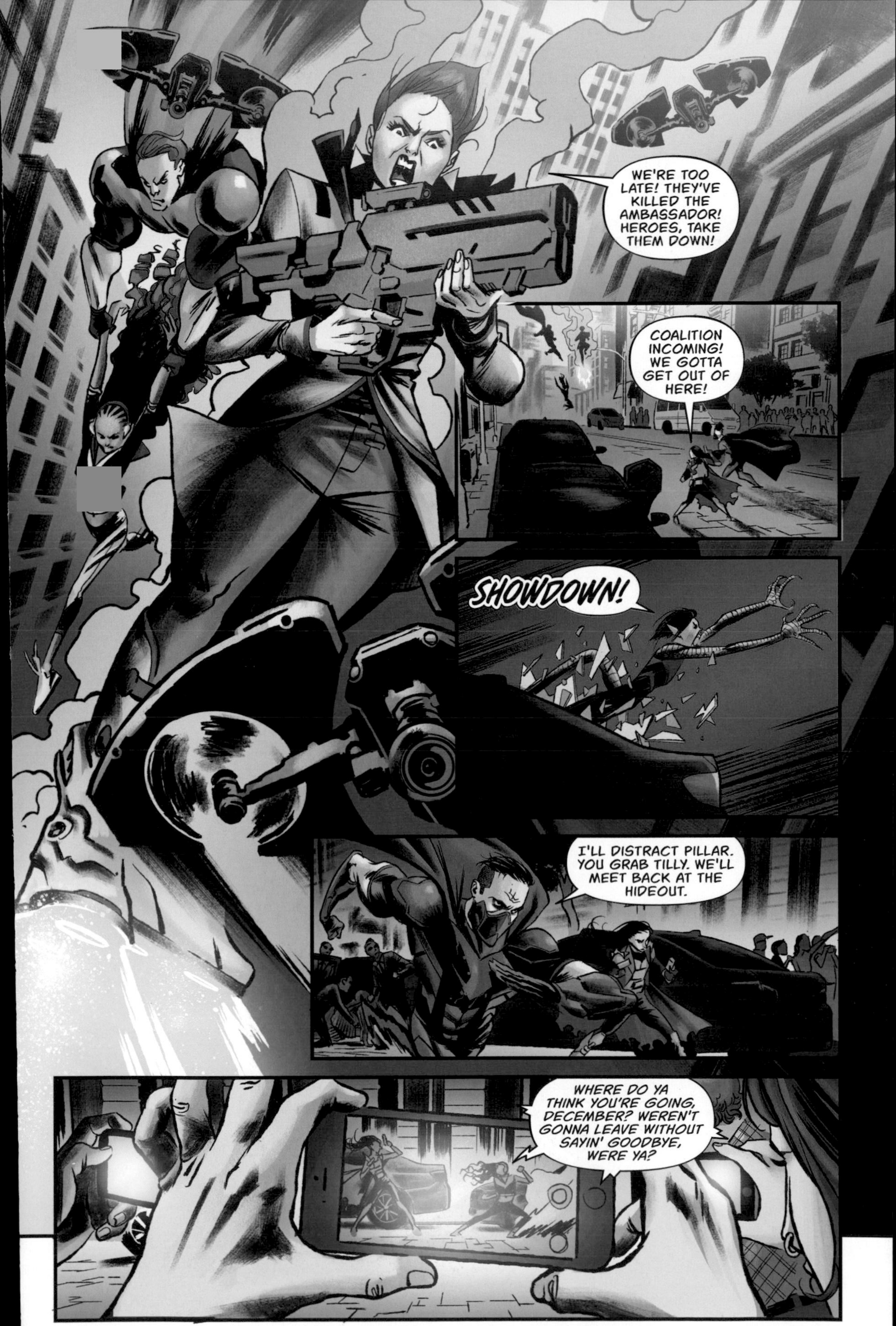
WE'RE TOO LATE! THEY'VE KILLED THE AMBASSADOR! HEROES, TAKE THEM DOWN!
COALITION INCOMING! WE GOTTA GET OUT OF HERE!
SHOWDOWN!
I'LL DISTRACT PILLAR. YOU GRAB TILLY. WE'LL MEET BACK AT THE HIDEOUT.
WHERE DO YA THINK YOU'RE GOING, DECEMBER? WEREN'T GONNA LEAVE WITHOUT SAYIN' GOODBYE, WERE YA?

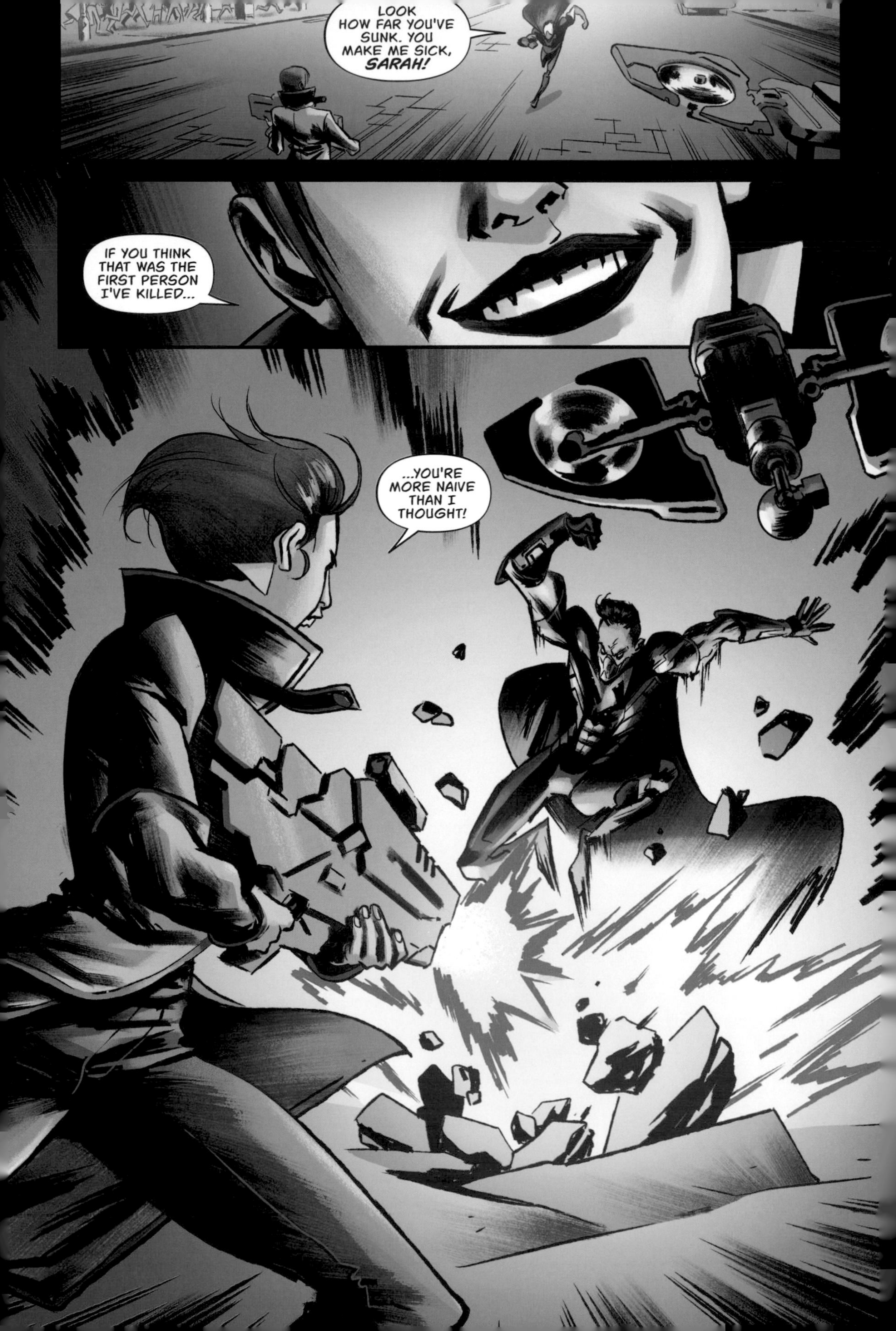
LOOK HOW FAR YOU'VE SUNK. YOU MAKE ME SICK, SARAH!
IF YOU THINK THAT WAS THE FIRST PERSON I'VE KILLED...
...YOU'RE MORE NAIVE THAN I THOUGHT!

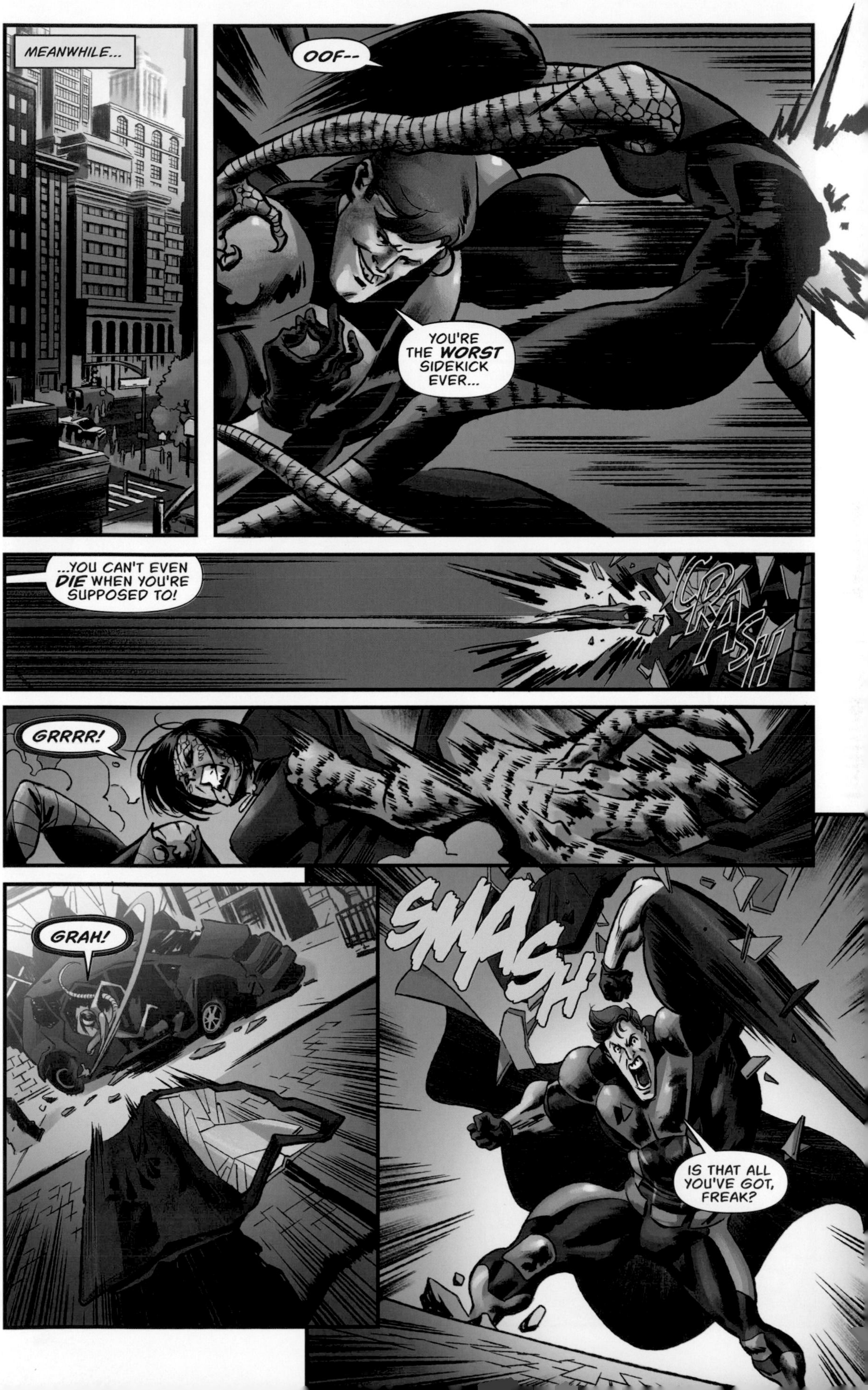
MEANWHILE...
OOF--
YOU'RE THE WORST SIDEKICK EVER...
...YOU CAN'T EVEN DIE WHEN YOU'RE SUPPOSED TO!
CRASH
GRRRR!
GRAH!
SMASH
IS THAT ALL YOU'VE GOT, FREAK?

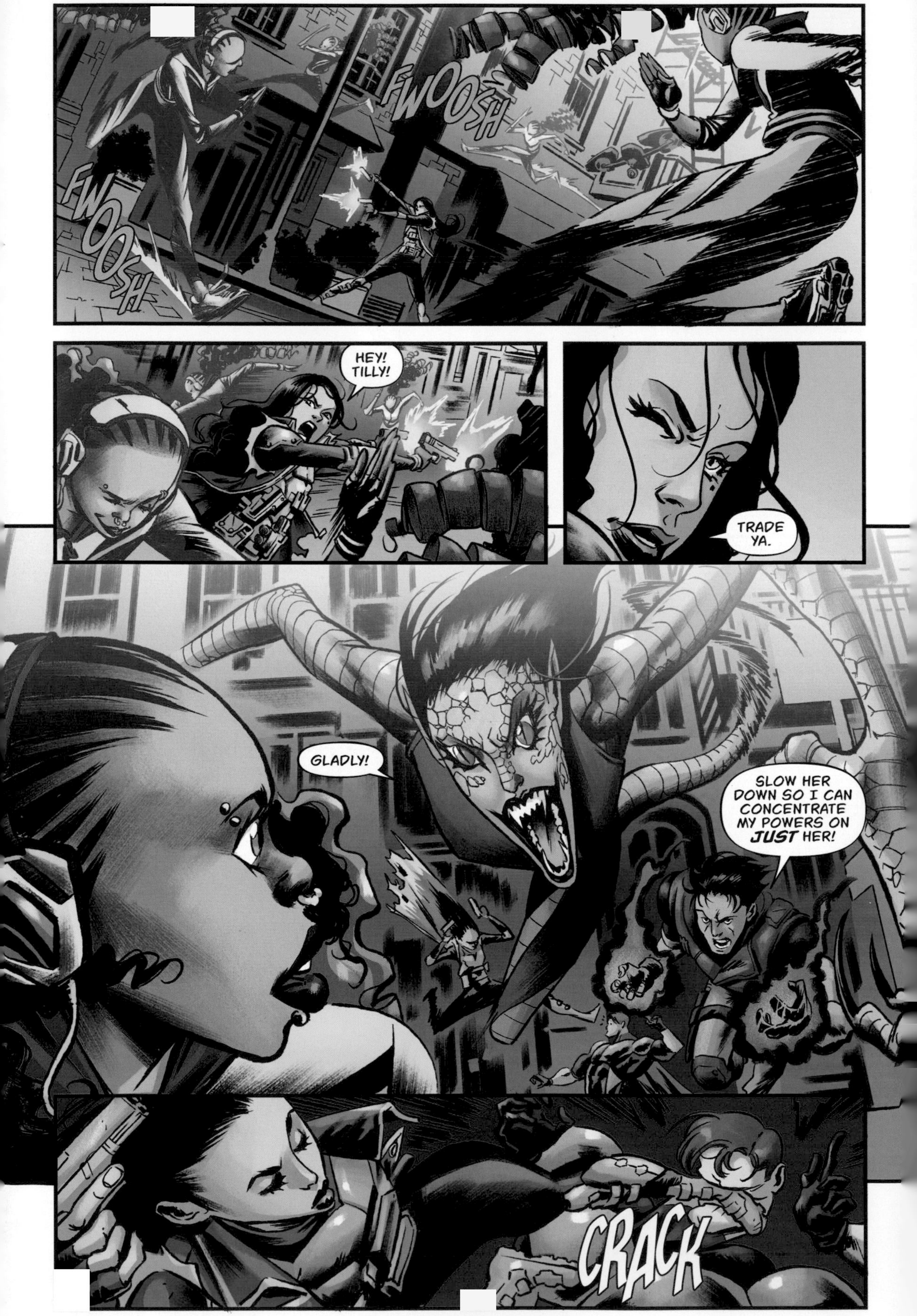
FWOOSH
FWOOSH
HEY! TILLY!
TRADE YA.
GLADLY!
SLOW HER DOWN SO I CAN CONCENTRATE MY POWERS ON ***JUST*** HER!
CRACK

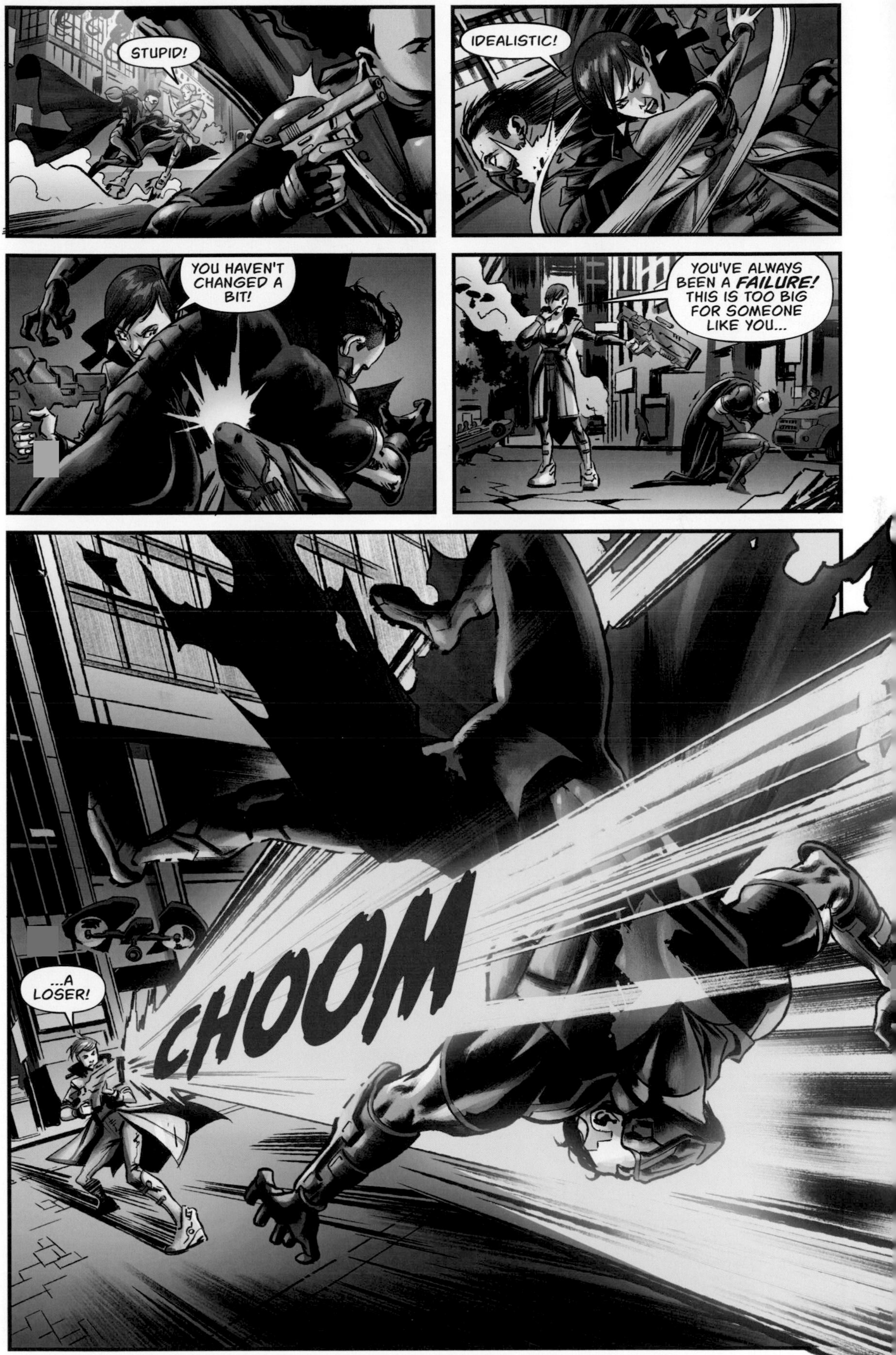
STUPID!
IDEALISTIC!
YOU HAVEN'T CHANGED A BIT!
YOU'VE ALWAYS BEEN A **FAILURE!** THIS IS TOO BIG FOR SOMEONE LIKE YOU...
...A LOSER!
CHOOM

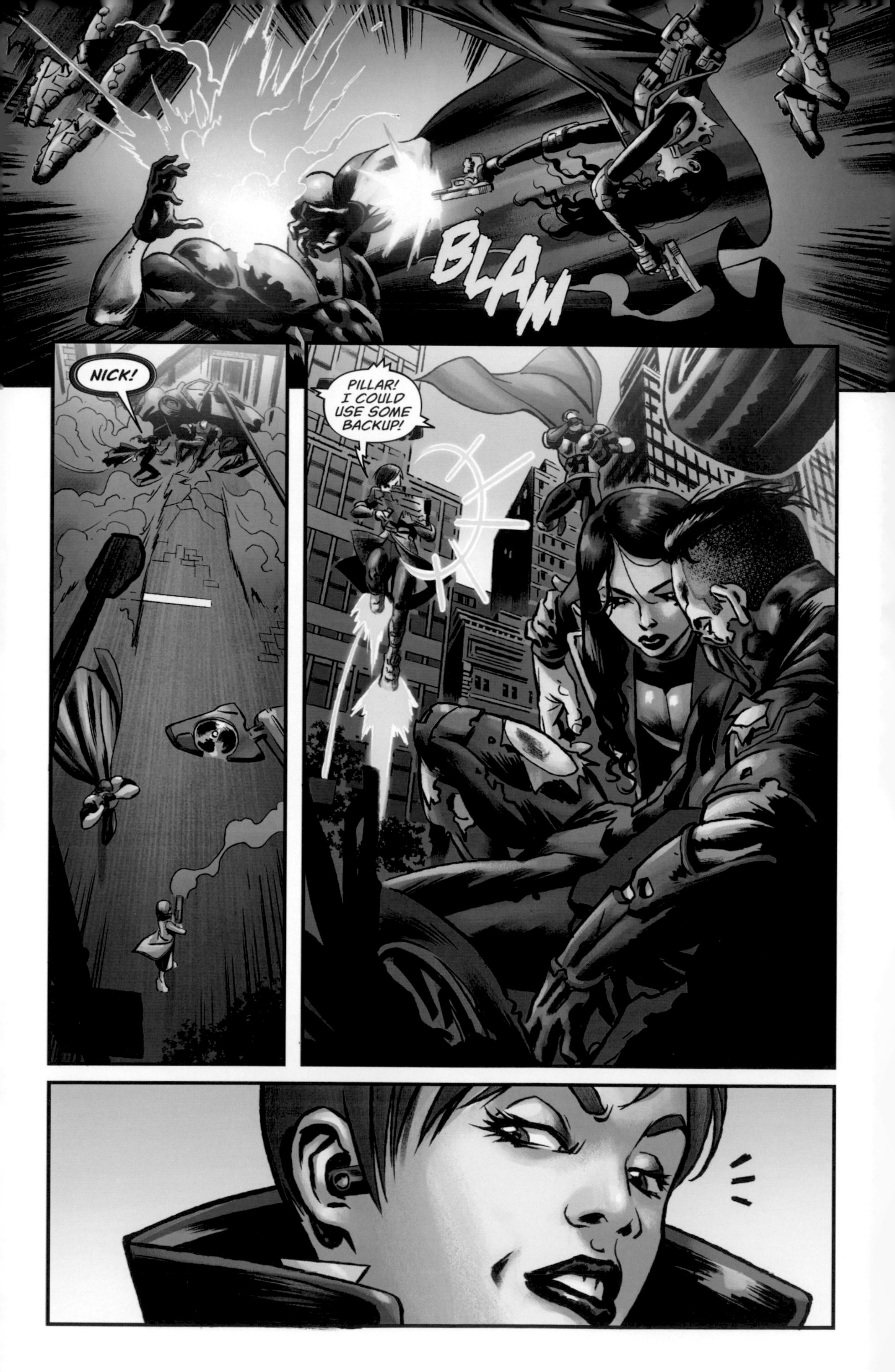
BLAM
NICK!
PILLAR! I COULD USE SOME BACKUP!

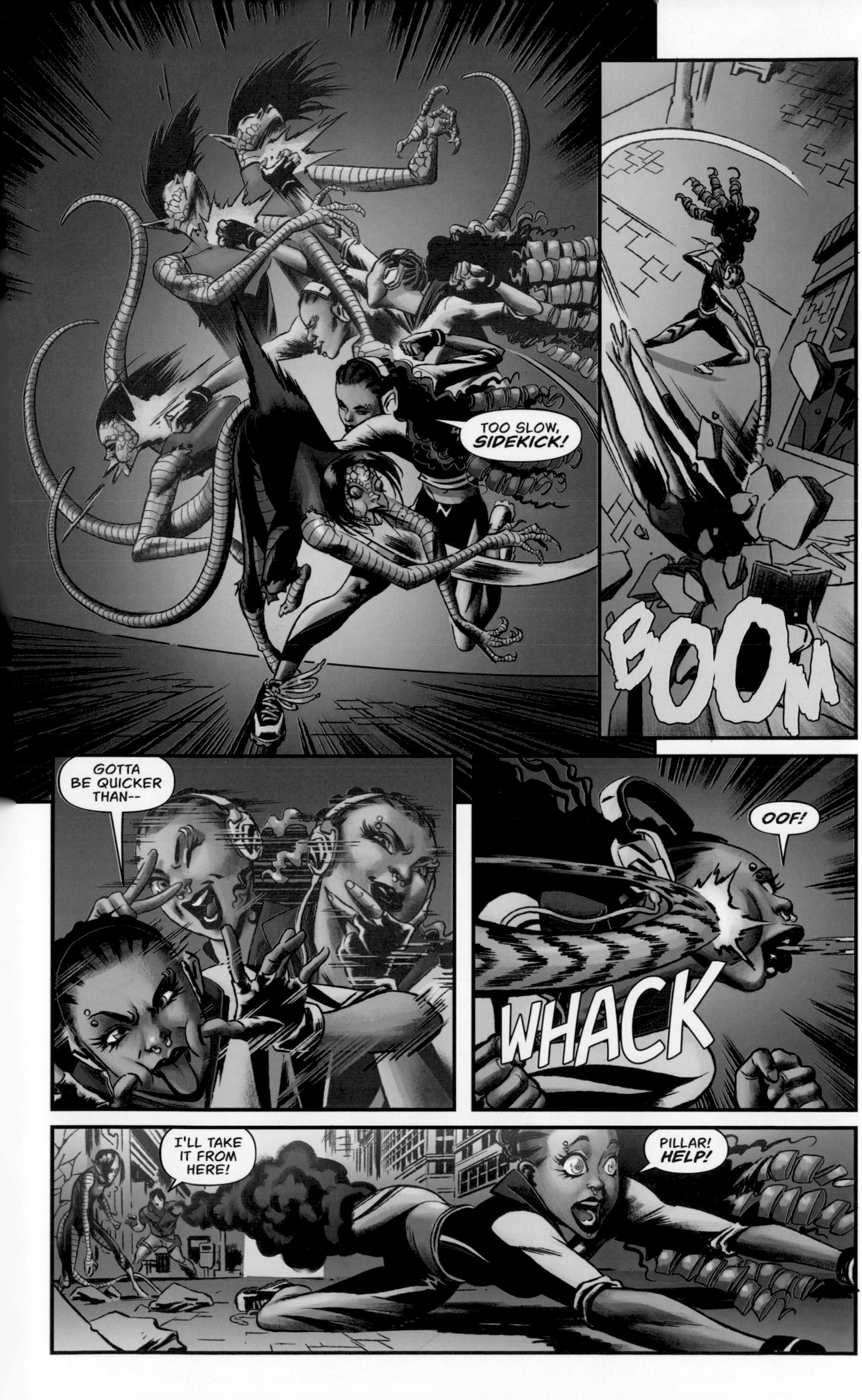
TOO SLOW, SIDEKICK!
BOOM
GOTTA BE QUICKER THAN--
OOF!
WHACK
I'LL TAKE IT FROM HERE!
PILLAR! HELP!

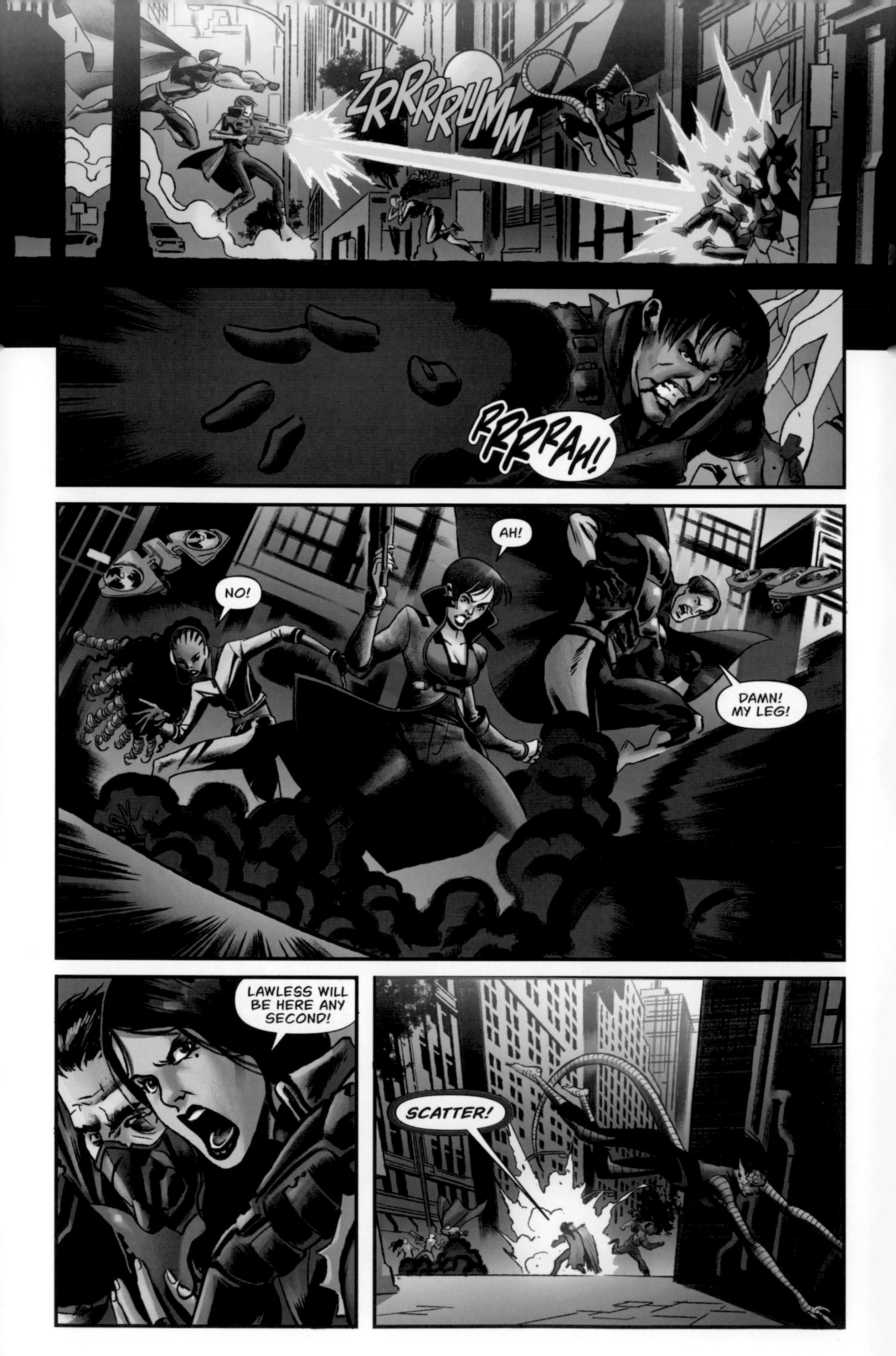
ZRRRRUMM
RRRRAH!
NO!
AH!
DAMN! MY LEG!
LAWLESS WILL BE HERE ANY SECOND!
SCATTER!

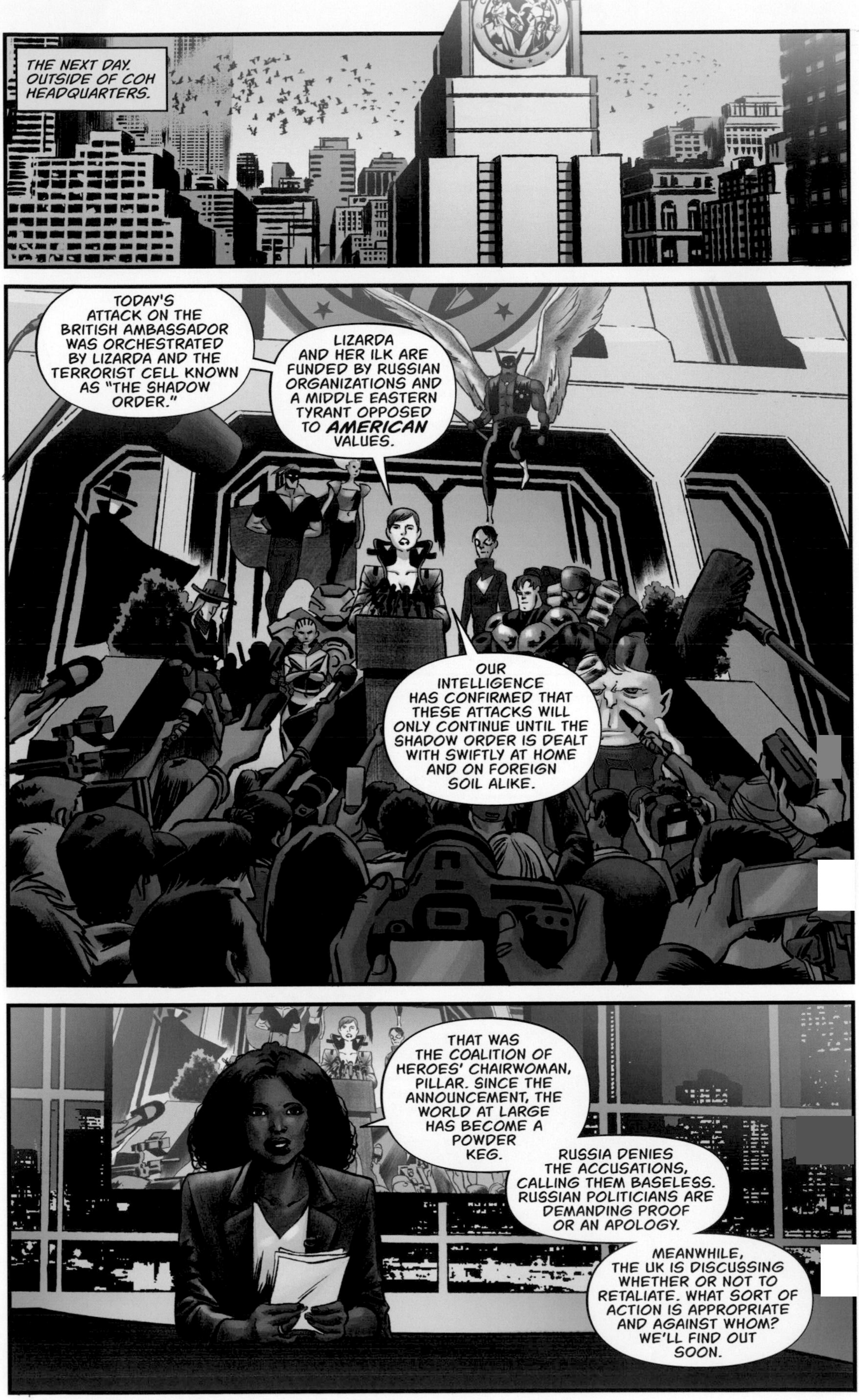
COALITION OF HEROES
THE NEXT DAY. OUTSIDE OF COH HEADQUARTERS.
TODAY'S ATTACK ON THE BRITISH AMBASSADOR WAS ORCHESTRATED BY LIZARDA AND THE TERRORIST CELL KNOWN AS "THE SHADOW ORDER."
LIZARDA AND HER ILK ARE FUNDED BY RUSSIAN ORGANIZATIONS AND A MIDDLE EASTERN TYRANT OPPOSED TO **AMERICAN** VALUES.
OUR INTELLIGENCE HAS CONFIRMED THAT THESE ATTACKS WILL ONLY CONTINUE UNTIL THE SHADOW ORDER IS DEALT WITH SWIFTLY AT HOME AND ON FOREIGN SOIL ALIKE.
THAT WAS THE COALITION OF HEROES' CHAIRWOMAN, PILLAR. SINCE THE ANNOUNCEMENT, THE WORLD AT LARGE HAS BECOME A POWDER KEG.
RUSSIA DENIES THE ACCUSATIONS, CALLING THEM BASELESS. RUSSIAN POLITICIANS ARE DEMANDING PROOF OR AN APOLOGY.
MEANWHILE, THE UK IS DISCUSSING WHETHER OR NOT TO RETALIATE. WHAT SORT OF ACTION IS APPROPRIATE AND AGAINST WHOM? WE'LL FIND OUT SOON.

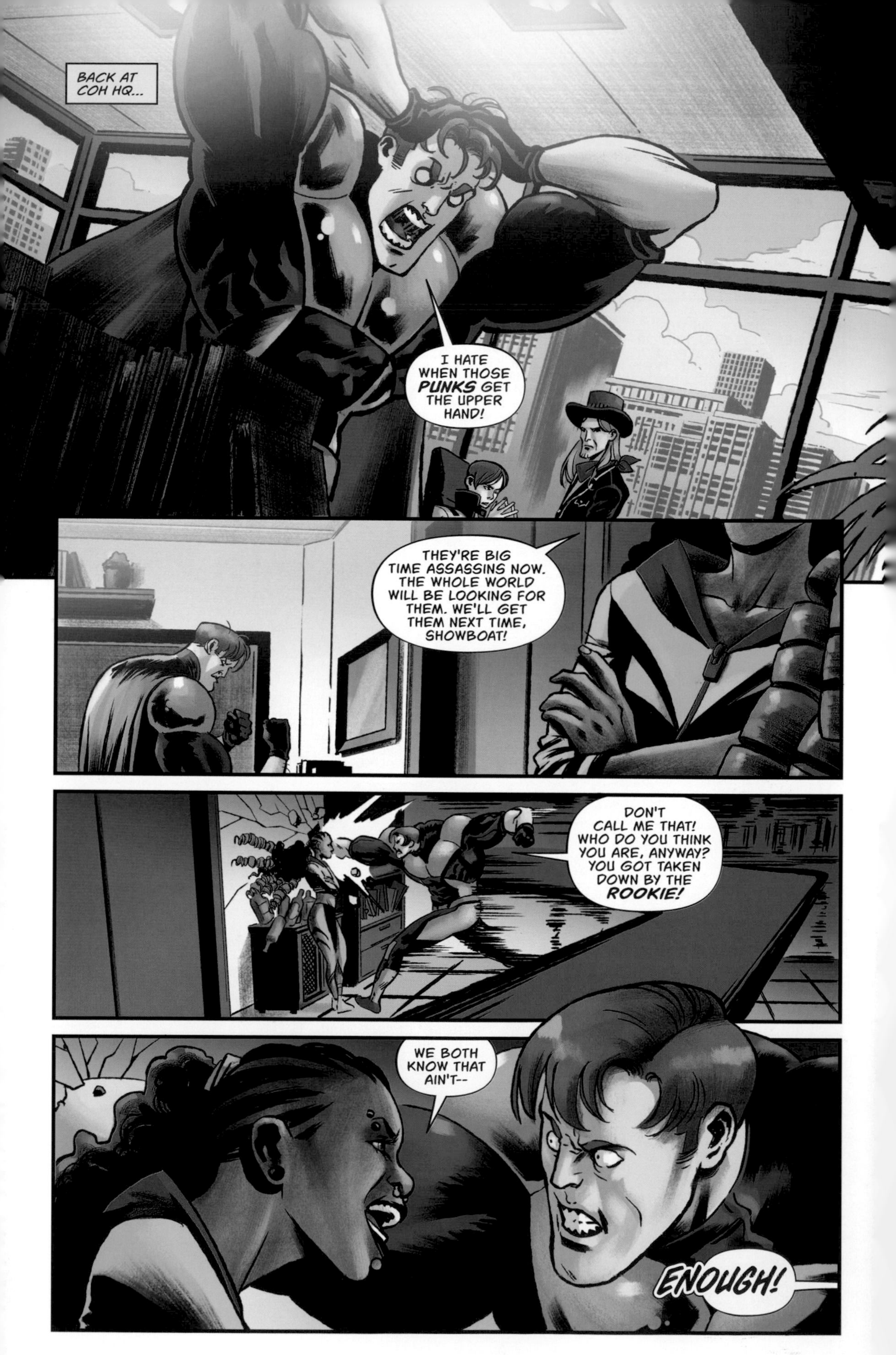
BACK AT COH HQ...
I HATE WHEN THOSE PUNKS GET THE UPPER HAND!
THEY'RE BIG TIME ASSASSINS NOW. THE WHOLE WORLD WILL BE LOOKING FOR THEM. WE'LL GET THEM NEXT TIME, SHOWBOAT!
DON'T CALL ME THAT! WHO DO YOU THINK YOU ARE, ANYWAY? YOU GOT TAKEN DOWN BY THE ROOKIE!
WE BOTH KNOW THAT AIN'T--
ENOUGH!

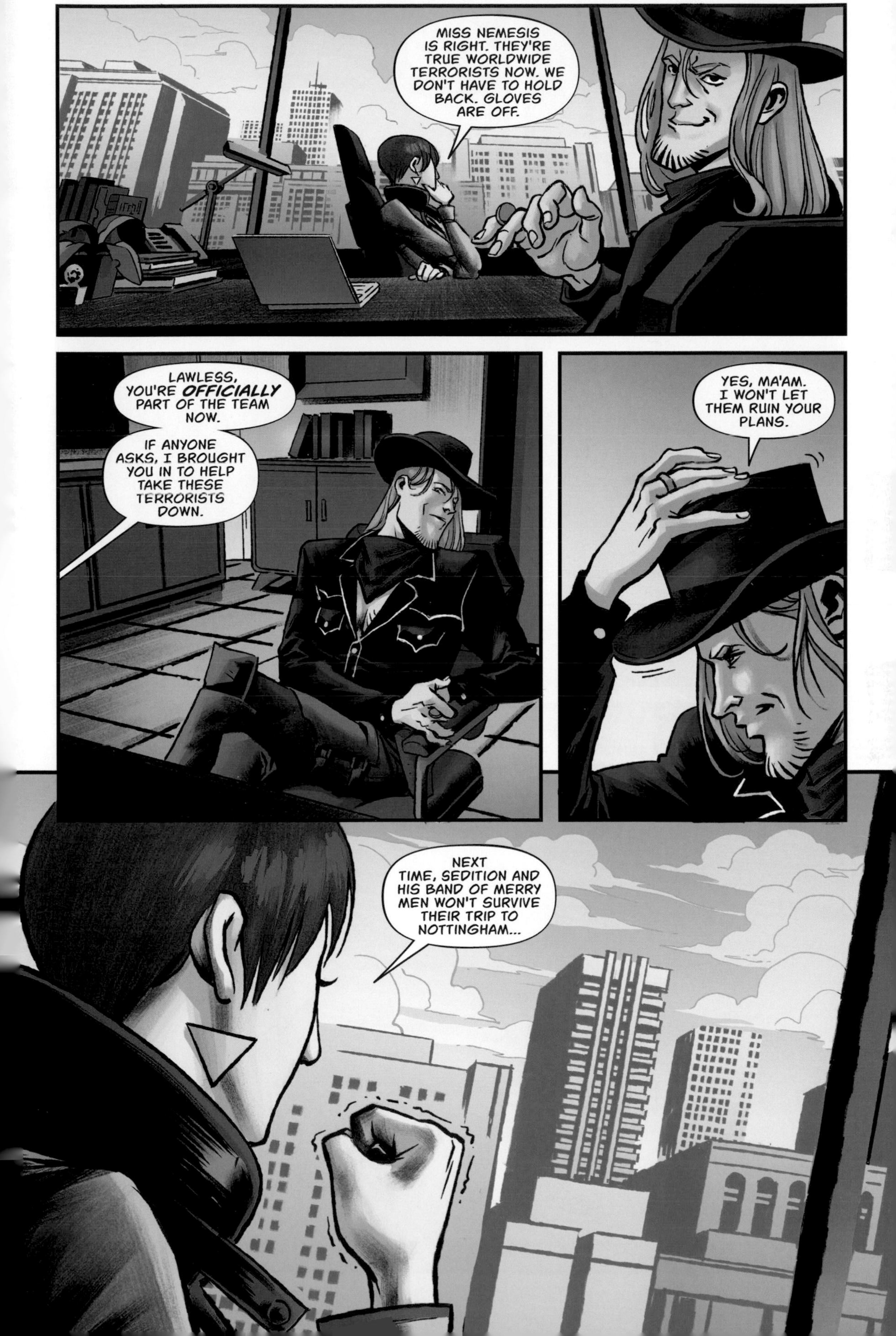
MISS NEMESIS IS RIGHT. THEY'RE TRUE WORLDWIDE TERRORISTS NOW. WE DON'T HAVE TO HOLD BACK. GLOVES ARE OFF.
LAWLESS, YOU'RE OFFICIALLY PART OF THE TEAM NOW.
IF ANYONE ASKS, I BROUGHT YOU IN TO HELP TAKE THESE TERRORISTS DOWN.
YES, MA'AM. I WON'T LET THEM RUIN YOUR PLANS.
NEXT TIME, SEDITION AND HIS BAND OF MERRY MEN WON'T SURVIVE THEIR TRIP TO NOTTINGHAM...

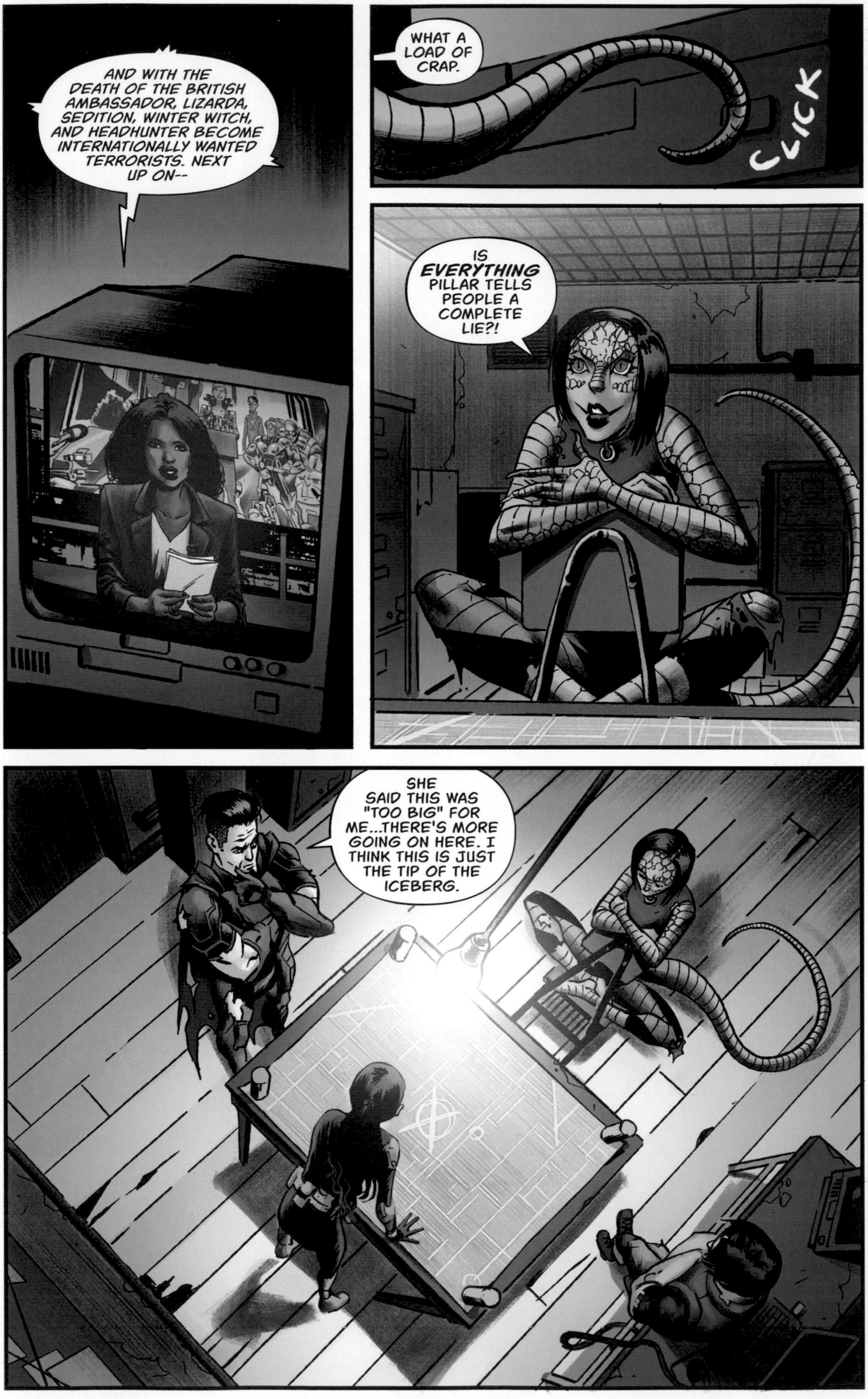
AND WITH THE DEATH OF THE BRITISH AMBASSADOR, LIZARDA, SEDITION, WINTER WITCH, AND HEADHUNTER BECOME INTERNATIONALLY WANTED TERRORISTS. NEXT UP ON--
WHAT A LOAD OF CRAP.
CLICK
IS EVERYTHING PILLAR TELLS PEOPLE A COMPLETE LIE?!
SHE SAID THIS WAS "TOO BIG" FOR ME...THERE'S MORE GOING ON HERE. I THINK THIS IS JUST THE TIP OF THE ICEBERG.

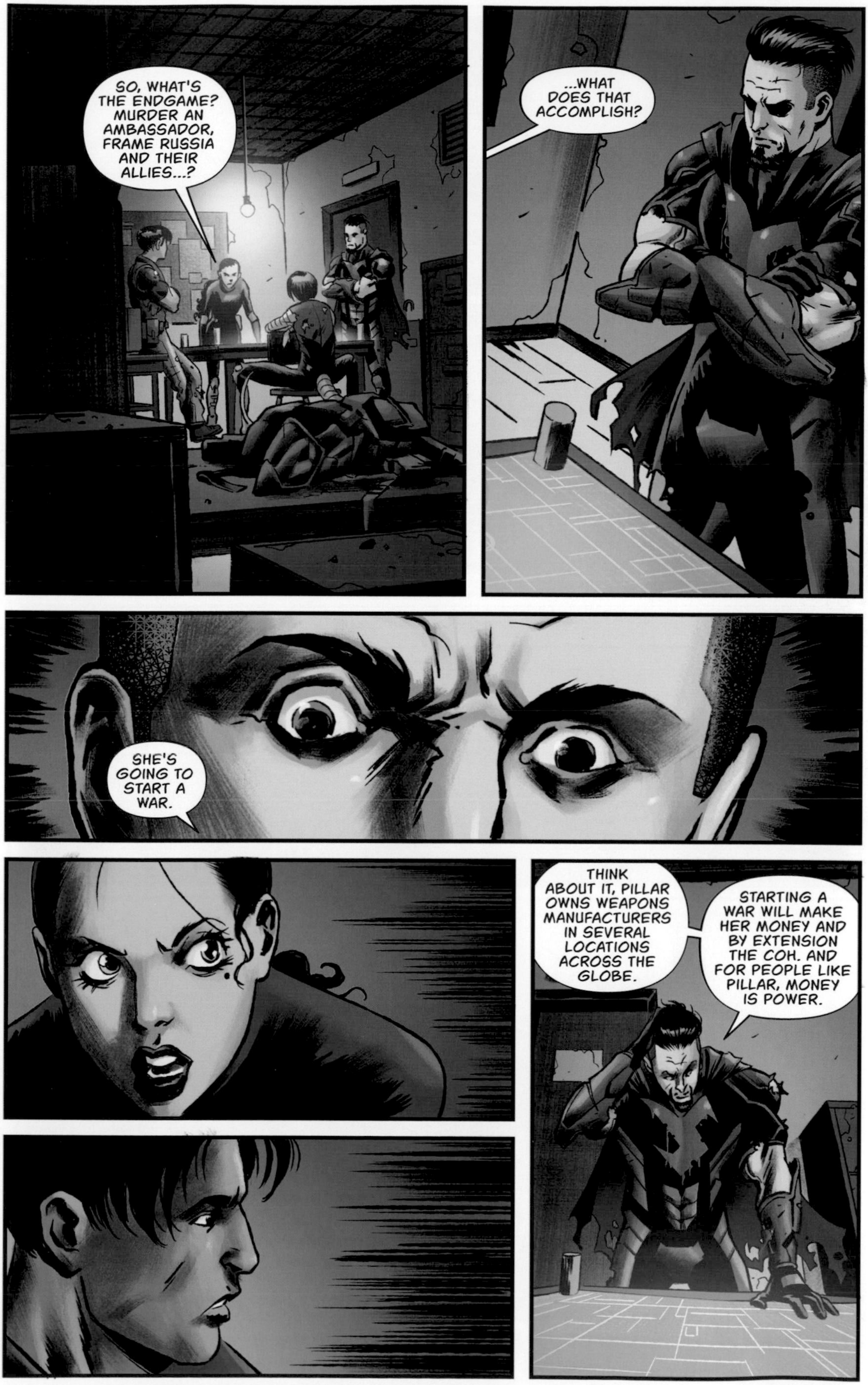
SO, WHAT'S THE ENDGAME? MURDER AN AMBASSADOR, FRAME RUSSIA AND THEIR ALLIES...?
...WHAT DOES THAT ACCOMPLISH?
SHE'S GOING TO START A WAR.
THINK ABOUT IT, PILLAR OWNS WEAPONS MANUFACTURERS IN SEVERAL LOCATIONS ACROSS THE GLOBE.
STARTING A WAR WILL MAKE HER MONEY AND BY EXTENSION THE COH. AND FOR PEOPLE LIKE PILLAR, MONEY IS POWER.

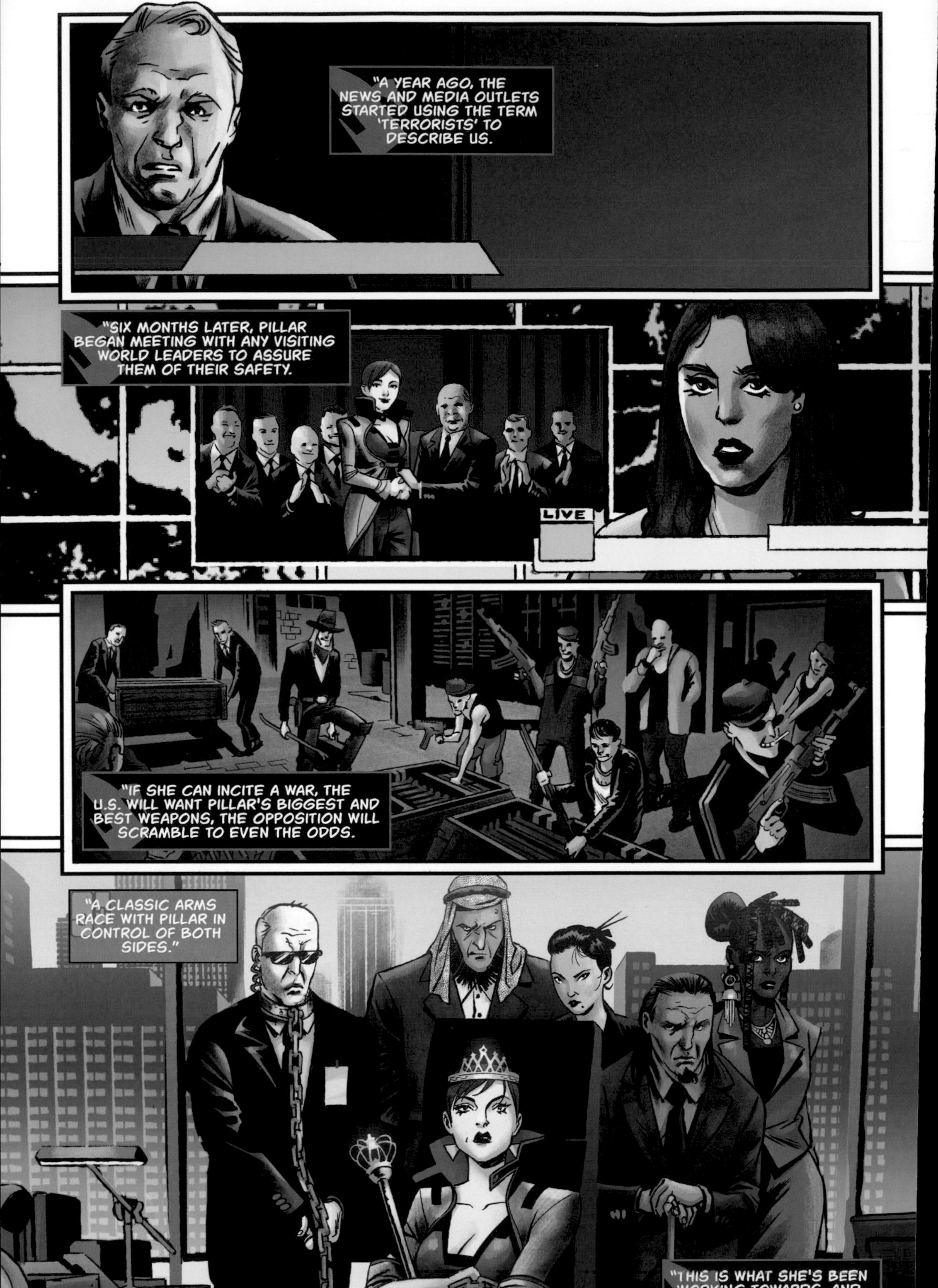
"A YEAR AGO, THE NEWS AND MEDIA OUTLETS STARTED USING THE TERM 'TERRORISTS' TO DESCRIBE US.
"SIX MONTHS LATER, PILLAR BEGAN MEETING WITH ANY VISITING WORLD LEADERS TO ASSURE THEM OF THEIR SAFETY.
LIVE
"IF SHE CAN INCITE A WAR, THE U.S. WILL WANT PILLAR'S BIGGEST AND BEST WEAPONS, THE OPPOSITION WILL SCRAMBLE TO EVEN THE ODDS.
"A CLASSIC ARMS RACE WITH PILLAR IN CONTROL OF BOTH SIDES."
"THIS IS WHAT SHE'S BEEN WORKING TOWARDS. AND WE'RE THE PERFECT SCAPEGOATS."

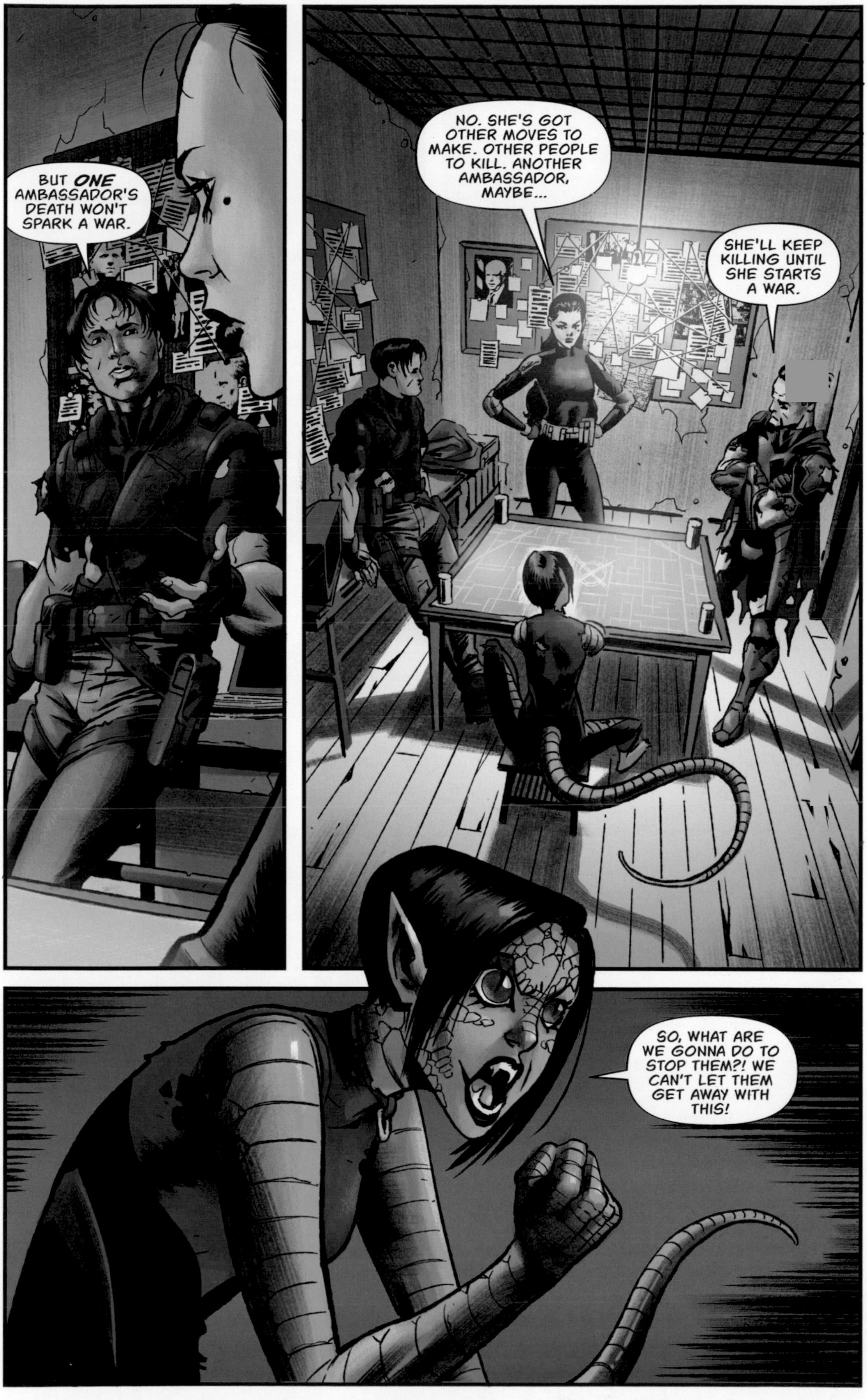
BUT ONE AMBASSADOR'S DEATH WON'T SPARK A WAR.
NO. SHE'S GOT OTHER MOVES TO MAKE. OTHER PEOPLE TO KILL. ANOTHER AMBASSADOR, MAYBE...
SHE'LL KEEP KILLING UNTIL SHE STARTS A WAR.
SO, WHAT ARE WE GONNA DO TO STOP THEM?! WE CAN'T LET THEM GET AWAY WITH THIS!

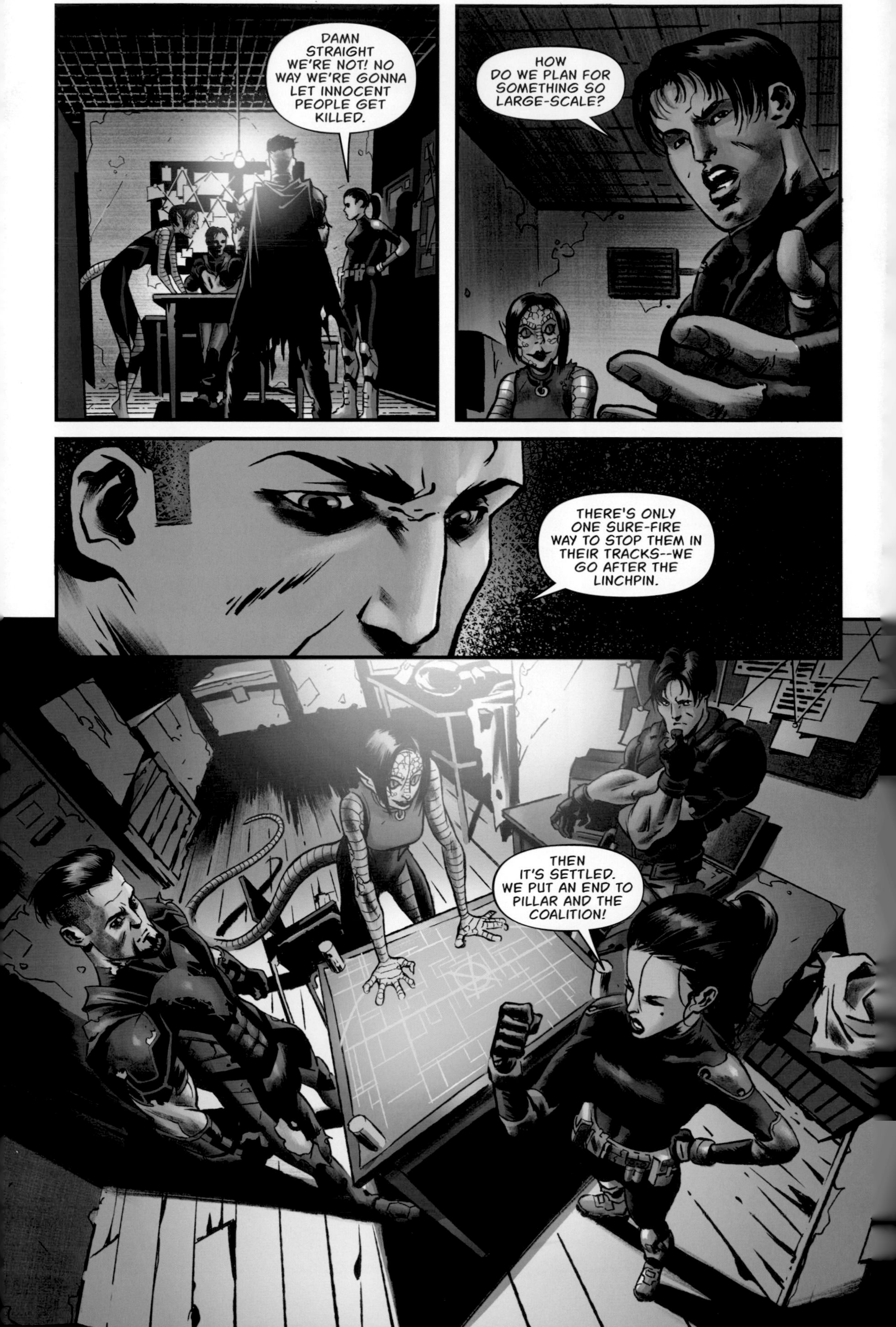
DAMN STRAIGHT WE'RE NOT! NO WAY WE'RE GONNA LET INNOCENT PEOPLE GET KILLED.
HOW DO WE PLAN FOR SOMETHING SO LARGE-SCALE?
THERE'S ONLY ONE SURE-FIRE WAY TO STOP THEM IN THEIR TRACKS--WE GO AFTER THE LINCHPIN.
THEN IT'S SETTLED. WE PUT AN END TO PILLAR AND THE COALITION!

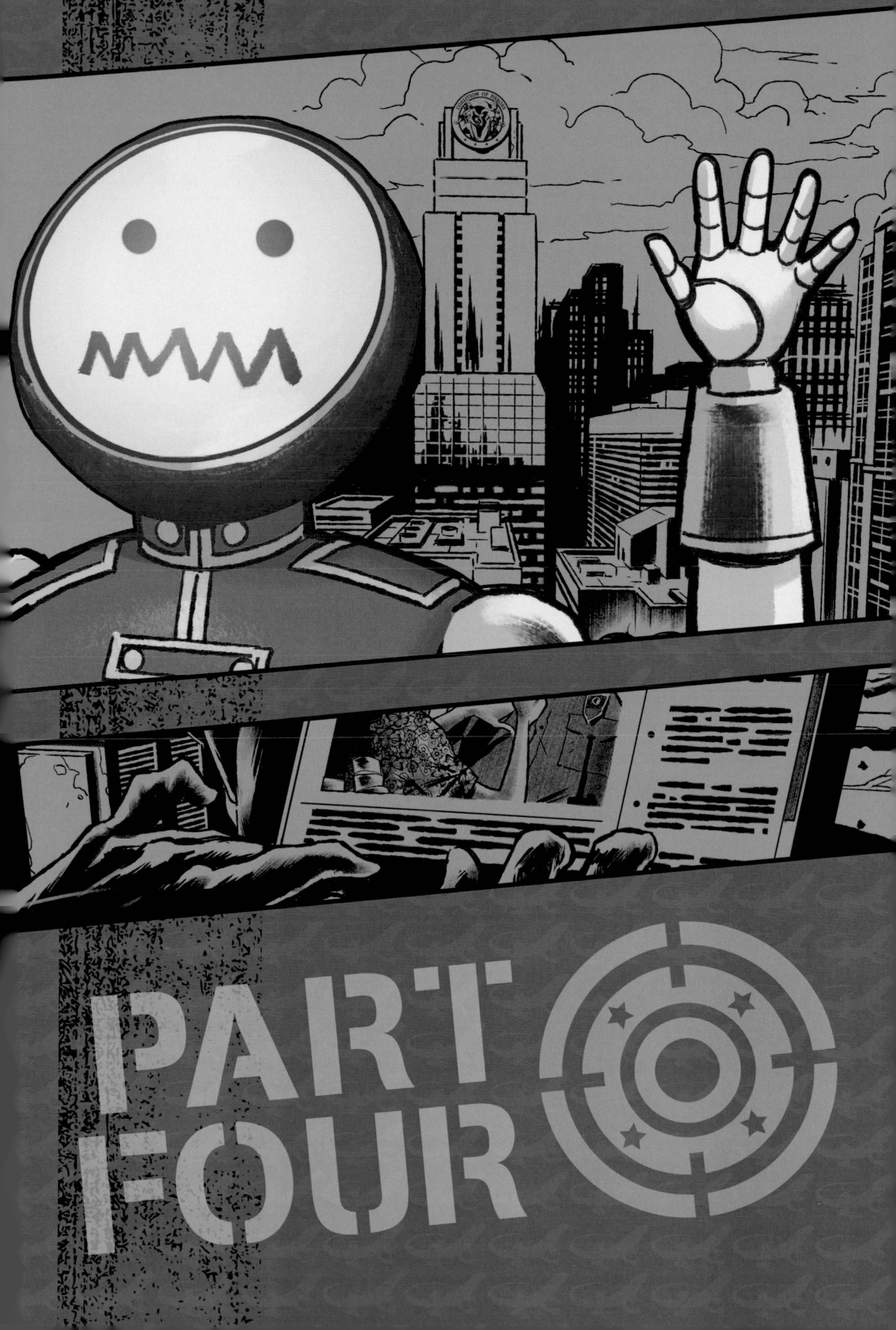

PART FOUR

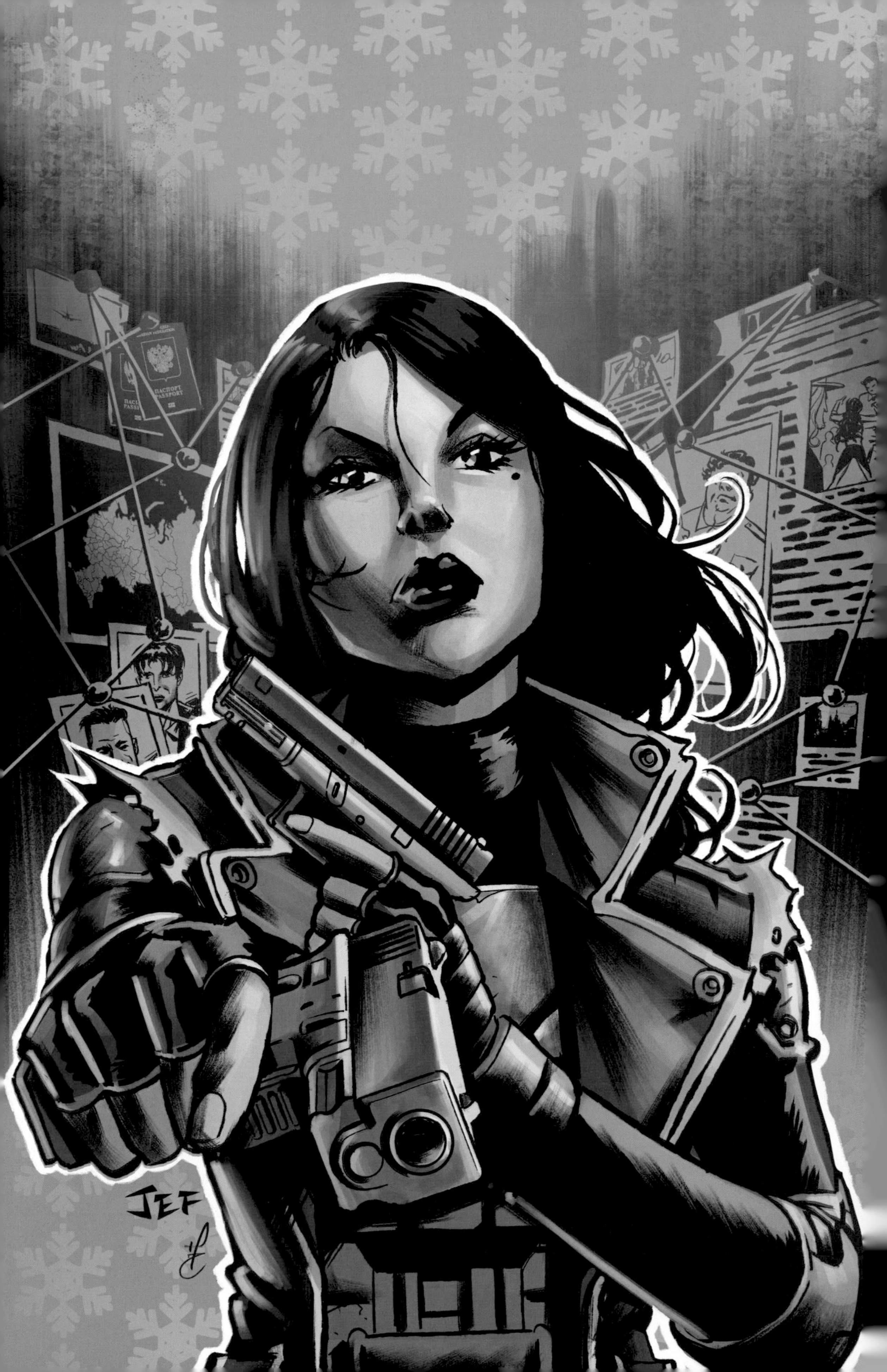
ПАСПОРТ
PASSPORT
JEF

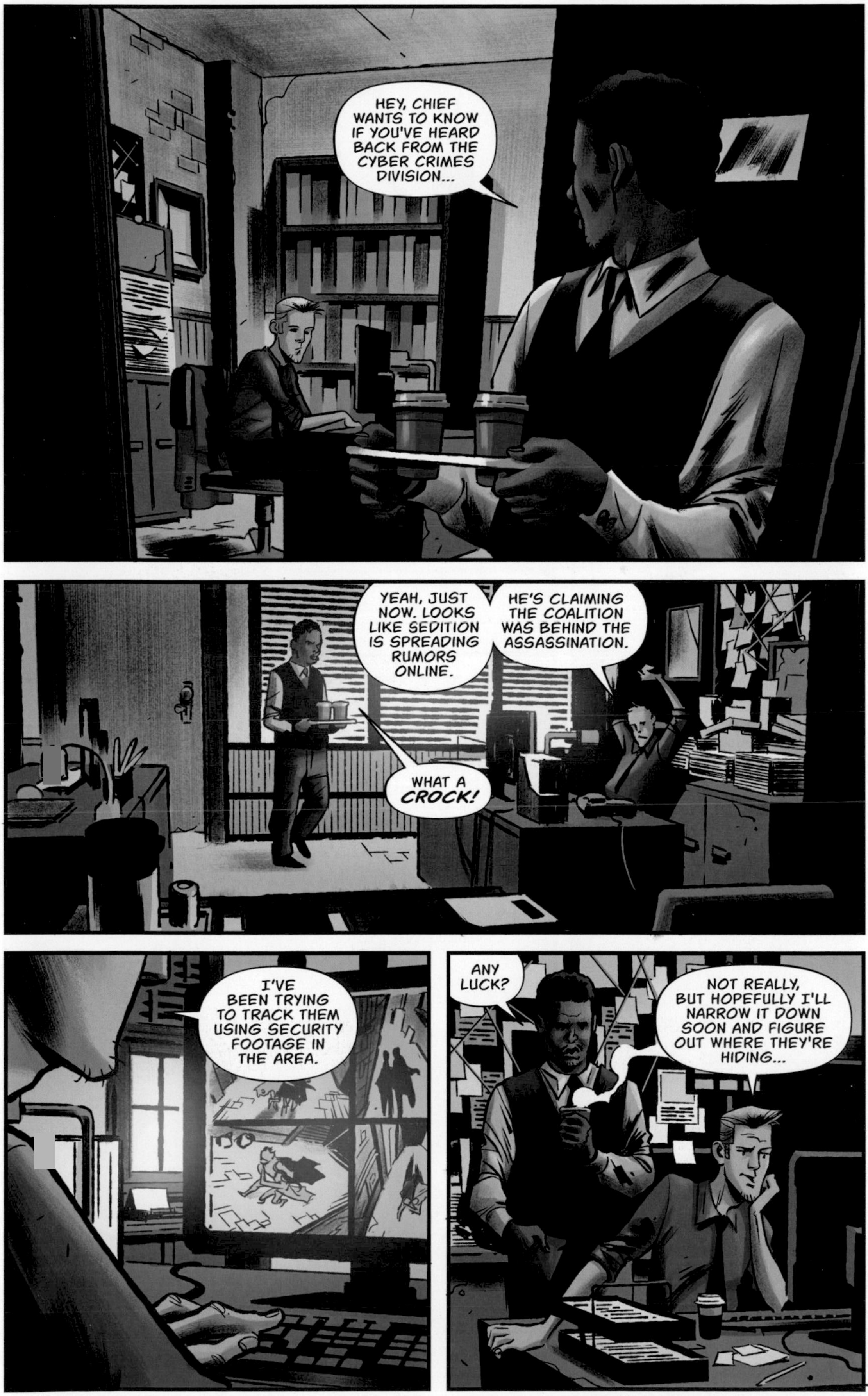
HEY, CHIEF WANTS TO KNOW IF YOU'VE HEARD BACK FROM THE CYBER CRIMES DIVISION...
YEAH, JUST NOW. LOOKS LIKE SEDITION IS SPREADING RUMORS ONLINE.
HE'S CLAIMING THE COALITION WAS BEHIND THE ASSASSINATION.
WHAT A CROCK!
I'VE BEEN TRYING TO TRACK THEM USING SECURITY FOOTAGE IN THE AREA.
ANY LUCK?
NOT REALLY, BUT HOPEFULLY I'LL NARROW IT DOWN SOON AND FIGURE OUT WHERE THEY'RE HIDING...

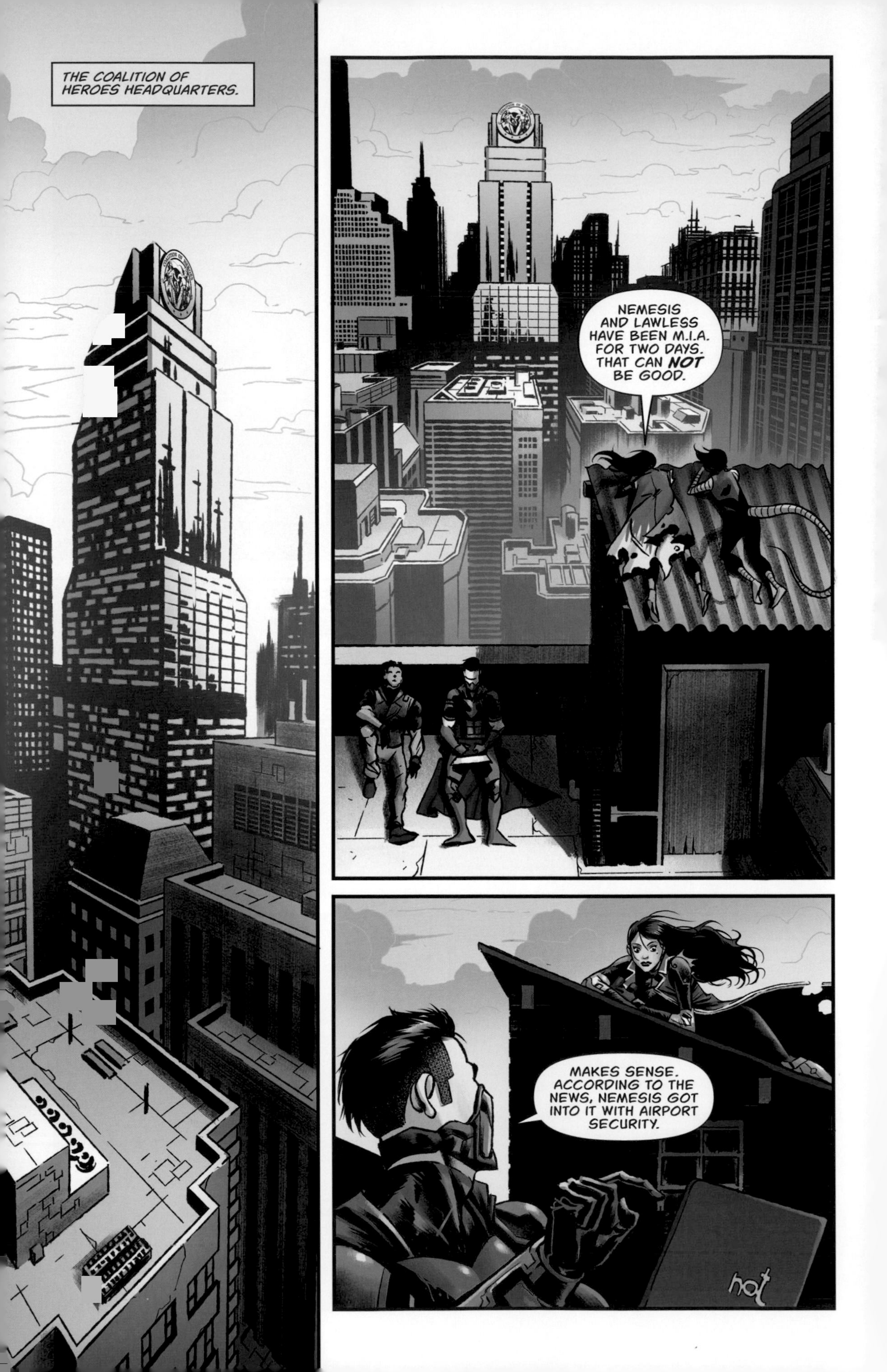
THE COALITION OF HEROES HEADQUARTERS.
NEMESIS AND LAWLESS HAVE BEEN M.I.A. FOR TWO DAYS. THAT CAN **NOT** BE GOOD.
MAKES SENSE. ACCORDING TO THE NEWS, NEMESIS GOT INTO IT WITH AIRPORT SECURITY.

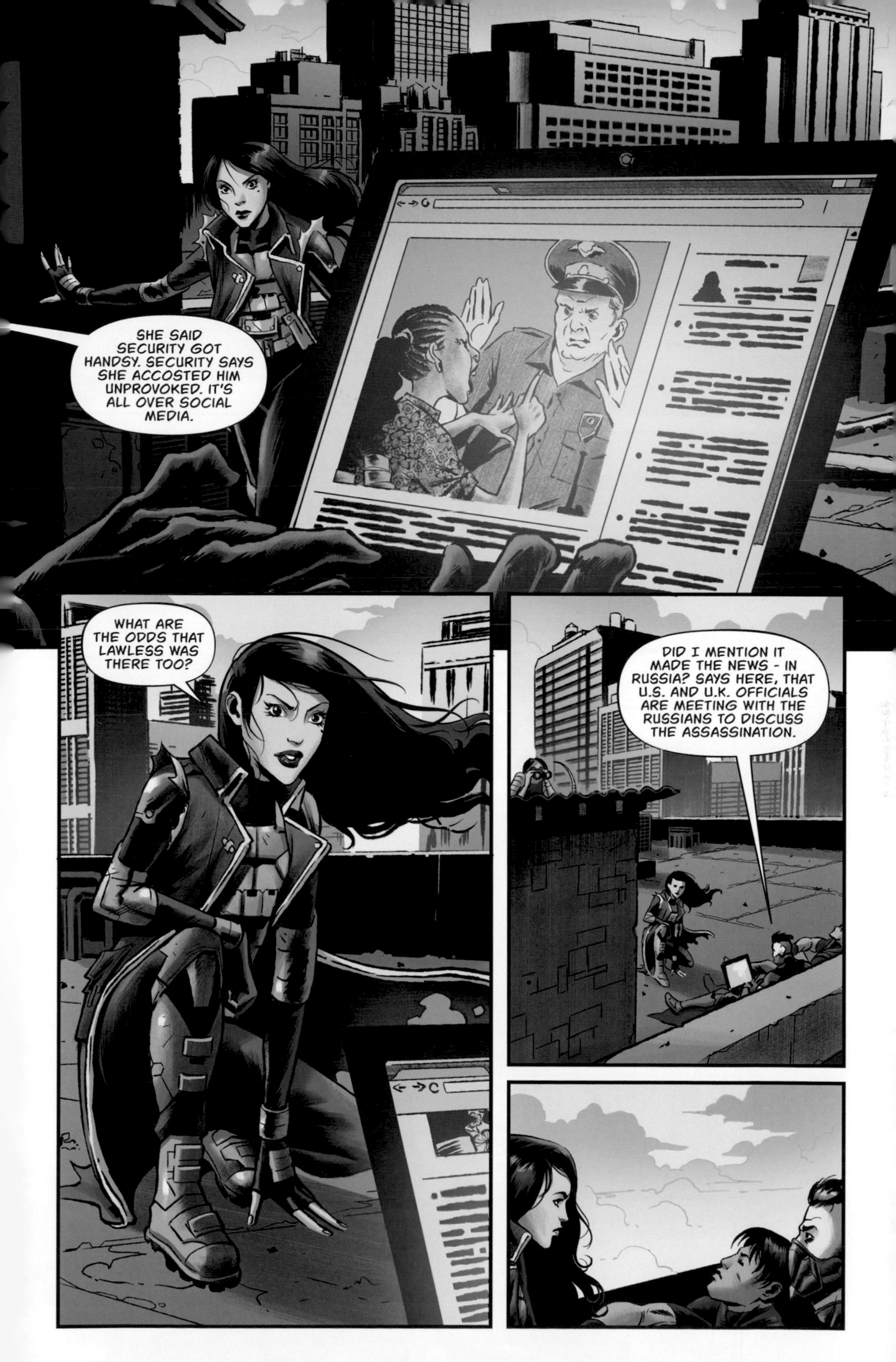
SHE SAID SECURITY GOT HANDSY. SECURITY SAYS SHE ACCOSTED HIM UNPROVOKED. IT'S ALL OVER SOCIAL MEDIA.
WHAT ARE THE ODDS THAT LAWLESS WAS THERE TOO?
DID I MENTION IT MADE THE NEWS - IN RUSSIA? SAYS HERE, THAT U.S. AND U.K. OFFICIALS ARE MEETING WITH THE RUSSIANS TO DISCUSS THE ASSASSINATION.

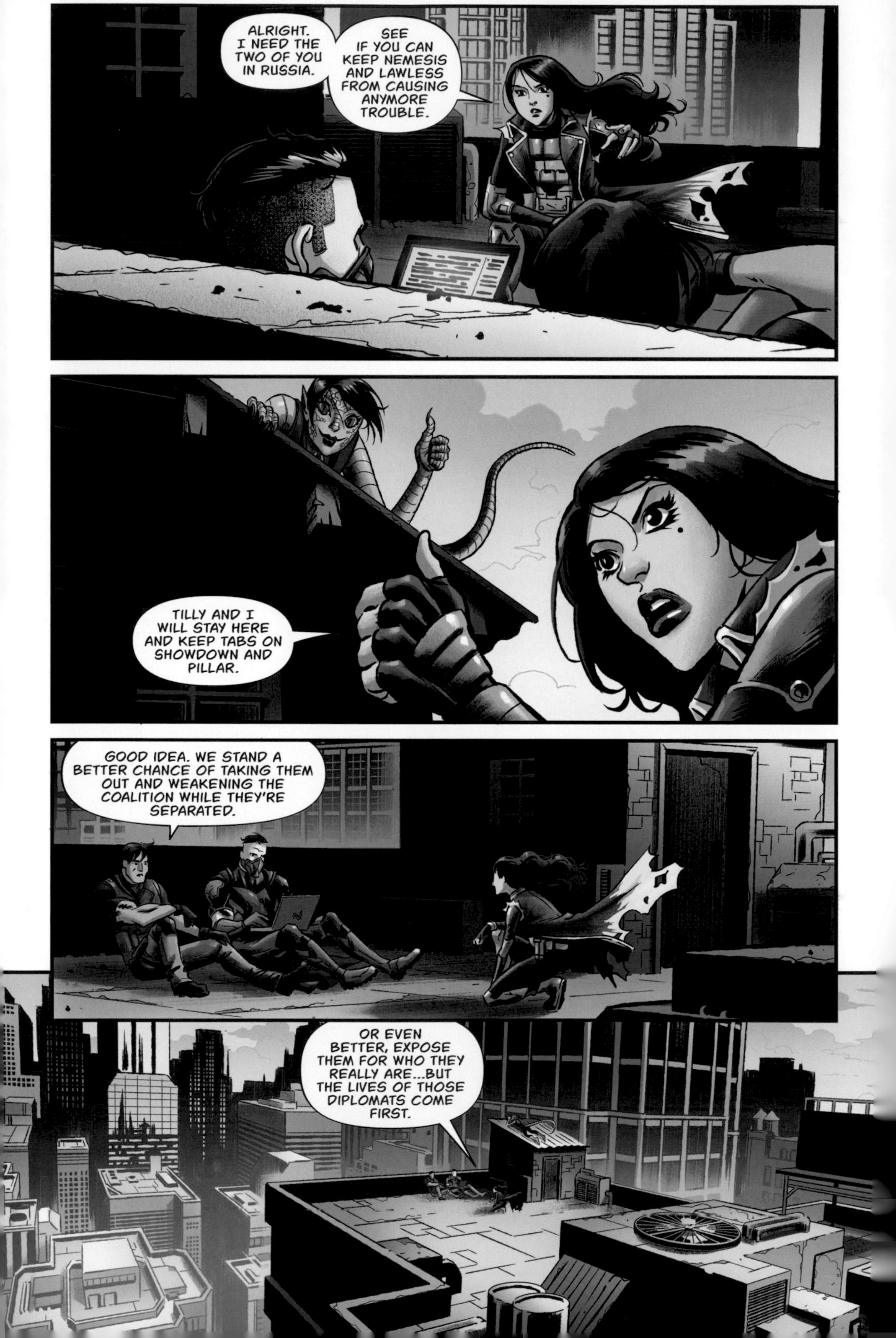
ALRIGHT. I NEED THE TWO OF YOU IN RUSSIA.
SEE IF YOU CAN KEEP NEMESIS AND LAWLESS FROM CAUSING ANYMORE TROUBLE.
TILLY AND I WILL STAY HERE AND KEEP TABS ON SHOWDOWN AND PILLAR.
GOOD IDEA. WE STAND A BETTER CHANCE OF TAKING THEM OUT AND WEAKENING THE COALITION WHILE THEY'RE SEPARATED.
OR EVEN BETTER, EXPOSE THEM FOR WHO THEY REALLY ARE...BUT THE LIVES OF THOSE DIPLOMATS COME FIRST.

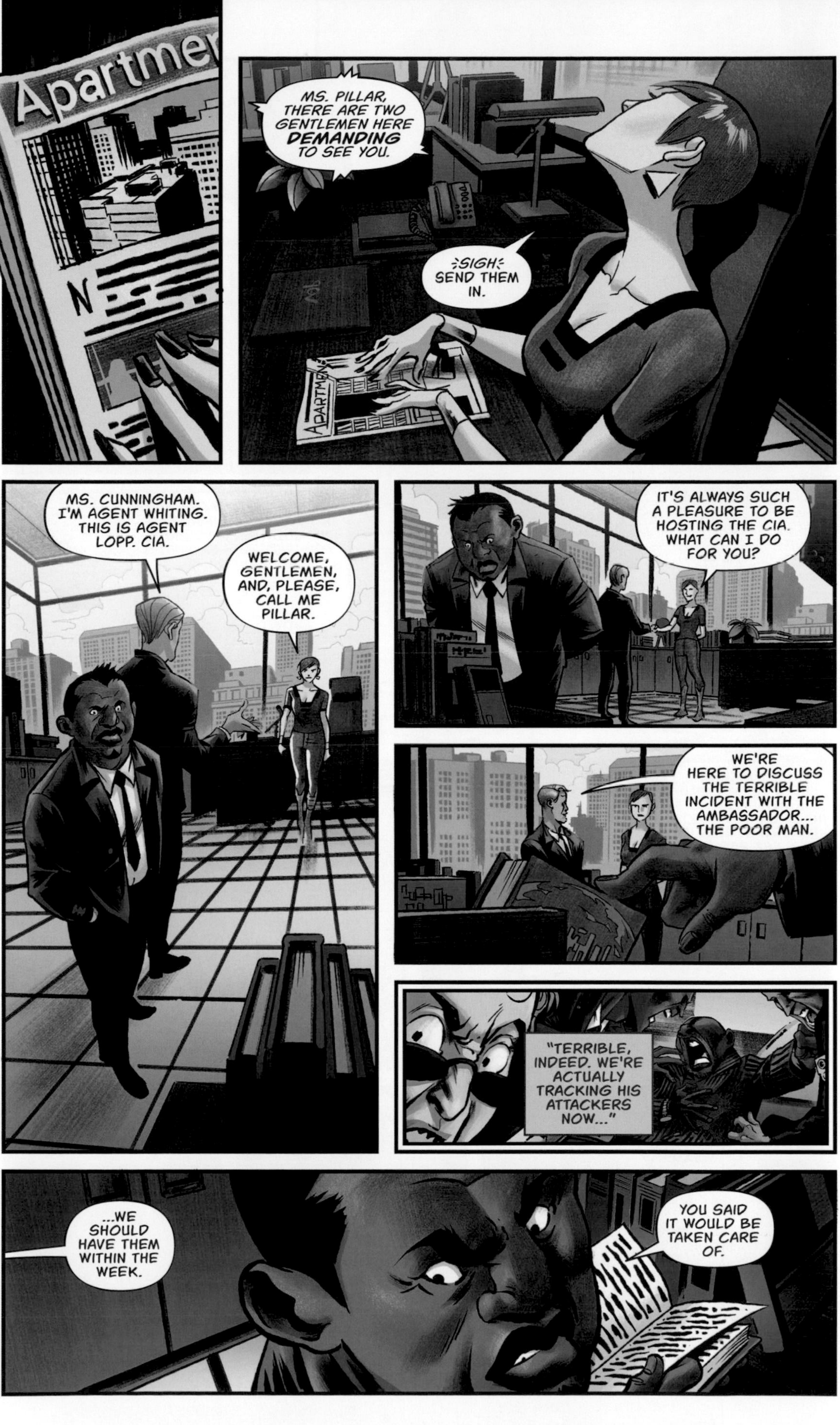
Apartmen
MS. PILLAR, THERE ARE TWO GENTLEMEN HERE DEMANDING TO SEE YOU.
SIGH SEND THEM IN.
MS. CUNNINGHAM. I'M AGENT WHITING. THIS IS AGENT LOPP. CIA.
WELCOME, GENTLEMEN, AND, PLEASE, CALL ME PILLAR.
IT'S ALWAYS SUCH A PLEASURE TO BE HOSTING THE CIA. WHAT CAN I DO FOR YOU?
WE'RE HERE TO DISCUSS THE TERRIBLE INCIDENT WITH THE AMBASSADOR... THE POOR MAN.
"TERRIBLE, INDEED. WE'RE ACTUALLY TRACKING HIS ATTACKERS NOW..."
...WE SHOULD HAVE THEM WITHIN THE WEEK.
YOU SAID IT WOULD BE TAKEN CARE OF.

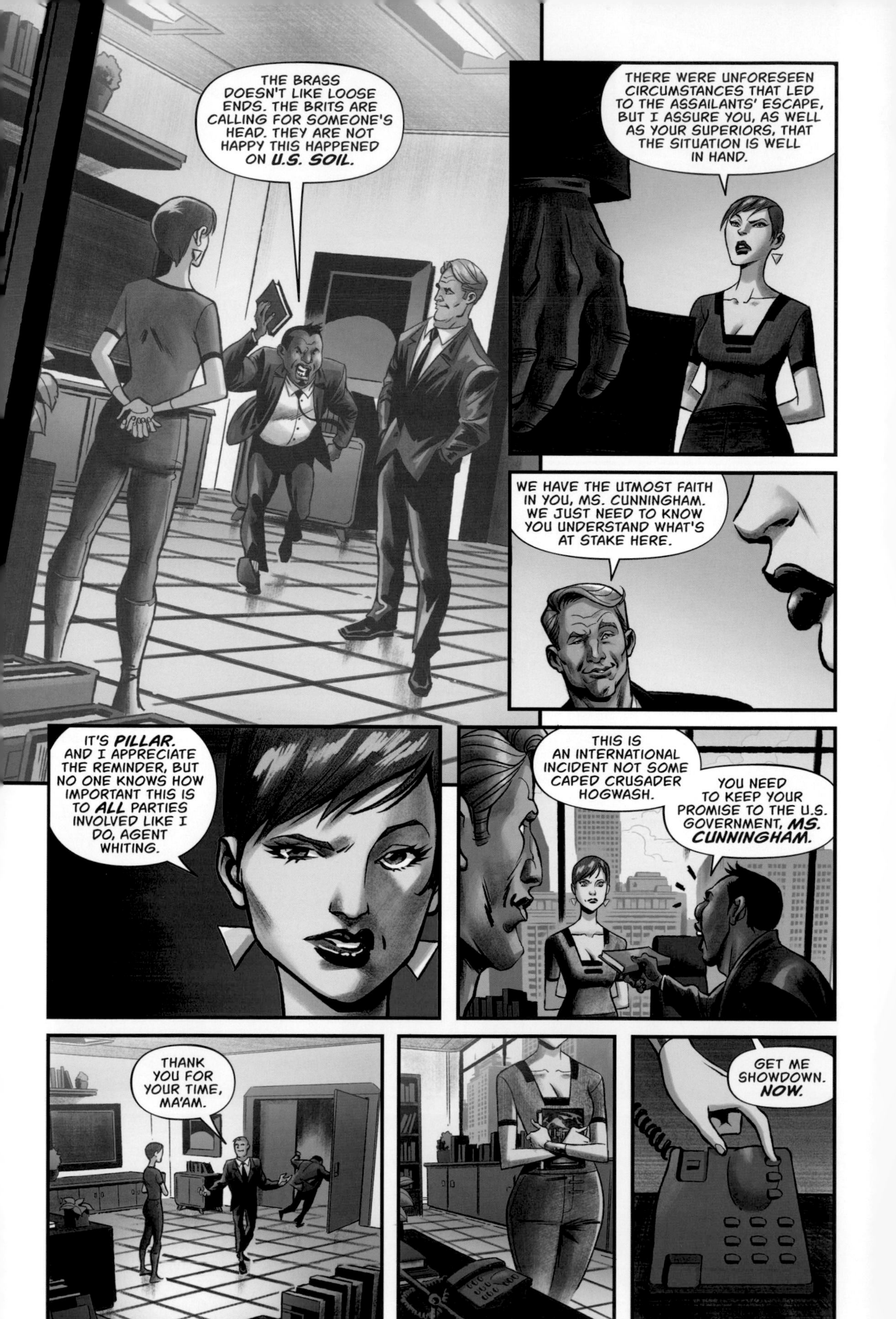
THE BRASS DOESN'T LIKE LOOSE ENDS. THE BRITS ARE CALLING FOR SOMEONE'S HEAD. THEY ARE NOT HAPPY THIS HAPPENED ON U.S. SOIL.
THERE WERE UNFORESEEN CIRCUMSTANCES THAT LED TO THE ASSAILANTS' ESCAPE, BUT I ASSURE YOU, AS WELL AS YOUR SUPERIORS, THAT THE SITUATION IS WELL IN HAND.
WE HAVE THE UTMOST FAITH IN YOU, MS. CUNNINGHAM. WE JUST NEED TO KNOW YOU UNDERSTAND WHAT'S AT STAKE HERE.
IT'S PILLAR. AND I APPRECIATE THE REMINDER, BUT NO ONE KNOWS HOW IMPORTANT THIS IS TO ALL PARTIES INVOLVED LIKE I DO, AGENT WHITING.
THIS IS AN INTERNATIONAL INCIDENT NOT SOME CAPED CRUSADER HOGWASH.
YOU NEED TO KEEP YOUR PROMISE TO THE U.S. GOVERNMENT, MS. CUNNINGHAM.
THANK YOU FOR YOUR TIME, MA'AM.
GET ME SHOWDOWN. NOW.

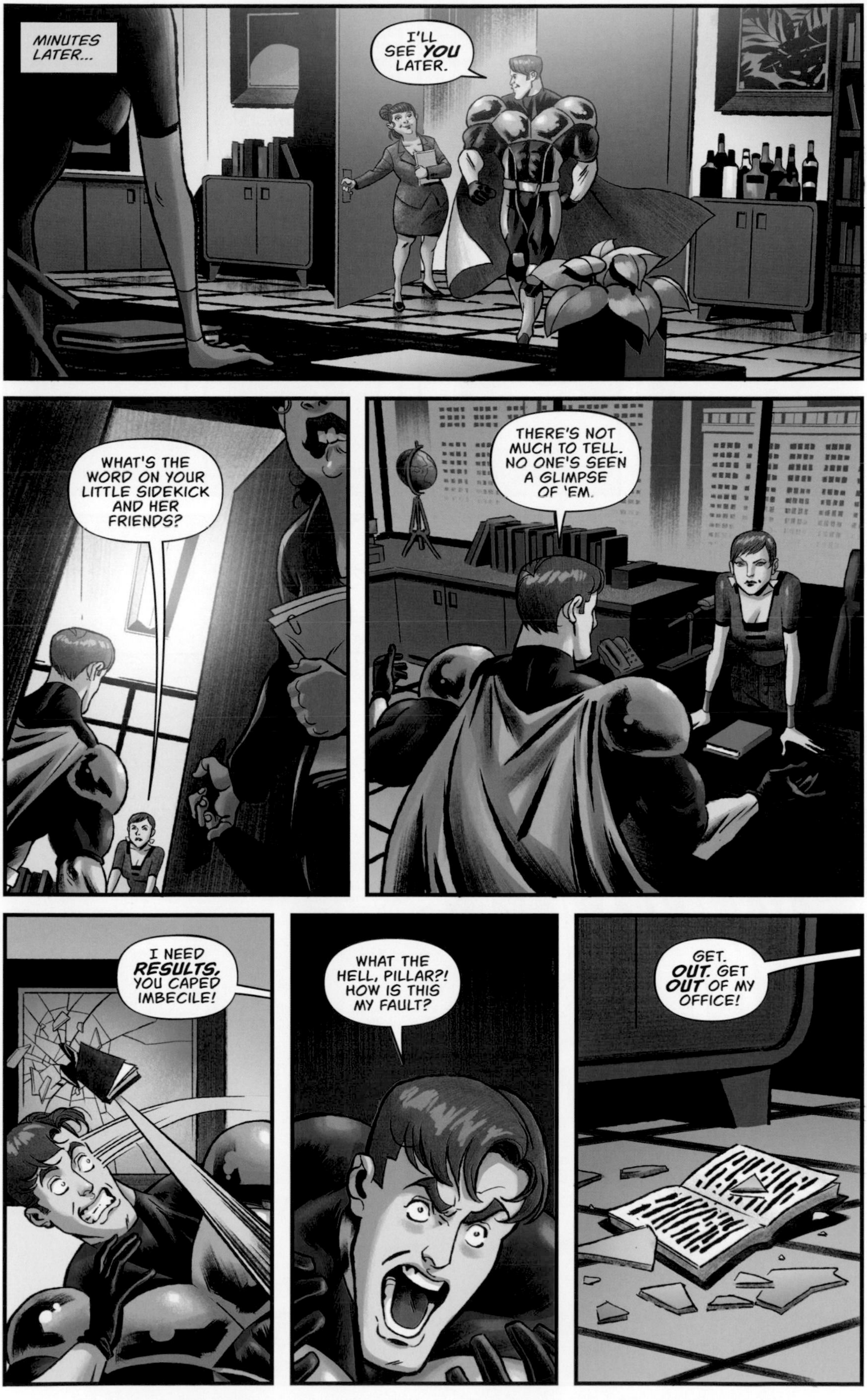
MINUTES LATER...
I'LL SEE YOU LATER.
WHAT'S THE WORD ON YOUR LITTLE SIDEKICK AND HER FRIENDS?
THERE'S NOT MUCH TO TELL. NO ONE'S SEEN A GLIMPSE OF 'EM.
I NEED RESULTS, YOU CAPED IMBECILE!
WHAT THE HELL, PILLAR?! HOW IS THIS MY FAULT?
GET. OUT. GET OUT OF MY OFFICE!

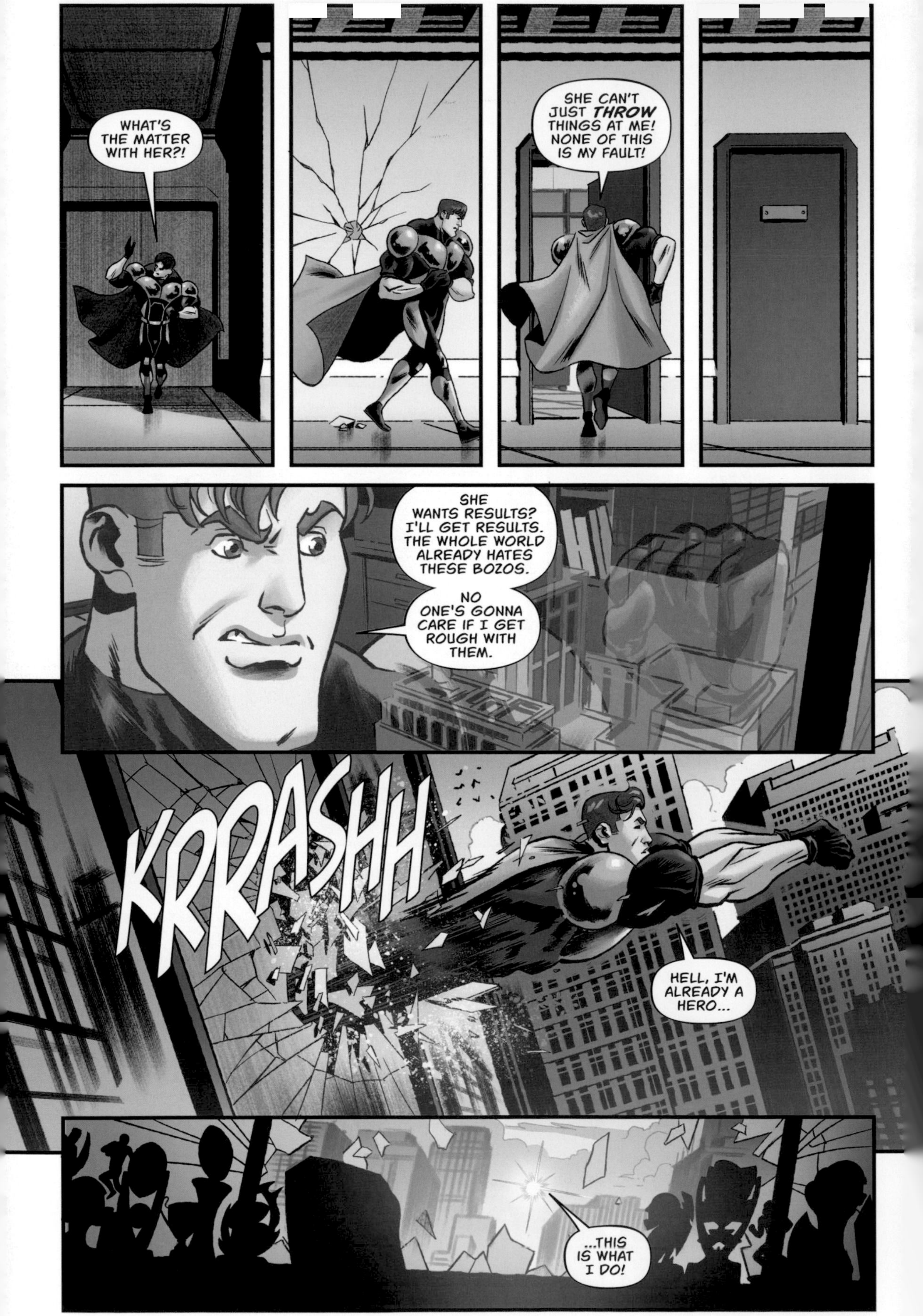
WHAT'S THE MATTER WITH HER?!
SHE CAN'T JUST THROW THINGS AT ME! NONE OF THIS IS MY FAULT!
SHE WANTS RESULTS? I'LL GET RESULTS. THE WHOLE WORLD ALREADY HATES THESE BOZOS.
NO ONE'S GONNA CARE IF I GET ROUGH WITH THEM.
KRRASHH
HELL, I'M ALREADY A HERO...
...THIS IS WHAT I DO!

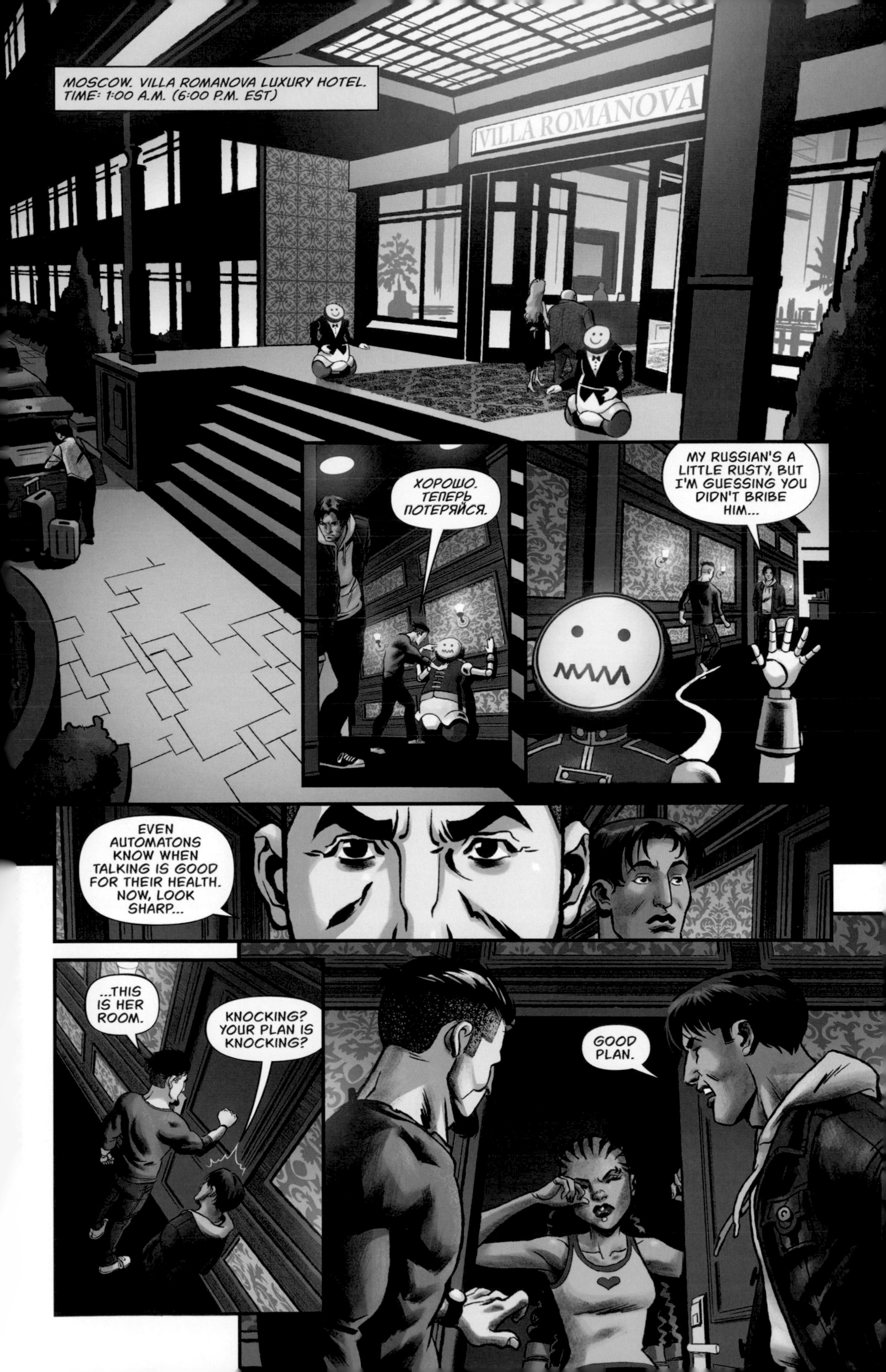
MOSCOW. VILLA ROMANOVA LUXURY HOTEL.
TIME: 1:00 A.M. (6:00 P.M. EST)
VILLA ROMANOVA
VILLA ROMANOVA
ХОРОШО. ТЕПЕРЬ ПОТЕРЯЙСЯ.
MY RUSSIAN'S A LITTLE RUSTY, BUT I'M GUESSING YOU DIDN'T BRIBE HIM...
EVEN AUTOMATONS KNOW WHEN TALKING IS GOOD FOR THEIR HEALTH. NOW, LOOK SHARP...
...THIS IS HER ROOM.
KNOCKING? YOUR PLAN IS KNOCKING?
GOOD PLAN.

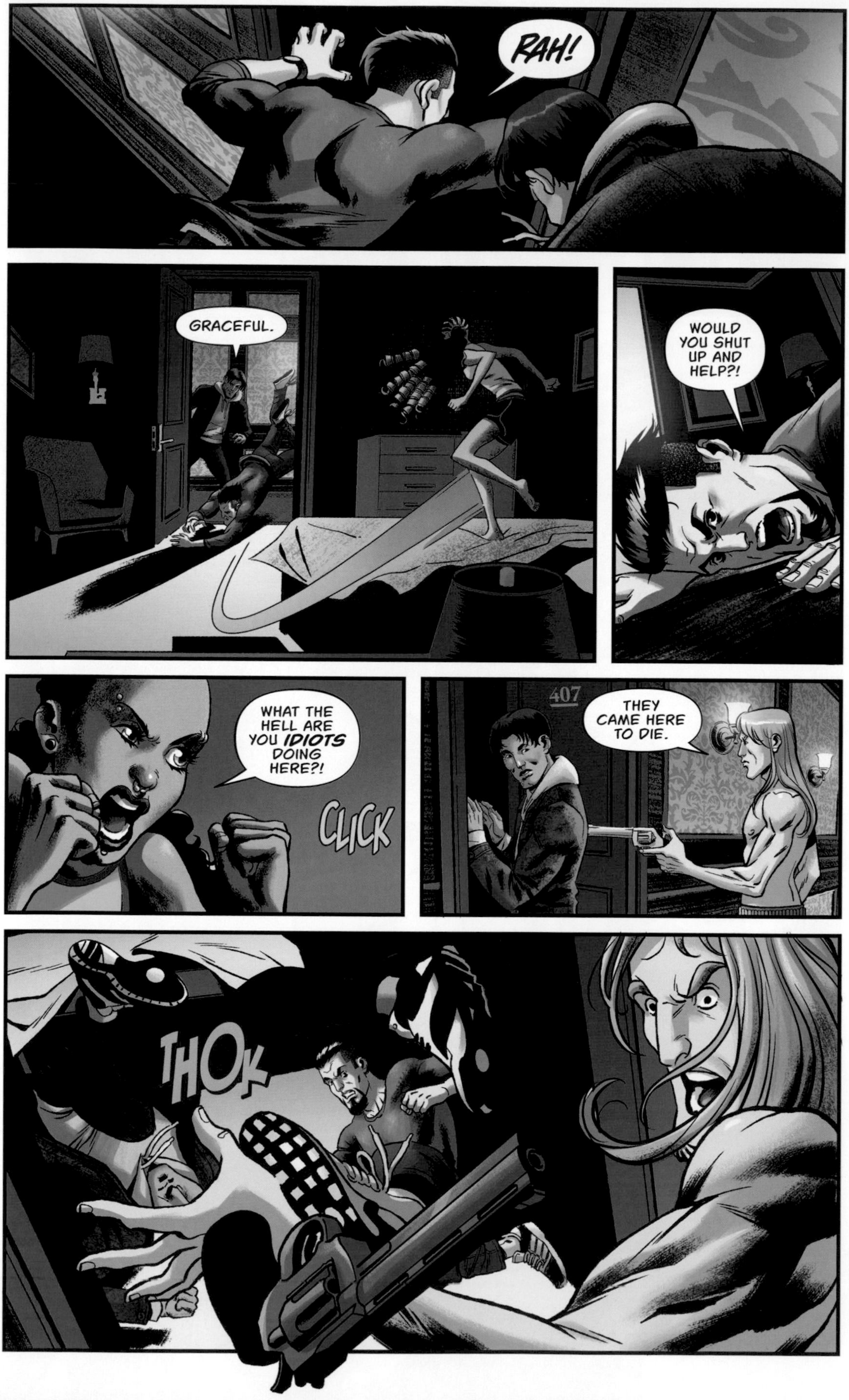
RAH!
GRACEFUL.
WOULD YOU SHUT UP AND HELP?!
WHAT THE HELL ARE YOU IDIOTS DOING HERE?!
CLICK
407
THEY CAME HERE TO DIE.
THOK

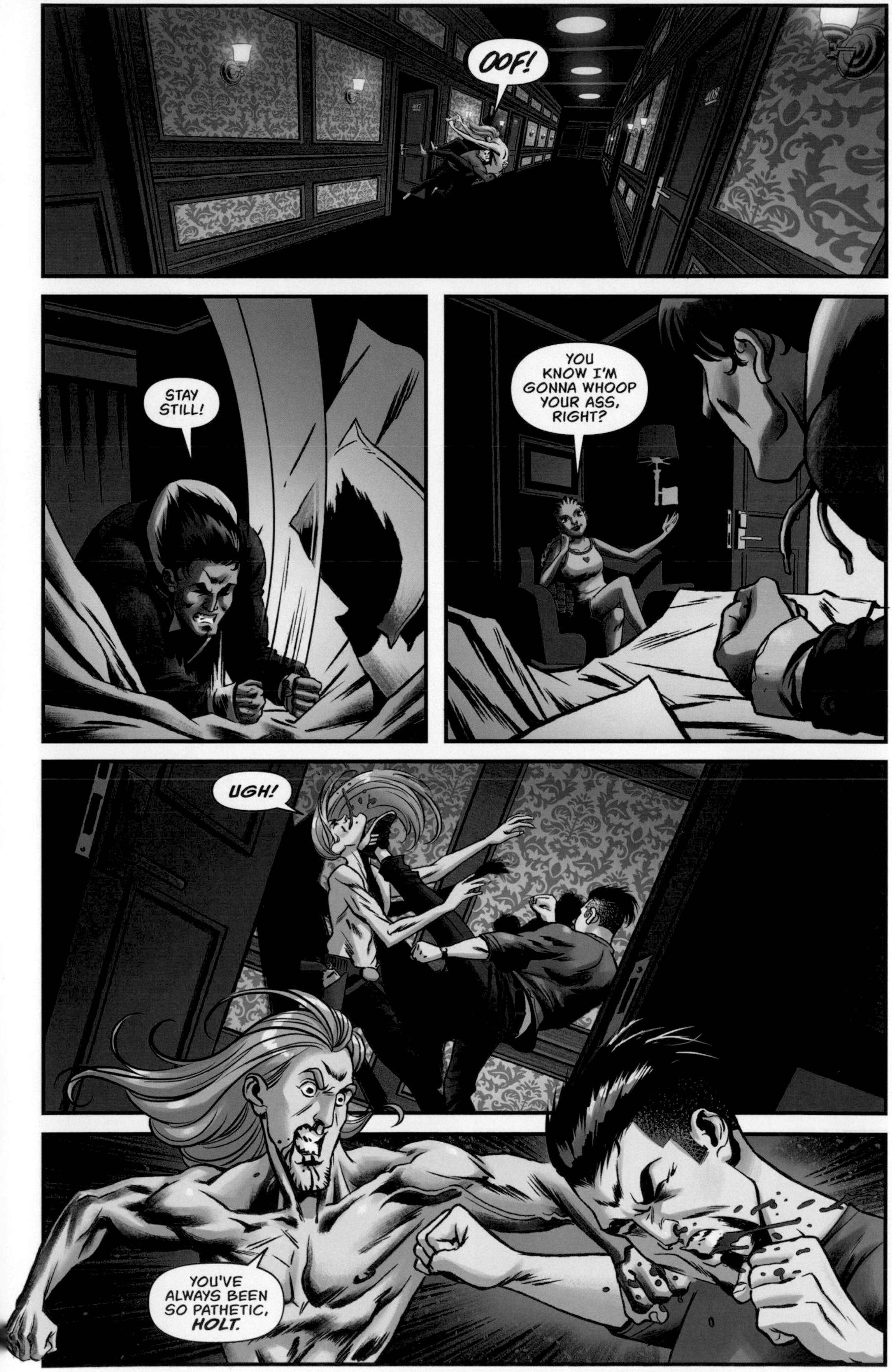
OOF!
STAY STILL!
YOU KNOW I'M GONNA WHOOP YOUR ASS, RIGHT?
UGH!
YOU'VE ALWAYS BEEN SO PATHETIC, HOLT.

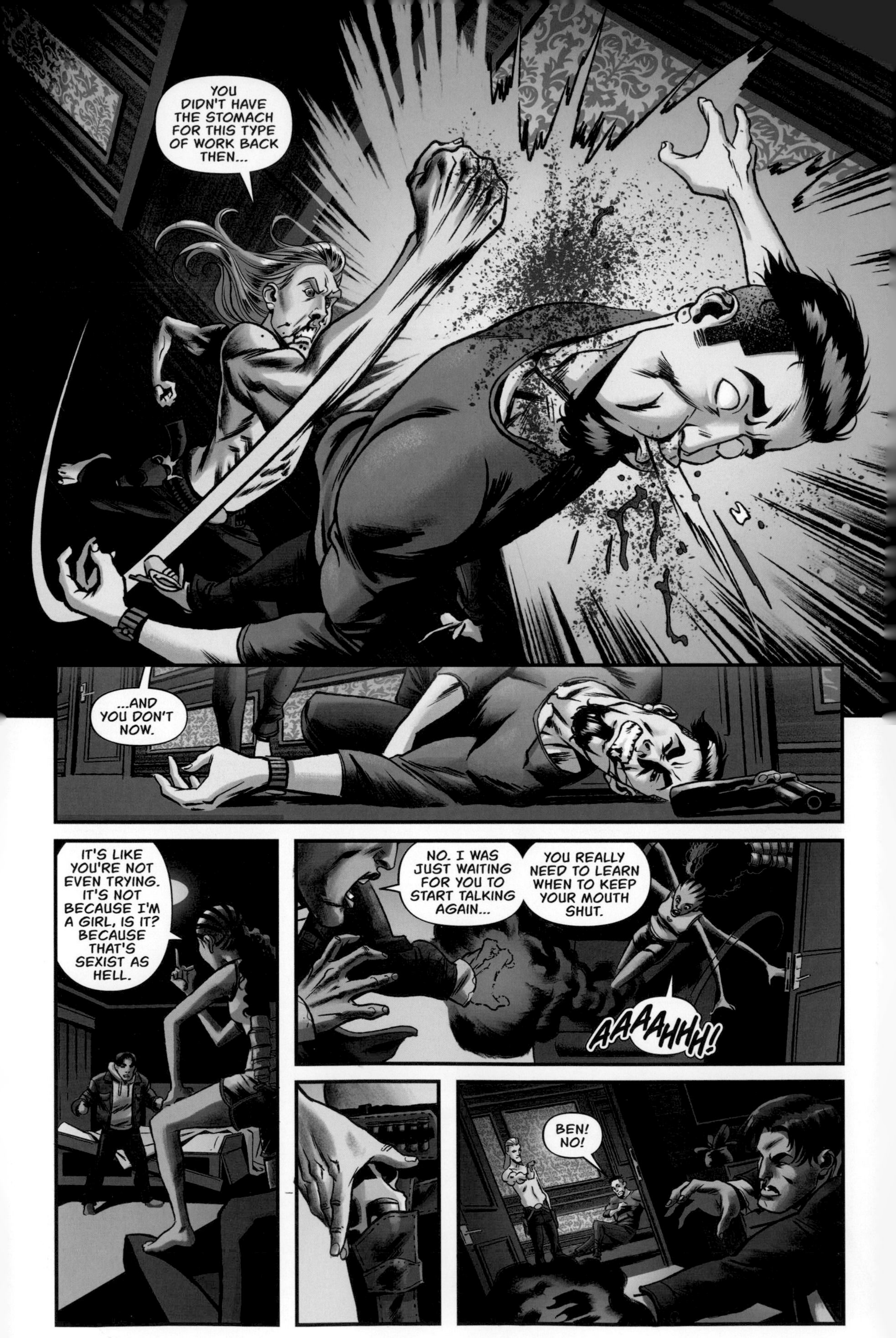
YOU DIDN'T HAVE THE STOMACH FOR THIS TYPE OF WORK BACK THEN...
...AND YOU DON'T NOW.
IT'S LIKE YOU'RE NOT EVEN TRYING. IT'S NOT BECAUSE I'M A GIRL, IS IT? BECAUSE THAT'S SEXIST AS HELL.
NO. I WAS JUST WAITING FOR YOU TO START TALKING AGAIN...
YOU REALLY NEED TO LEARN WHEN TO KEEP YOUR MOUTH SHUT.
AAAAHHH!
BEN! NO!

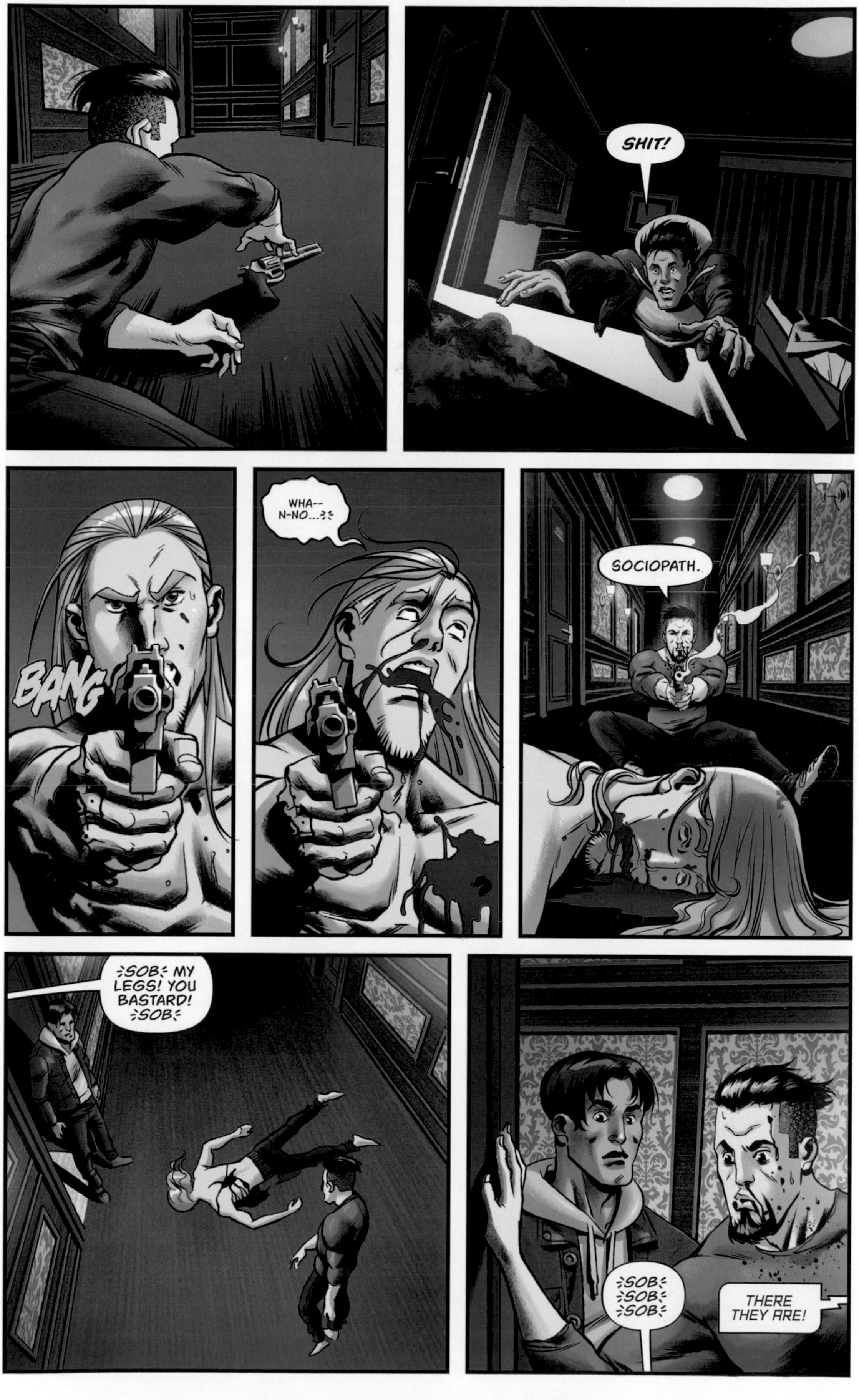
SHIT!
BANG
WHA-- N-NO...
SOCIOPATH.
SOB MY LEGS! YOU BASTARD! SOB
SOB SOB SOB
THERE THEY ARE!

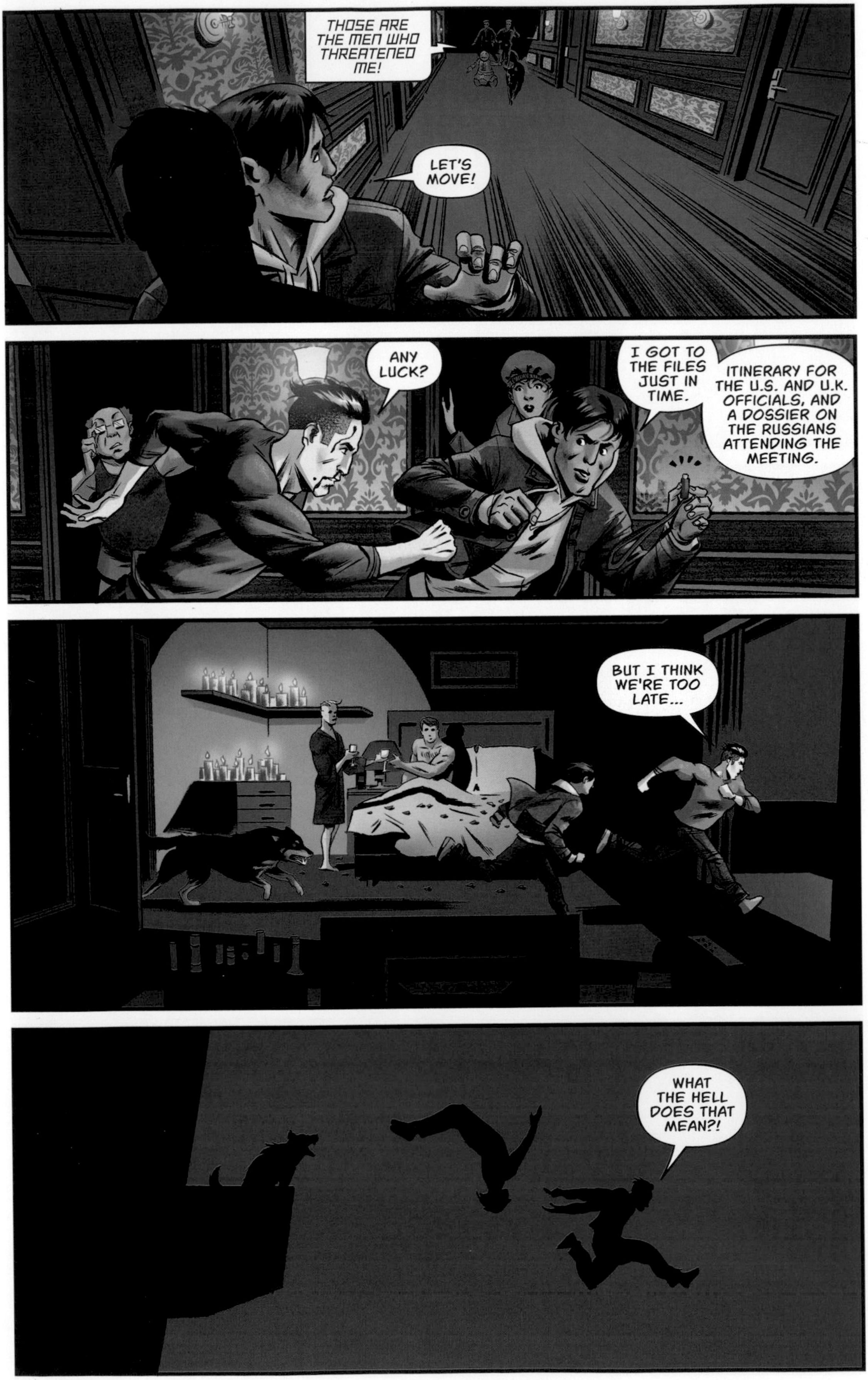
THOSE ARE THE MEN WHO THREATENED ME!
LET'S MOVE!
ANY LUCK?
I GOT TO THE FILES JUST IN TIME.
ITINERARY FOR THE U.S. AND U.K. OFFICIALS, AND A DOSSIER ON THE RUSSIANS ATTENDING THE MEETING.
BUT I THINK WE'RE TOO LATE...
WHAT THE HELL DOES THAT MEAN?!

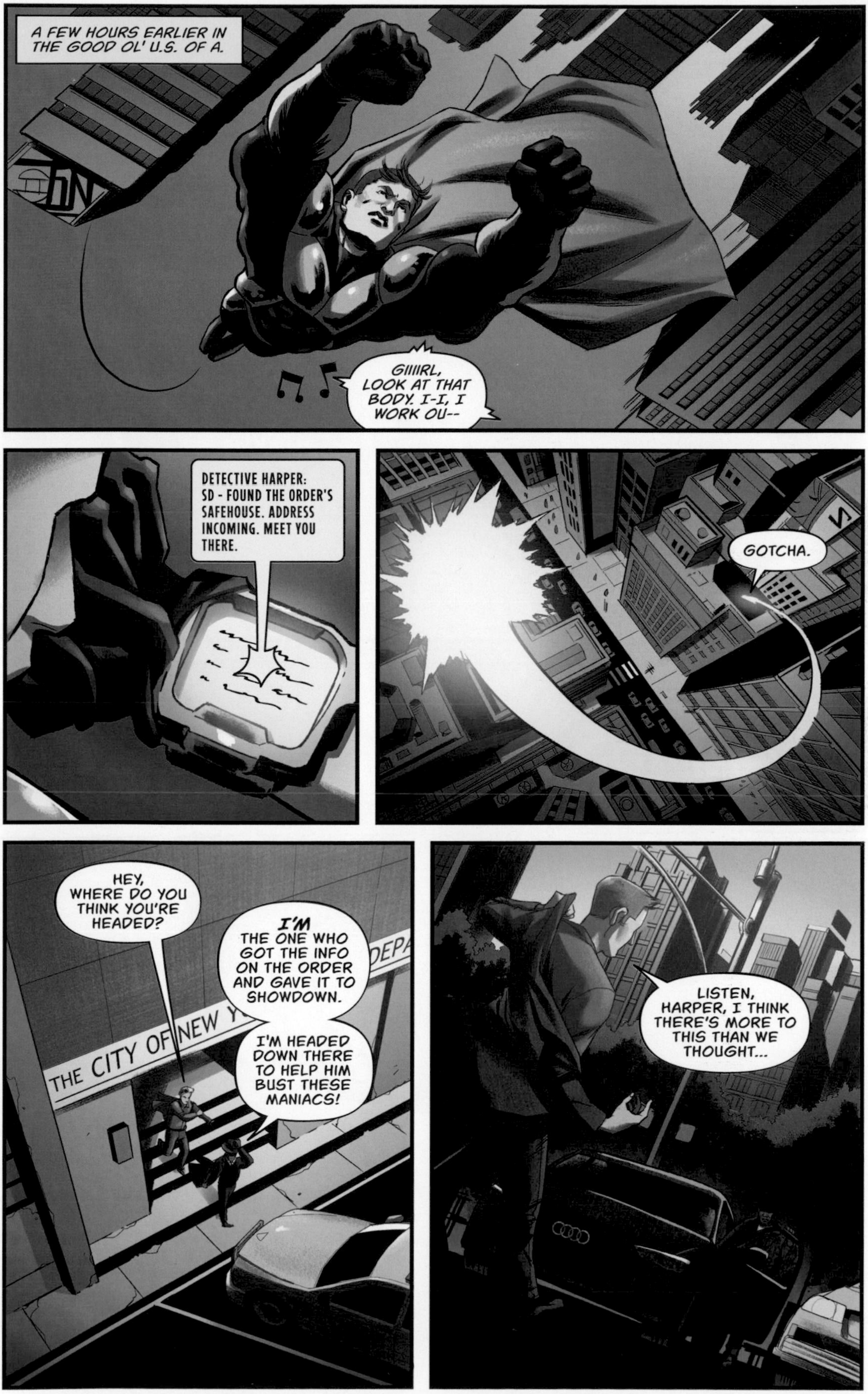
A FEW HOURS EARLIER IN THE GOOD OL' U.S. OF A.
GIIIRL, LOOK AT THAT BODY. I-I, I WORK OU--
DETECTIVE HARPER: SD - FOUND THE ORDER'S SAFEHOUSE. ADDRESS INCOMING. MEET YOU THERE.
GOTCHA.
HEY, WHERE DO YOU THINK YOU'RE HEADED?
THE CITY OF NEW Y
DEPA
I'M THE ONE WHO GOT THE INFO ON THE ORDER AND GAVE IT TO SHOWDOWN.
I'M HEADED DOWN THERE TO HELP HIM BUST THESE MANIACS!
LISTEN, HARPER, I THINK THERE'S MORE TO THIS THAN WE THOUGHT...

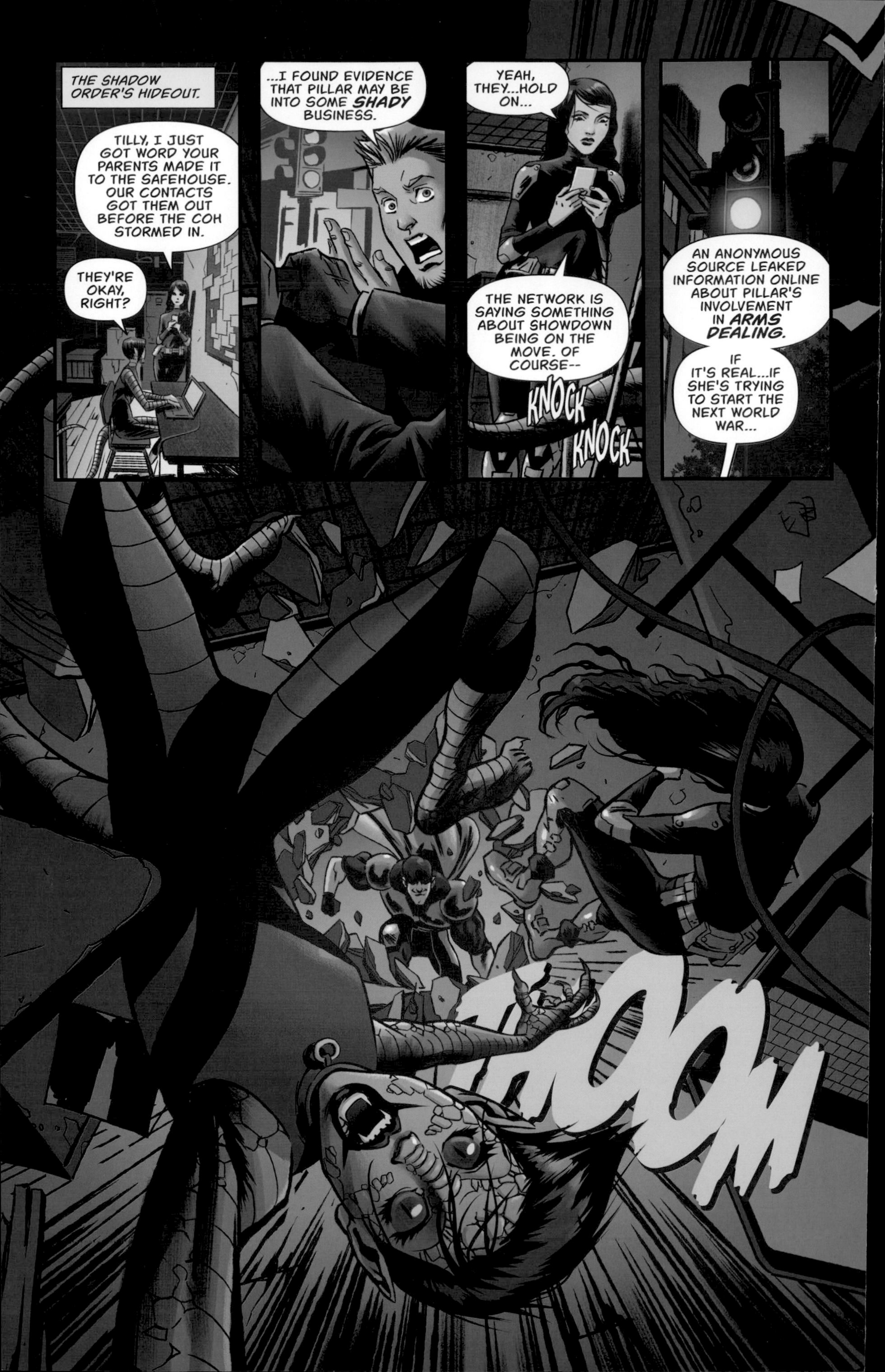
THE SHADOW ORDER'S HIDEOUT.
TILLY, I JUST GOT WORD YOUR PARENTS MADE IT TO THE SAFEHOUSE. OUR CONTACTS GOT THEM OUT BEFORE THE COH STORMED IN.
THEY'RE OKAY, RIGHT?
...I FOUND EVIDENCE THAT PILLAR MAY BE INTO SOME SHADY BUSINESS.
YEAH, THEY...HOLD ON...
THE NETWORK IS SAYING SOMETHING ABOUT SHOWDOWN BEING ON THE MOVE. OF COURSE--
KNOCK KNOCK
AN ANONYMOUS SOURCE LEAKED INFORMATION ONLINE ABOUT PILLAR'S INVOLVEMENT IN ARMS DEALING.
IF IT'S REAL...IF SHE'S TRYING TO START THE NEXT WORLD WAR...

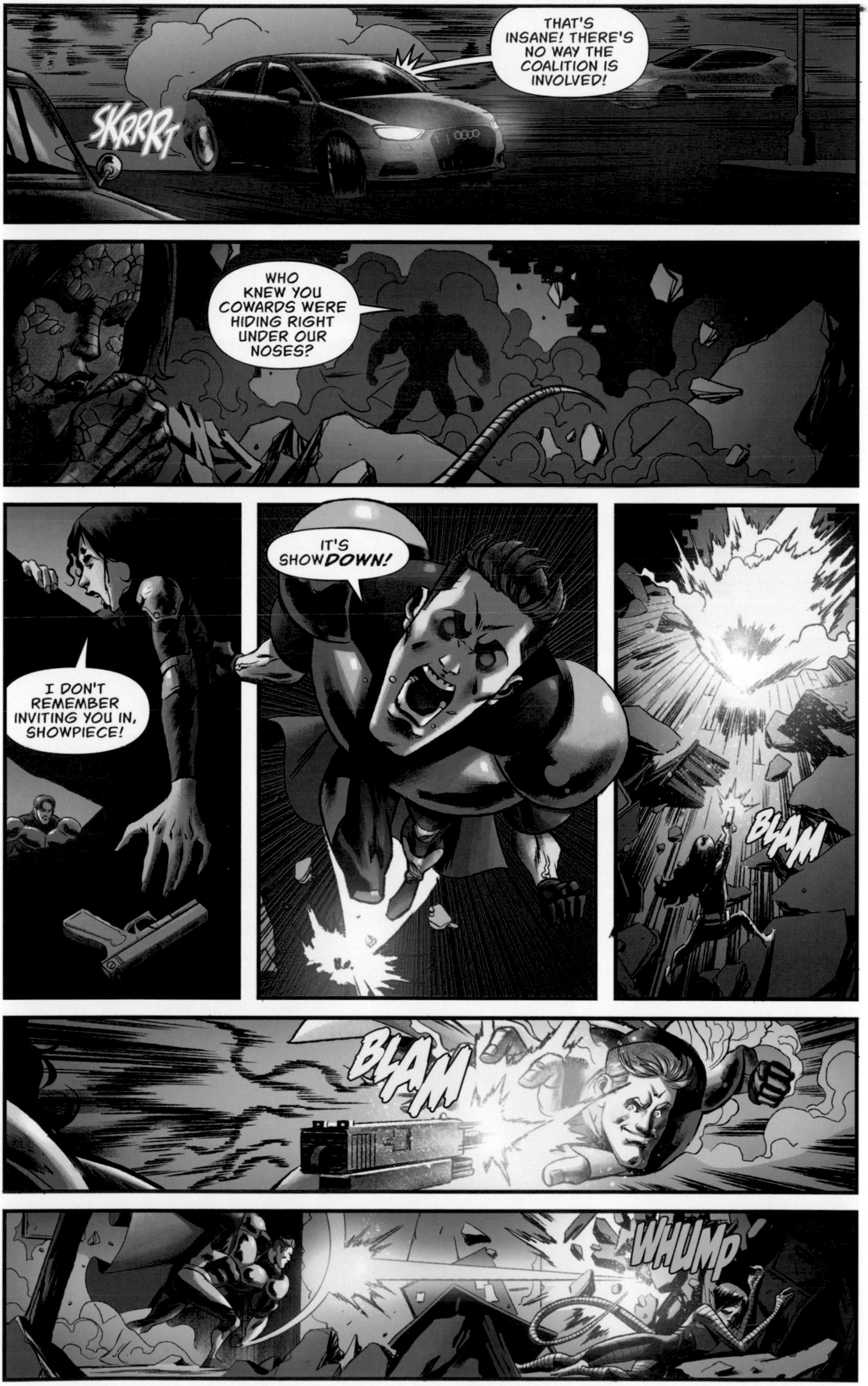
THAT'S INSANE! THERE'S NO WAY THE COALITION IS INVOLVED!
SKRRRT
WHO KNEW YOU COWARDS WERE HIDING RIGHT UNDER OUR NOSES?
I DON'T REMEMBER INVITING YOU IN, SHOWPIECE!
IT'S SHOWDOWN!
BLAM
BLAM
WHUMP

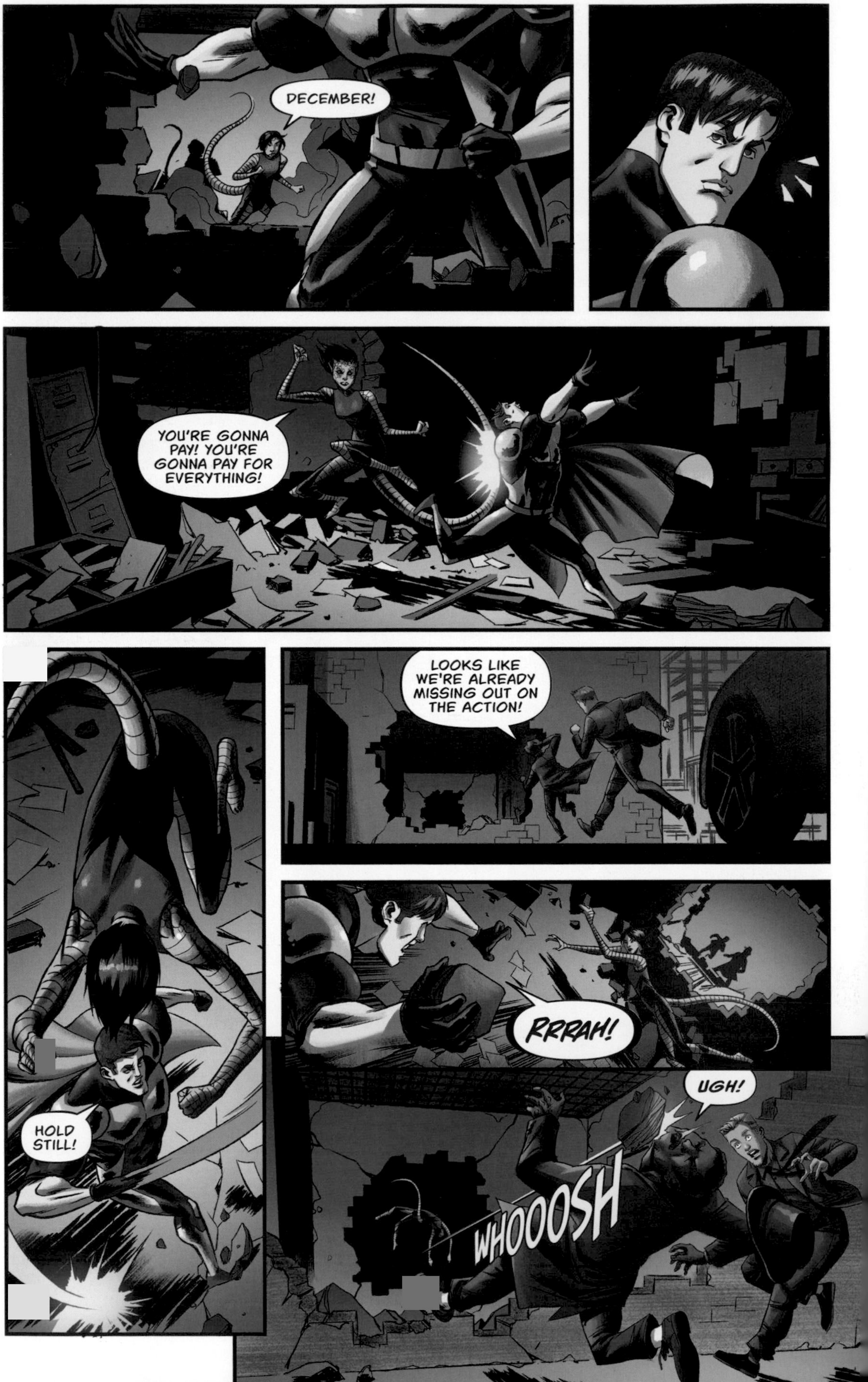
DECEMBER!
YOU'RE GONNA PAY! YOU'RE GONNA PAY FOR EVERYTHING!
HOLD STILL!
LOOKS LIKE WE'RE ALREADY MISSING OUT ON THE ACTION!
RRRAH!
UGH!
WHOOOSH

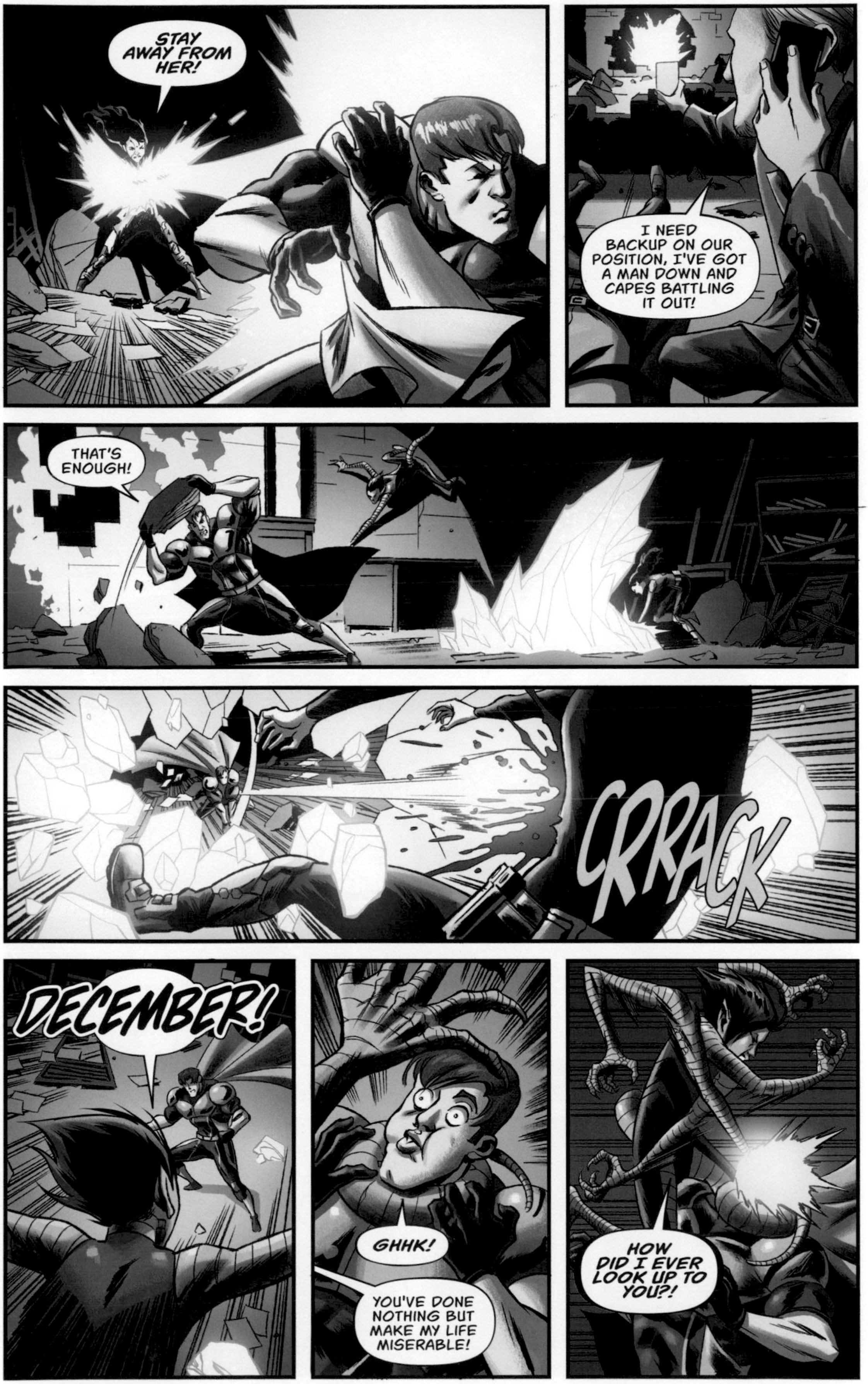
STAY AWAY FROM HER!
I NEED BACKUP ON OUR POSITION, I'VE GOT A MAN DOWN AND CAPES BATTLING IT OUT!
THAT'S ENOUGH!
CRRACK
DECEMBER!
GHHK!
YOU'VE DONE NOTHING BUT MAKE MY LIFE MISERABLE!
HOW DID I EVER LOOK UP TO YOU?!

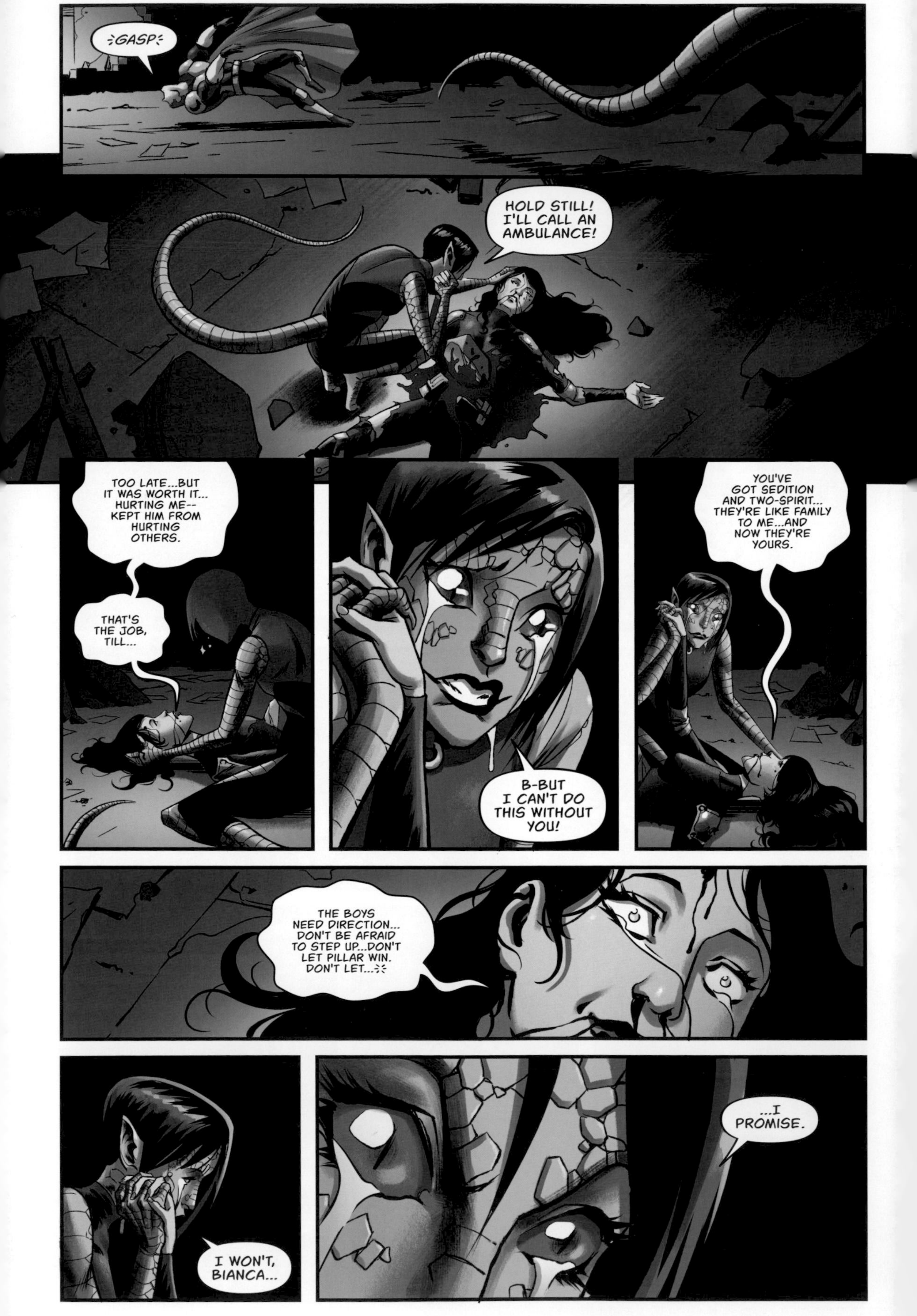
GASP
HOLD STILL! I'LL CALL AN AMBULANCE!
TOO LATE...BUT IT WAS WORTH IT... HURTING ME-- KEPT HIM FROM HURTING OTHERS.
THAT'S THE JOB, TILL...
B-BUT I CAN'T DO THIS WITHOUT YOU!
YOU'VE GOT SEDITION AND TWO-SPIRIT... THEY'RE LIKE FAMILY TO ME...AND NOW THEY'RE YOURS.
THE BOYS NEED DIRECTION... DON'T BE AFRAID TO STEP UP...DON'T LET PILLAR WIN. DON'T LET...
I WON'T, BIANCA...
...I PROMISE.

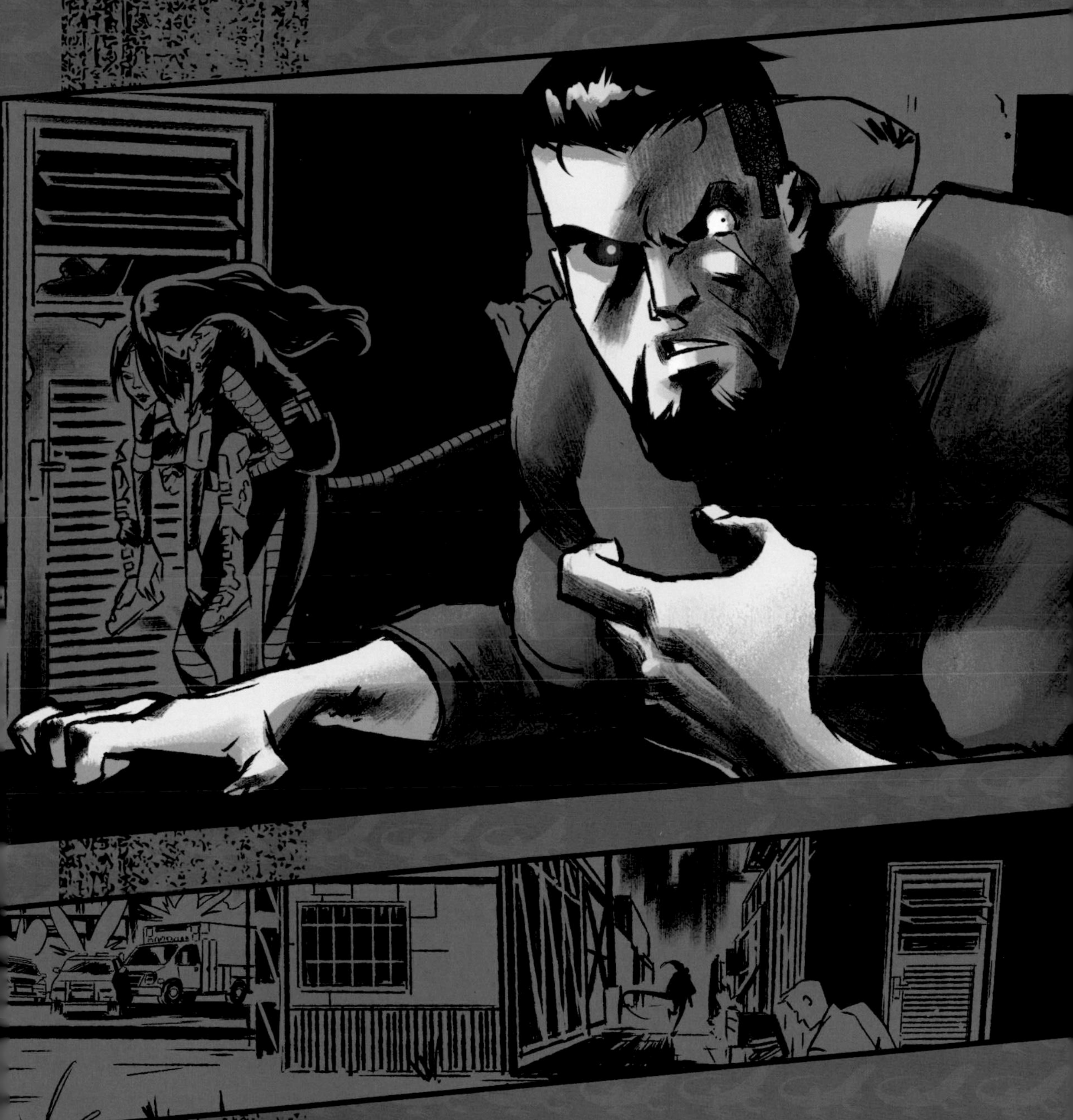

PART FIVE

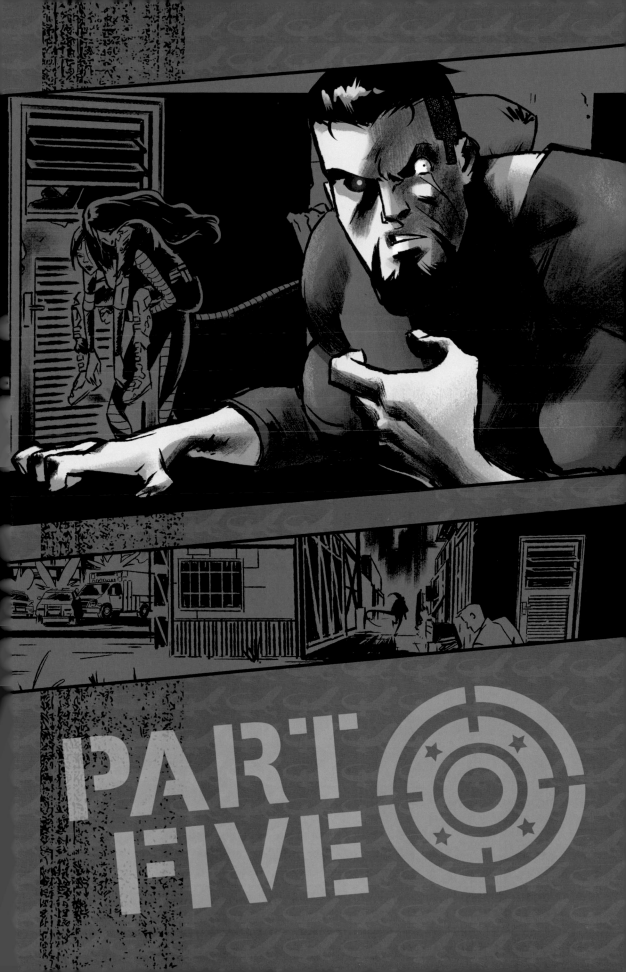

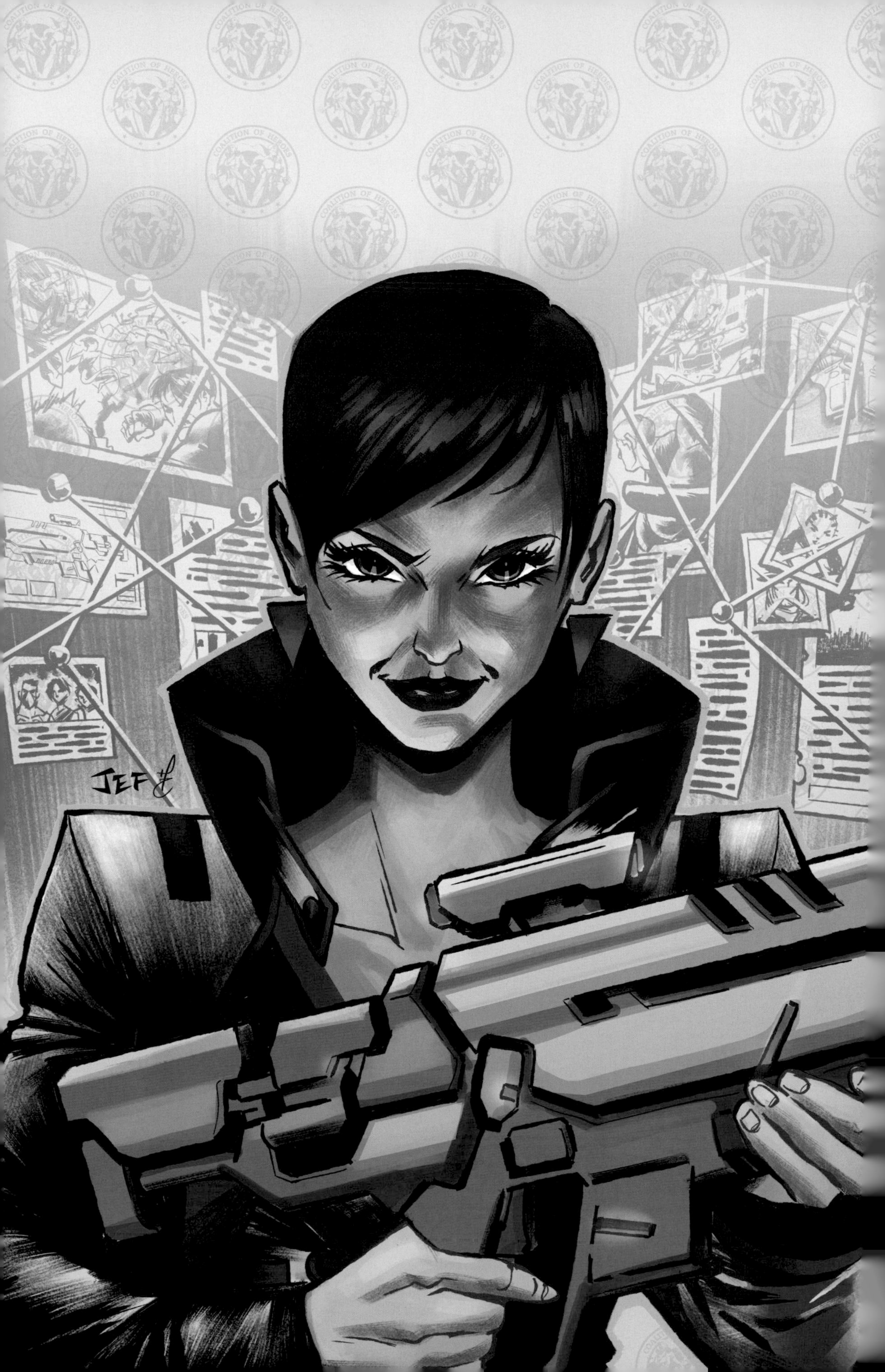
COALITION OF HEROES
JEF

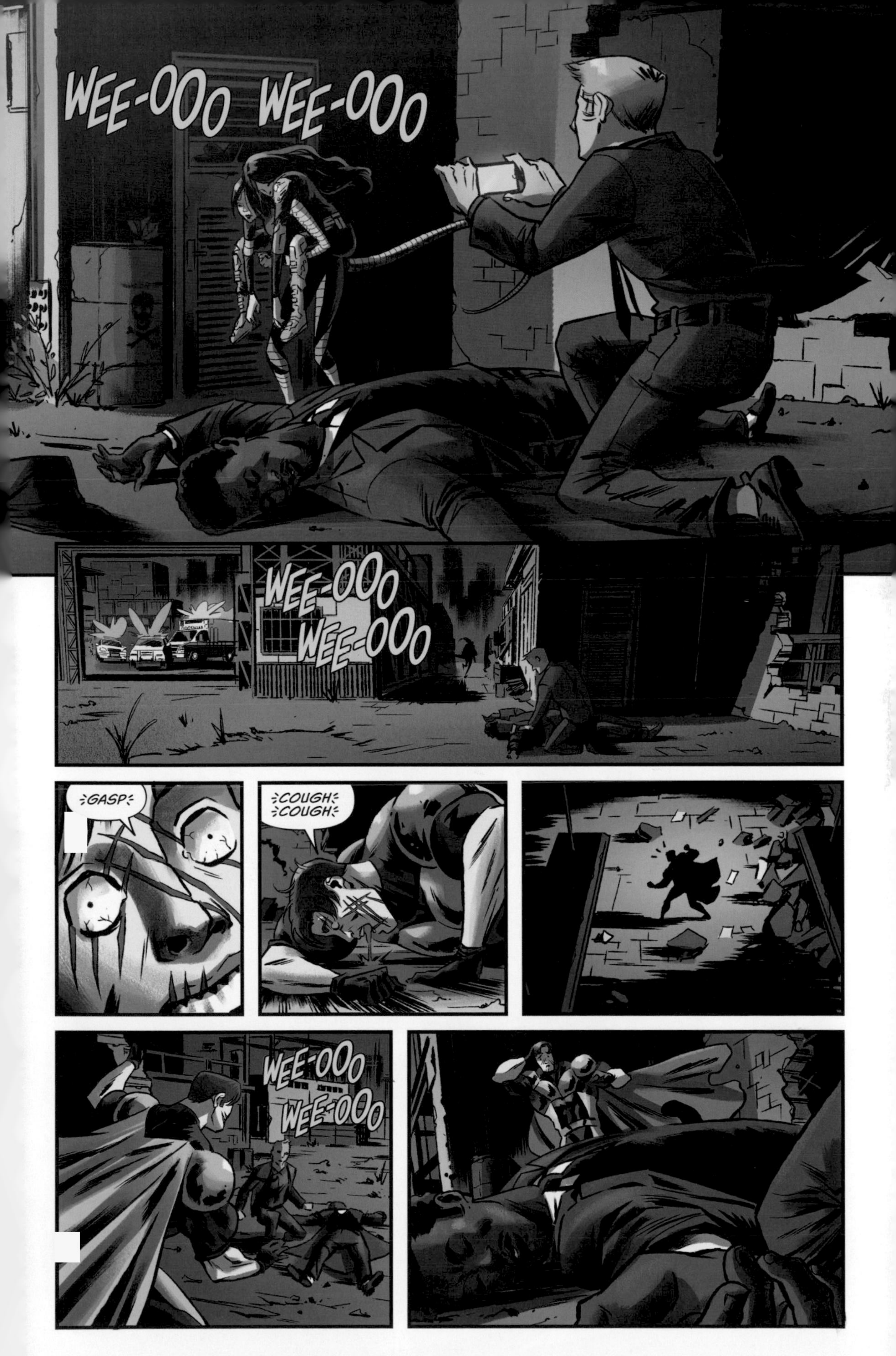
WEE-OOO WEE-OOO
WEE-OOO
WEE-OOO
GASP
COUGH COUGH
WEE-OOO
WEE-OOO

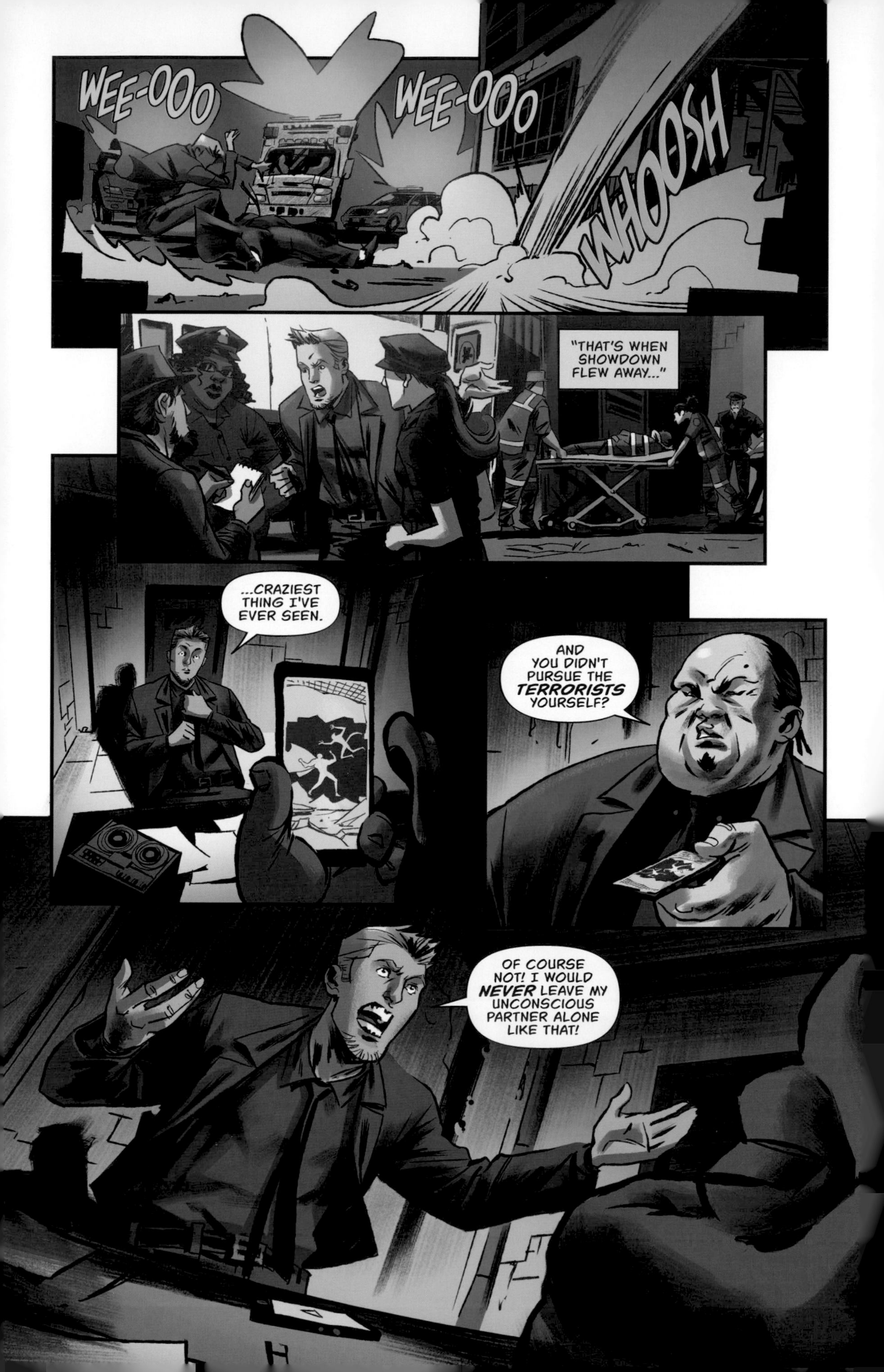
WEE-OOO
WEE-OOO
WHOOSH
"THAT'S WHEN SHOWDOWN FLEW AWAY..."
...CRAZIEST THING I'VE EVER SEEN.
AND YOU DIDN'T PURSUE THE **TERRORISTS** YOURSELF?
OF COURSE NOT! I WOULD **NEVER** LEAVE MY UNCONSCIOUS PARTNER ALONE LIKE THAT!

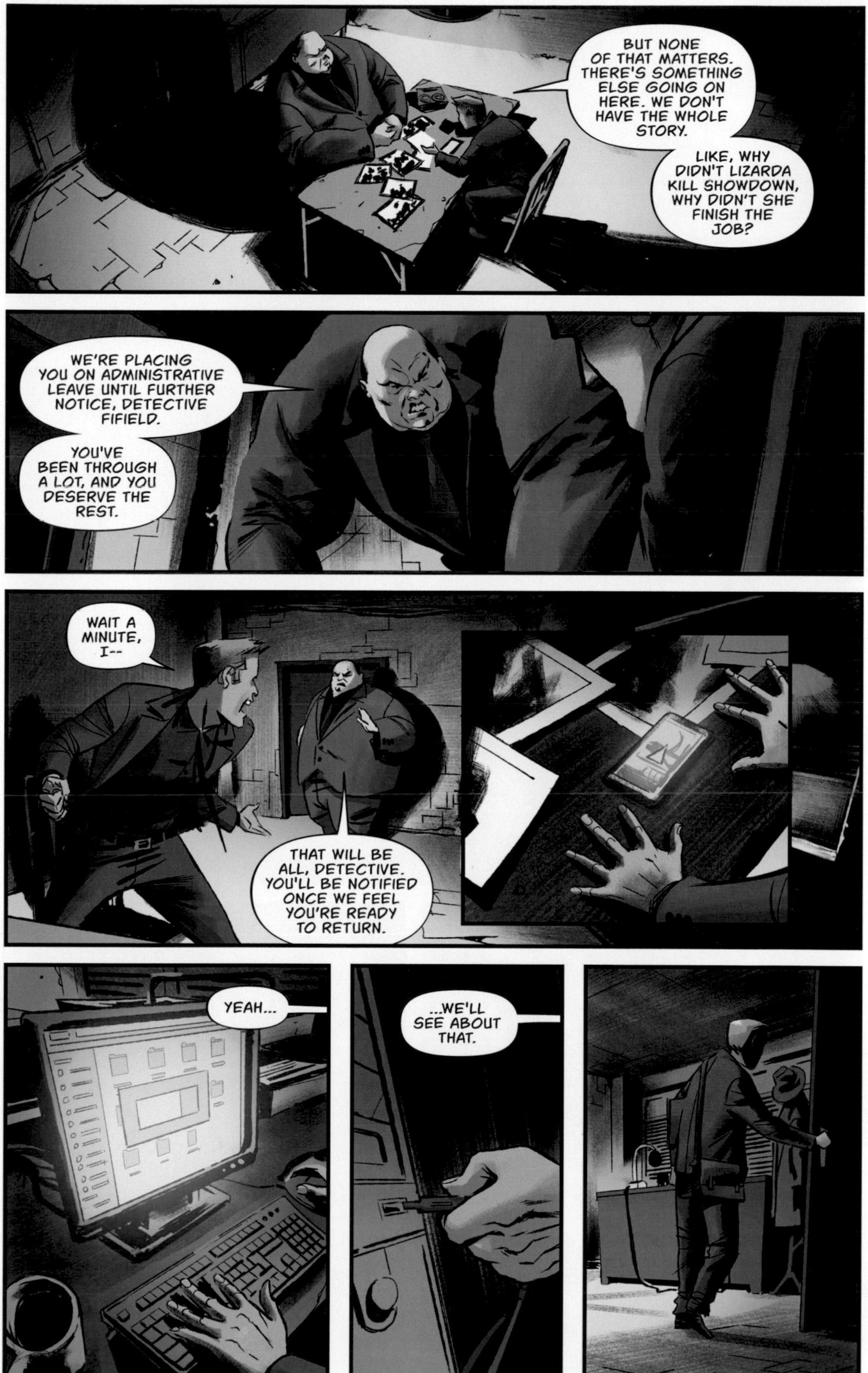
BUT NONE OF THAT MATTERS. THERE'S SOMETHING ELSE GOING ON HERE. WE DON'T HAVE THE WHOLE STORY.
LIKE, WHY DIDN'T LIZARDA KILL SHOWDOWN, WHY DIDN'T SHE FINISH THE JOB?
WE'RE PLACING YOU ON ADMINISTRATIVE LEAVE UNTIL FURTHER NOTICE, DETECTIVE FIFIELD.
YOU'VE BEEN THROUGH A LOT, AND YOU DESERVE THE REST.
WAIT A MINUTE, I--
THAT WILL BE ALL, DETECTIVE. YOU'LL BE NOTIFIED ONCE WE FEEL YOU'RE READY TO RETURN.
YEAH...
...WE'LL SEE ABOUT THAT.

I DON'T TRUST THE NEWS...

...I WANT TO HEAR IT FROM *YOU*. WHAT THE HELL HAPPENED OUT THERE?

TILLY...?

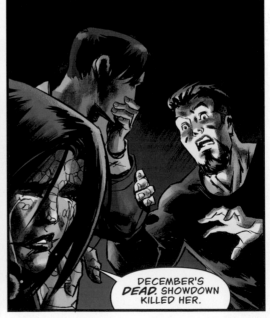

DECEMBER'S *DEAD*. SHOWDOWN KILLED HER.

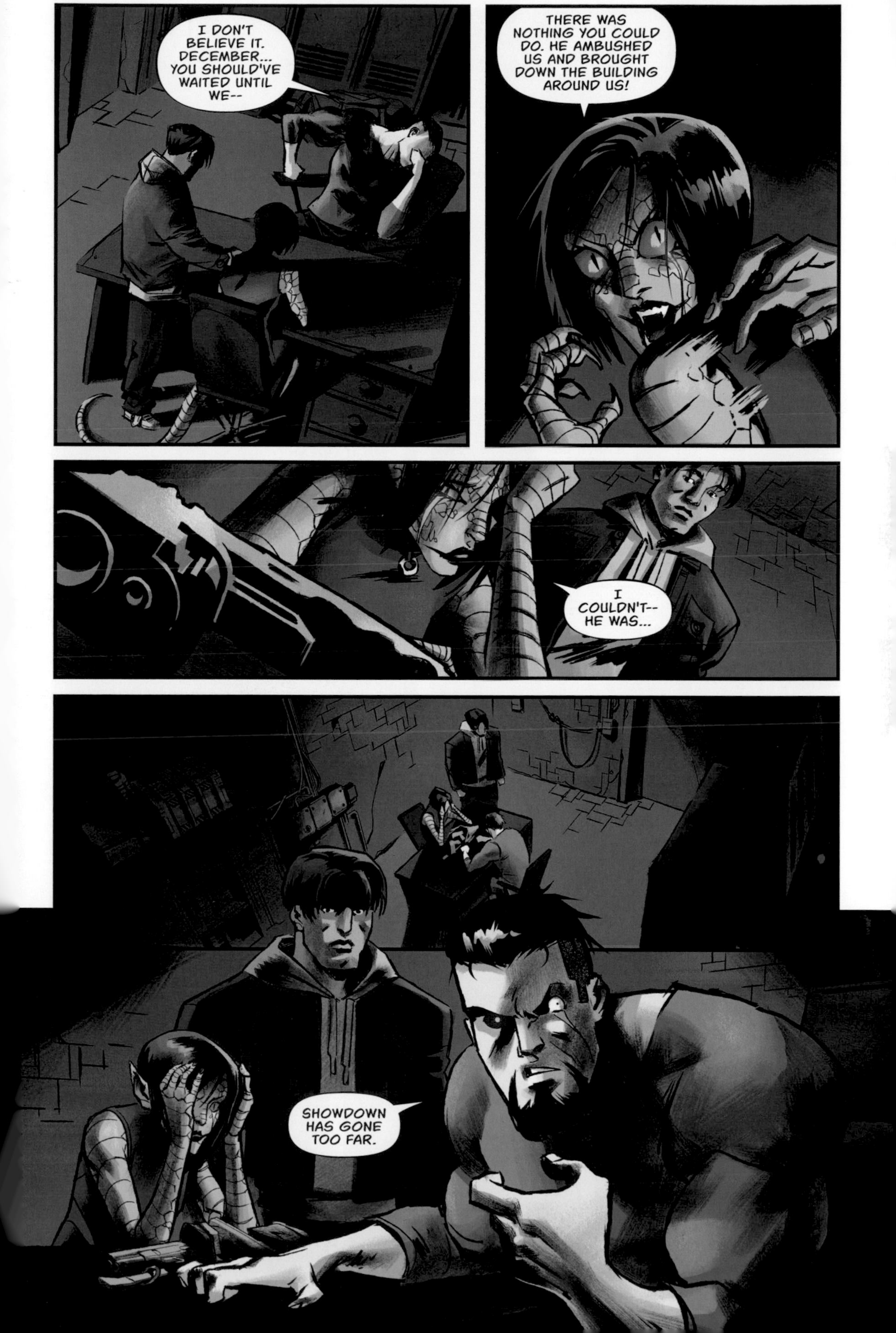
I DON'T BELIEVE IT. DECEMBER... YOU SHOULD'VE WAITED UNTIL WE--
THERE WAS NOTHING YOU COULD DO. HE AMBUSHED US AND BROUGHT DOWN THE BUILDING AROUND US!
I COULDN'T-- HE WAS...
SHOWDOWN HAS GONE TOO FAR.

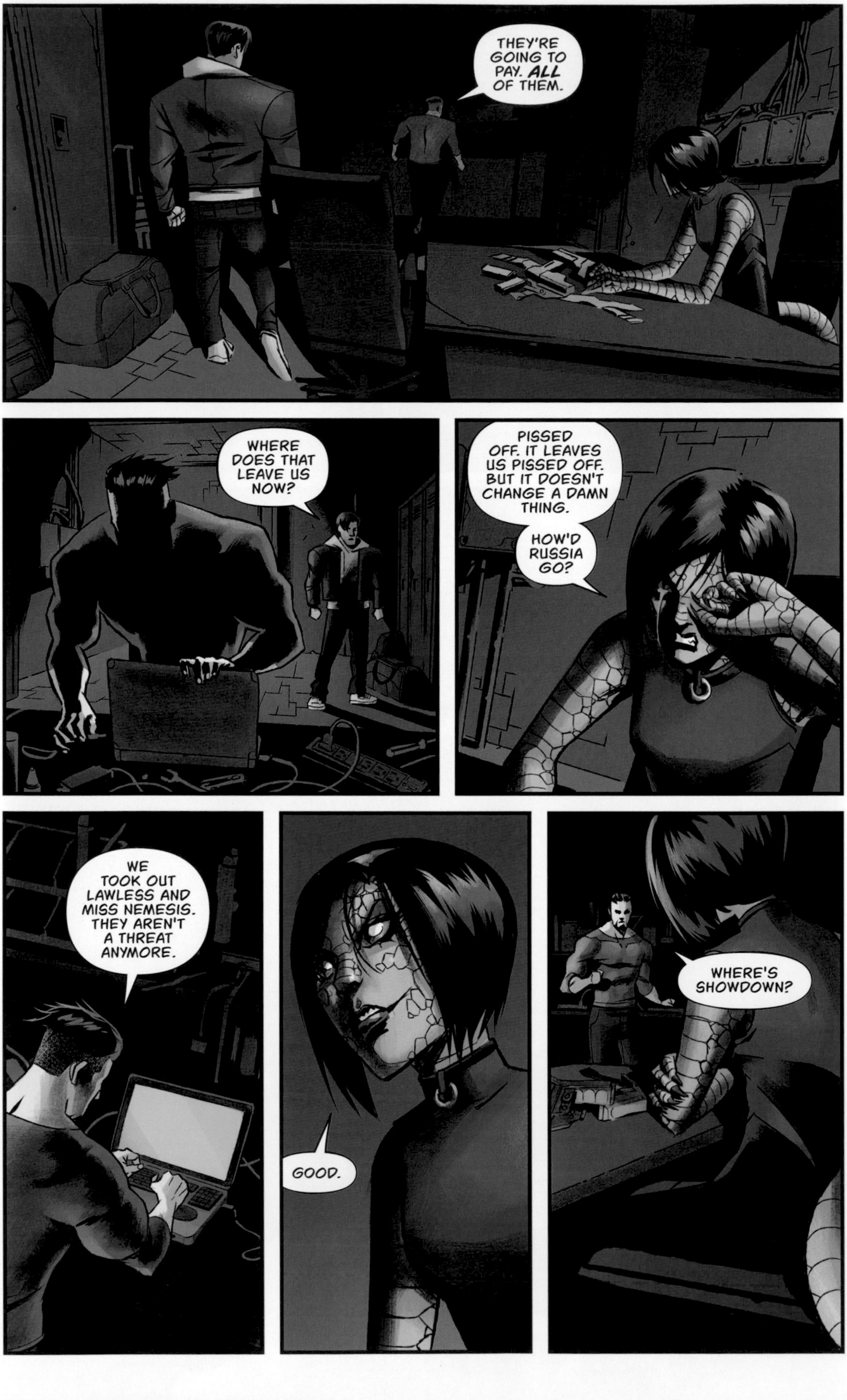
THEY'RE GOING TO PAY. ALL OF THEM.
WHERE DOES THAT LEAVE US NOW?
PISSED OFF. IT LEAVES US PISSED OFF. BUT IT DOESN'T CHANGE A DAMN THING.
HOW'D RUSSIA GO?
WE TOOK OUT LAWLESS AND MISS NEMESIS. THEY AREN'T A THREAT ANYMORE.
GOOD.
WHERE'S SHOWDOWN?

HE'S BEEN M.I.A. SINCE THE FIGHT. REPORTS SAY HE FLEW OFF, BUT NO ONE KNOWS WHERE.

WE CAN'T LOSE SIGHT OF THE MAIN OBJECTIVE. NOW'S THE TIME TO TAKE OUT PILLAR.

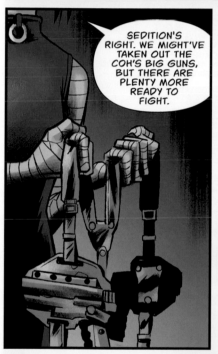

SEDITION'S RIGHT. WE MIGHT'VE TAKEN OUT THE COH'S BIG GUNS, BUT THERE ARE PLENTY MORE READY TO FIGHT.

JUST TO BE CLEAR, WHAT DO WE MEAN BY 'TAKE OUT'? I PROBABLY MAIMED NEMESIS FOR LIFE, BUT THAT WAS IN BATTLE. ARE WE GOING TO *KILL*--

WE HAVE NO CHOICE. PILLAR'S GOT SHOWDOWN AND THE REST OF THE COH ON A LEASH. SHE'S THE REASON DECEMBER AND COUNTLESS OTHERS ARE DEAD.

THUD

THEN WE SUIT UP. HIT HER HARD. SHE'LL SEE IT COMING, BUT IF WE PLAY IT SMART, WE CAN STOP HER FROM HURTING ANYONE ELSE.

YEAH...OKAY. LET'S SUIT UP. FOR BIANCA. ONE WAY OR ANOTHER, THIS NEEDS TO END...

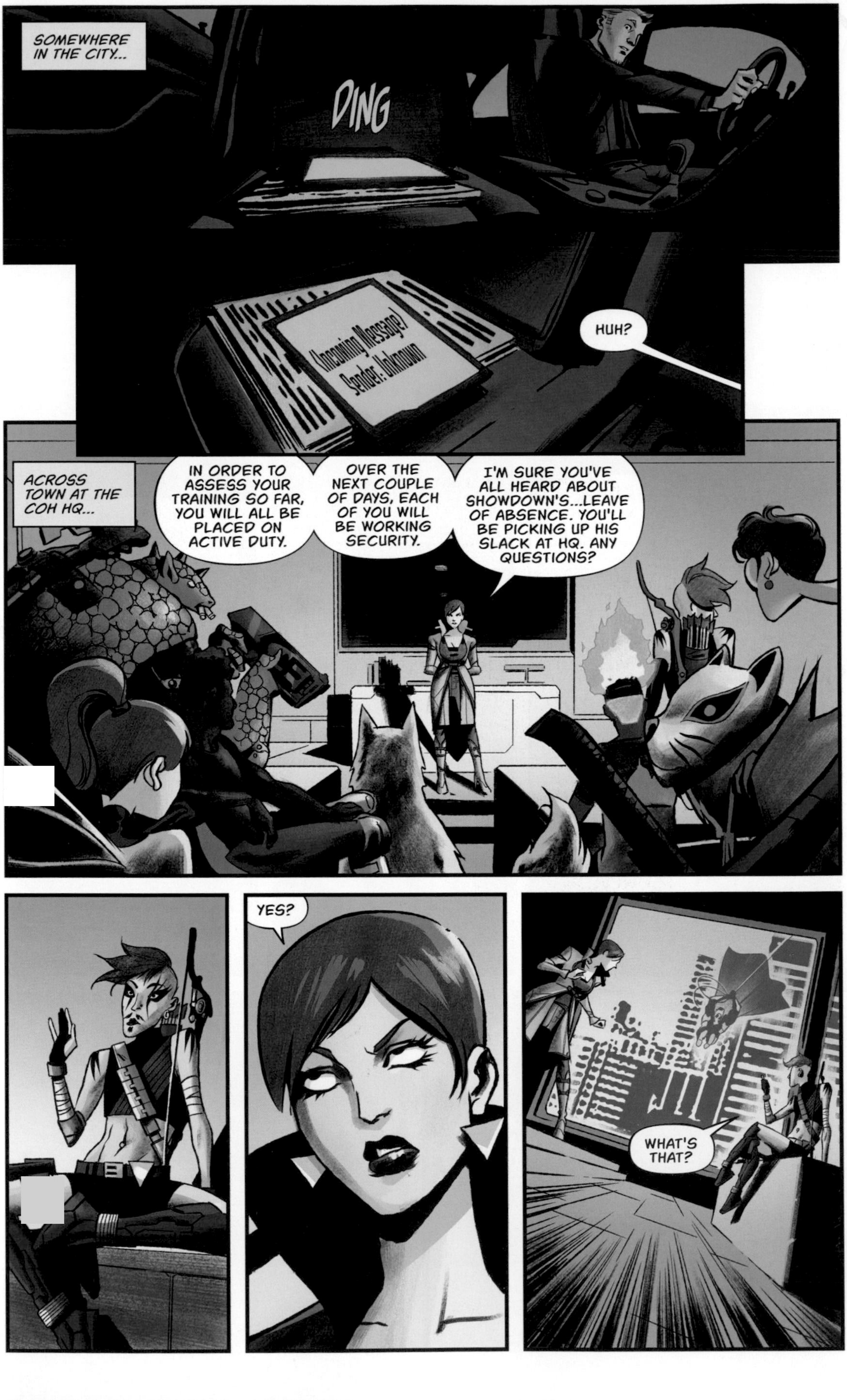
SOMEWHERE IN THE CITY...
DING
(Incoming Message)
Sender: Unknown
HUH?
ACROSS TOWN AT THE COH HQ...
IN ORDER TO ASSESS YOUR TRAINING SO FAR, YOU WILL ALL BE PLACED ON ACTIVE DUTY.
OVER THE NEXT COUPLE OF DAYS, EACH OF YOU WILL BE WORKING SECURITY.
I'M SURE YOU'VE ALL HEARD ABOUT SHOWDOWN'S...LEAVE OF ABSENCE. YOU'LL BE PICKING UP HIS SLACK AT HQ. ANY QUESTIONS?
YES?
WHAT'S THAT?

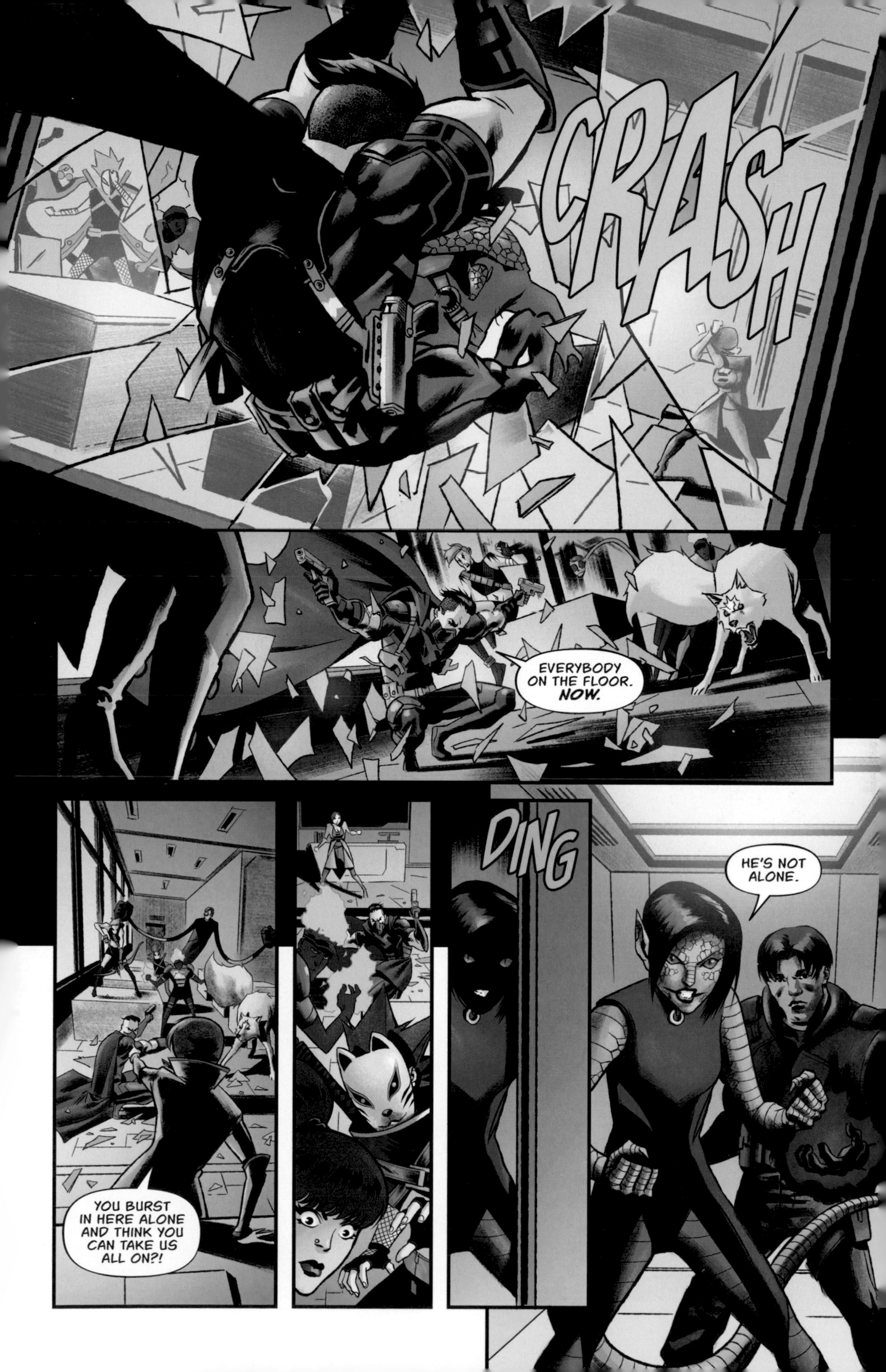
CRASH
EVERYBODY ON THE FLOOR. NOW.
YOU BURST IN HERE ALONE AND THINK YOU CAN TAKE US ALL ON?!
DING
HE'S NOT ALONE.

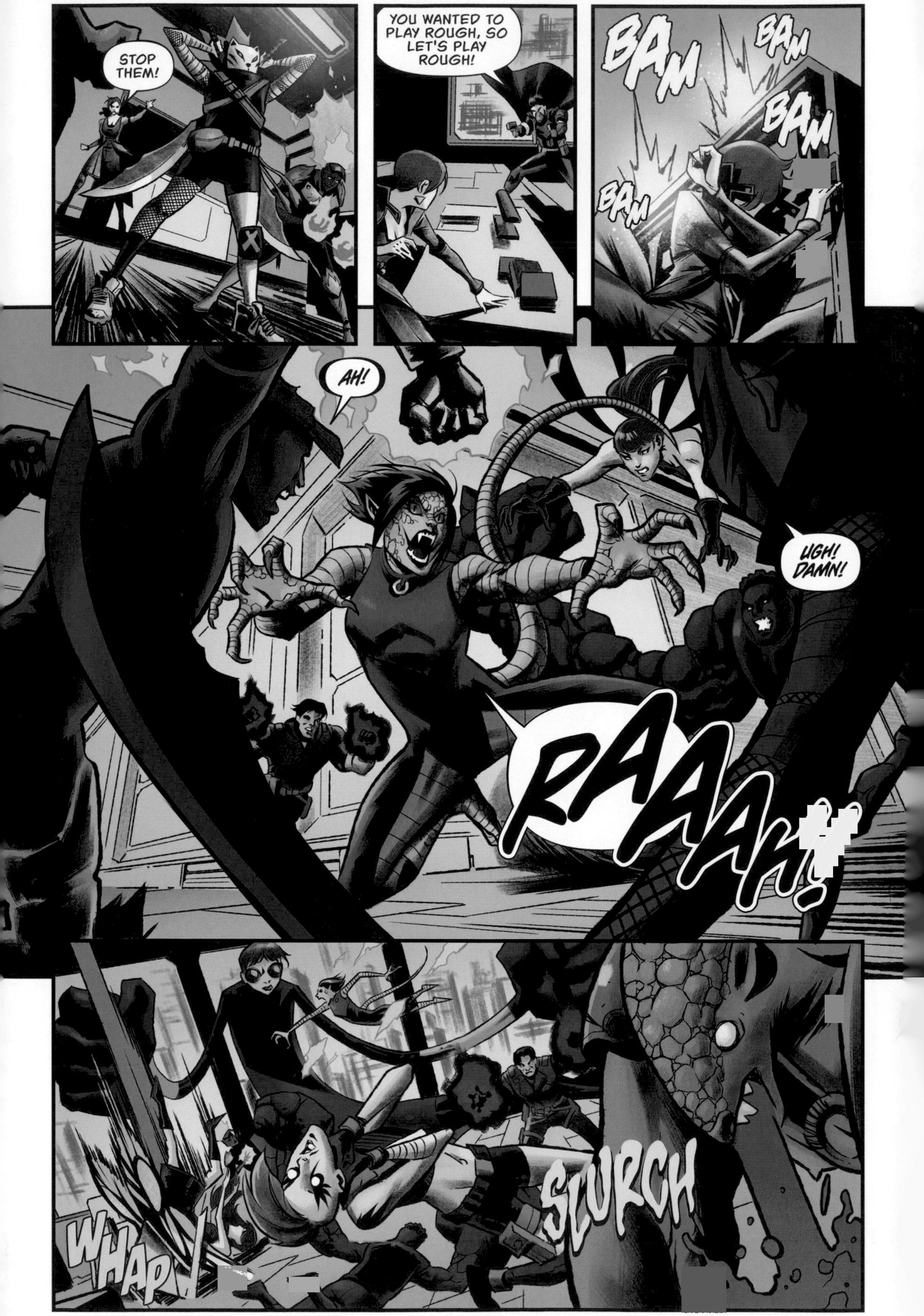
STOP THEM!
YOU WANTED TO PLAY ROUGH, SO LET'S PLAY ROUGH!
BAM
BAM
BAM
BAM
AH!
UGH! DAMN!
RAAAAH!
WHAP
SLURCH

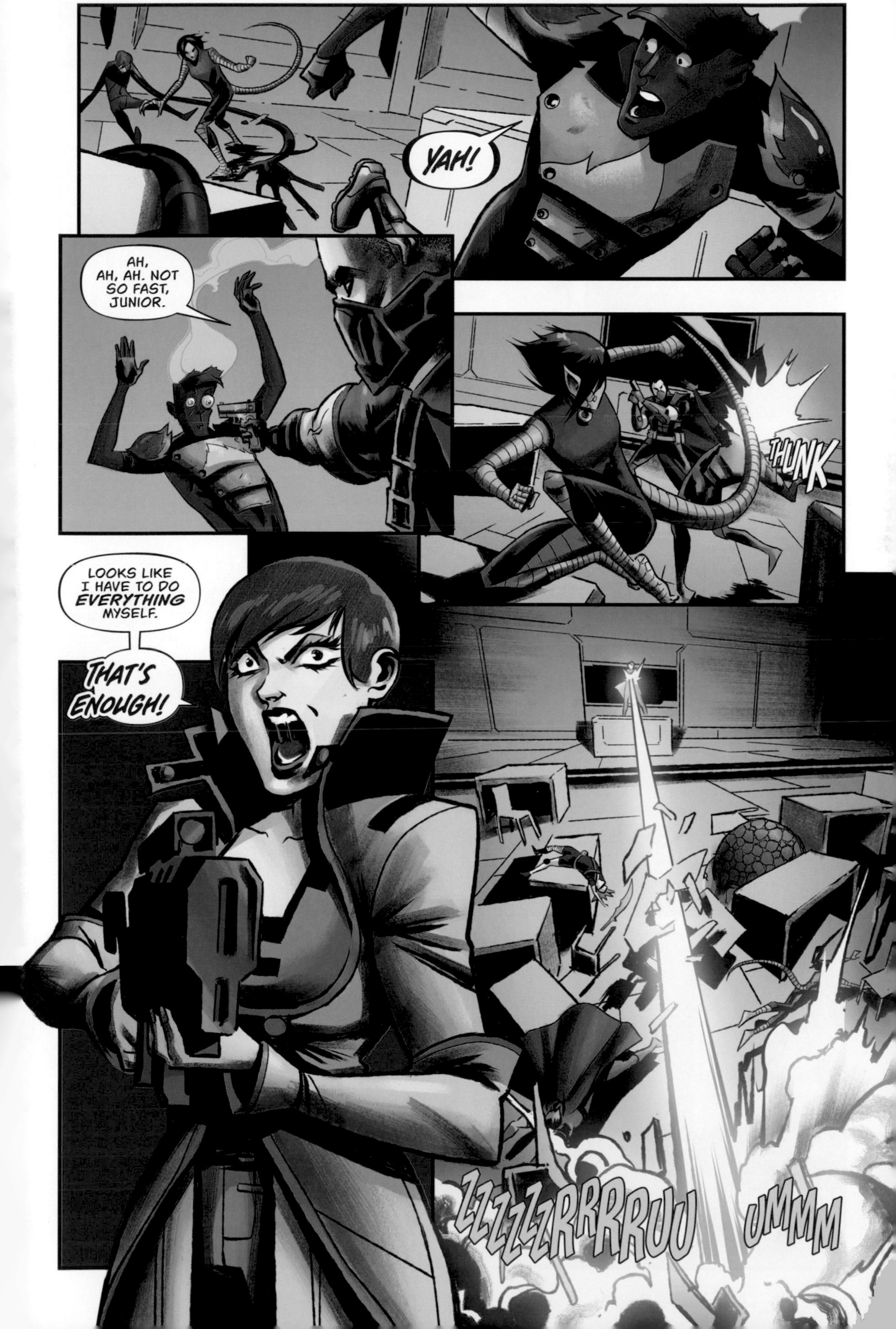

YAH!
AH, AH, AH. NOT SO FAST, JUNIOR.
THUNK
LOOKS LIKE I HAVE TO DO EVERYTHING MYSELF.
THAT'S ENOUGH!
ZZZZZRRRRUU UMMM

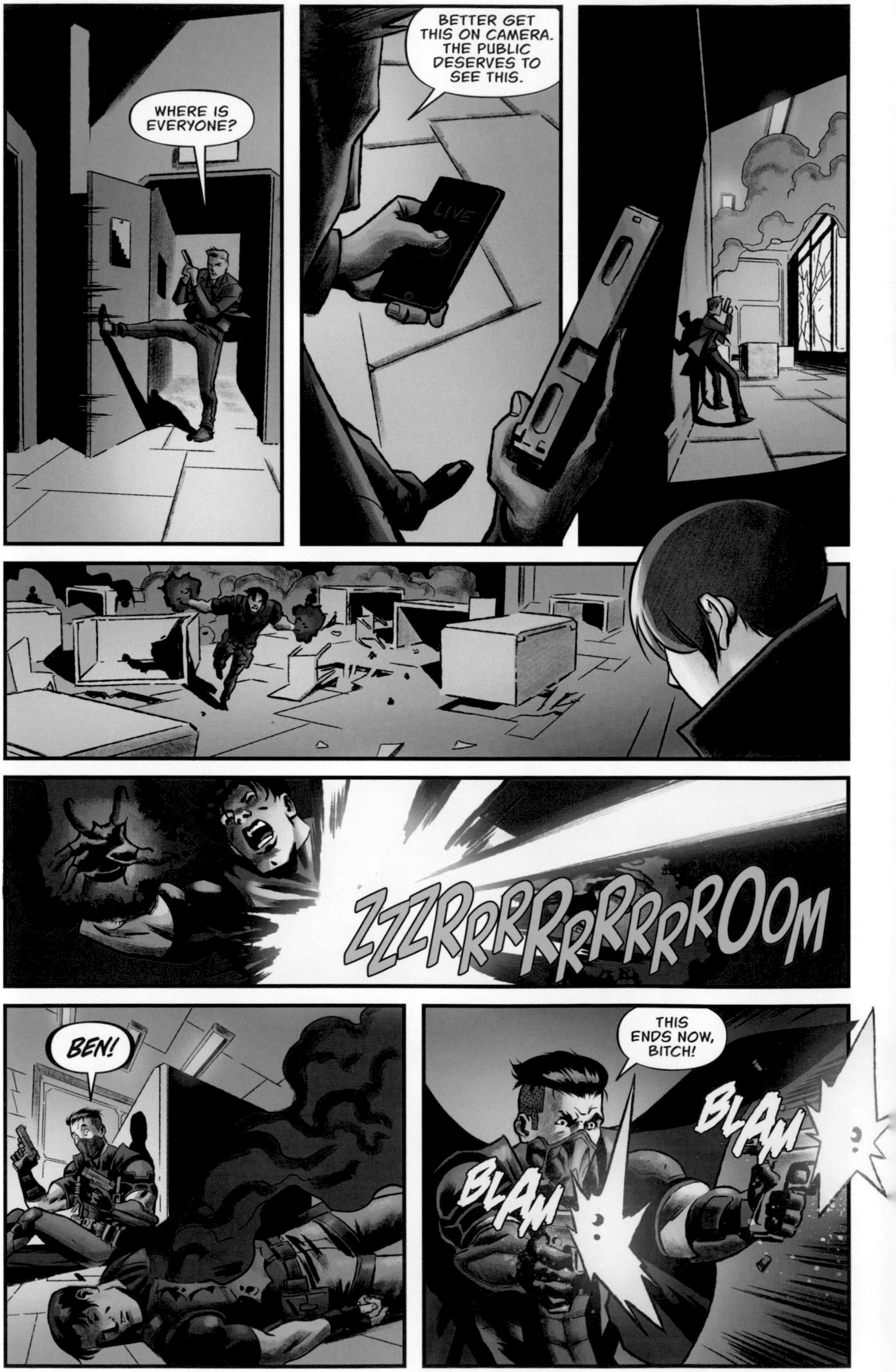
WHERE IS EVERYONE?
BETTER GET THIS ON CAMERA. THE PUBLIC DESERVES TO SEE THIS.
LIVE
ZZZRRRRRRRRRROOM
BEN!
THIS ENDS NOW, BITCH!
BLAM
BLAM

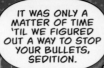

WHAT'S THE MATTER? DON'T YOU LIKE THE NEW COH BULLET SHIELD?

IT WAS ONLY A MATTER OF TIME 'TIL WE FIGURED OUT A WAY TO STOP YOUR BULLETS, SEDITION.

BOOM

GUNS WORKED WELL ENOUGH WITH LAWLESS. KILLED HIM WITH HIS OWN.

THIS IS HOW IT ENDS, SARAH! I'M NOT LETTING YOU WALK OUT OF HERE!

OH, JUST *DIE* ALREADY!

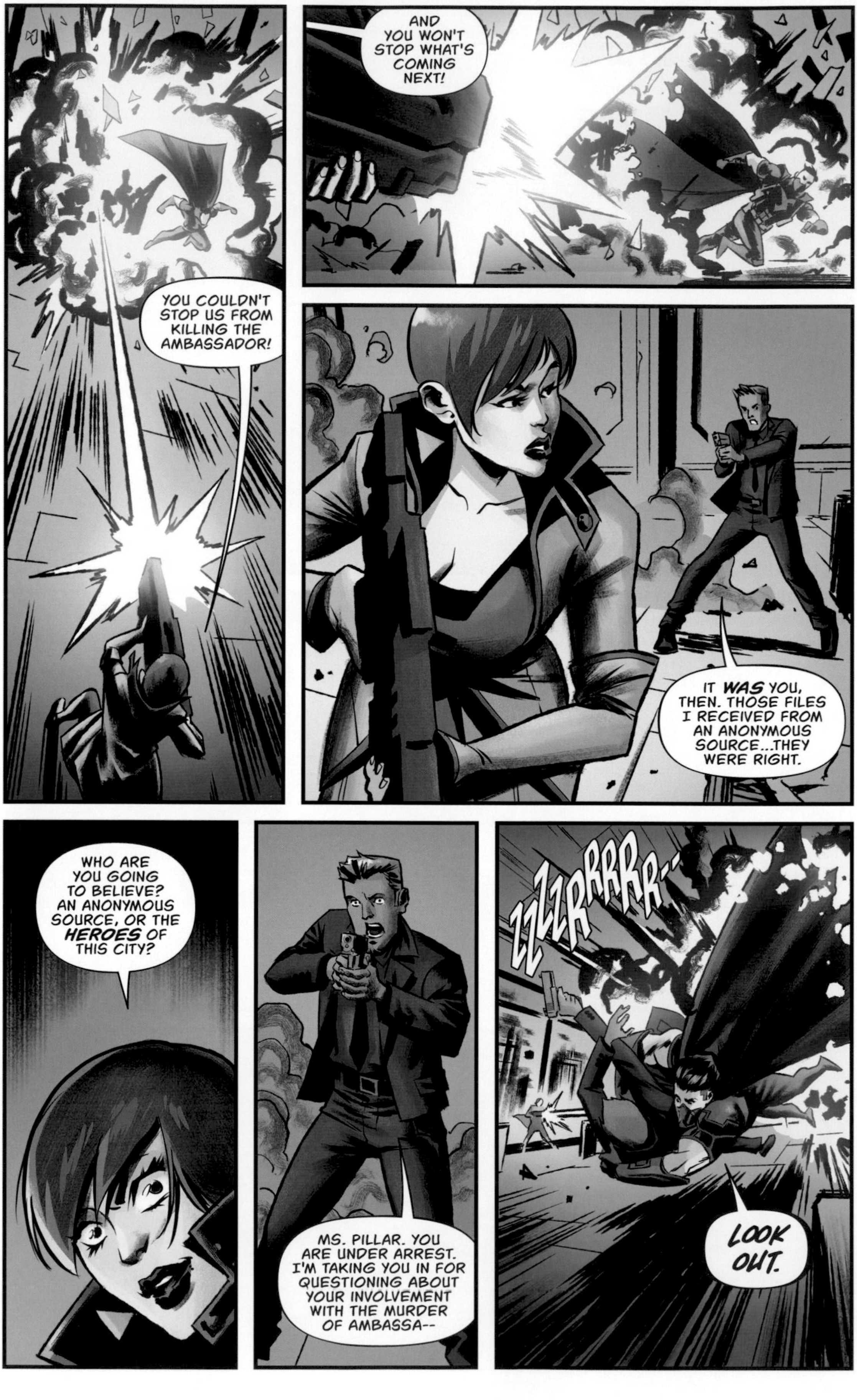
YOU COULDN'T STOP US FROM KILLING THE AMBASSADOR!
AND YOU WON'T STOP WHAT'S COMING NEXT!
IT **WAS** YOU, THEN. THOSE FILES I RECEIVED FROM AN ANONYMOUS SOURCE...THEY WERE RIGHT.
WHO ARE YOU GOING TO BELIEVE? AN ANONYMOUS SOURCE, OR THE **HEROES** OF THIS CITY?
MS. PILLAR. YOU ARE UNDER ARREST. I'M TAKING YOU IN FOR QUESTIONING ABOUT YOUR INVOLVEMENT WITH THE MURDER OF AMBASSA--
ZZZRRRRR--
LOOK OUT.

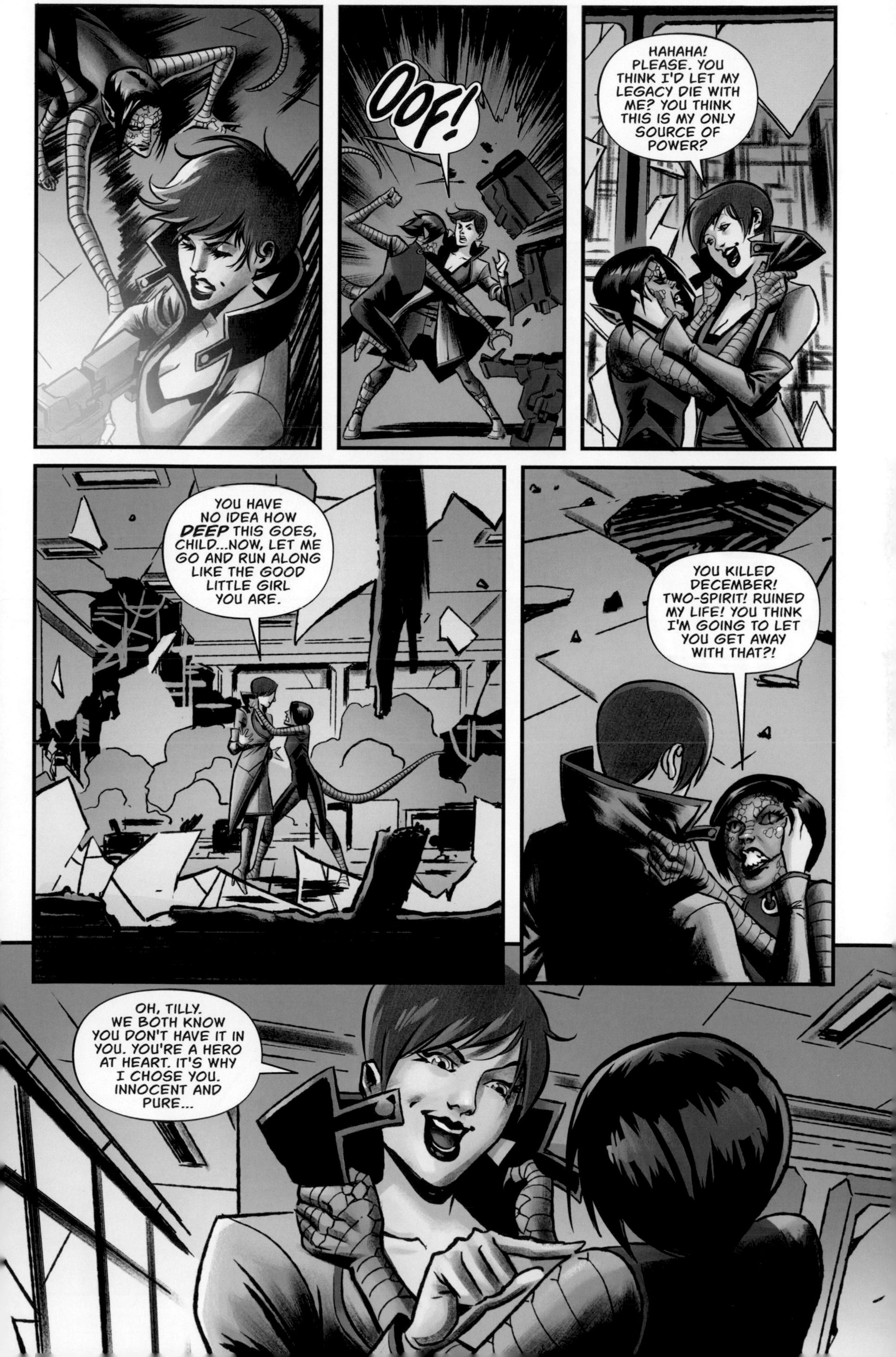

OOF!
HAHAHA! PLEASE. YOU THINK I'D LET MY LEGACY DIE WITH ME? YOU THINK THIS IS MY ONLY SOURCE OF POWER?
YOU HAVE NO IDEA HOW DEEP THIS GOES, CHILD...NOW, LET ME GO AND RUN ALONG LIKE THE GOOD LITTLE GIRL YOU ARE.
YOU KILLED DECEMBER! TWO-SPIRIT! RUINED MY LIFE! YOU THINK I'M GOING TO LET YOU GET AWAY WITH THAT?!
OH, TILLY. WE BOTH KNOW YOU DON'T HAVE IT IN YOU. YOU'RE A HERO AT HEART. IT'S WHY I CHOSE YOU. INNOCENT AND PURE...

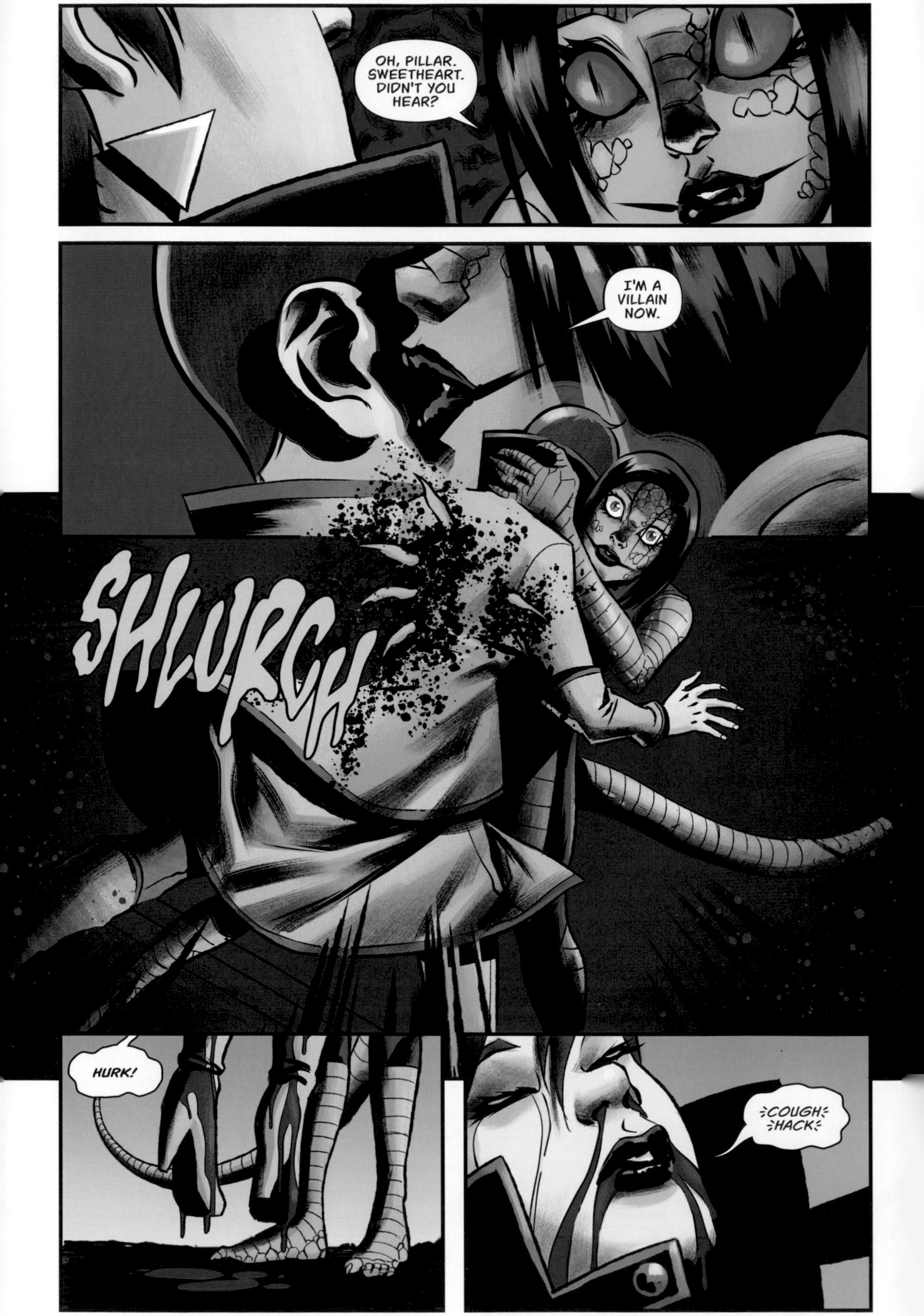
OH, PILLAR. SWEETHEART. DIDN'T YOU HEAR?
I'M A VILLAIN NOW.
SHLURCH
HURK!
COUGH HACK

IT'S NOT OVER... SHE'LL HAVE HAD CONTINGENCIES. WAYS TO PROTECT HER LEGACY.

THERE WILL BE OTHERS WAITING TO PICK UP THE PIECES...

THEN WE SHOULD PREPARE FOR THEM.

I'LL GET TWO-SPIRIT. BURN THE BUILDING TO THE GROUND.

THEY DON'T DESERVE ANYTHING LESS.

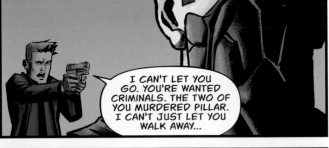

I CAN'T LET YOU GO. YOU'RE WANTED CRIMINALS. THE TWO OF YOU MURDERED PILLAR. I CAN'T JUST LET YOU WALK AWAY...

WE JUST TOOK OUT THE MOST DANGEROUS, WOMAN IN THE COUNTRY...

...AND YOU WANT TO ARREST US? ARE YOU SURE THAT'S A GOOD IDEA, DETECTIVE?

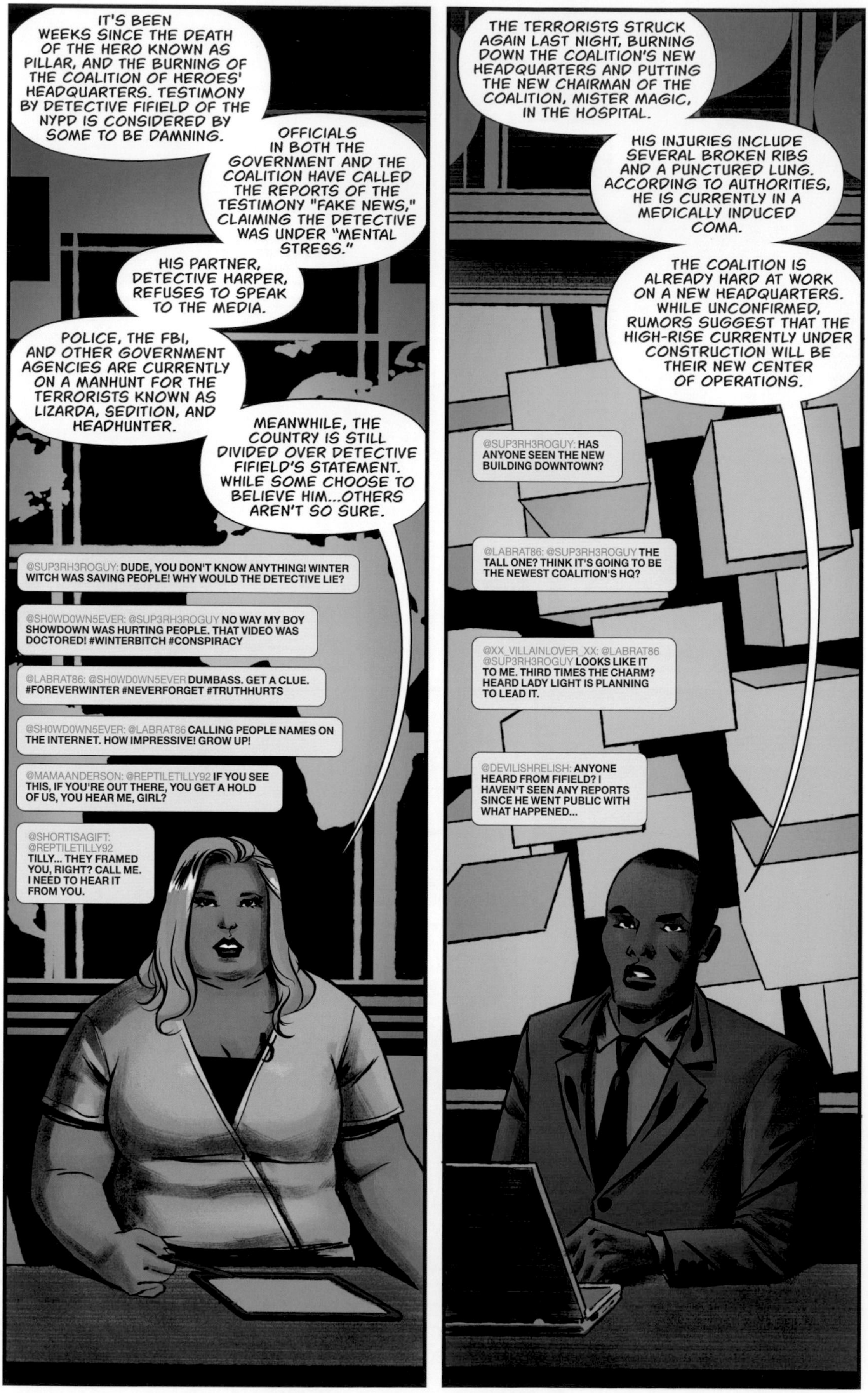
IT'S BEEN WEEKS SINCE THE DEATH OF THE HERO KNOWN AS PILLAR, AND THE BURNING OF THE COALITION OF HEROES' HEADQUARTERS. TESTIMONY BY DETECTIVE FIFIELD OF THE NYPD IS CONSIDERED BY SOME TO BE DAMNING.
OFFICIALS IN BOTH THE GOVERNMENT AND THE COALITION HAVE CALLED THE REPORTS OF THE TESTIMONY "FAKE NEWS," CLAIMING THE DETECTIVE WAS UNDER "MENTAL STRESS."
HIS PARTNER, DETECTIVE HARPER, REFUSES TO SPEAK TO THE MEDIA.
POLICE, THE FBI, AND OTHER GOVERNMENT AGENCIES ARE CURRENTLY ON A MANHUNT FOR THE TERRORISTS KNOWN AS LIZARDA, SEDITION, AND HEADHUNTER.
MEANWHILE, THE COUNTRY IS STILL DIVIDED OVER DETECTIVE FIFIELD'S STATEMENT. WHILE SOME CHOOSE TO BELIEVE HIM...OTHERS AREN'T SO SURE.
@SUP3RH3ROGUY: DUDE, YOU DON'T KNOW ANYTHING! WINTER WITCH WAS SAVING PEOPLE! WHY WOULD THE DETECTIVE LIE?
@SH0WD0WN5EVER: @SUP3RH3ROGUY NO WAY MY BOY SHOWDOWN WAS HURTING PEOPLE. THAT VIDEO WAS DOCTORED! #WINTERBITCH #CONSPIRACY
@LABRAT86: @SH0WD0WN5EVER DUMBASS. GET A CLUE. #FOREVERWINTER #NEVERFORGET #TRUTHHURTS
@SH0WD0WN5EVER: @LABRAT86 CALLING PEOPLE NAMES ON THE INTERNET. HOW IMPRESSIVE! GROW UP!
@MAMAANDERSON: @REPTILETILLY92 IF YOU SEE THIS, IF YOU'RE OUT THERE, YOU GET A HOLD OF US, YOU HEAR ME, GIRL?
@SHORTISAGIFT: @REPTILETILLY92 TILLY... THEY FRAMED YOU, RIGHT? CALL ME. I NEED TO HEAR IT FROM YOU.
THE TERRORISTS STRUCK AGAIN LAST NIGHT, BURNING DOWN THE COALITION'S NEW HEADQUARTERS AND PUTTING THE NEW CHAIRMAN OF THE COALITION, MISTER MAGIC, IN THE HOSPITAL.
HIS INJURIES INCLUDE SEVERAL BROKEN RIBS AND A PUNCTURED LUNG. ACCORDING TO AUTHORITIES, HE IS CURRENTLY IN A MEDICALLY INDUCED COMA.
THE COALITION IS ALREADY HARD AT WORK ON A NEW HEADQUARTERS. WHILE UNCONFIRMED, RUMORS SUGGEST THAT THE HIGH-RISE CURRENTLY UNDER CONSTRUCTION WILL BE THEIR NEW CENTER OF OPERATIONS.
@SUP3RH3ROGUY: HAS ANYONE SEEN THE NEW BUILDING DOWNTOWN?
@LABRAT86: @SUP3RH3ROGUY THE TALL ONE? THINK IT'S GOING TO BE THE NEWEST COALITION'S HQ?
@XX_VILLAINLOVER_XX: @LABRAT86 @SUP3RH3ROGUY LOOKS LIKE IT TO ME. THIRD TIMES THE CHARM? HEARD LADY LIGHT IS PLANNING TO LEAD IT.
@DEVILISHRELISH: ANYONE HEARD FROM FIFIELD? I HAVEN'T SEEN ANY REPORTS SINCE HE WENT PUBLIC WITH WHAT HAPPENED...

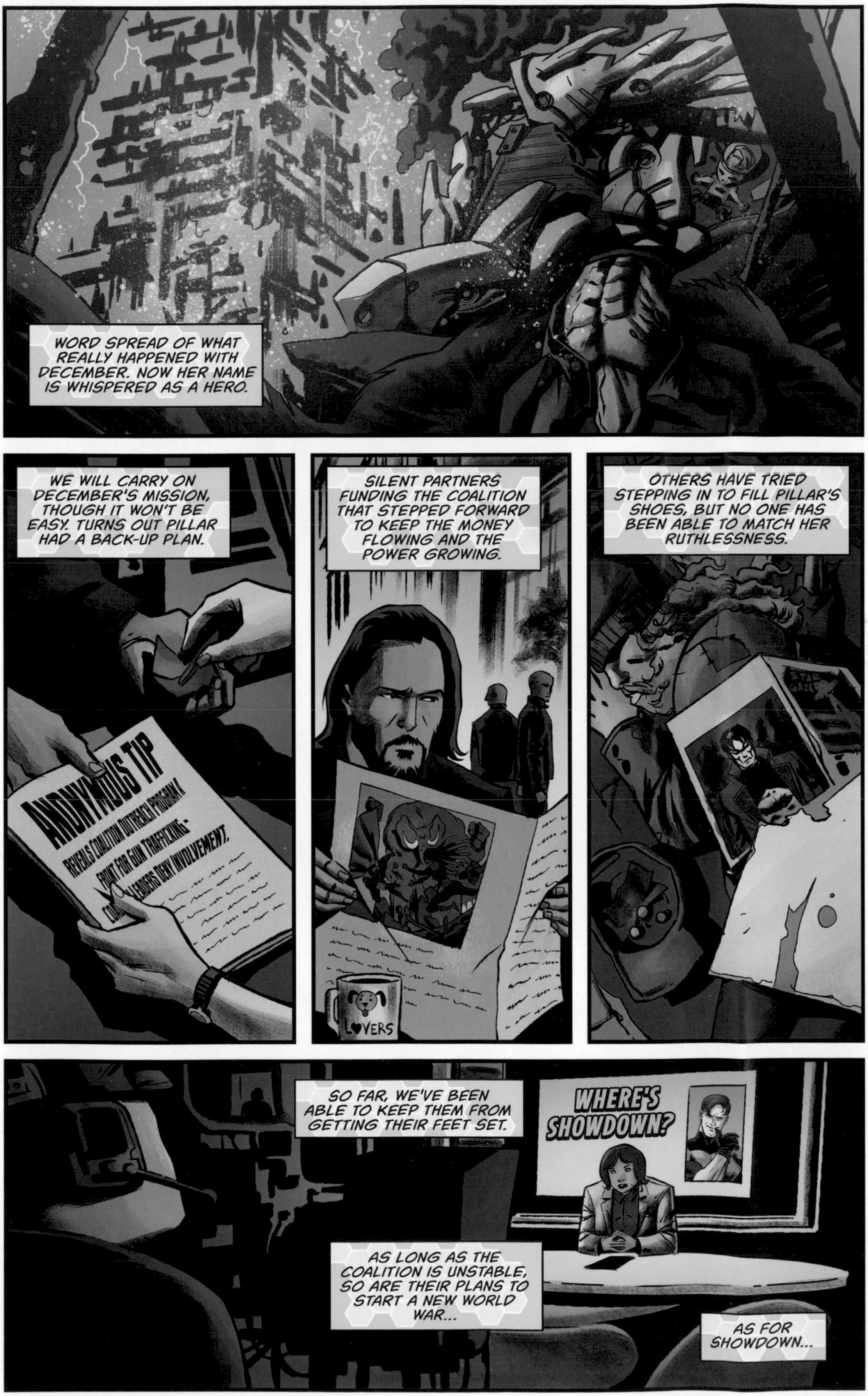

WORD SPREAD OF WHAT REALLY HAPPENED WITH DECEMBER. NOW HER NAME IS WHISPERED AS A HERO.
WE WILL CARRY ON DECEMBER'S MISSION, THOUGH IT WON'T BE EASY. TURNS OUT PILLAR HAD A BACK-UP PLAN.
ANONYMOUS TIP
REVEALS COALITION OUTREACH PROGRAM A FRONT FOR GUN TRAFFICKING -
LEADERS DENY INVOLVEMENT.
SILENT PARTNERS FUNDING THE COALITION THAT STEPPED FORWARD TO KEEP THE MONEY FLOWING AND THE POWER GROWING.
L♥VERS
OTHERS HAVE TRIED STEPPING IN TO FILL PILLAR'S SHOES, BUT NO ONE HAS BEEN ABLE TO MATCH HER RUTHLESSNESS.
SO FAR, WE'VE BEEN ABLE TO KEEP THEM FROM GETTING THEIR FEET SET.
WHERE'S SHOWDOWN?
AS LONG AS THE COALITION IS UNSTABLE, SO ARE THEIR PLANS TO START A NEW WORLD WAR...
AS FOR SHOWDOWN...

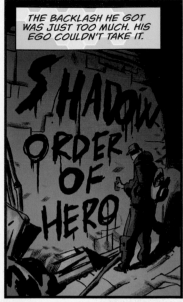

...HE LEFT FOR KOREA TO LEAD A NEW DIVISION OF HEROES FOR THE COALITION.

THE BACKLASH HE GOT WAS JUST TOO MUCH. HIS EGO COULDN'T TAKE IT.

#FOREVERWINTER

THE WORLD HASN'T LOOKED AT HIM OR PILLAR THE SAME SINCE THE DAY DECEMBER DIED.

THE SAME CAN BE SAID ABOUT US. WE'LL NEVER BE HEROES, BUT TITLES DON'T MATTER TO US. WHAT DOES MATTER IS THAT THE PEOPLE OF THIS CITY ARE SAFE.

AND WHILE WE DON'T LET JUST ANYONE INTO OUR GROUP, THOSE THAT PROVE THEIR LOYALTY ARE GIVEN A CHANCE.

THE TRUTH IS THAT WE NEED ALL THE HELP WE CAN GET...

...BECAUSE A VILLAIN'S WORK IS NEVER DONE.

THE END.

CLASSIFIED INFORMATION

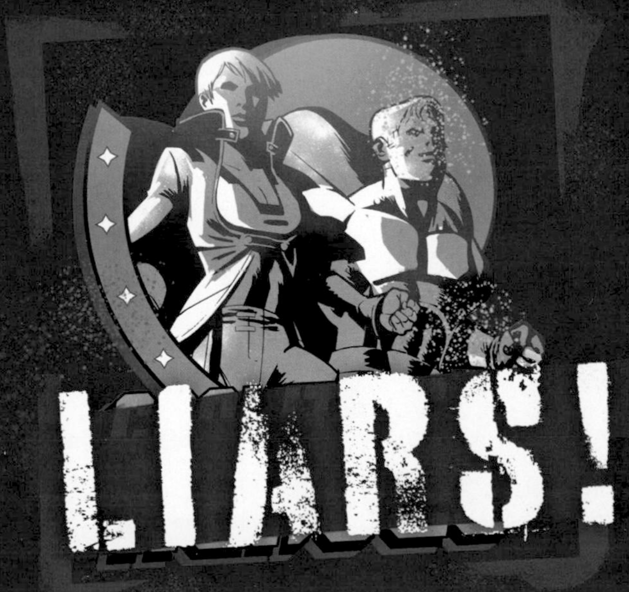
LIARS!

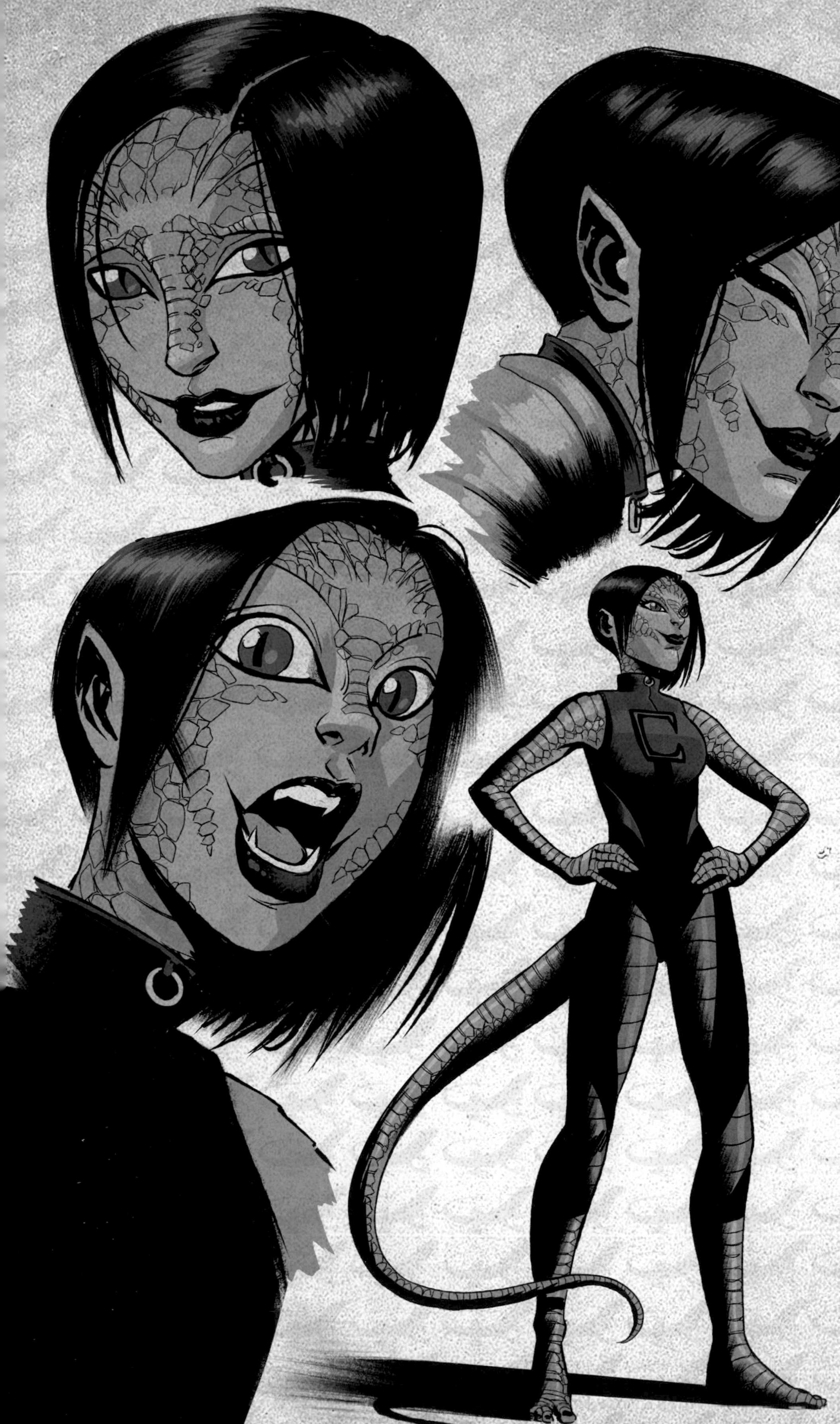

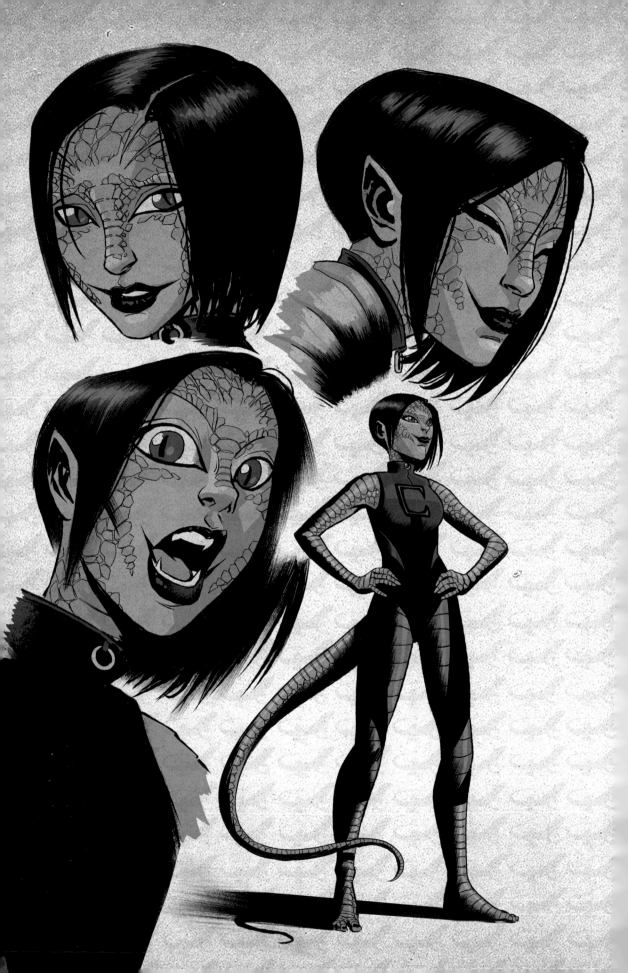

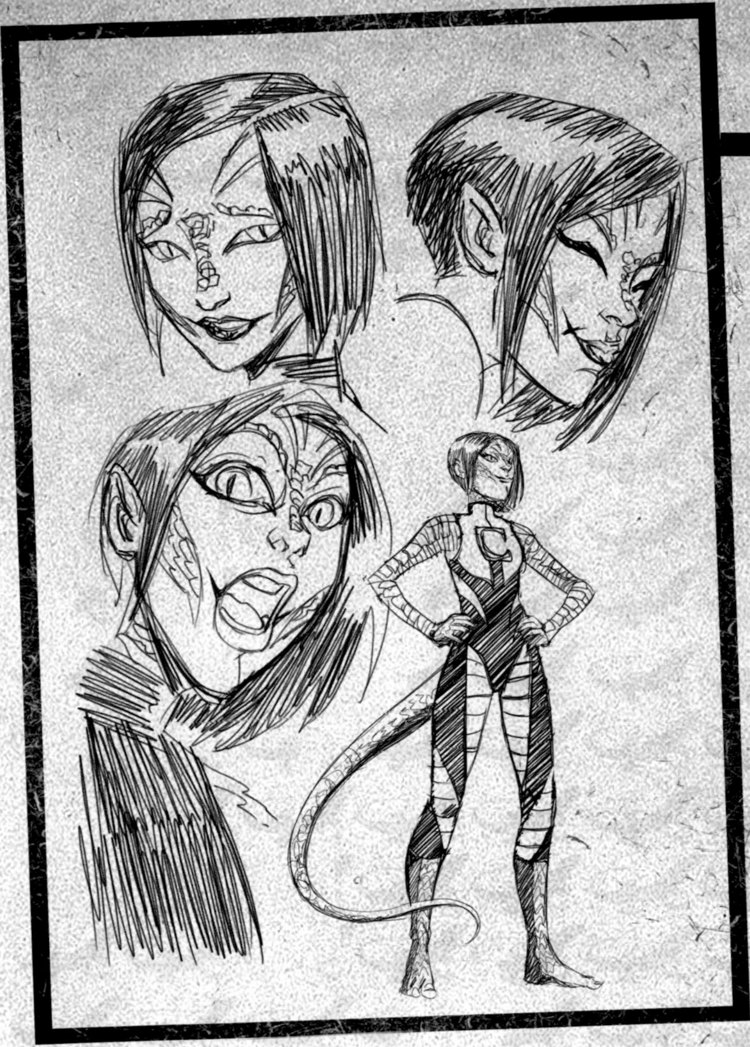

Name:
Matilda 'Tilly' Anderson
Codename: ***Rep-Tilly***
Age: ***21***

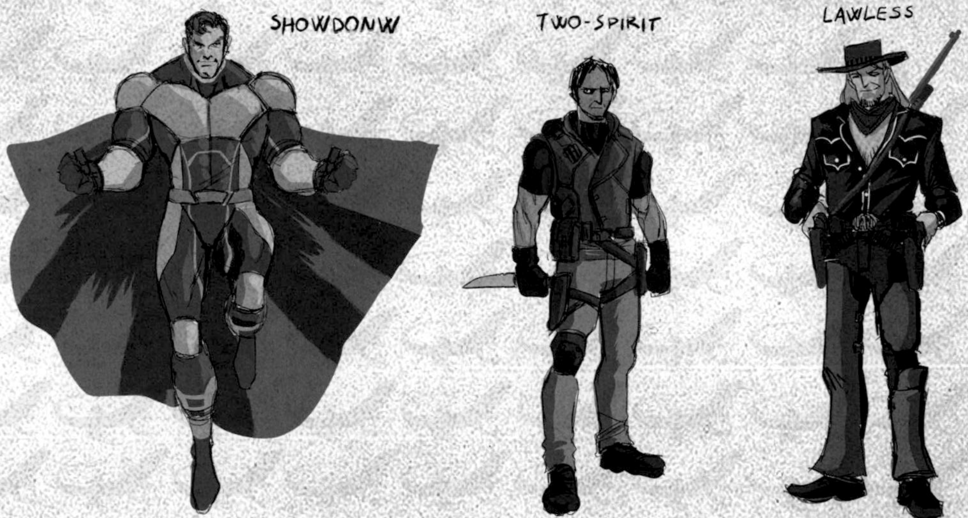

SHOWDONW
TWO-SPIRIT
LAWLESS

Name:
Cody Langstrom
Codename: ***Showdown***
Age: ***26***

Name:
Benjamin Turner
Codename: ***Headhunter***
Age: ***37***

Name:
Marcus Lawton
Codename: ***Lawless***
Age: ***35***

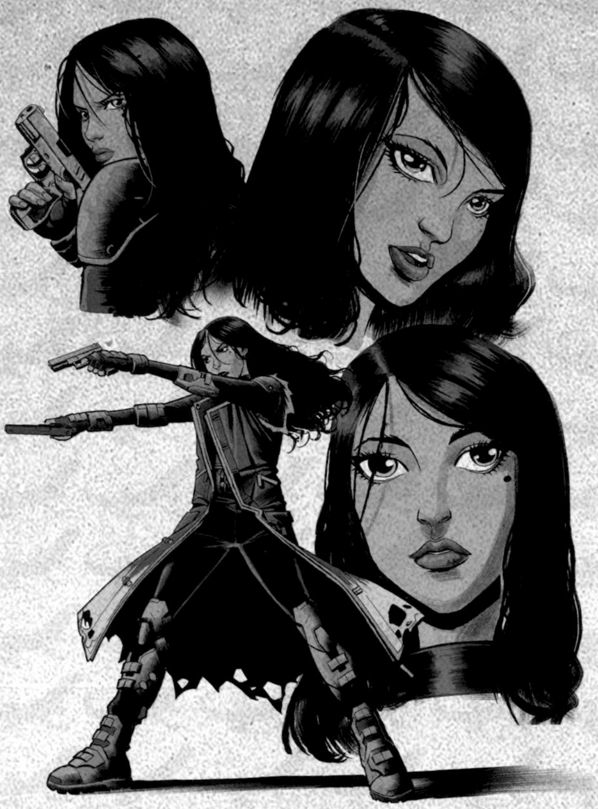

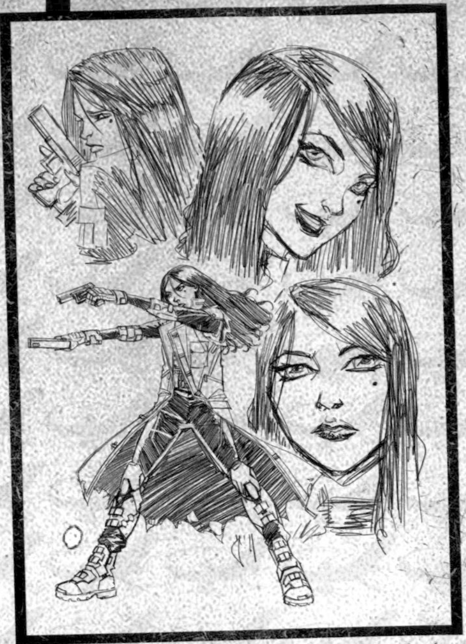

Name:
Bianca Cardiel
Codename: **December/Winter Witch**
Age: **33**

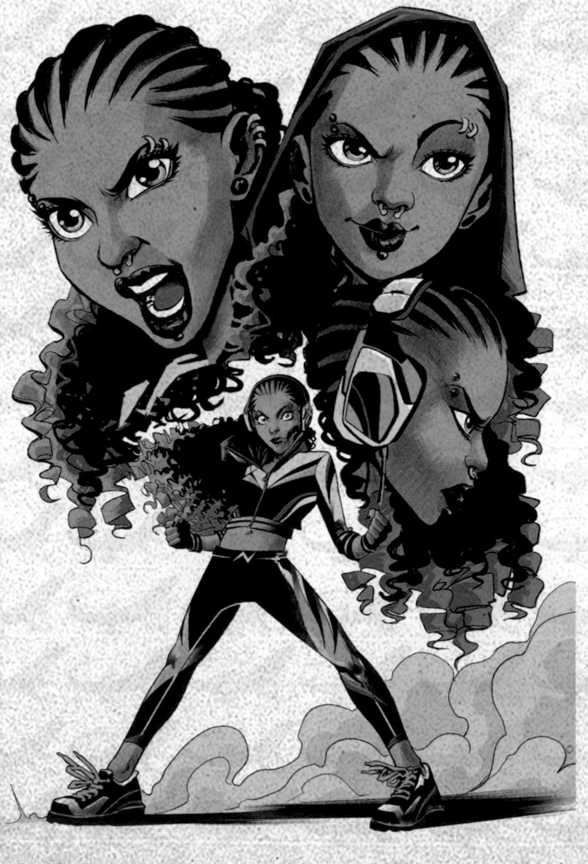

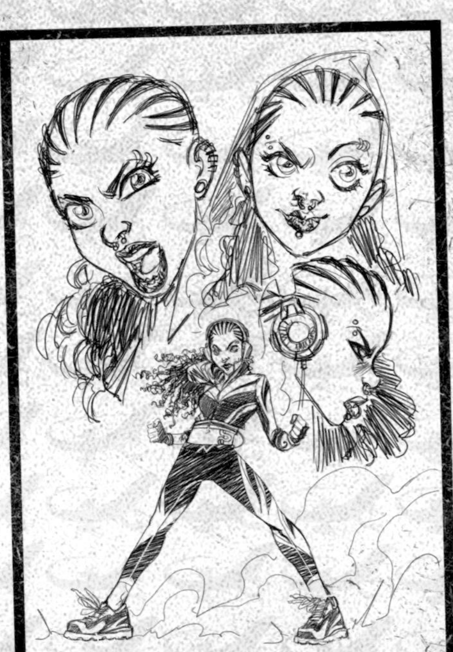

Name:
Trina Brennan
Codename: ***Miss Nemesis***
Age: **24**

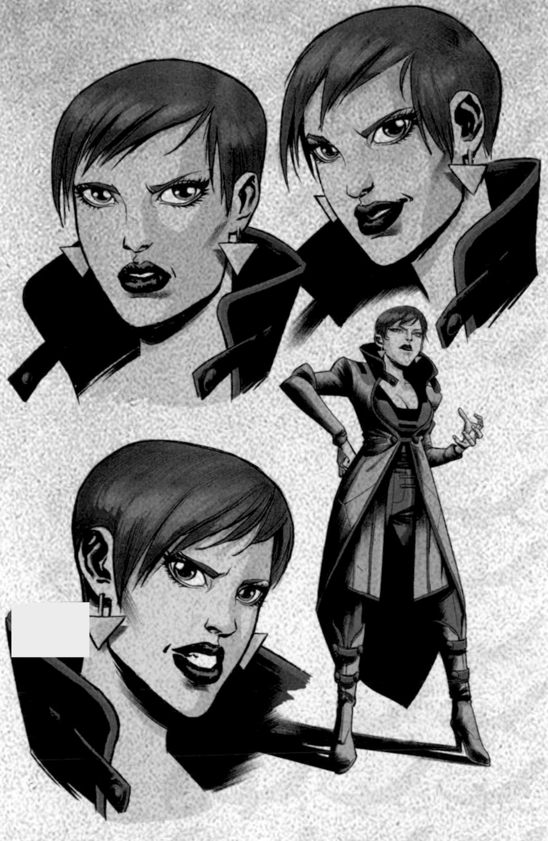

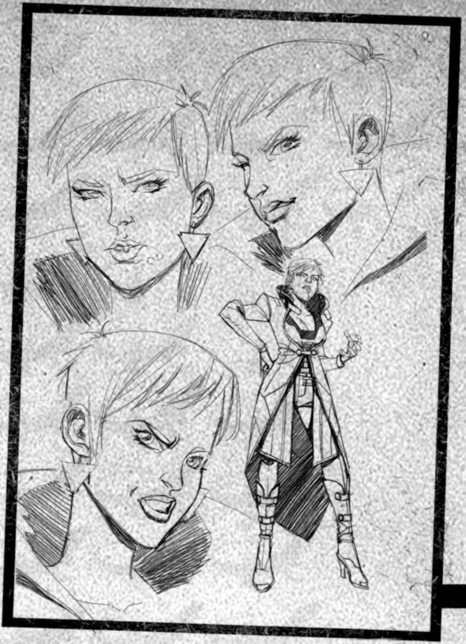

Name:
Sarah Cunningham
Codename: ***Pillar***
Age: ***38***

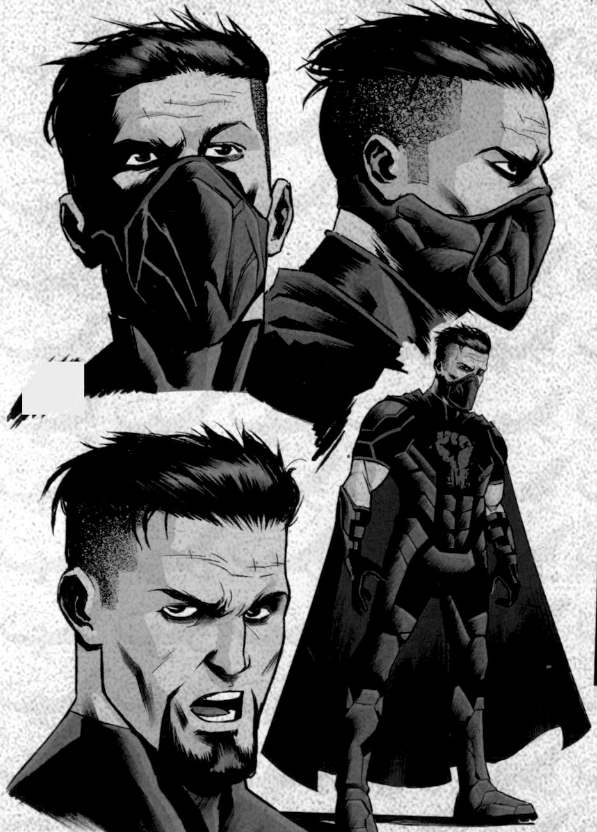

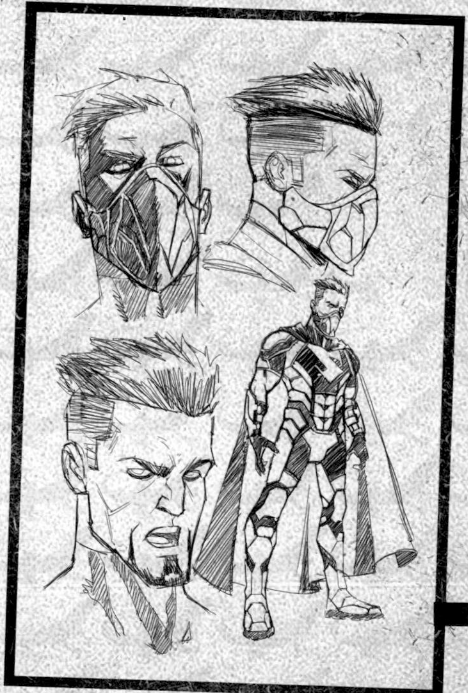

Name:
Nick Holt
Codename: ***Sedition***
Age: ***38***

DISCOVER MAD CAVE COLLECTED EDITIONS

Wolvenheart Vol. 1: Legendary Slayer
ISBN: 978-0-9981215-8-1

Honor and Curse Vol. 1: Torn
ISBN: 978-0-9981215-5-0

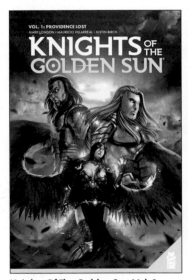

Knights Of The Golden Sun Vol. 1:
Providence Lost
ISBN: 978-0-9981215-4-3

Battlecats Vol. 2: Fallen Legacy
ISBN: 978-0-9981215-6-7

Show's End Trade Paperback
ISBN: 978-0-9981215-7-4